'Never mind tomorrow eveni excitedly, running into the mids.. .. .. lighting the one on Barrow Hill *tonight*! I heard it from the vicar himself. He says the war'll be over at midnight so that's when it should be lit, and he wants everyone who can get there up on the hill in time to see it. Kiddies and all – they can sleep in tomorrow, keep 'em out of the way while we get the bunting and flags up and the party ready.' She stopped, panting for breath, and they all looked at each other, excitement dawning in their eyes at last.

'Tonight!' Heather exclaimed. 'The party's starting *tonight*!' She whirled round and pulled Ruth into a fierce hug. 'Ruth – Joyce – the war's going to be over *tonight* – at midnight! We're going to have the biggest and the best party this village has ever seen before, because the war's going to be *over*!'

They stared at each other and burst into wild laughter. In another moment, they were all joining in the dance and then the men, talking in a different group, and the children who were racing around the green, joined in as well. The entire village was there, leaping and skipping in frenzied joy, as the meaning of the word *over* dawned on them at last and they glimpsed a future that would be free of fear, free of death, free of loss and pain and anguish.

Lilian Harry's grandfather hailed from Devon and Lilian always longed to return to her roots, so moving from Hampshire to a small Dartmoor town in her early twenties was a dream come true. She quickly absorbed herself in local life, learning the fascinating folklore and history of the moors, joining the church bell-ringers and a country dance club, and meeting people who are still her friends today. Although she later moved north, living first in Herefordshire and then in the Lake District, she returned in the 1990s and now lives on the edge of the moor with her ginger cat and two miniature schnauzers. She is still an active bell-ringer and member of the local drama group, and loves to walk on the moors. Her daughter and two grandchildren live nearby. Visit her website at www.lilianharry.co.uk or you can follow her on Twitter@LilianHarry.

A Farthing
Will Do

LILIAN HARRY

A ORION PAPERBACK

First published in Great Britain in 2005
by Orion Books
This paperback edition published in 2005
by Orion Books,
an imprint of The Orion Publishing Group Ltd,
Orion House, 5 Upper St Martin's Lane,
London WC2H 9EA

The Orion Publishing Group's policy is to use papers that
are natural, renewable and recyclable products and
made from wood grown in sustainable forests. The logging
and manufacturing processes are expected to conform to
the environmental regulations of the country of origin.

A CIP catalogue record for this book
is available from the British Library.

Printed in Great Britain by
Clays Ltd, St Ives plc

www.orionbooks.co.uk

In loving memory of Mum and Dad –
the original Lilian and Harry

Chapter One

'Christmas is coming, the goose is getting fat,
Please put a penny in the old man's hat.
If you haven't got a penny, a ha'penny will do,
If you haven't got a ha'penny, a farthing will do.
If you haven't got a farthing – God . . . Bless . . . You!'

The voices rang out like bells in the crisp night air and
Ruth Purslow felt her throat tighten as she saw Sammy's
bright head gleaming amongst those of the other children
gathered around the farmhouse door. It was three years
since that first Christmas he had spent with her at Bridge
End in 1941 – three years of a war that it had sometimes
seemed would never end. Now it looked at last as though
the Allies were winning. The D-Day invasion, back in
June, had turned the tide and the enemy were being slowly
beaten back.

'Let's hope this will be the last Christmas of the war,'
her sister Jane Warren murmured in her ear. 'We've all had
enough, even out here in the country. God only knows
what they must be feeling like in towns and cities like
Portsmouth and Southampton – not to mention London.'

'It'll end soon,' Ruth said. 'It's got to. And then the
men'll come home and we can go back to normal.' But her
voice trembled a little.

Jane glanced at her in the moonlight. 'And the rest of the
kiddies'll go back home,' she said quietly. 'That's what
you're thinking, isn't it? *Sammy*'ll go home.'

Ruth hesitated, then admitted, 'Well, I've got so fond of

1

him. He's been like my own little boy these past three years. And he loves being in the country – he even talks like us now! I just don't know how he'll take to going back to a little street in Pompey. And there's that brother of his, too. He'll be coming out of the Army and goodness knows how they'll get on together.'

'Hasn't his dad said anything?' Jane asked. 'I thought you and he were – well, quite friendly. Hasn't he talked it over with you at all?'

Ruth felt herself blush. 'No, not really. Well, he hasn't been able to get out here much lately, what with all the work on the ships. He goes to sea a lot, you know. And it seems a bit early days to be – well, making any plans.' She felt her cheeks redden deeper and was glad of the darkness. Even so, she knew her sister was looking at her curiously. 'Your Lizzie will be glad when Alec can come home,' she added hastily. 'They'll be able to start their married life properly then. They haven't had much of it so far.'

'He's got to be let out of POW camp first,' Jane said grimly. 'And God knows when that'll be. Poor Lizzie's at her wits' end over it. And it seems so unfair – he wasn't even in the Armed Forces. It doesn't seem right that merchant seamen should be taken prisoner. Nor that their ships should be sunk.'

Ruth, whose own husband had been a merchant seaman, sighed. 'You know what they say – all's fair in love and war. And I suppose preventing supplies getting to us is just another way of fighting.'

The children were singing a different carol now. There were eighteen or twenty of them – largely village children, for most of the evacuees had gone home now that the bombing seemed to have stopped, but there were a few who, like Sammy Hodges, had stayed on for one reason or another. Sammy's mother had died early in the war, leaving his father Dan unable to care for the boy properly, and since he still worked long hours in the shipyard Ruth had been only too happy to keep the boy with her.

'*God rest ye merry, gentlemen,*' the carol-singers warbled, '*let nothing you dismay.*'

The carol-singing was a feature of village life. It had been dropped in the second Christmas of the war, when everything had seemed so dark and dismal and the blitzing of the cities had begun, but started again in 1941 when Ruth and Jane and Lizzie had made up their minds to give Sammy Hodges a Christmas to remember. Almost everyone in the village had joined in, bringing back life to the dark lanes and the huddled cottages, and every Christmas Eve since then there had been a grand tour of the village, ending at the Knights' farm where they would be plied with mulled ale, cider and mince pies.

Even there, things had changed. Arthur and Emily Knight had aged during the past few years and the farm had been taken over by their son Ian. At first, it had seemed that he would be allowed to stay at home, but as the war progressed he was called up and went into the Army while three Land Girls were brought in to work the farm under the direction of his wife, Heather, and Arthur. Eli, the stockman who had been on the farm since he was a boy, had hobbled out of retirement and together they'd kept the land worked and the animals tended.

'Heather'll be glad to see her man back,' Jane commented as they trooped into the big kitchen. 'She'll be able to hand over the reins and settle down to raising the family. Three kiddies are a lot to look after as well as running a farm.'

'I'm not sure she'll find it all that easy, just the same.' Having lived alone for so many years since her own husband had died, Ruth understood what it was like to have your independence. 'It seems to me she enjoys being a farmer. She might not want to go back to the kitchen – especially with her mother-in-law already there!'

Jane laughed. 'They won't have any trouble. Emily Knight'll be only too pleased to sit back. It's the natural way of things, isn't it – the younger generation taking over while the older ones take it easy. They'll all slot into place all right when Ian comes home, you'll see.'

Sammy came over and took Ruth's hand. 'Did you like the singing, Auntie Ruth? We've been practising for ages.'

'You don't have to tell me that! Even Silver knows most of the words,' Ruth said, smiling at the thought of her big grey parrot squawking them out in his creaky voice. 'He'll still be singing "See Amidst the Winter Snow" in the middle of July.' She gazed affectionately at the boy. He had changed so much since he had first come to her, a thin and frightened little waif, so dirty that she hadn't even known his hair was fair until after she'd bathed him. Now he had grown and filled out so that, while still on the small side for eleven, he was a sturdy little chap, his rosy face shining with confidence. The thought of losing him brought a pain to her heart.

Heather Knight arrived with a tray of steaming glasses. 'Mulled cider,' she offered. Her brow beneath the mane of rich brown hair was smooth despite the cares of war, her hazel eyes lively and her wide mouth smiling. 'Our own – we had such a good crop of apples. There's hot milk with honey in it for the children.'

'Just what we need on a cold night,' Ruth said, taking a glass. 'Have you had any word from Ian?'

Heather nodded. 'He'll be in Italy for a bit longer yet, but they're not putting up much of a fight now. I don't think their heart was ever really in it, you know. It was Mussolini, in cahoots with Hitler, who pushed them in.'

'Just think,' Jane said, looking into her glass, 'it could be all over by this time next year and we'll be able to have a proper peacetime Christmas again. Things do seem to be getting more hopeful, don't they?'

'What's a peacetime Christmas like?' Sammy asked, and

they all turned to look at him, startled. Ruth opened her mouth to say that surely he remembered Christmases before the war – he'd been five years old when it started – but then she recalled what his home life had been like and smiled at him.

'Not so very different from the ones we have now, really,' she said. 'But all the men will be home – Ben and Terry, and Alec, and young Mr Knight – and they won't have to go away again. And we won't have to think about bombs and air raids and the blackout. And there'll be all sorts of nice things to eat, things we haven't seen for years – bananas and coconuts, and ice cream – all sorts of things.'

There was a short pause. She glanced at the other women, knowing they were thinking the same as her. Then Sammy spoke the words that were in all their minds.

'And I'll have to go back to Portsmouth,' he said. 'I'll have to go back, because there won't be any need for me to be evacuated any more.'

When everyone had gone, trooping out into the cold night with laughter and a few snatches of song still on their lips as they wished each other a Merry Christmas, Heather Knight and her mother-in-law started to clear the big kitchen. There wasn't too much to do – Ruth and Jane and some of the others had already washed up the cups and glasses, and the plates were stacked in a neat pile to be rinsed. Once they were all put away, Emily went into the larder and brought out the big turkey, already stuffed and in its enamel roasting pan.

'This can go in the oven now. If it cooks slow overnight we can just fire up the stove in the morning and have dinner ready for twelve. Then everyone'll have the chance for a sit-down in front of the fire till it's time to see to the animals again.'

Heather nodded. The three Land Girls and Eli would all be joining them for Christmas dinner, and there would be

Eli's widowed sister Clara who lived with him in the farm cottage, and Heather's own three children, Roger, Pat and Teddy. That would make eleven faces around the table. A nice number for Christmas dinner; though however many there were, she knew that the most important face of all – her husband Ian's – would be missing, just as he had been missing for the past three Christmases. But surely, if the war ended soon, as everyone seemed to think it would, he would be home for next Christmas. And then we'll be a proper family at last, she thought. For the first time, really, since he's never even seen little Teddy yet.

Ian had spent most of the war in Africa and Italy. Letters came infrequently, often months out of date, and in them he referred to letters Heather had written so long ago she had forgotten them. He asked constantly what was happening on the farm, whether the cows were giving a good yield, had there been many heifer calves born, how had the lambing gone, and he complained that she wasn't telling him the things he wanted to know. But Heather knew she had reported all these things faithfully, along with family news, and could only assume that some of her letters had got lost. And she was just too tired, after working on the farm all day, to write it all over again – it would all be out of date by that time anyway.

I can't wait to get home, he wrote. *The farm must be going to rack and ruin with just you and Eli and a few town girls to look after it. What do they know about animals and crops? I know you're doing your best, Heather, and you've got Dad to tell you what to do, but it needs a man around the place. Never mind – the minute this war's over, I'll be home and we'll soon get the place back on its feet.*

Heather raised her eyebrows a little as she remembered this. Born and brought up on a farm herself, she considered that she was making a good job of looking after this one. Mr Knight – 'Dad' to her – was old now and had arthritis, so couldn't do much more than advise. To begin with,

6

feeling rather as if she were trying to steer an avalanche, she had turned to him almost all the time, but after the first few months her confidence had begun to grow. The sight of tiny points of green shimmering over the fields as shoots of new wheat she had sown herself pricked through the earth had been a real thrill, and the arrival of her first lambs almost as amazing as the births of her own babies. From then on, she had taken more and more control, and Arthur Knight had come out into the fields more to congratulate than to advise.

The Land Girls had been a tremendous help too. They lodged in one of the farm cottages and old Aggie Clutter had been glad to move in and look after them. She gave them breakfast and supper and the girls had their midday dinner with the family in the farmhouse kitchen.

'It'll seem strange when they go home,' Heather said to Emily now as the oven door was closed on the turkey. 'They're part of the farm. You wouldn't think they were the same girls as those townies who came here, scared stiff of the cows and cooing over the lambs as if they were cuddly toys!'

'You wouldn't,' her mother-in-law agreed with a chuckle. She went to the sink and pumped up some water to rinse her hands. 'But they've turned out real well. I must say, when I saw them I thought they'd be more trouble than they were worth – especially young Stevie with her gold ringlets and all. More like a film star than a farmhand, she was.'

'She can't help her looks,' Heather said, as if Stevie had been ugly rather than pretty. 'And it was handy that Pam and Jean already knew each other in Southampton. I did think Stevie might take longer to settle in but when it turned out she knew the Budd family and some of the other evacuees – well, it seemed to make it easier. I suppose it must help if you're in a strange place, to see a few familiar faces about.' She sighed. 'I'll be sorry to see Stevie go back to Portsmouth, I really will.'

Stevie and Heather had hit it off right from the start. The other two were nice enough girls, and they all worked well together but, to Heather, Stevie had become more like a sister.

'That won't happen for a while yet,' Emily said, wiping her hands on the roller towel behind the door. 'I know everyone's talking as if the war'll be over soon, but you never know what dirty trick that Hitler might have up his sleeve.'

Heather nodded. There'd been a lot of talk lately about 'secret weapons' and bombs even bigger than the ones that had already been used by both sides. You couldn't take anything for granted.

When Ian comes home, we'll work the farm together, she thought as she began to set the big kitchen table for breakfast. The older kiddies are more or less off my hands now and Teddy'll be at school in a couple of years – I'll be able to show him all the changes there've been and we can plan what we're going to do next. All these hardships will be past then, and we can look forward to a happy future. It'll be different – I don't suppose he realises how much things have changed here, especially for women – but it'll be good. And the main thing is, we'll be able to share it all.

It had been so long since she had been able to share anything with her husband.

Jane, Lizzie and Ruth walked back down the lane together. Jane's husband, George, had slipped back early to make a final check on the animals and Sammy was walking ahead, putting his feet down very quietly in the hope of seeing a badger. The three women linked arms and sauntered along in the moonlight, talking softly.

'Another Christmas,' Ruth said, with a little sigh. 'It doesn't seem possible that a war can drag on so long. D'you realise, this is the *sixth* since the war started? Six Christmases of war! A lot of the kiddies don't know anything else. They've grown up with bombs and air-raid warnings and their daddies away fighting, and they don't even know that life can be different.'

'And some of them will never see their daddies again,' Lizzie said in a sombre voice. 'Some men never even got the chance to *be* daddies.' Her voice cracked a little.

Ruth took her arm quickly. 'Lizzie, I'm sorry. I didn't mean to upset you. Me and my big mouth! I should've known better than to remind you of Alec, especially after having such a nice evening.'

'You didn't remind me. There's not a minute goes by when I don't think about him. I just live for the day he comes home again. Thank goodness I've got my nursing to keep me occupied.' Lizzie drew in a deep breath and turned to her mother. 'Is there anything else to do for dinner tomorrow, Mum? Don't forget we've got company.'

Jane laughed. 'I'm not likely to forget, with you reminding me every five minutes! But just in case you think I can't count, there'll be eight of us – you, me and your father, Ruth and Sammy here, and Dan Hodges if he manages to get over from Portsmouth, and the two Americans. Not a crowd, but enough to make a bit of noise and give young Sammy a party.' She hesitated, then added, 'It may be our last chance to do that.'

There was a small silence. Lizzie glanced at her aunt but before Ruth could speak there was a cry of excitement, quickly hushed, from Sammy and they all stopped. He tiptoed back to them and even in the moonlight Ruth could see that his face was glowing with delight. 'I saw one, Auntie Ruth! I saw a badger! He came out of the hedge and ran across the lane – I saw the stripes on his face. I knew there was one here!'

'There's a sett in the woods,' Lizzie told him. 'You went to see it with Ben last time he was home, didn't you?'

9

'Yes, and Ben showed me the track he makes coming over the bank and across the lane. It's his own path. But I didn't know what time he'd come. He doesn't come out until very late, Ben said.'

'In that case,' Ruth said, taking his hand, 'it must be very late now and time for us all to be in bed. Come on, Sammy. You know who's coming tomorrow, don't you?'

He glanced up at her and for a moment she thought he was going to tell her scornfully that he didn't believe in Father Christmas any more. But then his smile broke out and he gripped her hand tightly and said, 'Dad! Dad's coming tomorrow, for Christmas dinner. And I've got a present for him.'

'Which still needs to be wrapped up,' Ruth said, walking on briskly. 'Come on. You won't see the badger again tonight – he's probably three fields away by now, scared out of his wits by all the noise we're making. Let's get home and make sure everything's ready for tomorrow. It's Christmas again and we're going to give your dad the best Christmas he's ever had!'

The best Christmas he's ever had? Lizzie thought, as she and her mother turned away up the farm track. Well, I don't begrudge Dan Hodges his Christmas, even if he is an odd sort of a bloke. But I wish I could be saying the same about my Alec. I wish I could be giving *him* the best Christmas he's ever had.

As it was, she knew that he probably wouldn't be having any sort of Christmas at all, hundreds of miles away in a German prisoner-of-war camp.

Chapter Two

Dan Hodges woke early on Christmas Day. The little house in April Grove felt cold and empty, but he was used to that by now and barely noticed it as he shuffled downstairs in his socks and an old coat to make a pot of tea. There were no decorations – he knew that somewhere there was a box of paperchains that Sammy and Nora had made years ago – but he didn't see any point in putting them up when it was just for himself. It would have been different if the boys were home – if Nora was still alive.

There were a few cards on the mantelpiece, though. The Budds from further down April Grove had popped one through the door. It looked home-made, probably that little Maureen had made it, carefully drawing a snowman and giving him a bright orange nose that might be a carrot, and a black bowler hat and red scarf. And there was one from Tommy and Freda Vickers next door, one from the Taylors and, rather to his surprise, one from Annie Chapman, Jess Budd's sister, who'd looked down her nose at him and Nora when they'd first moved here but had been a good friend later on. He felt a bit ashamed now of some of the things he'd said about Annie Chapman and her stuck-up ways.

Pride of place, however, was taken by two cards that had come from Bridge End. One from Sammy – another home-made one, quite well drawn with Father Christmas on his sleigh and eight really lifelike reindeer on the roof of a cottage that you could see was Ruth Purslow's. And one from Ruth herself – a bought one this time, showing a pretty village scene with a coach arriving in the square and snow-covered thatched cottages all around. There were kiddies playing in the snow and someone – a man – getting off the coach and being welcomed by a woman in a red cloak. Arriving for Christmas, Dan thought, just as he'd be arriving later on, and his heart lifted.

Not that he'd be arriving at all if he didn't get his skates on! The kettle was whistling now and he hastily poured some boiling water into the teapot the way Ruth had shown him, swilled it around and tipped it out again before making the tea. Nora had done it that way too, but he'd always thought it one of those daft things that women did until Ruth had explained the reason.

While the tea was brewing, he made some porridge. It was a nuisance having to wash the saucepan but he had a long bike-ride in front of him, all the way from Portsmouth to Bridge End, and he needed a bit of sustenance. There were no buses or trains on Christmas Day and he wouldn't have wanted to spend the money anyway. Better to use it for Christmas presents for Sammy and Ruth.

He sat down to his breakfast in the cold room, thinking of Ruth. She'd come into his life just when it had been at its lowest point, after Nora had died and he'd been forced to let Sammy go for evacuation. He'd tried to keep the boy at home, knowing Nora hadn't wanted him to go away, but it had been impossible. The neighbours had helped, especially the Vickers and Jess and Frank Budd – keeping an eye on the kiddy, giving him a bit of dinner – but in the end someone had come to see him and told him he couldn't go on that way, leaving the nipper on his own for days on end while he went off to sea. There were air raids at that time too, and although Dan thought Sammy had enough sense to go down the shelter, he had to admit that at eight years old he needed someone to look after him. The trouble was, he'd been so dazed with misery at losing Nora that he hadn't been able to see what was happening under his own nose. And Sammy was miserable too, a poor little scrap frightened of his own shadow, which irritated Dan because he couldn't understand how a boy of his could be like that.

Not like Gordon, he thought, spooning up the lumpy porridge straight from the saucepan. Gordon took after him – a big, confident boy who'd stand up to anyone and would never let himself be bullied. A boy who knew what he wanted and went after it, a boy Dan had been proud of. And just look where that had got him – two years in an approved school for thieving, breaking his mother's heart and maybe even making her illness worse.

Gordon was in the Army now. He'd joined up the minute he was out of the approved school and done all right, too. He was somewhere in France at the moment, but he didn't write home much and there was no Christmas card from him on the mantelpiece. Dan sighed. He supposed his elder son would come home when it was all over, maybe go back to work at Camber Dock, but it would never be the same again; he'd been away too long. And Dan didn't even know if he'd still be at Camber himself when the war ended. Nothing had been decided, nothing could be until things got back to normal but, ever since he'd started going out to Bridge End to see Sammy, he'd been wondering if a country life might suit him better. Portsmouth hadn't ever been very kind to him; he'd lived in its poorest parts, and although he'd always put up with the mean streets and poverty because he knew nothing else, the trees and fields of the countryside had eased his mind and comforted him. And Ruth was there, too. Ruth . . .

Dan finished his porridge and poured a second cup of tea. It would be getting light soon and he wanted to set off as soon as possible. He'd dragged in the old tin bath last night and it was still in the scullery, with five inches of scummy water waiting to be tipped out. He'd do that and then he'd wash up this saucepan and cup. Time was when he'd have left them, but Ruth had taught him that things left had to be dealt with eventually, and the longer you left them the harder it was. That certainly applied to cold baths and porridge saucepans!

The morning was still cold and grey when he pulled his bike out of the shed and set off, an old Army pack on his back holding a clean shirt, his toothbrush and a bit of soap, and his Christmas presents for Sammy and Ruth and the other folk out at Bridge End. He bent and fastened cycle clips round his ankles and wheeled the bike out of the back gate.

Tommy Vickers was at the bottom of his garden, putting something in the dustbin. He gave Dan a cheery grin and a salute and said, 'Merry Christmas, Dan. Off to see your nipper, then?'

'That's right,' Dan said. 'Been invited to stop for the night too, up at the farm. I'll ride back tomorrow afternoon, before it gets dark. Merry Christmas to you and your Freda, Tom. Your Eunice home?'

Tommy shook his head. 'She'll be here for New Year's Eve. We've got Clifford, though. Not that we'll see much of him, mind – you know he's sweet on young Gladys Shaw. We've been wondering if they might announce their engagement today.'

'Well, I'll be getting along.' Dan wasn't much interested in Tommy's nephew and Gladys Shaw. He wheeled the bike up the narrow alley and out into April Grove, by the allotments. But even then he wasn't able to get away immediately, for the whole Budd family were coming up the street on their way to the Chapmans' house.

'Mr Hodges!' Jess exclaimed, stopping while young Maureen jigged impatiently at her side. 'Are you going to ride all the way out to Bridge End?'

'Well, it wouldn't be much good riding halfway, would it?' said her husband, Frank. 'Anyway, it's not that far. I used to do it when you and the boys were out there.'

Jess poked her elbow into his side and smiled at Dan.

'Well, you give young Sammy our love, won't you? And wish everyone a Merry Christmas from us.' Jess had been evacuated to Bridge End for a few weeks at the start of the war but had come home to be with Frank, bringing the baby Maureen with her. The two boys, Tim and Keith, had stayed for longer but they were both back home now. Tim was now an apprentice on the Gosport ferry while Keith was going to the technical school; Frank was hoping he'd take up a Dockyard apprenticeship when he left.

'I'll do that,' Dan said and swung his leg over the saddle. 'Merry Christmas.' He cycled off up the road and the Budds watched him go.

'You know, Dan Hodges has changed a lot since he first came here,' Jess observed. 'Remember what a surly man he used to be – wouldn't even give you a good morning, let alone a Merry Christmas. Now he's turning into a really nice sort of chap.'

'There was always a lot of good in him,' Frank said. He'd known Dan before the Hodges family had come to April Grove, when they lived over the pub in one of the roughest streets in Old Portsmouth. 'He had a lot of bad luck, getting turned out of the pub like that, and then the trouble with that older boy of his, and losing his wife. But he always worked hard and he played fair too, for all his faults.'

'It was his manner that put people off,' Jess said as they walked the last few yards to Annie's house. 'It was as if he didn't know how to be pleasant. But there, I suppose he was always worrying about the family and how to make ends meet, with Nora being so poorly. Anyway, he's a lot easier to talk to now, and Sammy's doing well out in the country, by all accounts.' She sighed. 'I wonder how they'll get on when the war's over and he comes home again. They might not find it so easy to settle down after all these years.'

Frank made no comment. He liked Dan Hodges well enough, but it was Christmas Day and he was more

15

interested in his own family. Just now, he was also more interested in what they were going to have for dinner. Annie had managed to get a really big turkey and she could be relied on to set a good table for Christmas. 'Come on,' he said, quickening his step. 'Me stomach thinks me throat's been cut. And those two boys will have eaten the lot if we don't hurry up!'

Tim and Keith were already at the gate, and as Jess and Frank drew near the front door opened and Annie came out, smiling. The two sisters kissed and then Annie reached up to give Frank a kiss as well.

'Merry Christmas!' she said. 'Come on in, out of the cold. And just think – this time next year, we could be at peace again.'

'Peace!' Jess said. 'I can hardly remember what it is. And Maureen's never known it at all. Oh, *won't* it be wonderful!'

Ruth and Sammy were waiting in the cottage when Dan arrived. He was breathless from having cycled as fast as he could against a sharp wind, and his face was reddened. He jumped off his bike and gripped Sammy's shoulder in greeting, then gave Ruth a nod and a smile. 'Merry Christmas!'

'Merry Christmas, Dan,' Ruth said softly. She'd wondered if he might kiss her, since it was such a special day, but even after three years they still hadn't progressed that far – at least, not in public. And she supposed that Sammy was 'public' as far as that went. 'Come in and have a hot drink,' she added, leading the way into the cottage. 'You look shrammed.'

'It's a bitter wind,' he allowed, unwinding the long scarf from round his neck. 'It's warm enough in here, though. And how are you, Silver?' he asked, addressing the big grey parrot on its stand. 'Still as noisy as ever?' He dropped into the big wheelback chair beside the range.

'I'm a little teapot,' the parrot informed him. 'Short and

16

stout. I've got sixpence, jolly little sixpence. Tuppence to spend. *Sod* the little buggers! It's a bleeding *eagle!*'

'All right, all right,' Dan said, giving him a sunflower seed to shut him up. 'I only asked. Blimey, he don't change, does he!'

'Silver'll never be any different,' Ruth said, lifting the kettle from the fire and pouring hot water into a large enamel mug. 'It's when he goes quiet that I start to worry.' She mixed the cocoa and handed him the mug. 'You'll never guess what your Sammy's taught him to say now.'

'Do I want to?' Dan curled his big hands round the mug. The cocoa was too hot to drink yet but he tried a sip just the same. 'Mm, that tastes good. I hope it's not more bad language.'

'Silver knows more bad language than anyone else,' Ruth said wryly. 'I don't know what those sailors thought they were up to on that ship while my Jack was bringing him home . . . No, it's nothing bad, just some more Christmas carols. Well, songs, really – you know, like "Christmas is Coming" and "We Wish You a Merry Christmas". He knows all the words and half the tunes.'

'I wanted to take him carol-singing,' Sammy said. He was leaning against his father, and Ruth thought how different they were with each other now from the first time Dan had come to the house. It had been an awkward meeting and she'd been glad to see Dan leave again. She thought Sammy had been equally glad.

'It's too cold outside for parrots,' Dan said. 'They're used to hot countries. Anyway, you know what he's like, he wouldn't sing the carols you wanted him to and you'd probably all end up singing "I'm a Little Teapot" at every house.'

They all laughed and Dan sipped his cocoa again. He closed his eyes for a few moments, relaxing in the warmth of the little cottage. It was so different from his house in April Grove. You could smell the cleanliness and the scent of the fir cones and apple wood that Ruth put on the fire. You could feel the peace and the contentment of those who lived here. You could sense that the same feelings had been a part of this cottage for the past two, perhaps three, hundred years. Generations of countryfolk, living plain, simple lives in a tiny cottage that had no real modern facilities – no running water, no electricity, no gas – just a range to cook by, a pump for drawing water, an earth privy outside the back door. And trees outside – trees and grass and sky, in place of tarred roads and smoke and buses and cars. I could live in a place like this, he thought. And if that's how I feel, what must my Sam be thinking?

If only he could find some sort of work out here in the country. But what could a man like him do, who'd worked all his life on ships' engines and welding?

'Finish your cocoa, Dan,' Ruth said gently, and he opened his eyes to find her standing over him, her coat and gloves on, and Sammy beside her in what looked like a new overcoat – new to Sammy, anyway – and a thick blue scarf. For a moment, as Dan looked at him, he looked so much like his mother Nora that Dan caught his breath and felt a sudden heat in his eyes. He gulped his cocoa down, not caring that it was still a bit too hot, and was glad of the excuse for his watering eyes. He rubbed the back of his hand across them and grinned, then put his hands on the arms of his chair and pushed himself up.

'Come on, then. Christmas dinner, here I come! What are we having – turkey or chicken?'

'Neither,' Ruth said, her eyes sparkling, and Sammy, hopping up and down with excitement, chimed in, 'It's *goose*, Dad! A huge fat goose from Auntie Jane's own flock!'

'Goose?' Dan said. 'Well, d'you know, I don't think I've ever eaten goose. I can see this is going to be a Christmas to remember.' He remembered something else and paused as they started towards the door. 'Just a mo – I've brought

18

you a Christmas present, Ruth. Open it now, will you, before we go up to the farm.'

'But we're all having our presents together, after dinner,' she began, and caught his eye. 'Oh, all right, then.' She took the little parcel he gave her and unwrapped it, then gave a cry of pleasure. 'Dan, it's lovely. Thank you! Thank you very much.'

She lifted the brooch, shaped like a parrot, from its nest of cotton-wool and pinned it on her frock. Then she raised her face and said, 'Happy Christmas, Dan.' And she got her kiss, after all.

It was a merry party that ate goose in the big farm kitchen that day. George and Jane had marked the bird out weeks ago and had been fattening it up, and when it was brought to the table everyone exclaimed in admiration. Dan was transfixed. He hadn't seen such a piece of meat in his entire life. The most he and Nora had ever been able to afford was a rabbit, or a small chicken that had lasted the family for only one meal. This giant looked as if it would last even the Warren family for a week.

'Blimey,' he said in tones of awe, 'it's a blooming ostrich!'

Everyone laughed, but Ruth felt sudden tears prick her eyes. He had sounded exactly like Sammy when he had first laid eyes on Silver and called the parrot a 'bleeding eagle'. No matter how different they looked, there was no doubt that Sammy was Dan's son.

Lizzie gave Sammy a smile. This was her first Christmas with the family for two years and she felt especially glad that Sammy was still with them. She had started her nursing in Southampton Hospital but had later transferred to Haslar Royal Naval Hospital, in Gosport, as a Voluntary Aid Detachment Nurse and knew she was lucky not to be on duty over the holiday.

She looked around the table, feeling the warmth of a big

19

Christmas gathering, for as well as the family there were the two American airmen from the nearby camp, who had been 'billeted' on the Warrens for occasional meals. Nobody was quite sure whether this was because the Americans didn't have enough food for their men – which seemed doubtful, since the two often brought generous food parcels – or whether it was an attempt to forge good relationships between the two nations, but Floyd and Marvin were such pleasant young men that nobody really cared. They were part of the family now, and it would be difficult to imagine the place without them.

'Say,' said Floyd, the older of the two. He gazed at the golden-breasted bird, resting on a huge willow-pattern meat platter with crisp roast potatoes and parsnips piled all around it. 'That's some dinner! I thought you British were supposed to be on strict rations?'

'Most of us are,' Jane said ruefully. 'At least, the ones who live in towns and cities. Out here in the country we're lucky – we can grow our own food, and that includes Christmas dinner! But you know we don't eat like this all the time, Floyd.'

'Sure, I know that. But there's generally enough milk and eggs and butter to go around. What about these ration books we hear about?'

'Well, we have them too.' Ruth was beginning to feel a little uncomfortable. The table certainly didn't give any hint of hardship, with its dishes heaped with vegetables and that enormous goose. 'We can't buy any more in the shops than city folk. It's just that we've got more space to grow things – and we're farmers too. It's what we do for our living.'

'We're feeding the country too, don't forget,' George put in. 'And we can't just help ourselves to whatever we like. Most of what we grow goes to the Ministry. We have to watch it, same as anyone else.'

'Not really the same,' Dan cut in. He'd listened in silence

but now he couldn't help butting in. 'I don't see many countryfolk queueing for hours at the baker's or butcher's shop. You ought to see the women where I come from – half the morning spent in queues, and all their work to do when they get home. Tired out, they are, and pale as death. And that's on top of the bombing, when the Blitz was on – having to leave dinners to spoil in the oven while they dashed down the shelter during the daylight raids, then having to get up not five minutes after they'd gone to bed and get the family down there at night, in the freezing cold and rain and all. And never knowing what they'd find when they came out – their own house blown to bits, maybe, or a copper standing in the street waiting to tell 'em their family's all killed. You haven't had none of that here.'

There was an uncomfortable silence. Ruth, sitting next to Dan, laid her hand on his thigh and he bit his lip and glanced at her. 'Sorry, Ruth,' he mumbled. 'Didn't mean to blast off like that.' He looked round the table and cleared his throat. 'Sorry, everyone. That was bad manners, at Christmas dinner and all.'

'That's all right, Dan,' Jane said. 'You're right, anyway. We don't know what war's like, out here away from it all. Not but what we haven't had our moments,' she added. 'I remember the night Southampton was blitzed. You could read your paper by the light of the fires. And that time when Portsmouth went, too. I remember how frightened the evacuees were, not knowing what was going on at home.'

'Still, I think we ought to leave the subject for now,' George declared. 'As Dan says, it's Christmas dinner and we ought to enjoy it. It won't help anyone if we're miserable, so let's cheer up and pull these crackers our Lizzie's made and see what sort of jokes she's given us.'

A babble of agreement broke out and they crossed their arms around the table and pulled the crackers. Lizzie had spent a good deal of her off-duty time during the past few weeks, making the crackers out of coloured crêpe paper; inside each one she had put a home-made paper hat, a tiny present and a slip of paper with a joke or riddle on it. They all put on their hats and read out the jokes while George began to carve the goose.

'When is a sailor not a sailor?' demanded Ruth. 'When he's aboard!'

'Why should you never put a clock at the top of the stairs?' Floyd asked. 'Because it will soon run down!'

'Why did the butterfly?' Sammy read. 'Because it saw the kitchen sink. That's a good one, isn't it, Dad? Because it saw the kitchen sink – get it?'

'Yes, I get it,' Dan said. 'I fell out of my cradle laughing at that one. Listen to this. Why couldn't the viper viper nose? Because the adder adder 'andkerchief!'

The Americans roared with laughter. 'I never heard that one before,' Floyd declared. 'How about this?' He cleared his throat and began:

> *'Can you tell me why*
> *A hypocrite's eye*
> *Can better descry*
> *Than you or I,*
> *On how many toes*
> *A pussy-cat goes?'*

There was a bewildered silence. 'Can we do *what?*' George asked. 'I didn't even understand half the words.'

Floyd repeated the rhyme more slowly, making sure they understood each word, but they still looked baffled. Jane shook her head, her lips moving as she mouthed the words to herself. 'I just don't get it at all,' she said at last. 'You're saying a bad man would be able to count a cat's toes better than a good one. Well, I don't see why he should.'

'Or even why he'd want to,' Lizzie put in, and looked

accusingly at the young American. 'You never got that out of my cracker.'

He grinned. 'I know. But you put all the others in, so you knew them. I wanted to give you something to puzzle over, too.' He glanced round the table, his dark eyebrows lifted in a mischievous quirk. 'Well, d'you want to know the answer?'

'If we can understand it,' George said, laying the last slice of goose on the plate Jane had placed beside the big platter.

'Okay, here goes. Listen carefully, now.' He cleared his throat again.

> *'A man of deceit*
> *Can best counterfeit.*
> *And so, I suppose,*
> *He can best count 'er TOES!'*

There was another short silence while they disentangled this, and then a universal groan. Only Sammy still looked puzzled. 'I don't understand it. Everyone knows cats have four feet.'

'It's not that sort of feet, Sammy,' Ruth said, and explained. 'Anyway, I think that's enough riddles now. How much goose do you want?' She began to help him to meat and vegetables. For several minutes the conversation was reduced to requests to pass the sprouts or carrots and enquiries as to whether everyone had gravy or redcurrant jelly. Then there was another, more satisfied silence as they all began to eat.

When conversation began again Lizzie, who was sitting next to Floyd, glanced sideways at him. 'When did you manage to put that riddle into your cracker?'

'I didn't. I've known it since I was a kid. Kinda clever, isn't it?'

'Too clever for us,' Lizzie said. 'We're more accustomed

to things like *"When is a door not a door? When it's ajar."* That kind of riddle. We're just simple countryfolk here, you know.'

'And what makes you think I'm any different?' he demanded. 'I grew up on a farm too. OK, it's a mite bigger'n yours here, but it's basically not much different. And in some ways our life out there was a lot less sociable. The nearest neighbours live three miles away and the nearest town's ten. We still manage to have quite a bit of fun, though – the odd get-together for a party or a barn dance, that kind of thing.'

'Barn dances?' Lizzie said. 'We have them too. D'you do dances like the Veleta or the St Bernard's Waltz?'

He shook his head. 'I guess ours are more American than those. We do square dancing – hoedown kinda stuff. It's fun.'

'It sounds a bit like our country dancing.'

'Yeah, I guess it is. Probably started from that. But it's pretty energetic too.'

'I'd like to try it,' Lizzie said wistfully. 'It's ages since I've been to a dance.'

Floyd looked at her. 'We ought to get one up at the camp. We do ordinary dancing – strict tempo and jiving, that kind of thing – but we've never put on a square dance. D'you reckon folk would come along?'

'I'm sure they would. *I* would.' Her eyes were sparkling. 'I love dancing.'

'So why have you never been to any of our other dances?'

'Oh . . .' She looked away, blushing a little. 'Because I'm married, I suppose. And my hubby's a POW in Germany. It doesn't seem right to dance with someone else when he's shut up in a cell.'

'Plenty of girls do. It's like your dad said just now – it doesn't help anyone else for us to be miserable. I bet your man wouldn't mind you having a bit of fun. And it doesn't have to mean anything. It's just a nice thing to do.'

'I know.' She knew just how nice it would be, to be held in a man's arms again. Too nice. 'I just don't want to do it, that's all. But country dancing – square dancing – that would be all right.'

'We'll get it fixed up,' he said with decision. 'I know we can get up a band – a piano accordion, a fiddle or two. We'll get to work on it as soon as we get back to camp.'

'Will you? Will you really?' Lizzie felt a sparkle of excitement. She looked into his dark blue eyes. 'That'll be lovely, it really will. You'll make sure it's on one of my weekends off, won't you?'

'Yes,' Floyd said, holding her look for a moment. 'I will. It's a promise, Lizzie.'

Lizzie looked away. Her heart had quickened and she wondered if she had done right in allowing herself to get all het up over the idea of a square dance. Then Ruth, on her other side, nudged her and said, 'D'you want any more goose, Lizzie? You didn't take much first time round.'

'Oh, thanks.' She took the plate and looked at it. 'No, I think I've had enough, actually. Here, Floyd, you have some.' She passed the plate to him and turned quickly back to her aunt. 'How's Sammy enjoying his dinner, then? And Dan?'

'It's smashing,' Sammy said. He had almost disappeared behind his plate, it had been heaped so high, but she could see him now, working manfully to clear it. 'It's the best Christmas dinner I've ever had. Isn't it, Dad?'

'Yes,' Dan said, but his voice was quiet and his expression looked far away. 'The best I've ever had too.'

He's thinking of Nora, Ruth thought, glancing at his face. He's wishing she could be here to enjoy a dinner like this. I don't suppose she'd ever had such a good one either.

She sighed, and wondered if Dan would ever really recover from his grief at losing his wife.

25

So many people were separated this Christmas, Heather Knight thought as she watched her father-in-law carve their goose. She and Ian had been apart for more than three years now and there was still no sign of his coming home. With the situation as it was there, she could only be thankful that he was still alive, but it was tragic that he had missed so much of their children's growing up. Roger, at twelve, was turning into a lanky youth, their daughter Pat was ten and he'd never even seen Teddy, conceived during his last leave and now a sturdy toddler, coming up to three and a half years old and already doing his own little jobs about the place – feeding the hens, collecting their eggs, staggering on fat little legs across the yard with a small bucket of milk for the kitchen.

Well, nothing could be done about the things that Ian had missed but she could at least try to make up for some of them. She'd tell him all those little things that she'd left out of her letters, to help him get to know his children all over again. She'd take him round the farm and show him all that she'd done, the new ways of working she had developed. She'd help him learn and understand the new ways they'd all had to get used to – the wartime regulations, the restrictions – for even though they would surely be relaxed as soon as the war was over, it would take time to get back to normal. Ian might not understand that, after being away for so long, but with her beside him to explain it all he would soon settle in. And they'd work together. Partners, she thought with a glow of anticipation, that's what we'll be – partners.

'Wake up, Heather,' Stevie said suddenly from across the table, and she realised that they were all looking at her. 'Where are you? I've asked you twice if you want cabbage.'

'Sorry,' Heather said, blushing as they all laughed at her. 'I was just thinking how lovely it'll be next Christmas, when Ian's home again.' She helped herself from the bowl of cabbage Stevie had pushed across the table and then spooned a small pile on to Teddy's plate.

'Now, don't you be too previous,' her father-in-law warned her. 'We don't know he will be. I know they're saying the war'll end soon but we can't be sure. There's a lot more water to flow under the bridge before we can start thinking along those lines.'

'I know, Dad. But I've got to hope, haven't I? We've all got to hope.' She looked round the table at the children's faces. 'He's been away from us for too many Christmases as it is. I can't bear to think he might not be here for the next one.'

'We all want him back,' Emily said sadly. 'And if hope could bring him, he'd be here now.'

'He will be,' Stevie said. She brushed her pale golden hair back from her face and smiled at Heather over the piled vegetable dishes. 'I know he will be. The war'll be over and all the men will be back.' She gave them a wry smile. 'And we'll have to go back, too. All us Land Girls – back to the cities, where we belong.'

The other two Land Girls squeaked in dismay. 'Don't say that!' Pam exclaimed. 'We're country girls now. We won't know what to do with ourselves back in Southampton. Anyway, it's not the same any more, with all the bomb damage.'

'You want to go home though, surely?' Emily asked. 'I'm sure your parents will want you back after all this time.'

Jean shrugged. 'Reckon mine have got used to not having me around. They think I ought to be married and in my own home by now, anyway. So do I, if I'm honest.'

'Well, there'll be plenty of young men around soon for you to choose from,' Emily declared. 'Once all the boys come home from the war they'll be looking for nice girls to settle down with. This war's held a lot of that up.'

'Not for everyone,' Heather said. 'Look at all the girls who've got married quickly because their sweethearts are

27

going away. And the ones who've got engaged to Americans.' She fixed Roger with a stern look. 'Yes, you *do* have to have carrots, even if it is Christmas Day. Remember what Ben Warren told you when he was on leave last time – all the pilots eat them to help them see in the dark.'

'Cats don't eat carrots,' he objected, 'and they can see in the dark all right.'

'Well, they must have a different sort of eye.' She gave a little sigh. Roger was getting altogether too argumentative lately. He was growing up, of course, and he didn't have a father to keep him in line, that was the trouble. It would be better when Ian came home.

Everything would be better when Ian came home.

Chapter Three

Floyd was as good as his word and a few weeks later the whole village was invited to the square dance being held in one of the hangars at the airfield. Most of them had done English country dancing and a few square dances as well, and some had tried Scottish country dancing. 'They're all much the same,' Lizzie told her Auntie Ruth when she popped in for a cup of tea on her day off. 'You'll come, won't you? It'll be fun.'

'I'd like to, but I can't leave Sammy on his own.' Sammy had been left on his own plenty of times when he was living in Portsmouth, but Ruth had firm opinions about that. And Silver, who had firm opinions on just about everything, wouldn't be much good as a babysitter.

'You can bring him over to the farm. Mum and Dad aren't going. Dad says it'll be too late for him – he needs his beauty sleep for the cows! Sammy can sleep in Ben's room.'

Lizzie's younger brother, Ben, was in the RAF. The clever one of the family, he'd been planning to go to university once he left school, but he'd been called up as soon as he turned eighteen and his plans had had to be shelved for the duration of the war. To everyone's surprise, he'd become a pilot and had managed to survive hundreds of operations. At twenty-five, he was now a Squadron Leader and had won the DFC and a bar.

His mother Jane was proud of him but hoped he'd take up his university place once it was all over and he was demobbed, but George sucked his teeth and shook his head. The boy would have other ideas by then, he said. He'd have seen and been through more than they'd ever dreamed possible and he wouldn't want to go back to school, or what amounted to school, after all that. He didn't add: *That's if he survives*, but everyone knew the words were hanging in the air. Pilots had short lives and Ben had already lived longer than most.

'All right, I'll do that,' Ruth said, offering her a biscuit. 'Perhaps Dan would come too. I always liked country dancing. It's a shame we never managed to keep the classes going in the village hall but it's all been so difficult, what with so many people going away. We've put on a few village hops, I know, and the Land Girls have been good coming to those, but they won't do regular classes. Say they're too tired.'

'I expect they were to begin with,' Lizzie said. 'They weren't used to the hard work and long hours then. Anyway, they can come to this. I'll go up to the Knights and ask their girls. Heather'll probably come too. That's the nice thing about this sort of dancing, we old married women don't mind doing it with strangers. Not that they're *all* so fussy,' she added, rolling her eyes. 'I hear Susie Brown's been seen with that GI again. It's a shame, that's what it is, with her hubby away fighting. I don't know how she can do it.'

'Well, she's not the first and she won't be the last,' Ruth observed. 'I must say I was a bit concerned when your mother said she'd agreed to have Floyd and Marvin over for Sunday dinner when they weren't flying. A couple of handsome young Americans could have been quite a temptation. But they're decent young chaps, I could see that straight away, and not likely to—'

'Not likely to what?' Lizzie demanded, her brown eyes flashing. 'All right, Auntie Ruth, you don't need to answer – I know what you mean. What annoys me is that you seem to think that *I* might be tempted! Well, I can tell you, I'm not, nor ever have been, not even for a minute!'

Her aunt stared at her in dismay. 'Lizzie, Lizzie, don't take it like that! I never meant that at all. Oh, I'm sorry.' She came across to put her arms around the angry young woman. 'Of course you'd never do anything like that. I don't know what I was thinking of to say such a thing.'

'Nor do I,' Lizzie said, still sounding slightly aggrieved. She allowed herself to be pushed back into the wooden armchair by the range and picked up her cup. 'Floyd and Marvin are more like brothers to me. But if people are going to be thinking otherwise maybe I won't go to this square dance after all.'

'Oh, you must! It wouldn't even be happening if it wasn't for you. And of course people won't think anything of it. I really am sorry, Lizzie. I didn't mean it to come out that way, truly I didn't.'

'Well, all right.' Lizzie sipped in silence for a minute or two, then said, 'Silver's very quiet this afternoon. He's not sickening for anything, is he?'

'I hope not!' They both looked at the stand where the big grey parrot was holding a sunflower seed with one foot and probing it with his beak. 'He's just having one of his silent days. I think Sammy's been wearing him out, teaching him all those Christmas carols. He's not sorry the boy's back at school and he can get a bit of peace!'

Lizzie laughed. 'I shouldn't think you're sorry, either, are you? You can have a bit too much of Christmas carols.'

'Especially when it's Silver singing them,' Ruth agreed, thankful that her niece's good humour seemed to have been restored. They finished their tea and Lizzie got up to go. She only had a short time before returning to Gosport, and wanted to spend most of it with her mother. She pulled on her dark blue coat and kissed her aunt. 'So that's settled, then? You'll come to the dance.'

Ruth nodded. 'So long as your mother doesn't mind

having Sammy.' She saw Lizzie out and watched her swing away along the lane, then shivered and went back to the warmth of the kitchen.

I don't know why I said that about being worried about those two Americans, she thought, stirring the coals in the range. I didn't even know I had been! And I've never doubted Lizzie, not for a moment.

All the same, it wasn't surprising that young women left on their own for years at a time sometimes slipped a little way down the primrose path. As Ruth had said, Susie Brown wasn't the first and wouldn't be the last. And Lizzie was a healthy young woman, who needed her man.

It'll be a good thing when all this is over and the men come back to their rightful places, she thought, going outside for more coal. It'll be a good thing for any number of reasons.

Floyd came over to the farm several times to consult Lizzie about the dance. He wanted to know what sort of food the villagers would enjoy and what kind of dances they could do. 'There'll be a caller,' he said, 'so they won't be expected to remember everything. They just have to listen and do what he says – so long as they know the moves.'

'Well, we used to do a bit of square dancing when we had our own classes,' she said. They were in the farm kitchen and Lizzie was knitting a Fair Isle pullover for Sammy from a pile of different-coloured wools. 'We know things like do-si-do and ladies' chain and allemande left, and that sort of thing. Is that what you mean?'

'Yeah, that's it. And trail through and U-turn?'

'I'm not so sure about those.' She slipped a thread of blue wool on to her needles.

'Well, we'll start off with some easy dances and see how it goes. It's meant to be fun – no one has to be scared they won't be able to do it.' He handed over some sheets of paper. 'I brought a few posters over, see? One of the guys is good at art.' The posters showed pictures of men in check shirts and work trousers, twirling girls in gingham skirts and white blouses under their arms. Lizzie laughed.

'They're lovely! Everyone will want to come when they see those. I'm not sure we'll all be able to dress like that, though.'

'Doesn't matter. It's all simple stuff. I dare say most girls have got a blouse or skirt not too different from these.' He glanced at her. 'Wear that pretty lacy thing you had on at Christmas. You looked real cute in that.'

Lizzie blushed. The blouse had been made from an old lace tablecloth, but she wasn't going to tell Floyd that. Come to think of it, there was a gingham tablecloth in the sideboard too – she wondered if it could be turned into a skirt.

'How will we get there?' she asked, thinking out loud, but Floyd took it as a serious question.

'We'll send some lorries. There'll be benches in the back. It won't be like going by limousine, but you'll be in the dry.' He grinned at her. 'It's going to be fun, Lizzie. I'm real glad you're coming.'

Lizzie met his eyes and then looked down at her knitting. Her life, which had become very much a matter of routine in the past few months, had been brightened by the arrival of the two Americans. Nursing at Haslar Hospital seemed to be going through a quiet phase; since D-Day, when they had had an influx of patients, the war had taken a different turn and although wounded men were still arriving, the urgency had transferred to other theatres of war. There had been no bombing for a long time, and everyone was hoping the fighting would soon be over. It makes you feel restless, she thought. We're fed up with it. We want to get back to normal life but somehow we can't. It's like one of those nightmares where you're walking down a long road without ever reaching the end. Life had become tedious and dull. And Floyd and Marvin's visits to the farm had been a

33

bright spot in the dullness, rather like the bright red she was now knitting into the soft blue.

The visits wouldn't last for ever, though. If the war did end soon, the Americans would be gone. They were bomber pilots and went over to Germany night after night, bombing the cities there as the Luftwaffe had bombed Britain. You never knew if they would come back, and one day they would be gone for good.

Lizzie felt suddenly depressed. The end of the war, which would bring back Alec, would also take away these new friends. It would take away Floyd.

'Hey,' he said gently. 'Why the sad face? I thought you were looking forward to the dance.'

'I am,' she said, laying her knitting down and looking up at him. 'I was just thinking – it's been so nice, having you here. You and Marvin. We will keep in touch, won't we? After you've gone back to America, I mean.'

'Sure we will,' he said. He looked at her, his blue eyes suddenly dark, and she felt something twist inside her. 'Coming over here has been one of the best things in my life, Lizzie. I'll never forget it, or you.'

She wanted to look away, but couldn't; she felt mesmerised, like one of the rabbits her brothers used to catch in torchlight. Floyd leaned a little closer and opened his mouth to speak. Lizzie's heart thumped; and then, with both relief and dismay, she heard her mother's voice at the door. Hastily, she picked up her knitting and began to click the needles furiously.

'My goodness, it's bitter out there this morning,' Jane was saying. 'We'll be getting more snow, I can feel it in the air. Your father's taking the sheep down to the near field already – oh hello, Floyd.' She was inside, her cheeks rosy with cold, shucking off her boots on the doormat and unwinding a long blue scarf from her neck. 'I didn't know you were here. Come over to make some more arrangements about that dance, have you?'

Floyd stood up. 'That's right, Mrs Warren. Lizzie and I have been going over the programme. It's going to be a really good evening – are you sure you won't come?'

Jane shook her head. 'George and me have to be in our beds early. There's a lot to do on a farm this time of year, with the beasts being in the barn. Has Lizzie been looking after you?' She went across to the stove and slid the kettle on to the hotplate. 'Given you something hot to drink?'

'Floyd brought some coffee over, Mum. There's some left in the pot if you'd like it.'

'I won't, thanks, so long as you don't think I'm being rude,' Jane said, dumping a trug full of potatoes and turnips on the table. 'I can't seem to get used to that ground coffee you Americans drink. I'll just have Camp.' She took the bottle from the shelf and poured a spoonful of dark liquid into a cup.

Floyd grinned and turned to Lizzie. 'Well, I guess that's just about it. I'll get the lorries down at the green by seven and I'll stick these notices up on my way back to camp. Right – I'll see you there.'

'Are you sure there's nothing else I can do?' Lizzie asked, laying down her knitting.

He looked at her as if he wanted to say something, then shook his head. 'Not a thing. This party's on us. A kind of thank you for all the hospitality we've been given here-abouts.' He met her eyes for a moment longer, then nodded at both women and let himself out of the back door.

Lizzie and her mother stared at each other across the big kitchen.

'Oh dear,' Lizzie said, her voice quivering a little. 'He said that almost as if it was going to be a goodbye as well. As if they'll be going away soon.'

'Well, and so they will,' Jane said, sipping her coffee. 'We all know that. As soon as the war ends, maybe even before. And I've got to say this, Lizzie, but to my mind the sooner that is, the better.'

'What do you mean?' Lizzie stared at her. 'What are you saying, Mum?'

Jane gave her daughter an inscrutable look. 'I'm not saying anything, Lizzie. Only that the sooner the war's over, the better it'll be for all of us. Even if it does mean that some people will be leaving the village.' She paused. 'Just remember that it'll mean some people coming back as well. Your Alec. Our Ben and Terry. Ian Knight. The Americans might be going away, but our own men will be coming back, and that's what matters.'

Heather too was thinking of the end of the war and Ian's return to the farm. She came in from the milking parlour, pulling off her wellingtons, and brushed her hair back from her face. Damp from sweat in the warmth of the steamy barn, it had now frozen, so that the strands were stiff, like wire. She dragged off her old jacket and hung it behind the door.

Emily had a pot of tea ready. The kitchen smelled of beef casserole and potatoes baked in their jackets, and a large pan of cabbage was simmering on top of the stove.

'It's bitter,' Heather said. 'I'm sure it'll snow tonight. The girls have gone back to the cottage and Eli finished off for me. The cows are looking well, though. We'll get some good calves this year.'

'You've done well,' Arthur Knight said from his chair in the corner. He drew on his pipe. 'Our Ian'll be proud of you.'

'I'm quite proud of myself!' Heather said with a grin, and sat down at the big scrubbed table. Emily poured a cup of tea and set it in front of her. 'Thanks, Mum.' She rubbed her face with the back of her wrist. 'I'll just drink this and then go and wash. Something smells good.'

'It's a nice bit of braising steak. You've earned a decent meal. Dad and I were just saying what a fine job you've made of taking over the farm. You've only had old Eli to help you – those girls weren't much use when they first came, but you've licked them into shape and the farm's looking as good as ever it did. It was a lucky day for us, the day our Ian brought you here as a bride.'

'A lucky day for me, too,' Heather said. 'I love farming, and you've been really kind to me. It could have been awkward, me taking over when Ian was called up.'

'Kind!' Emily said scornfully. 'Why, you've been like a daughter to us, Heather. Kindness doesn't come into it.' She hesitated. 'I just hope Ian will appreciate it, that's all. It might not be easy for him, you know – coming back to find you doing so well. He never did like playing second fiddle.'

Heather looked at her in astonishment. 'Second fiddle! Why, he won't be second fiddle at all – we'll be partners. I'm looking forward to it.'

Arthur leaned forward and knocked out his pipe. 'All the same, there's been quite a few changes around the place. It'll take a bit of time for him to get used to things again.'

'Well, I'll be here to help him do that. I can show him just what we've done. And Eli says he'll stay on a bit, just until all the men are back.' Her face saddened for a moment. There were quite a few young men who wouldn't be coming back, and whose names would be added to the memorial of the Great War of 1914–1918 which stood on the village green. 'Pam and Jean are going to go home, but Stevie says she'll stop on too. She likes the country and she's in no hurry to go back to Portsmouth.'

Emily lifted the lid on the saucepan and poked a fork into the cabbage. 'Well, maybe we're being a bit previous, talking as if the war's going to be over next week. There's a long way to go yet, if you want my opinion.' Her words were drowned by a sudden roar of aircraft overhead, and they all looked up. 'That's those Americans going over again. They're bombing Germany to bits, from what I can make out. But I can't see Hitler taking that lying down – people are still talking about his "secret weapon".' She poked at the cabbage again. 'This is just about ready now, Heather. Go and have your wash and call the kiddies in – they're playing Ludo in the back room. And after supper we'll have a game of cards.'

Heather went through to the scullery to do as she was told. It was cold out there and she washed quickly, splashing her face with icy water and rubbing warmth into it with a rough towel. Then she went to tell the children supper was ready.

What was Ian going to think of it all, she wondered, picking up Teddy and cuddling him against her while Roger and Pat put away the counters. The children growing so big, the farm doing so well. Her mother-in-law's words came back to her mind and she frowned a little.

Second fiddle? Ian must never feel he was 'second fiddle'. It was up to her to make sure he didn't.

'Square dancing?' Dan Hodges said. He'd cycled over from Portsmouth to see Sammy and Ruth, but he was keeping an eye on the weather. If it looked like snow he'd have to go back early, or even use the train. You couldn't ride your bike out on these dark country roads in a snowstorm. 'You mean that American stuff?'

'Well, it's at the American camp so I suppose that's what it will be,' Ruth said with some amusement. 'Those two young airmen that come over to Jane's of a Sunday, they're arranging it all. There's posters all over the village – you must have seen them.'

'I did notice something,' he acknowledged. 'Didn't stop to read 'em, though. I just wanted to get here, in the warm. When is this square dance, then?'

'Next Saturday night. I thought you might come over in the afternoon and – and stop the night,' she added, blushing a little. 'Jane says you can use Ben's room, like you did at Christmas.'

'I'm stopping with Auntie Jane and Uncle George,'

Sammy put in. He was over by Silver's stand, feeding the parrot sunflower seeds. 'You can have Ben's bed and I'll sleep on cushions on the floor.' He gazed at his father entreatingly. 'Say you will, Dad.'

'Well, I dunno.' Dan looked at Ruth. 'You're going anyway then, are you?'

'It'll be a nice night out,' she said a little defensively. 'And it's not like ordinary dancing.'

'Blimey, don't say it like that!' he exclaimed. 'You go to the dance if you want to, Ruthie. It's none of my business what you do. Tell the truth, I'd like to come, only I might have to work next weekend. We got a big job on – I might need to go to sea.'

'Oh, Dan!' Ruth's voice betrayed her disappointment. 'That's a shame. I was really hoping you'd come.' Her voice dropped and she looked down at her sewing. She was mending one of Sammy's shirts, turning the collar so that the worn edge would be on the inside. She bit her lip, feeling a sudden heat in her eyes. 'We've never had a night out together,' she said in a low voice.

Dan too was disappointed. He looked over at her, sitting in her armchair on the other side of the range, mending his son's clothes. She always had some sort of work in her hands, he thought – darning, mending, a bit of knitting. You never saw her sitting idle. And she didn't get out much, not even to the mobile pictures that some of the Yanks set up in the village hall every other Wednesday night. She'd taken Sammy once or twice, but mostly she was too tired after her day's work at the Cottage Hospital. He felt a sudden stab of fear. Nora's illness had started with feeling tired . . .

'You're all right, ain't you, Ruth?' he asked sharply. 'Not doing too much, are you?'

She smiled at him. 'We all do too much these days, Dan. I don't see as it does us any harm, though. I'm all right, just sorry you can't come to the dance.'

'So am I.' He slanted her a humorous look from beneath his dark brows. 'I'll be wondering if you're getting off with one of them Yanks. Maybe I should tell 'em at Camber that I can't work next weekend after all.'

'No, don't do that. Your work's important.' She finished the shirt and held it up in front of her, looking for parts that might soon need patching. 'And I shan't get off with any American, don't you worry. I'm fussy about the men I make friends with, after my Jack.'

Dan said nothing. Ruth had told him a good deal about her husband, who had been in the Merchant Navy and died of malaria when they hadn't been married long. He even knew the sound of Jack's voice, from the remarks he'd taught Silver as he'd brought the parrot home on one voyage. It still gave Dan a bit of a shock to hear another man's voice telling Ruth he loved her and asking if he could call her sweetheart. But that was something he'd had to get used to. It was a case of love me, love my parrot – and Dan knew that he loved Ruth. He just hadn't told her yet – not in so many words.

In truth, he was half afraid to tell her, because although he knew she was fond of him, he didn't know if she could ever let her feelings go any deeper. And he was afraid that telling her would somehow spoil things between them. She'd be embarrassed and, although he would still be able to come to the cottage to see Sammy, the easy friendship that had grown up between himself and Ruth would disappear.

'Ding-dong bell,' Silver said suddenly. 'Pussy's down the well. I've got sixpence, jolly little sixpence. Tuppence to lend, tuppence to spend, tuppence to take home to my wife. *Sod* the little buggers!'

They all laughed. Silver had an enormous repertoire of sayings and Ruth lived in hope that he would forget some of the ruder ones. He never did, though, probably because they brought him more attention than the others. He tilted

40

his head sideways now and gave them an evil look before scratching his eyebrow with a scaly grey claw. 'Silver's a *good* boy,' he said wheedlingly. 'Silver's a *clever* boy.'

'Clever you may be,' Ruth told him, thankful that the moment of awkwardness was over. She was pretty sure she knew what thoughts had been passing through Dan's mind, and wished he'd come out with them. 'I'm not so sure about *good*.' She folded the shirt and laid it aside. 'Now, what about a cup of tea? Sammy, d'you fancy sardines on toast?'

Sammy nodded and made for the cupboard where the tinned food was kept. Ruth added a tin or two to the store every week during the summer, knowing that winter snow might make shopping difficult. It was Sammy's job to bring logs to the shed as well. Do something every day in summer towards winter, that was Ruth's motto, and it had kept her and Sammy comfortable during even the worst of the weather.

She had everything so well arranged, Dan thought, comparing the snug neatness of the cottage with the bleak discomfort of his own home in Portsmouth. Not that it was as bad as it used to be – Ruth's example had shown him how to look after a place – but the house in April Grove had never had a chance. It had been a mess when he and Nora had moved in, and she'd never been up to the job of taking care of it. She'd done her best and so had young Sam, bless him, but it had been hopeless. And after she'd died Dan had just let everything slide. He'd had neither the time nor the heart for housework. It wasn't until he'd come out to Bridge End and seen how Ruth Purslow managed, with a job and all, that he'd realised how different life could be.

'D'you reckon you will be able to come next week?' Sammy asked wistfully as they sat round the kitchen table to sardines on toast. 'I wish you could.'

'So do I, son.' Dan's eyes rested on him for a moment,

then he looked across at Ruth. 'But you know what it is –
the war comes first.'

Sammy nodded. He could barely remember a time when
the war hadn't dominated their lives. Like most people, he
took it for granted that, whatever you wanted to do, the war
would come first.

'Brian Collins told me the war's going to be over soon,'
he said. 'Hitler's going to give in and we'll be the winners.'
He looked at his father. 'I don't really have to go back to
Portsmouth, do I, Dad? I could stay here. You'll be able to
come out to Bridge End every weekend then, won't you?
You'll be able to come and see me and Auntie Ruth
whenever you like.'

Chapter Four

The dance was held in an empty hangar at the airfield, and it had been decorated for the occasion. Lizzie laughed when she saw it, for it could have been a barn on any of the farms in the area – an enormous barn, it was true, but still a barn, with bales of hay to sit on and straw scattered over the floor. Floyd, who was waiting for her just inside the door, grinned.

'What's so funny?' he asked her.

'I was just wondering where the cows were.'

'Whaddya think this is, a rodeo?' He took her hand. 'It's a square dance – a hoedown. We have them when we finish the harvest or raise a new barn or someone gets hitched – whenever there's anything to celebrate. And a barn's the place we have them. It's the only place where there's room.'

Lizzie nodded. 'I know. It's lovely that you've gone to so much trouble. You must have been cadging hay from all the farmers in Hampshire.'

'Even your dad,' he agreed. 'Didn't he tell you? Anyway, never mind all that – we're here to dance. Listen.'

At the far end of the hangar was a stage on which stood a band of five musicians – an accordionist, two fiddlers, a piper and a drummer. They were beginning to play, and the tune set Lizzie's feet tapping at once. A caller, dressed in the chapped trousers and wide stetson of a cowboy, stepped forward and held out his hands for silence.

'Howdy folks, and welcome to the Big Hangar Barn. Tonight we're going to tread the boards, cut the mustard and dance on the seat of our pants. Now, I know a lot of you folks have your own way of dancing and we have ours, so what I've done is try to put the two together so we can all have fun. Take your partners now, boys and girls, form your squares – and let's dance!'

The American servicemen, all smartly dressed in uniform trousers and shirts, made at once for the local girls. Only a few had brought their husbands or sweethearts; most were alone, their men all away at the war. A little tentatively, they allowed themselves to be led on to the floor and stood in square formation, waiting for the caller to issue his instructions.

'We'll walk it through once for each couple and then we're away.' After he had completed his instructions, the musicians struck up and he began in a rapid, high-pitched voice: 'Allemande left your corner . . . do-si-do your own . . . allemande left your corner and go back to your own . . . give that girl a right-hand turn and promenade the ring . . . allemande left your corner, and everybody swing! Now the figure. First couple, go on swinging . . .'

Lizzie found herself whirling in the middle of a stamping, clapping ring of people. Floyd was gripping her tightly against him, one arm around her waist, the other hand holding hers as they pivoted on the spot. When they stopped she was dizzy but there was no rest as he led her around the ring, 'visiting' each couple in turn and then returning to their place to join hands in a circle and dance round. Listening to the calls and trying to follow where he led took all her concentration, and when the dance finished she was breathless and laughing.

'Well done!' he congratulated her. 'You've done this before, haven't you?'

'We used to have country-dance classes in the village and we did some square dances then. They weren't as fast as this, though.'

'Fast?' he echoed. 'Gee, if you think *that* was fast, you've got a real surprise coming.' The caller was already announcing the next dance. 'Come on, Lizzie. This is a real humdinger, you just got to do this one.'

'I haven't got my breath back yet—' but he took no notice and hauled her into another square. The rest of the girls were laughing and protesting in much the same way, but it was clear all were enjoying themselves. As they stood waiting for their instructions, Lizzie smiled at Floyd. 'This was a good idea.'

'Glad you're having a good time.' He looked into her eyes. 'So'm I.'

By the time the interval was announced, the ice had been well and truly broken. Each girl had a partner and they collected their plates of food and found seats where they sat eating and chatting. Lizzie, following Floyd to a pair of chairs in a corner, smiled a little wryly.

'What's that look for?' he asked as they sat down.

'I was just thinking . . . it's a good thing our men can't see us now. Most of the girls here have got someone away in the war, you know – a husband or a boyfriend. They wouldn't dream of going dancing with other men in the normal way, but the war's changed everything.'

'And you think the husbands and sweethearts wouldn't like it. I know what they say about us Yanks, Lizzie – that we're overpaid, oversexed and over here. I can understand it. But this isn't meant to be anything more than a bit of fun. A thank-you for all the hospitality we've been offered here. And I mean that in the nicest possible way!' he finished with a grin.

Lizzie smiled, then grew serious again. 'I know that, Floyd. But you know as well as I do that some of your boys have done a bit more thanking than they should.'

'Some of 'em have fallen for your girls,' he acknowledged. 'Is that so terrible? Seems pretty natural to me.'

'Maybe. But you can't expect our men to like it, especially when they thought the girls were going to stay faithful to them. And especially when they're married.'

Their eyes met. Then he said quietly, 'I agree that's a bad scene. But it's still natural, Lizzie. These things happen all the time. It don't take a war to make a coupla people fall in love when maybe they shouldn't.'

'It makes it easier though,' she said.

There was a short silence. Floyd put a forkful of ham into his mouth and chewed. Then he swallowed and said, 'OK, but look at it this way. Maybe a man and a girl get married when they shouldn't. Maybe just because they've known each other a long time, grown up together, their families expect it and they've never met anyone else. But they're not really right for each other. And then someone else comes along – someone who *is* the right man for that girl. Someone who can make her really happy, give her the life she ought to have. Are you saying that those two shouldn't ever be together? Are you saying she's got to stay with the first feller, the feller who just happened to be around at the time?'

'If she's married to him, yes. That's what marriage is.'

'What? Being unhappy? Being stuck with the wrong guy for life?'

'No! Staying faithful – sticking with the vows you made. For better, for worse. It doesn't have to be for worse, anyway. If it's someone you've always known, grown up with, you know them pretty well. You know the way they want to live – it's the same as the way *you* want to live. You might not know anything about – about this new person. They might live a completely different way of life, one you could never understand.' She realised that her voice was rising and stopped, biting her lip. More quietly, she went on, 'That's what's happening with some of the Americans who are taking up with our girls, Floyd. They're walking into their lives and most of them will walk out again, and they won't care what sort of mess they leave behind. And those who don't – those who actually get married – well, neither of them knows what they're taking on and it isn't fair to our men. It just isn't fair!'

The silence this time was longer. Then he said stiffly, 'You don't think much of us, do you, Lizzie?'

She looked up at him and her face changed. She put out her hand and laid it on his sleeve, feeling the warmth of his skin through the cotton. 'Floyd, I'm sorry! I didn't mean that. Most of your men are really nice – and that's half the trouble.'

'We're a long way from home,' he pointed out. 'A lot of our fellers are just kids. They've never been out of their home towns, a lot of 'em. They're country hicks. They're glad to be shown a bit of friendliness and it's not surprising if they react to it.'

'No, it's not. It's not surprising either way. I just think it's going to cause trouble when our own men come home.' She sighed.

Floyd glanced at her. She was looking down at her plate but he fancied he caught the glitter of a tear on her eyelashes. He set his plate on the floor and took hers from her lap, putting it with his. Then he took both her hands.

'Lizzie,' he said. 'You don't have to worry – not about me. I'm not going to walk into your life and out of it again. I think too much of you to do that.'

She looked up at him. Her eyes were wet. 'I just miss him so much,' she whispered. 'He's been away so long, and we hardly had any time together before he went. We never even got started with our lives.'

'I know. And I know just how dangerous it can be, when you miss one person that badly and there's someone else around, maybe getting a little close.' He paused. 'Would you rather I stopped coming to the farm, Lizzie?'

'No!' Her reply was sharp and instantaneous. She stared at him, shocked by her own reaction, and then went on more quietly, 'No, Floyd, don't do that. I – I'd miss you too, and what would be the point of that? We're – we're not going to do anything silly.'

'No,' he said, a little ruefully. 'No, we're not.' The musicians were striking up and he bent and picked up their plates. 'Time to start the dance again. That's what we're here for, after all.'

Ruth, too, had been enjoying the dance, but she was careful not to allow herself to be monopolised by one partner. Instead, she returned firmly to her own seat after every dance and on several occasions partnered one of the other women. One sergeant showed interest in escorting her back to the lorry afterwards, but Ruth smiled and shook her head. 'I promised to stay with my friend. She's a bit shy.'

Joyce Moore would have been amused to hear herself described as shy, but she was bidding an airman a loving goodnight at that moment just out of sight and came back a moment later with smudged lipstick and a wicked grin on her face. Ruth shook her head at her.

'You needn't look like that,' Joyce said. 'It's just a bit of fun. I'm not going to see him again.' She grinned more widely. 'I'm just enjoying feeling like a young girl again, at my first dance!'

'And you a married woman with a houseful of boys!' Ruth said, and laughed. 'You always were a naughty girl, Joyce.'

'I was not. I didn't have to get married, you know, whatever people with dirty minds thought. Johnnie really *was* a seven months baby! Anyway, Alf's safe enough – I'd never have time for a fling.' She glanced at Ruth. 'There's nothing to stop you, though. I saw the way that sergeant was looking at you.'

'And that's all he's going to get the chance to do – look,' Ruth said a little sharply. 'I'm not interested in having a "fling". You ought to know that by now.'

'Not with an American, anyway,' Joyce said slyly.

'What do you mean by that?'

'Oh, come on, Ruth, I'm your friend! You can't expect me not to notice. It's Dan Hodges you're carrying a torch for, isn't it? Has been for a long time.'

Ruth met her eyes, opened her mouth and then closed it again. She bit her lip, then laughed a little, blushing. 'Well, I suppose I do like him quite a lot. But it's not that easy, Joyce. We live such different lives. He's a shipbuilder or an engineer or something in Portsmouth – I've never really known exactly what he does, to be honest – and I live out here in the country. How can we ever settle down together? I really don't think I could move to the town.' She sighed. 'And then there's his boys.'

'His boys? Oh yes, I remember. He's got an older lad, hasn't he? Isn't he in the Army?'

'Gordon, yes. But he's a bit of a handful, I gather. He was at an approved school when Sammy first came out here, you know. He went straight into the Army when he left there and he's done well, by all accounts. But I don't know how I'd cope with him. I've never even met him. There's an awful lot to consider before I say "yes" to Dan – even if he ever asked me,' she added a little dolefully.

'You mean to say he hasn't? But I thought you two had an understanding, at least.'

'Yes, an understanding that we couldn't do anything until after the war. And it's been like that for three years now. I sometimes think it'll never be any different. It's gone on too long, you see, Joyce, and I don't think Dan's ever going to say anything. I don't even know what he thinks about it.'

'But he comes out to see you pretty often.'

'He comes to see Sammy,' Ruth corrected her. 'And he comes to see me too, I suppose. But when the war ends – well, Sammy'll go back to Portsmouth, and will Dan come out to Bridge End then? I don't know.'

Joyce was silent for a moment. They had been waiting to

climb up into the lorry and it was her turn to hoist herself into the back. She frowned and said, 'Does Sammy want to go back? He's settled so well here.'

'That's another problem,' Ruth said, climbing up beside her. 'He doesn't. And I've no idea what Dan thinks about that.'

Floyd and Lizzie were standing together in a dark corner close to the doors of the hangar.

'It's been a lovely evening,' she said softly. 'Thanks for organising it, Floyd.'

'It was a pleasure, ma'am,' he said gravely, and she gave his arm a little punch. 'Truly, Lizzie, it's been great. We'll do it again sometime soon. Can't say when, exactly – maybe I shouldn't tell you this, but we're due for another tour of operations in the next week or so. Machines are all spruced up and the guys have had a break, so we'll be back in the air.'

'Oh.' She was silent for a moment. 'I don't like to think of you flying again, Floyd. Bombing the German cities . . . it seems like tempting fate. You've been so lucky for so long.'

'Hey, what's this about luck? Pure genius, that's what it is.' He put his hands on her shoulders and spoke quietly. 'You don't want to worry about me, Lizzie. I'm going to come through this war without a scratch. I know it.'

Lizzie shivered. 'Don't talk like that – it *is* tempting fate. Floyd, I know just how many pilots get shot down. My nephew Ben's told me. He's another one who thinks he's got a charmed life.'

'Well, maybe we have, both of us.' His hands tightened a little and she looked up at him, seeing the gleam of his eyes in the faltering moonlight. She felt her heart leap a little and as she drew in her breath, her lips parted.

'Lizzie,' he murmured, and drew her against him. 'Look, I know what we were saying earlier . . . and I'm not going to make trouble for you. But if I asked you for just one kiss . . . ?'

'I can't,' she whispered, her eyes half closed. 'Oh Floyd . . .'

'Just one,' he breathed, his face now very close to hers. 'That's all. Just to take with me and remember when we're in the air. To bring me back safe again . . .'

She could not refuse. She felt his lips touch hers, softly at first, then with increasing pressure. Sudden longing pierced her and she clung to him, half crying. For a moment the world swung about them, the sounds of voices and laughter and engines drowned by the roaring of their own senses. Then, gently again, he broke the kiss and held her away.

'Thanks, Lizzie,' he said huskily. 'That'll bring me back safe.'

She stared at the pale shape of his face. 'Floyd—'

'It's all right. I won't read anything into it you don't mean. I won't ask again.' He gave a small, dry laugh. 'That's not a promise, by the way, just an intention. I'm not entirely sure I'll be able to stick to it.'

'Floyd, I meant what I said earlier. I'm not going to let Alec down. And it's not just because we grew up together. I love him, Floyd.'

'I know.' He turned his head. 'They're going. You'd better hop aboard that last lorry. And – I'll see you on Sunday, hey? That's if I'm still invited.'

'Of course you're still invited,' she said, and sped away from him. Hands reached down and hauled her up, and she almost fell into the back of the lorry. The driver, thinking everyone was aboard, was just putting it into gear and the girls squealed and laughed as it lurched away from the hangar.

Floyd stood in the shadows, watching as the vehicle gathered speed and disappeared into the darkness. He drew in a deep sigh and turned back to help clear up the debris of the evening's festivities.

She means it too, he thought. She does love her husband, and she won't let him down.

Tough luck, Floyd, buddy.

Chapter Five

As signs of spring began to appear in the fields and woods around Bridge End, the war entered yet another new phase. The newly formed United Nations was gathering strength, with South American countries almost vying to declare war on Germany and the Axis in order to qualify for membership. At the same time, British and American bombers were flying almost every night to rain destruction on the German cities, just as the Luftwaffe had blitzed Britain during 1941. The newspapers were filled with stories of heavy saturation bombing on cities such as Vienna and Berlin, and the ancient city of Dresden was almost flattened in one night, with a firestorm that killed over fifty thousand people.

'It can't be right,' Ruth said when Dan cycled out to see her and Sammy the following Sunday. 'Why do we need to do that, with the war almost over? There wasn't anything in Dresden to threaten us, was there? They make china there, not bombs.'

'It's war, Ruth. It's not for people like us to know the rights and wrongs of it.' Dan leaned back in his chair and passed a hand over his face. He looks tired out, Ruth thought. Somehow, the more they talk about the war being nearly over, the worse it seems to get. 'There was a nipper killed in the Dockyard the other day,' he said suddenly, without opening his eyes. 'Messing about with a German shell, he was, and it exploded in his face. Never stood a chance, poor little sod.'

'Oh Dan, that's awful!' Ruth exclaimed. 'But where did

he get such a thing? There hasn't been a raid for a long time.'

Dan shrugged. 'Nobody knows. Bloody things are still lying about, that's the trouble. There's unexploded bombs all over the flaming shop. Sorry about the language, Ruth, but it's no worse than you hear from that parrot of yours.'

Ruth smiled, although she didn't really like to hear Dan swearing. She didn't really like to hear Silver either, but there wasn't anything you could do about that. However, Dan didn't often let his tongue slip; it just showed how weary and fed up he was. 'You feeling all right, Dan?' she asked. 'Not had any bad news about your Gordon, have you?'

'Not had any news, good or bad. Boy never was much of a hand at writing letters. I dare say he's all right – Army life seems to suit him. It's when he comes out that the trouble'll start.' He glanced quickly at Ruth. 'No, I don't mean that really. He'll settle down all right. He was working down the Camber dock alongside me before – before his bit of trouble. I expect he'll pick up again there.'

Ruth wasn't so sure. From all she'd heard about Gordon he wasn't the sort to settle down easily anywhere. He was the sort who did well in the Army because he was tough and liked a fight, but that didn't mean he'd do as well in civilian life. She wondered if Dan realised this too and was worrying about him.

'Well, at least he knows he's got a home to come back to,' she said carefully. She still wasn't sure what Dan wanted to do after the war. He'd talked wistfully of living in the country, perhaps working in the forest, but if he had to keep a home for Gordon . . . 'It must be terrible for those whose families have been bombed out. Where are they all going to live? The authorities will never be able to build enough houses for all those thousands.'

'There's been a bit of news about that,' Dan said. 'They're going to build what they call Phoenix houses.

Prefabricated, they are – means they've been half built already, so they can be put up quick. Pompey's going to be the first place to get them.'

Ruth stared at him. 'Half built already? How can they do that, then? They surely can't bring great slabs of brick wall on a lorry.'

'They're not brick, they're sort of compressed board. Asbestos, so they won't catch fire. They're going to have proper kitchens with cupboards and refrigerators and an inside lav and bathroom.' He shook his head wonderingly. 'Refrigerators! Bathrooms! Most of the people that get them won't ever have had anything like that before. Makes you wish you *had* been bombed out.'

'Dan, don't say such things.' She still looked dubious. 'They don't sound very substantial. I mean, a house made of cardboard – I wouldn't like it, not even with a fridge and bathroom.'

'Well, they're supposed to last ten years, while they get the proper houses built,' Dan said. 'Anyway, they'll be something to be going on with.'

Ruth nodded, then went back to her earlier subject. 'I'm pleased to hear about that, but I still feel sorry for the lads whose whole families have gone while they've been away. Whatever can they do when they're demobbed?'

'I dunno.' Dan sighed. 'I dunno what any of us are going to do, Ruthie, if you want the truth. I dunno what sort of a state the country's going to be in – or the whole world, come to that. It seems a right bloody mess to me.' He bit his lip. 'Sorry. I'm not fit company for anyone today, and that's the truth. I never oughter come.'

'Don't be silly, Dan!' Ruth came across the room towards him. 'Of course you should have come. You're always welcome here, you know that. Sammy and I both like to see you. You're his dad, and I—' She stopped abruptly and then went on, 'I like to see you too. You don't have to put yourself out to be good company if you don't feel like it. I just like to see you here, sitting in that chair.'

There was a brief silence, then Dan looked up and met her eyes. She returned his look steadily and saw his eyes darken, his expression change. She drew in her breath and waited for him to speak. He opened his mouth.

'Dad!' Sammy was at the door, wiping his feet hastily as he pushed it open. 'Dad, I saw your bike outside. Have you come to dinner? It's rabbit today – Uncle George gave it to us. I skinned it myself, took its eyes out and everything! Auntie Ruth's done it in a stew. There's enough for Dad, isn't there, Auntie Ruth? You said there'd be enough for Dad if he came.'

'Yes, I did,' she said, smiling a little ruefully. Trust Sammy to come bursting in at just the wrong moment. Never mind, if Dan had something important to say, he'd find a way of saying it, she was sure. She gave Sammy a stern look. 'You'd better take those boots off. You'll never get all that mud off just by wiping them. Wherever have you been – in the slurry? It's almost up to your knees. You never got into that state at Sunday School, *I* know! I suppose you did go?'

'Course I did,' Sammy said indignantly. 'And afterwards I went looking for birds' nests with Roger Knight. He says the birds mate on St Valentine's Day so they ought to be nesting by now. How long does it take for a bird to make eggs after it's mated, Auntie Ruth, d'you know? D'you know, Dad?' He pulled off his boots and left them leaning drunkenly against each other on the doormat. 'Has Silver had his sunflower seeds this morning? Can I give him some?'

He dashed through to the scullery without waiting for an answer. Ruth and Dan looked at each other and she was pleased to see that he was grinning.

'Proper little country boy he is now,' Dan said. 'Birds'-nesting, skinning rabbits – why, he's not the same nipper as

56

come out here all that time ago. Frightened of his own shadow, he was then. You've made a lot of difference to him, Ruth.'

'Well, it's not surprising he was frightened, after all he'd been through. But he's still your boy, Dan. I wouldn't want you to think I'd changed him too much.'

'I don't think that. I just wonder sometimes – well, what his ma would say if she could see him now. She'd be pleased, Ruth, don't think she wouldn't, but I reckon she'd be surprised too. He was always her boy, see. More than Gordon ever was.' He sighed. 'Took more after me, *he* did, and not for the best, neither.'

Ruth saw that the anxiety had come back to his eyes. She said gently, 'I'm sure he's a son to be proud of now, Dan. He must have a lot of your good qualities.'

'Ah well, maybe.' Dan didn't sound convinced. 'Look – I didn't come out here to burden you, Ruth, not more than I've already done, anyway. I thought maybe we could go for a bit of a walk this afternoon, the three of us. That's if there *is* enough rabbit to go round?' he added enquiringly.

'Of course there's enough, Dan – isn't there always? And a walk will be grand. We'll go up to Top Field. The snowdrops are a real picture on the edge of the wood. And we can walk back through New Plantation.'

She knew that New Plantation was one of Dan's favourite places. It was, despite its name, one of the oldest parts of the forest and the trees were magnificent oaks, some twelve or fifteen feet around. However weary and anxious he was, he always seemed to feel easier when he had been there, amongst the huge trunks and beneath the canopy of deep green leaves. Even in winter the swaying branches and pencilled twigs seemed to give him pleasure, and the sight of the snowdrops and early primroses in the hedgerow were enough to brighten anyone's spirits.

'We'll make toast when we come back,' she said.

'Nothing like a slice of hot buttered toast for Sunday tea by the fire after a winter walk.'

In the other room, she could hear Sammy talking to Silver as he fed him with sunflower seeds. She wondered if Dan would take the opportunity to say what had been in his mind just before the boy had burst into the cottage. But Dan had got up from his chair and was putting some more coal on the range. It seemed that the moment had passed.

Floyd had made it to the farm for Sunday dinner the week after the dance, but after that he and Marvin were put back on operations and Lizzie saw almost nothing of him. Haslar Hospital was going through another busy period and she was too tired to go home on her days off. Instead, she stayed at the hospital and slept, and if she did go out it was with the other VADs, to walk along the sea wall or out to Stokes Bay. The barbed wire had been removed after D-Day last year, and people were allowed on the beach for the first time in several years. It was a treat just to be able to wander along the shingle at the edge of the waves and look across the Solent to the Isle of Wight.

Truth to tell, she was relieved not to be meeting Floyd for a while. She was aware that he was too much in her thoughts, that she'd looked forward too much to seeing him. She'd begun to make an effort to get Sundays off so that they could meet at the farm, and she'd been feeling dangerously excited when they were together. She'd even seen her mother looking quizzically at her once or twice, as though she thought Floyd and Lizzie were getting too friendly.

We're not really, she thought, picking her way across the beach. The remains of the building work on the Mulberry Harbours were still much in evidence – great slabs of concrete paving, broken up and scattered on the shingle. There was oil too, in sticky black patches, and if you got it on your shoes it was almost impossible to remove. Almost as impossible as it was to remove Floyd from her mind, she thought ruefully.

I'm not *in love* with him, she argued, not really. It's just that he's an attractive man, and he's different, and he's *here*. And Alec, the man I really love, is so far away, and it's so long since we were together – and sometimes I can hardly remember what he looks like. And when he comes home, he might have changed, or he might think I've changed, and – oh, it's all so difficult, and our lives are just ticking away, and we *still* don't know when all this will be over.

She stopped and gazed out across the sea at the island. Beyond it was France, and beyond that Germany. And Alec? Where – *where* – was he?

'Do you realise,' Stevie said, leaning on her pitchfork, 'that we've been here exactly four years?'

Heather, who was washing the floor of the milking parlour by dint of throwing a bucket of water and disinfectant across it and sweeping with a stiff brush, paused and looked at her. 'Is that all? It seems more like a lifetime.'

Stevie made a face at her and forked the last of the hay into the feeding racks, ready for afternoon milking. 'I don't know whether to take that as a compliment or an insult.' She leaned on the fork, looking pensive. 'It'll seem funny, going back to Portsmouth. I've got used to the country now. I'm not sure I'll be able to settle down in the city again.'

'I didn't think you'd ever settle down in the country,' Heather said. 'You were so glamorous – well, you still are, of course, even in baggy brown breeches and a cowboy hat! But the day you arrived, you looked as if you'd stepped straight out of the hairdresser's after a perm. I remember Dad calling you Goldilocks behind your back! We just couldn't believe those ringlets were real.'

Stevie tossed her head and the blonde curls danced.

'Well, now you know they're absolutely natural. Mind you, I *had* just been to the hairdresser. I thought I'd better get a decent cut before I came out to the back of beyond. I mean, a girl has to look her best on all occasions, you know!'

They both laughed and began to gather up their brushes and forks. Heather picked up a galvanised steel bucket and looked round at the milking parlour.

'All clean and tidy, ready for the little dears to come and muck it all up again,' she observed. 'It must have come as quite a shock to you three, when you realised what you'd have to do. Forty cows to clean up after, twice a day, not to mention the milking and all the work out in the fields. I wonder you all stuck it.'

'Well, we had to, didn't we. Same as everyone else has had to stick at jobs they never thought they'd have to do. Same as people have had to stick being bombed out.' Stevie frowned. 'I think the worst of it was not knowing what was going on at home during the raids, wondering if Mum and Dad were all right. Portsmouth had been having a really bad time when I came out here. I felt as if I was running out on them. But it was either that or one of the other women's services. I'd have had to go away, whichever it was.'

'Well, I'm glad you came here and I'm glad you stayed,' Heather declared. They left the milking shed and walked across the yard towards the stable where the two big Clydesdale horses, Boxer and Barty, were waiting to start their own work. She glanced at Stevie and added quietly, 'You've been like a sister to me. I always wanted one. I don't want you to go away, but we'll always keep in touch, won't we? You'll come back and see us sometimes?'

Stevie looked at her and they both stopped. Their eyes met and then she smiled.

'Of course we will,' she said a little huskily. 'You won't get rid of me that easily. No matter where I go after the war, or what I do, I'll always come back.'

Ruth was not the only person to feel disturbed by the bombing of Dresden. Questions were asked in Parliament and some newspapers published critical articles, calling it 'terror' bombing and arguing that the massacre of so many civilians, in a city that was of no strategic importance and at this stage of the war, was unnecessary and vengeful. The authorities replied that the town was an important railway junction, but it seemed a weak argument. It was as if the Allies were determined to leave no one in any doubt that they were winning. They rained firebombs over Berlin as well, and then Cologne, driving the German army into retreat from the Rhine.

'I just want it to be over,' Ruth said when she met Heather Knight in the baker's shop. 'I should think you do, too.'

Heather nodded. 'I want Ian back. I want to get on with our lives. Somehow, it seems to be harder than ever to wait now, with the end almost in sight. It's been such a long time, Ruth. And it's not just Germany. There's all this fighting in Japan as well. Do you know what I heard this morning? There was a firebomb attack on Tokyo – something like a hundred thousand people killed. What's it all for, Ruth? How can it have got this bad, just from us trying to stop Hitler marching into Poland? How did it spread all over the world like this?'

'It's as if war's a sort of huge machine,' Ruth said, 'and once you've started it, you can't stop it. There aren't any brakes. I don't know, they say it'll be over soon, but how can they stop it all at once? All these countries fighting each other – how can they possibly get them all to agree to stop at the same time? It just doesn't seem possible. I think it's going to drag on and on, and never really come to a stop.'

Heather stared at her in dismay. 'What an awful thought! I hope you're wrong.'

'So do I,' Ruth said, and then tried to smile. 'Don't take any notice of me, Heather. I'm just feeling a bit low. Time of the year, I suppose. I always feel a bit sad when the crocuses are out. They remind me of my Jack. It was in March that he died, you know.'

'Ruth, I'm sorry. I didn't realise. It was cholera or something, wasn't it?'

'Malaria,' Ruth said. 'He'd had it before and thought he'd got over it. But it comes back, and sometimes it's worse. That's how it was for him.'

Heather glanced at the posy of primroses in her basket. 'Are they for his grave?'

'No – Jack doesn't have a grave. He was buried at sea. These are for my dad. Me and Sammy always take him some primroses from the garden.' She glanced up and nodded towards a group of children coming along the lane. 'Here he comes now, out of school. I promised to meet him so we could take them together. Even though he never knew Dad, he likes to take a few flowers to put on his grave.'

Heather looked at Ruth's face. As she caught sight of Sammy amongst the other children, it had brightened and a soft smile spread across her lips. I know what's making her feel low, Heather thought. It's not just grief for her husband or her father. It's the thought that the war's going to end and Sammy will go back to Portsmouth.

She turned and made her way back to the farm. The end of the war was going to bring a lot of changes, she thought. People coming home – and people going away. Ian and Alec, Terry and Ben, coming back to the village with all the other men who had been away. And Sammy and Stevie leaving, along with the few evacuees who were still in the village and the other Land Girls.

It's not going to be as easy as we think, she thought. Some of it is going to be really hard.

Chapter Six

The Allies might have been throwing all they had at their enemies, but Hitler and the Japanese were fighting back. In mid-March the Dambuster Squadron dropped the biggest bomb yet on the Bielefeld viaduct, releasing thousands of tons of water; less than three days later, more of the dreaded V2 rockets hit London, landing on West Hampstead. Ten days after that, the United States bombed Kobe and Kure in Japan; the Japanese responded with kamikaze attacks on aircraft carriers, killing over eight hundred men on *USS Franklin*.

Yet as April came in, with softer breezes and the banks clothed in the purple and gold of violets and primroses, the tide seemed at last to have turned and those last vicious attacks the final death throes of a desperate foe. Driving the German armies before them, the Americans marched into the Ruhr, and white flags greeted the British as they closed in on Hanover, Bremen and Berlin. Vienna was liberated, and Arnhem captured. The noose was tightening on Hitler's capital and Winston Churchill announced that the war would be over in a matter of weeks.

'It's going to be over!' Heather exclaimed, meeting Lizzie as she came home for a day off. 'It's really going to be over! Your Alec will be home again – and my Ian. Oh Lizzie, it doesn't seem possible that it's all going to be over, after all this time. Peace is coming. *Peace*!'

'I hardly know what it means any more,' Lizzie confessed. 'It'll be strange in a way, not having the war in our minds all the time. It's been such a big thing, Heather –

what will there be to replace it? Oh, that sounds stupid, but – well, you know what I mean, don't you?'

Heather nodded. 'It's ruled our lives, hasn't it? And now it won't be there any more, but there'll be other things, Lizzie, *better* things. We'll have our men back, we can start to live our lives again. I know it'll be different, but I think it's going to be even better. I'm looking forward to working with Ian on the farm instead of just being a housewife. A farmer, instead of a farmer's wife.' She glanced at Lizzie's VAD uniform of grey dress and cape. 'What will you do? Will you go on nursing?'

'I don't think so. I'll be demobbed from the VADs. I could go back to training for State Registration at Southampton, like I did to start with, but I don't really want to. I think I've had enough of it. And Alec won't want me to be on shift work.'

'Specially night shift, eh!' Heather grinned, poking her in the ribs. 'I don't mind telling you, Lizzie, that's one of the things I'm looking forward to again – being able to get into bed of a night-time with my husband. And you needn't pretend to be shocked. You're looking forward to it too. It's only natural.'

'Well, maybe I am,' Lizzie said, laughing. 'And Alec and me've got a lot of catching up to do – not like you, with three kiddies already.'

She continued up the lane towards the farm, thinking of Alec and wondering how soon he would be released from the prisoner-of-war camp. Although she hadn't said anything to Heather, she had read the accounts of the horror felt by the Allied soldiers entering the German concentration camps and couldn't get rid of the idea that the atrocities that had been reported might have happened in the POW camps too. It was said that even Eisenhower and Patton, the toughest of the generals, had vomited and wept at the sights that had met their eyes, and Lizzie had seen them for herself at the cinema – piles of naked bodies, little more than skeletons, just thrown into trucks and driven away to mass graves, men, women and little children, starved and sore-ridden, staggering helplessly behind the wires, reaching out bony hands in a desperate plea for help. The whole audience in the cinema had been struck dumb, watching appalled as they realised that this had been going on throughout the war. Worse still, millions of Jews had been slaughtered in huge gas chambers, driven like cattle to an abattoir. How could such things happen? How could any human being be so callous?

'It just proves we were right to go to war against that man,' her father George said, when the family talked about it at dinner-time. 'I know there's been millions killed fighting him, but who's to say he wouldn't have killed even more if we hadn't stood up to it? He'd have taken over the whole world if he'd had the chance, and what a world it would have been.'

'I know. I must say, Dad, when I heard about all the bombing we've been doing – Dresden and places like that – I couldn't help wondering if we weren't going too far. But when you hear about this . . .' Lizzie shook her head. 'And yet, we were killing innocent people too – little children, babies, who never had a chance. I just can't make sense of it.'

'And it's better not to try,' Jane told her. 'People like us can't expect to make sense of these things. We don't have the brains or the education. We have to leave it to those who do, and trust in them to do right. And I believe they did. Now, let's try and forget it for a bit and enjoy being together again. Who wants a bit more apple crumble?'

It was good to be home again, Lizzie thought as she passed her plate, but she couldn't help being disappointed that the two American pilots weren't there. Well, if she were honest, that *Floyd* wasn't there. It was weeks since she had seen him, and then only briefly. They'd had no time to talk together since the night of the square dance.

I was a bit daft then, she thought, pouring custard on to the pudding. I read too much into what happened that night. We were just enjoying ourselves and I thought – well, whatever I thought, I was wrong. I was wrong to stay away too, because we're just friends, that's all. And if the war ends soon he'll go away and I'll never see him again, and that will be a shame. We'll have missed a few more chances to enjoy each other's company.

'If you don't stop pouring that custard soon, it'll overflow on to the table,' her mother said tartly, and Lizzie jumped. 'There, now look what you've done! All over the tablecloth!'

'Sorry,' Lizzie said, blushing and trying to scoop up some of the custard with her spoon. 'I was thinking about something else.'

'We could see that,' Jane said, and Lizzie had a feeling that her mother knew exactly what – or who – she'd been thinking about. 'Well, we'll all have something to think about soon. The end of the war! We're already planning a big village party. It would be nice if you could get home for it.'

'A party?' Lizzie said. 'In the village hall?'

'No, on the green. There's going to be games and children's races, and tea, and then dancing and a huge bonfire up on top of Barrow Hill. There'll be bonfires all over the country – beacons, like when the Armada came.'

Lizzie gazed at her. 'But how will you know when to have it? Nobody's going to know exactly when it will end, are they? How *do* wars end?'

'The last one ended when they signed the Armistice in that railway carriage,' George said. 'I don't see this one ending that way. I can't see Hitler signing any armistice.'

'It doesn't matter how it ends,' Jane said, a little impatiently. 'They'll tell us, won't they? And as soon as they do, we'll have the party. I told you, we're getting things together already.'

'We'll just have to take a chance that I can get home,' Lizzie said. 'They're not going to let everyone just leave the hospital to go home at a moment's notice, are they? We do still have some patients to look after, you know.'

The end of the war. It was being talked about wherever you went. It was coming, and coming soon.

And when it did so, Alec would come home. And Floyd would go away.

All through the war everyone had listened to the news programmes on the Home Service. *The Nine O'Clock News* had been especially important, often followed by a speech from Mr Churchill, or some of J. B. Priestley's *Jottings*. There had been a period when the traitor Lord Haw-Haw had broadcast at that time too, but nobody bothered about him now. Everyone knew the Allies were winning. It was just a matter of time.

One of the most famous of all the POW camps, Colditz, was liberated the day after Arnhem's capture. The next day another concentration camp, Belsen, was entered and there were yet more sickening pictures in the newspapers and on Pathé Pictorial. You hardly knew whether to smile or weep, Ruth thought, staring at the horrors. You had to be glad it was nearly all over – but oh, those poor, poor souls. Why couldn't something have been done to save them?

'We done as much as we could,' Dan said. 'We didn't know, not for certain. And we've been fighting as hard as anyone could. We can't blame ourselves for what the Jerries done.'

'It's just so terrible. I can't get them out of my mind. Men and women who've never done anything wrong, treated worse than animals. And the children – little *babies*, Dan. It's wicked. It's evil.'

'It won't happen again,' he said, coming to stand beside her and look at the newspaper she held. 'Nobody will ever let that happen again.'

She sighed. 'I hope you're right. But it seems to me there's always someone as wicked as Hitler, wanting to take over other countries. And if you don't know what they're doing, how can you stop them?'

'By showing them we won't allow it,' he said grimly. 'That's what we got to do, and we done it. Anyone else who thinks he'll go the same road as Hitler will know who he's got to reckon with.'

Ruth put down the paper. 'The village is going to have a party when the war ends,' she said. 'Will you be able to come out for it, Dan? I know Sammy'd like it if you could.'

'Well, I'll do me best. I dare say there'll be a bit of a holiday for everyone. I'll come out the first minute I can get away.'

'And then I suppose you'll be thinking about taking Sammy back home,' she said tentatively.

He glanced at her. 'Don't see there's no hurry about that,' he said gruffly. 'What I thought, he ought to stop on till school breaks up anyway, end of July. And then maybe for a week or two to help with the harvest, he likes doing that. And by then, well, we'll have a bit more idea . . .' His voice trailed away and Ruth gave him a quick look but he was staring into the glowing coals on the range and she couldn't decipher his expression.

She said, 'Of course, your Gordon will be coming home then too. There'll be a lot for you to think about.'

'That's right,' he said, still looking into the fire. 'There's Gordon as well. I dunno quite what—' He shook himself a little and gave her a rueful grin. 'Sorry, Ruth, what with Gordon and me job at Camber and all, I don't seem able to see me way clear at all. Better wait till we know it's over, eh? Then maybe we'll know what to do.'

'Yes,' Ruth said, trying to keep the disappointment out of her voice. 'That's the best thing, Dan.' She went to the sink and began to pump up some water. 'Let's have a cup of tea, shall we? Sammy'll be in soon and there's a nice shepherd's pie in the oven. After that I thought we'd have a game of cards. Sammy always enjoys that.'

'Sammy, Sammy, shine a light,' Silver piped up suddenly in his gravelly voice. 'Ain't you playing out tonight? I love you, Ruthie,' he added in a soft, coaxing tone. '*Let* me be your sweetheart.'

Ruth stayed quite still by the sink. She didn't dare turn round. It was Jack's voice that had spoken those words, it was Jack who had taught the parrot to say them. But Jack, she realised suddenly, was in the past. She would never stop loving his memory, but it was another man she wanted to hear speak those words to her now. It was another man whose sweetheart she wanted to be.

On 26 April, Russian soldiers reached Berlin. Mr Churchill announced that the war would be over in a matter of weeks. The battle for Berlin had begun and was being fought, street by street. GIs entered Dachau and were so outraged by what they saw that they killed every SS guard they saw, including over a hundred who had surrendered. The last days of the war in Europe seemed to be the bloodiest of all, and those at home could only pray that it would soon be over.

By 2 May the rumours began to spread: Hitler and Eva Braun were dead; Goebbels had killed his six children and then committed suicide; Goering had been shot. When someone asked Mr Churchill if the rumours were true, the Prime Minister replied that it was 'wishful thinking'. But within a few days everyone knew. And on 7 May came at last the longed-for statement to the nation. Hostilities were at an end. At one minute past midnight on 8 May, the war would be finally over.

Over . . . Such a small, simple word and so difficult to understand. It was the word they'd repeated again and again since the very beginning. *Over by Christmas. Over by the summer. Over by this time next year. Over . . . Over . . .*

Over . . . It had been spoken so often that they scarcely understood what it meant any more. They tried it out in their mouths, twisted their tongues around it, tasted it on their lips, and still it made no sense.

'I can't believe it,' Heather said. She had been away for two days, visiting her mother in Sussex, and had come back to find that everyone had gravitated to the green to meet each other, to try this strange word out to see if anyone else understood it. 'We've waited such a long time. I can't believe it's over at last.'

Jane and Ruth were in the middle of a knot of women who were taking refuge in practical thoughts. 'There's all the cakes to bake, we've been keeping the flour and sugar back and thank goodness there's plenty of eggs at this time of year. And jellies to make as well – we'll have to look out plenty of bowls – and we'll need enough sandwiches to feed an army. Oh!' Ruth put a hand to her mouth and giggled. 'An *army*! Well, I dare say some of the Americans will come down from the air base . . . Jane, is George going to organise the kiddies' games and races in the afternoon? And then there'll be the bonfire in the evening . . .'

'Never mind tomorrow evening!' Joyce Moore shouted excitedly, running into the midst of the circle. 'They're lighting the one on Barrow Hill *tonight*! I heard it from the vicar himself. He says the war'll be over at midnight so that's when it should be lit, and he wants everyone who can get there up on the hill in time to see it. Kiddies and all – they can sleep in tomorrow, keep 'em out of the way while we get the bunting and flags up and the party ready.' She stopped, panting for breath, and they all looked at each other, excitement dawning in their eyes at last.

'Tonight!' Heather exclaimed. 'The party's starting *tonight*!' She whirled round and pulled Ruth into a fierce hug. 'Ruth – Joyce – the war's going to be over *tonight* – at midnight! We're going to have the biggest and the best party this village has ever seen before, because the war's going to be *over*!'

They stared at each other and burst into wild laughter. In another moment, they were all joining in the dance and then the men, talking in a different group, and the children who were racing around the green, joined in as well. The entire village was there, leaping and skipping in frenzied joy, as the meaning of the word *over* dawned on them at last and they glimpsed a future that would be free of fear, free of death, free of loss and pain and anguish.

By ten-thirty that night, the village was ready. Flags and strings of bunting had been dug out of boxes, lofts and basements where they'd languished for six long years, and were festooned from house to house. The Union Jack fluttered from the pole on top of the church tower and Bill Fry, the butcher, had hung another one, almost as big, right across the front of his shop. Every house and cottage had a lamp on in the front window and the curtains drawn back, so that for the first time in years light spilled out into the lanes and across the village green. Windows were open, despite the coolness of the evening and the drizzle that had begun to fall, and every wireless was tuned to the Light Programme where joyful music was playing. The village was alive with both light and music, and even those who were still grieving for loved ones who would never come back could not fail to feel their hearts lift.

As darkness fell the villagers began to make their way up Barrow Hill to where some of the men and the older boys had been busy constructing a huge bonfire. Heather gasped when she saw it towering above her, its sides built into a palisade of rough-hewn planks, with the branches of fallen trees rearing out of its centre towards the sky. 'It's as big as a house!' she exclaimed, and Stevie giggled beside her.

'I should think there's enough wood there to keep your stove going for a whole winter. Most of it's that tree that

71

fell in Top Field last winter. Eli's had us chopping and sawing for the past three days.'

'I thought you were ploughing Long Acre!'

'We were. This was in our spare time.' Stevie craned her neck to admire the edifice. 'The vicar's going to light it at exactly one minute past midnight.'

'How will he know—' Heather began, but Stevie grinned and put her finger to her lips.

'Wait and see.'

Heather curbed her impatience and looked about her. Almost the whole village was there. Everyone who could walk had climbed the hill – even those who hadn't walked so far for years and had to be helped up the steep path. Small children had staggered up; babies had been carried. Everyone had come to experience the jubilation of the village at the end of the war. They had lit their way by a variety of torches, lanterns, even candles carried in jam-jars. The sparks and points of light danced in the air like fireflies.

'Where's Eli, then?' she asked suddenly. 'If he built it, he should be here to light it. And Solly Barlow, I can't see him either. I'd have thought he would be in charge of the fire, him being a blacksmith.'

'Oh, I expect he's around somewhere,' Stevie said vaguely, and Heather glanced at her suspiciously. The Land Girl was looking mischievous, as if she were about to burst out laughing, but she met Heather's eyes with a look of bland innocence. She knows more than I do about what's going on, Heather thought with a sudden, unexpected flash of annoyance; and then she quashed the momentary irritation with the reminder that she had been away from the village for the best part of two days and that events had moved swiftly in that time. Everyone had known the war was coming to an end, but nobody had known when it would be, and the end, coming with Hitler's death, had been quicker than anyone had thought. All this had been arranged as soon as the news began to filter through and although everyone else seemed to know what to expect, Stevie was obviously enjoying Heather's bewilderment.

'All right,' she said, 'you keep your secret. I'll find out soon enough.'

It was half past eleven; then a quarter to twelve. The villagers formed a circle around the towering bonfire and a tall figure moved forward with a long taper in his hand. Heather saw that it was the vicar – the 'new' vicar as everyone still called him – and she felt a pang of sorrow that old Mr Beckett could not be here. He had been a familiar and much-loved figure, cycling about the parish with his long, spindly arms and legs sticking out at all angles, or flitting through the churchyard like a great bat in his cassock, with his pyjama trousers visible tucked into his shoes. But the new vicar was liked and respected well enough, and it was right that he should be the one to welcome the return of peace.

Five to twelve. Four minutes. Three. Two. One.

'Someone must have a watch—' Heather began, and then stopped as the chimes of the church clock began to strike down in the village. She caught her breath. It was midnight. Only one more minute . . .

The crowd began to chant. 'Ten – nine – eight – seven – six – five – four – three – two – *one*!' With everyone else, Heather cheered, caught up in the wild excitement of years of endurance and suffering brought to an end, of a war won at last, of peace come to a world that had almost despaired of ever knowing it again. But their cheers, deafening as they were, were drowned by another sound – a sound that had been heard only occasionally during the past six years, a sound that would at one time have meant invasion. It was the most joyous, most English sound she knew – that of church bells, their peals as light and sparkling as if the stars themselves were chiming delight. Ruth knew then where Eli was, and Solly Barlow the blacksmith, and some of the other older men who had been bellringers until the war had silenced them.

As the glorious sound glittered on the night air, the vicar laid his taper against the beacon and it sprang into roaring, gold and orange life. The flames reached instantly towards the sky and as they did so, it was lit by other fires and beacons on hilltops and in valleys all about, and by a latticed network of searchlights, combing the skies with elation; and from the port of Southampton, only a few miles away, the muffled booming and hooting of ships' foghorns could be heard between the clamour of the bells, and it seemed as if the whole of southern England was alive and shouting for joy.

The whole of *England*, Heather thought, turning to hug Stevie and whirl her into the dance that had broken out by the searing light of the fire. England – Britain – the whole world. Everyone who knows anything about the war must be celebrating at this moment, because it's over. The world is free and we can have our lives back at last.

It wasn't over everywhere, of course. As the fire finally died down and the villagers began to make their way down the hill to snatch a few hours' sleep before the party on the village green, they realised that there was still a war to be won in the Far East. Japan had not surrendered. Nor, it seemed, was ever likely to.

'They're different, the Japs,' George Warren said as he and Jane walked along the lane with Sammy and Ruth. 'It's all to do with their pride. They'd rather die than give in. Trouble is, they want to take the rest of us with them.'

'But surely now that Europe's safe we can concentrate on beating them,' Jane said. 'It can't take too much longer. And – well, I know there are still men fighting and some of them will die, and I know there are all those POWs being treated so badly in their camps, but I still can't help feeling thankful it's finished here. It must be all right to celebrate that, surely?'

'Of course it is,' Ruth said. 'It wouldn't be right not to. Our boys have fought hard to give us tonight. We've got to celebrate for their sakes as much as for ours. It wouldn't be much of a thank-you for all they've done if we didn't.'

'Dad'll come tomorrow,' Sammy said. 'He said he would, if there was a holiday, and there's going to be two days off for everyone. He'll come on his bike, first thing.'

Ruth felt a twinge in her heart. Dan wouldn't be taking Sammy home straight away – he'd already said he'd like the boy to stay for the rest of the summer. But after that, had he made up his mind what to do then? There was Gordon to consider too. He had to put his sons first – both of them. He might want them both back with him in April Grove, where they could rebuild their old life. Of one thing Ruth was certain: from all she had heard of Gordon, he was unlikely to want to come out to the countryside.

'Come on, Sammy,' she said, pausing at the cottage gate. 'Time for bed. We've got a busy day tomorrow.'

'Today,' he said. 'It's after midnight, so it's today. The first day after the war, Auntie Ruth. Everything's going to be different now.'

Yes, she thought, opening the door. It's the first day after the war, and everything is going to be different.

Chapter Seven

Dan did not arrive next morning. Sammy went off to the village hall to help carry the long trestle tables to the green and set them up for tea and to mark out the lines for the races. Ruth stayed in the kitchen, baking rock buns and making sandwiches with the jam and fish paste she had been saving in the cupboard for the past month. Already there were three big bowls of jelly setting in the larder, and at twelve o'clock her sister Jane arrived with Boxer pulling the farm cart loaded with a churn of milk for the tea and several trays with more sandwiches and cakes which she had collected from various outlying cottages.

'Dan not here yet?'

Ruth opened the oven door and took out a tray of scones, puffed up and golden. 'No. I must say, I'd expected him a bit before this. Thought he'd be straight out on his bike. He said he'd come the first minute he could.'

'Perhaps he had to go to work,' Jane said doubtfully. 'I mean, I know it's a holiday but some people still have to turn up – train drivers and people like that. He might have had some important job on.'

'Yes, he might. I dare say he's on his way, anyway.' Privately Ruth suspected that Dan might have been out celebrating last night and woken late. After all, you couldn't blame him if he had. He'd worked night and day for six long years, during which he'd lost his wife, seen one son sent to approved school and then called up into the Army, and had to let the other be evacuated. Of course he'd want to celebrate.

All the same, she was disappointed that he hadn't made the effort to come out to Bridge End sooner. Disappointed and – if she was honest – rather hurt.

'I'll put these scones on my big meat-platter,' she said, pushing her feelings from her mind. 'They can be buttered later when they've cooled down. What about your Lizzie, Jane, has she managed to get home?'

'Not yet, but she's coming. Sent a telegram to say she'd be here by tea-time. She's got to go back to Haslar in the morning but at least she'll be here to share a bit of it with us. She must be so thrilled. It won't be long before Alec's home. They're letting POWs out of the camps as fast as they can now.'

Ruth nodded. 'And Ian Knight from the farm, he'll be back pretty soon, I should think. They won't want to pay men for longer than they've got to! Give them a demob suit and send them back to civvy street as soon as possible.'

Jane laughed. 'Well, maybe. It doesn't sound very grateful but I expect you're right. Anyway, we need the men back to get the country on its feet again.' She lifted the platter in both hands. 'I'll take this out to the cart. We're setting everything out and covering it with sheets to keep the flies and dust off till it's wanted. It's going to be a real spread.'

She went out to where Boxer was chomping in his nosebag, and Ruth heard his hooves clopping down the lane. She began to clear the kitchen table, piling used bowls and baking trays by the sink, and started to pump up water. She filled the kettle and put it on top of the range.

From the window, she could see the lane. People were passing all the time – women bearing covered trays, men with fencing posts destined to become goal posts for the football match or markers for the races, boys and girls running and shrieking with excitement. Some of them glanced at the window and waved at her, and she waved back, smiling at their joyous faces. Perhaps, in a minute, she would see Dan cycling from the Portsmouth road, or striding along from the little railway station. Perhaps that was what had happened – something had gone wrong with his bike and he'd had to wait for a train. Perhaps, today, there weren't any trains. But if not, how would Lizzie get here? Jane would be so disappointed if Lizzie didn't come.

And I'll be disappointed if Dan doesn't come, she thought. Sammy and me – we'll both be disappointed.

The kettle boiled and Ruth began to wash the dishes. She had been so sure that Dan would come early today. It was such a special day and she'd wanted them to spend it together – she, Dan and Sammy. She'd even believed that today would be the day Dan would make a decision about the future – their future.

I never thought I'd want to marry again, after my Jack, she thought. But all the time Dan's been coming here, I've felt more and more close to him. Funny really, when you think what sort of a state he was in that first time – dirty and shabby, scowling and hardly a word to say even to his own son. It was as if they barely knew each other. But since then, well, he's seemed to be really comfortable here. And I'm comfortable too – comfortable with him. More comfortable than I've ever been with anyone, since Jack. And I thought Dan felt the same. I know he said all that about waiting till the end of the summer but somehow, last time he was here, I thought he'd be the same as me and not want to wait any longer. I thought today might be the day he'd ask me to marry him.

She looked at the clock. It was twelve-thirty. The races were to start at two, and then there would be the tea party and the bonfire and dancing on the green. Sammy would be home at any moment for his dinner. She'd been hoping that there would be three of them to sit down together. She went to the window again, but there was still no sign of Dan.

The back door burst open and Sammy dashed in. His

socks were wrinkled around his ankles, his shoes were muddy and his jumper had a hole in the front. His fair hair was tousled and there was a streak of blood on one cheek.

'Sammy! Whatever have you been doing?'

'Helping put up the jumps for the races in Uncle George's big field.' He skidded to a stop and beamed at her. 'It's going to be ever so good, Auntie Ruth. There's going to be long jumps and high jumps and hurdling and egg-and-spoon races – we've got to take our own spoons – and three-legged races and a sack race – Uncle George is bringing the sacks – and a greasy pole over the stream, and sandwiches and cakes and jelly and *everything*. And after tea the big boys are going to do boxing and the Land Girls are doing a song and dance thing, I shan't bother to watch that, and – where's Dad?' He stared around the kitchen as if expecting his father to appear from some hiding place. 'I thought he'd be here by now.'

'Well, he's not, I'm afraid.' Ruth bit her lip, thinking that perhaps she had sounded too abrupt. 'I'm sure he'll be here as soon as he can. Perhaps his bike had a puncture or the train was late.'

Sammy nodded. 'Yes, he'll be here soon. What's for dinner, Auntie Ruth? I'm starving!'

She smiled, wishing that she could accept the explanation so easily and hoping that Dan would appear before Sammy began to wonder again. 'It's beans on toast. I haven't had time to cook—'

'Beans on toast! Smashing!' He dragged out a chair and dropped into it, then jumped up again as Ruth pointed at his hands. Giving them a sketchy wash at the sink, he said over his shoulder, 'I saw Lizzie coming down the lane. *She* must have got the train all right. I thought Dad might be on the same one.'

'Oh,' Ruth said a little bleakly. Dan could indeed have been on the same train as Lizzie, coming through Fareham from Portsmouth. Lizzie would probably have caught it at

Gosport and might either have changed or come straight through. Ruth realised that she didn't know, and shrugged it aside. Dan had obviously not been on the same train – that was all that was important. So why wasn't he here?

They ate their beans on toast and washed up. Sammy chattered on about the races, and they fed Silver some sunflower seeds before setting out. As they walked down the lane towards the village green, others joined them. Everyone was in a state of joy and excitement.

'I bet everyone in the country's having a party today,' Joyce Moore said, catching up with Ruth while her boys raced ahead with Sammy. 'They say the King and Queen and the Princesses are going to come out on the balcony of Buckingham Palace and wave at everyone. There'll be thousands there. I expect Mr Churchill will be there too. After all, it's him that's got us through it all.'

'Well, I don't think we'd have won if it hadn't been for the rest of the Allies,' Ruth said fairly. 'Especially America.'

'No, but it was him kept us going with his speeches when we were being bombed and losing all our men. It was seeing him looking like a bulldog and waving that cigar of his and giving the V sign that gave us heart and made us determined not be beaten. Well,' she grinned, 'him and Vera Lynn, perhaps!'

Ruth laughed. 'I reckon there are a lot of men who'd agree with you there. The Forces' Sweetheart kept a lot of men smiling through when they must have felt more like crying.' Her own smile faded a little. 'It's been hard for them, being taken away from their homes and families and jobs to become soldiers and sailors and airmen. I mean, if they'd wanted that sort of life, they'd have gone into the Services in the first place, wouldn't they? Like my Jack, joining the Merchant Navy – not that he ever wanted to fight. He just wanted to go to sea.'

'Well, they'll be back soon,' Joyce said, 'and then they'll have to get used to that. I reckon they'll have changed a bit, with all they've seen and done. Look at the places they've been to, the people they've met. It's bound to have altered them a bit.' She glanced at Ruth. 'Where's Sammy's dad, then? I'd have thought he'd be out here too, helping celebrate.'

'Oh, he'll be along later, I expect,' Ruth said, and then sighed. 'To tell you the truth, Joyce, I'm a bit worried. We were expecting him early on. I'd have thought he'd have sent a telegram or something if he couldn't make it for any reason, but we haven't heard a word. Sammy will be proper disappointed.'

'And he's not the only one,' Joyce observed, and gave Ruth's arm a squeeze. 'Come on, Ruth, I know you've got a soft spot for Dan Hodges. More than a soft spot! And why not? He's a good-looking man. I like 'em big and dark like that myself!' She rolled her eyes and Ruth laughed.

'All right, you hussy – yes, I am fond of him. He's not an easy man, mind, but then he's not had an easy life. But – well, I did think there was a sort of understanding between us.'

Joyce stared at her. 'You don't mean you think he's stood you up, just because he hasn't arrived yet? There must be a hundred reasons!'

'I know. I'm reading too much into it. But somehow, this being the day it is – well, I thought he'd be here first off, and I really thought he'd *say* something. And he hasn't even sent a message!' Ruth stared at her friend, feeling the tears come to her eyes. 'I don't know what to think, Joyce, I really don't.'

Joyce looked at her for a minute and then took her arm. 'I can tell you what to think,' she said firmly. 'You can think he's been held up somehow. His bike broke down halfway here and he's having to walk. He's stopped to give someone else a hand. Or maybe that other boy of his has come home unexpectedly and he can't just walk out and leave him. There's dozens of reasons why he hasn't come yet, but he *will*. I'd bet my bottom dollar he'll come before the day's out. You'll see.'

Ruth gave her a wobbly smile. 'I'm being daft.'

'We're all a bit daft today,' Joyce declared. 'Now you just come with me, Ruth Purslow, and be daft with the rest of us. Your Dan'll find you when he turns up, and you'll wonder why you ever let yourself get in such a state. Come on – the boys are waving at us. They're waiting to start the races!'

She walked briskly on along the lane and Ruth followed her. Joyce was right, she told herself. Something had held Dan up but he would come. Nothing would keep him from Bridge End on this day, of all days.

All the same, she couldn't help feeling a twinge of unease deep inside. As if there were something wrong – something that even she wouldn't be able to help Dan cope with.

The races and children's games took all afternoon. Sammy won both the egg-and-spoon and the three-legged race, his leg tied firmly to that of Joyce's youngest boy, Billy. He came last in the sack race, falling almost at once and struggling desperately in his sack while all the others bounded past him. He came second in the high jump but tripped over his own feet in the long jump, falling flat on his face in the sand. He came about halfway in the sprint and his face shone with pleasure as he ran back to Ruth with his prizes – a bar of chocolate and a bag of pear drops.

'They're for you,' he said, thrusting them into her hands. 'I won them for you.'

'Sammy, you can't give me your prizes. They're yours.' She tried to give them back but he shook his head.

'I wanted to give them to you. I *won* them for you.' As she gazed helplessly at him, he added, 'You can share them with me if you like. I don't mind that.'

'All right, Sammy,' she laughed. 'We'll start now. Let's have a pear drop each.' She opened the paper bag, already sticky, and he extracted a bright yellow sweet. Ruth had a pink one and they sucked companionably.

'It's good, isn't it,' Sammy said as they watched the football match start. The teams were bigger boys and they rushed about the field, kicking wildly and pushing each other over whenever they got the chance. The whole thing was degenerating into a brawl when the vicar, who was acting as referee, stepped on to the pitch, narrowly avoiding being knocked over himself, and waved his arms for them to stop.

'Really, this is disgraceful,' he shouted. 'If you can't play by the rules, we'll stop the game.'

'Mr Beckett wouldn't have minded,' one of the boys shouted back. 'It was him made up the rules!' The vicar flapped his arms in despair and retreated to the sidelines. He turned to Ruth and said, 'That's what happens all the time. Whatever I try to do, someone tells me that Mr Beckett would have done it differently. Usually, it seems that he would have done exactly what I'm telling them *not* to do!'

Ruth laughed. 'He wasn't much more than an overgrown boy himself, even though he was past seventy. But everyone loved him.'

'I know,' the vicar said gloomily, and waved his arms at the players again. 'Foul! That was definitely a foul! I warned you, Brian Collins!' He marched across the field, ignoring the other players, and dragged Brian Collins off by his collar. 'Right, now perhaps the rest of you can play in a civilised manner.'

Ruth turned to Sammy and found that he had gone. He was on the far side of the field, sharing the pear drops with some other boys. So much for winning them for me, she thought wryly, and wandered away from the noisy game of football. She glanced up at the church clock; it was nearly time for tea. Better go and start giving a hand with pouring out lemonade and milk.

Once again, she wondered what had happened to Dan. However much he'd been held up, he ought to have been here by now. He could almost have walked here and surely if he'd tried, he'd have been given a lift at some point. Something's happened to him, she thought with a cold feeling of dread. Something awful has happened to him.

And then she saw him. Walking slowly, his head bent, not returning any of the cheerful greetings given him by passers-by. Walking with drooping shoulders and dragging feet, so unlike his usual straight-backed, confident stride that at first she scarcely recognised him. Walking as if, amongst all the joy and jubilation, he had nothing to celebrate at all.

'Dan,' she whispered, frozen with dismay, and then ran across the field towards him. And as he glanced up and she caught the expression on his face, the empty desolation of his eyes: 'Oh, *Dan*. . .'

'It come this morning,' he said, twisting the scrap of paper in his big hands. 'Just before I shut the back door to get me bike out of the shed. I had a good breakfast – bowl of cornflakes, coupla slices of that bacon your Jane give me last week, bit of bread and jam, cuppa tea – and I washed it all up and then got meself ready. I went up the pub last night with Tommy Vickers, just to celebrate a bit, but I never drunk more'n a coupla pints, Ruthie, I didn't have a thick head or nothing. And I done all that and I was just going out the back door when the boy banged on the front door. I nearly didn't answer it, tell you the truth, only I thought maybe it was Jess Budd come along with something for Sam like she does sometimes, or to tell me about the street party they're having, so I went and answered it and – and it was one of them telegram boys with his red bike. And he give me this.' He stared at the paper, crumpled in his fingers, and began to straighten it out. His voice was thick and husky as if his throat were full of tears, and he spoke with incredulity. 'He give me *this*, Ruthie.'

They were sitting on a fallen tree a little way along the lane, away from the village green. It was quiet here, the sounds of celebration muffled by the trees. Ruth listened to the rambling account, knowing that he needed to go through it all before he could come to the point. He'd probably been going through it over and over again in his mind on the way out here. Gently, already certain in her mind as to what it said, she took the telegram away from him and looked down at the strip of typed message, stuck unevenly on the flimsy paper. Her heart sank as she saw her fears confirmed.

'Oh Dan,' she said, and laid her hand on his arm. 'Dan, I'm sorry. I'm *so* sorry.'

'He was doing all right in the Army,' Dan said in a bewildered voice. 'I mean, I know he was a bit of a varmint, he was always getting into trouble at school, and then there was that trouble with the shop in Pompey when he got sent away – but he'd got over that. He was doing all right. They give him a medal for what he done in Italy. A *medal*, Ruthie.'

'I know. He was a good soldier.'

'And when they went into France, his captain wrote and told me he was pleased to have my Gordon in his company. Wrote specially, he did. And it was nearly all over. He'd have bin coming home. I was going to tell you this, Ruthie: he wrote to me just last week and said he wanted to stop on in the Army when it was all over, wanted to sign up as a regular. The life suited him, see. It was what he was made for. And now – now this.' He gestured at the telegram. 'All finished. All over. He's dead, Ruthie. My Gordon. He's *dead*.'

'Yes,' she said, and took both his hands in hers. 'And I'm so sorry, Dan. I'm really, really sorry.'

'You never knew him,' he said. 'I wanted you to know

him, Ruthie. He wasn't like Sam, I know – but I wanted you to know him. He was my boy.'

'I know,' she said. 'I wanted to know him too.' That wasn't quite true – she'd dreaded meeting Gordon, not at all sure that she'd like him, anxious that it might affect her relationship with Dan. But Dan was right. Gordon was his son, a part of him, and he'd wanted them to know each other.

'And now I've got to tell Sam,' he burst out. His eyes were like dark hollows in his grey face. 'Poor little bugger. What's he going to feel like, hearing his brother's bin killed, today of all days. This was supposed to be a day he'll remember all his life. I don't want him to remember it like this.'

She thought for a moment. 'We could leave it until tomorrow, but it means we're both going to have to pretend there's nothing wrong. He's having such a good time, Dan, I really don't want to spoil it. But can you manage to do that, d'you think?'

He stared at the ground and sighed heavily. 'I seem to have done nothing but "manage" for six bloody years,' he said. 'All me life, in fact. I dare say I can manage one more day. But you'll have to help me, Ruth. I can't do it without you.'

'I'll help you, Dan,' she said, and slipped her hand under his arm to urge him to his feet. 'Let's find him now, before he comes looking for me. He's going to be so pleased to see you.' They stood together for a moment and she looked up into the dark, anguished eyes. 'I'm here, Dan. I'll help you all I can.'

Chapter Eight

Lizzie had reached the farm just in time for the hasty dinner Jane had cobbled together in the midst of all her other preparations. The three of them sat down to sausages and mashed potatoes with a few spring greens, followed by bottled plums and custard and a cup of tea. Then Lizzie ran upstairs and changed out of her nurse's uniform while Jane washed up and George gathered together some more bits and pieces for the children's games. He had found an old football belonging to Terry in the cupboard under the stairs, and a cricket bat and some stumps that the dog had chewed when he was a puppy. Some of the youngsters who weren't involved in races could mess about with them in a corner of the field.

'I'm glad you could get away,' Jane said as they set off. 'I thought the hospital might be too busy.'

'They're only doing emergency operations, and the wards are pretty quiet now. There haven't been half as many men coming in lately. A lot of the girls were going over to Portsmouth – there are going to be big celebrations in the Guildhall Square. But I wanted to come home.'

'I'm glad you did. Home's where everyone ought to be at times like this.'

Once they arrived, George was kept busy organising the children's games while Jane and Lizzie seemed to work non-stop in the village hall, cutting yet more sandwiches, setting out plates of cakes, spooning jelly into bowls and making huge jugs of lemonade. Then there were the tables to be laid on the green, away from the races, and all the chairs belonging to the hall to be dragged outside. The people living nearest the green brought theirs out as well and the women placed them around the tables, which were spread with an assortment of tablecloths and bedsheets and laid with cups and plates. Finally, the plates of food were set all along the middle.

'What a feast,' Jane said, standing back to admire it. 'I'd never have thought we could get up such a spread with hardly any notice.'

'Go on, people have been saving up for this for months,' Lizzie grinned. 'What about that cupboard we weren't allowed to open? You had all kinds of stuff hidden away there.'

'Well, we had to be prepared, didn't we?' Jane said. 'Like the Girl Guides. We couldn't let ourselves be caught on the hop.'

She went back to the hall to start making tea. Years ago, a small copper had been bought for heating water but it was rather temperamental and needed constant attention. The fire was almost out now and she poked it to let in more air.

Lizzie strolled away from the green, along the lane that led up to Barrow Hill. She noticed Ruth and Dan Hodges sitting on a log, talking seriously, and wondered if they'd made up their minds to get married. Everyone was half expecting it, although nobody knew what the couple would do. You couldn't imagine Ruth leaving the village to live in Portsmouth, and Dan was a dockyardman of some sort and knew hardly anything about country life.

She turned up a narrow path to avoid disturbing them, and climbed up through the woods. Tim Budd had been up here once after a plane had crashed nearby and found a German airman's hand, still in its glove. He'd had nightmares for weeks afterwards, Edna Corner had said. Lizzie wondered what Edna was feeling now. She'd gone to live with her mother after Reg had joined up, and now she was a widow with a young child who had never seen his daddy. War was a cruel thing. It couldn't be much comfort to Edna and people like her, to know that it was over.

Lizzie reached the top of the hill and looked at the remains of last night's bonfire. It must have been a wonderful celebration, she thought, wishing she'd been able to be there. Still, it had been fun at the hospital, with everyone excited at the thought of returning to civvy street. They'd all been talking about what they'd do with their new freedom – get married, in lots of cases, but there were quite a few who weren't so keen in swapping liberty for the kitchen sink, and even those whose families had money didn't seem interested in the butterfly life they'd led before the war. There was talk of careers, of travel and adventure. Lizzie had felt almost envious, listening to their dreams, but had reminded herself that that was probably all they were – dreams – and that once they'd been demobbed, the other girls would probably be glad to settle down and marry, just like everyone else.

There was no such decision for her to make. She was already married and would set up home with Alec in the farm cottage her father George had earmarked for them. Alec would go back to working on the farm and they would start their family straight away. Her life would follow the pattern already laid down by her mother, and by her grandmother before that – a pattern that had been set generations ago and followed without question. It was a good pattern, she told herself. It was the best life to live.

She sat on a rock and gazed out over the countryside. Down below, the village clustered around the grey stone church with its little square tower, and the green where she could see her mother and the other women laying out the long trestle tables. In her father's field next to the green, the children were running races, surrounded by an excited crowd; their cheers drifted up, mingled with the music of the village band that had set up at one corner of the green. It was a small band, composed mostly of older men who had not had to go away, but soon the younger ones would be back and the band return to full strength.

The church bells were ringing now, drowning out everything else. Their sound hadn't been heard at all for the first few years of the war and even when Mr Churchill decreed that, with the threat of invasion over, they could be rung again for Easter Day and then on other occasions, it had been difficult to find enough ringers. Eli and Joe had tried to teach a few of the boys and the older men, but without experience the band was still unsteady and the notes of the bells clashed together more than they harmonised. Yet it was a joyful sound and Lizzie tilted her head to hear it better.

A few miles away she could see the American air base, made out of a number of fields, their hedges ripped out and their ground flattened, with runways and roads built across them. The farmers there had lost their land but had been handsomely compensated and started up in other places, and some of the land had been rough scrub anyway. She wondered what would happen to it now.

Floyd's face drifted into her mind and she sighed. There were still men and aircraft at the base but she had heard nothing from either him or Marvin, and her mother hadn't mentioned them. Lizzie knew that Jane had noticed the closeness that was developing between herself and Floyd, and disapproved of it, so that was probably why she avoided the subject. But there was no reason why Lizzie shouldn't ask. The two young men had come regularly to the farm for Sunday dinner for months and it would be perfectly natural for her to enquire after them. In fact, it would seem strange if she didn't.

Since the night of the square dance, Lizzie and Floyd had seen each other only briefly, and never alone. She had tried hard to push him from her mind. He was a nice fellow – they both were, he and Marvin, and so were most of the other Americans she had met – but his life was very different and his home was thousands of miles away. They could never be more than friends and, once he had returned to America, they wouldn't even be that. They might keep in touch for a while but would soon drift apart as their own lives took up their time and attention. She would have Alec and her own family to occupy her, and no doubt Floyd would marry – he probably had a sweetheart waiting for him now – and in a few years they would both be just a memory. Ships that pass in the night, she thought. That's all we are.

It was a poignant thought, and brought with it a twinge of sorrow. As she sat on the top of the hill, looking down at the airbase, Lizzie felt tears prick her eyes. She brushed them away impatiently and heard a voice close behind her.

'Lizzie? Is that you?' Disbelievingly, she turned her head and saw the man she had been thinking of, standing a few yards away and watching her. She stared at him, her lips parted, her eyes wide, and he took a step forward. 'I couldn't believe it when I saw you sitting there. I was thinking about you – it was like I'd conjured you up out of thin air!'

'I was thinking about you too, Floyd,' she whispered, and rose to her feet. 'Where have you come from?'

He came towards her, then stopped a couple of feet away. 'I came over from the base in Norfolk. Took a helluva long time to do it, too – train to London and then on here, and what with all the folk trying to get home to celebrate VE Day, and the carriages stuffed with prisoners of war being repatriated – well, it was a bit of a nightmare. But I'm here now,' he concluded, grinning, 'and it was worth every second to see your face.'

Lizzie smiled back, still dazed by his sudden appearance. 'But – why have you come? Aren't they celebrating on the airbase as well?'

'Sure they are, but I wanted to be here with you. You and the family and all the village folk,' he added. 'And

91

when I got off the train I took it into my head to come this way, over the hill. I thought it'd be fun to look down at the village and see what was going on before I made myself known.' He paused, then said, 'I've got good memories of Barrow Hill.'

'We used to walk up here often,' she nodded. 'After Sunday dinner ... Oh, Floyd, it's *so* good to see you!'

'It's good to see you too, Lizzie,' he said quietly. There was a brief silence and then he held out his arms. 'Have you got a kiss for your old pal?'

Lizzie moved towards him a little uncertainly. The memory of that last kiss they had shared, before he went away, was sharp in her mind. She looked up at him and put out her hands. He took them in his and laid them on his lapels, then slipped his arms around her shoulders and pulled her gently against him.

'Lizzie,' he whispered as he touched her lips with his.

A little gust of wind caught at her hair and clothes, but she barely noticed it. Her whole being was taken up with the sensation of being in Floyd's arms, her lips meeting his. Dizzy, she felt as if the world were swinging around her, the hilltop where they stood the only stable piece of earth in the world. Unconsciously, she tightened her fingers on his lapels, drawing him closer still, and then released them to slide her hands up his shoulders to the back of his neck. She wrapped her arms about him, giving herself completely to his kiss until, at last, they drew slowly and reluctantly apart and stared at each other.

'Oh Floyd,' she whispered unsteadily, and felt the tears brim from her eyes.

'Lizzie,' he muttered. 'Lizzie, I never meant – I didn't dream ... Lizzie, I've upset you. I'm sorry.'

'No!' She shook her head, half laughing, the tears rolling down her cheeks. 'You haven't. I'm not upset – just surprised and – and so *glad* to see you! I was sitting here looking at the base and thinking about you – and then there you were, as if you *knew*. Floyd, I've missed you so much!'

'I've missed you too, Lizzie,' he said soberly, and took her hand, holding it firmly in his. 'I've missed you every minute I've been away. That's why I had to come today. When we heard the war was going to be finished, I knew I had to see you one more time.' He hesitated. 'Everything's going to change now, Lizzie. I'll be going away, and your husband will be coming home.'

'I know,' she murmured. 'And I want him to come back, Floyd. I love him.'

'Yes,' he said, looking down at her. His eyes were very dark. 'I know you do. But just for today, d'you think you could pretend you love me, just a little bit? I'm not asking for anything you can't give me,' he added hastily. 'I just want one day – today – to remember when we've said goodbye for the last time.'

'But you'll be back,' she cried, unwilling to admit that there would have to be a 'last time'. 'You'll come back to see us again. You'll still be in England. You're part of our family now, Floyd. You can't go away for ever.'

'No,' he said. 'I'm not part of your family, Lizzie. I felt I was for a while – a little while. But I'm not. I'll go away, back to the States, and we'll live different lives, like we did before. And I won't be back again after today. This really is goodbye, Lizzie. We're being posted to Germany. I shan't be coming back to England again.'

'Germany?'

'There's going to be a lot to do there,' he said. 'Us – the Yanks – and you British, and the Russians – we'll all be in it together, sorting out the mess, getting it all together again. And there's no time to hang around. We've got to start straight away.'

'You're going to Germany?' Her voice was desolate, a thin thread of sound almost drowned by the sounds of jubilation below: the brass band, the cheering, the church bells. 'You won't be coming back?'

'That's right, Lizzie,' he said quietly, watching her face. 'So – can we have this one day?'

Lizzie looked up into his eyes. Her tears had started afresh but she smiled through their glitter and put her other hand into his. She nodded shakily.

'One day, just for us.' She looked down the hill at the village below. 'Come on, then. Let's enjoy it together.' Her old impish grin broke through. 'There's going to be fish-paste sandwiches and lemonade! I bet you wouldn't be getting *those* back at the airbase!'

Floyd laughed, and swung her hands in his. 'I bet I wouldn't, too! But you know what, Lizzie? I'd rather share fish-paste sandwiches and lemonade with you than caviar and champagne with any other girl I know. And that's the honest truth!'

Hand in hand and laughing, they ran like children down the hill where the races had now finished and tea was about to begin. As they arrived at the green, Jane was just coming out of the hall with a huge jug of lemonade. She stopped and stared at them in astonishment. 'Floyd! Where in the world have you sprung from?'

'He's come to celebrate VE Day with us, Mum,' Lizzie told her, disengaging her hand to push back her flying hair. 'I told him we were having fish-paste sandwiches and he says he wants a whole plateful. And lots and lots of jelly.'

'Well, we'll just have to see if we can spare some, then.' Jane reached up and gave him a smacking kiss. 'Sit yourself down there, Floyd, and Lizzie will get you whatever you want. We're pleased to see you, all of us. You've made a special day even more special, and that's the truth.'

Floyd sat down and Lizzie ran to fetch another plate, which she heaped with sandwiches and cakes. She brought them back and handed them to him with a bow, then sat down beside him.

'Mum's right,' she said, looking into his eyes. 'You've made a special day even more special. And the rest of it is just for us – you and me.'

'You and me,' he echoed, lifting his glass of lemonade. And she felt a thrill run through her body.

It was like a toast. A toast – and a promise.

Everyone in the village sat down to tea at the long tables. Dottie Dewar and her family were at one end, the children grabbing the cakes before they'd had any sandwiches, and the Woddis sisters, sitting very straight, were beside them nibbling daintily at slices of bread and butter and looking very uncomfortable.

'I don't know how they came to be sitting next to that lot,' Jane whispered to her sister, giggling. 'I don't suppose they've ever exchanged a single word with Dottie. They wouldn't demean themselves.'

Ruth snorted. 'They didn't mind demeaning themselves to take in evacuees and treat them like slaves! Those poor kiddies – they'd have been better off with Dottie, slut though she is. I still feel guilty that one of us didn't do something about it.'

'At least they went home safe enough in the end,' Jane said. She turned to Dan, who was sitting silently at the table, steadily eating sandwiches without appearing to notice them. 'Are you all right, Dan? Have a rock cake – I made them fresh this morning.'

He shook his head. 'No thanks, Jane. I'm not really hungry.' He took another sandwich and crammed it into his mouth, chewing as if his life depended on it. Jane glanced at Ruth and raised her eyebrows. Ruth turned down the corners of her mouth and shook her head slightly, and Jane moved away, still wondering. You'd have thought that this day of all days, the man would have been able to take that grim look off his face. She hoped Ruth wouldn't do anything silly. They all knew that there was some sort of understanding between her and Dan, but Jane wasn't at all anxious to see her sister make a decision she would come to regret.

She was a bit worried about her daughter too. The way she and Floyd had come running down the hill, laughing like a couple of kids! Had Lizzie known he was coming, she wondered. Jane had been relieved when the American had been posted away to Norfolk; she'd had an idea those two were getting too close, especially after that barn dance. She hoped that there was nothing going on between them.

'Any more lemonade?' someone called out, and she hurried back to the village hall. By the time she got back, Dan was smiling – well, he'd stopped actually frowning which was halfway to a smile – and Lizzie was on her feet helping some of the kiddies to jelly. Jane relaxed a little. Maybe she'd been reading too much into things. Anyway, this wasn't a day for worrying. This was a day for putting away all the cares of the last six years and enjoying the first day of peace.

With tea over, the tablecloths were whipped off and taken home for washing and the tables folded and carried back into the hall. The brass band took up its position in the centre of one side of the green, and someone brought out a gramophone and a stack of dance records.

'When's the bonfire going to be lit?' Floyd asked, leading Lizzie into the circle. 'Hey, it's not very easy dancing on grass, is it!'

'Not very,' she grinned, 'but we British don't like to have things too easy. Not like you Americans!'

'Watch it!' he warned. 'A guy could get mad at that kind of insult.'

'Oh yes?' she challenged him. 'And what are you going to do about it?' She leaned back her head and gave him an impudent stare.

Floyd narrowed his eyes and puckered his lips. 'Wait till it gets dark. Then I'll show you!'

'Oo-er,' Lizzie said with a shiver. She moved sinuously in his arms, enjoying the feeling of wickedness. Nothing was going to happen between them, she knew – no more than a kiss or two, anyway – but she had a delicious sensation of danger: the kind of danger you might be in if you were walking on a high, narrow mountain path with only a fence between you and a drop of thousands of feet.

The dance came to an end and he walked her back to the edge of the green. The landlord of the Red Cow had brought out a barrel of beer and set it up beside a bench, and the men were clustered around it, drawing off pints. Floyd fetched a couple and handed one to Lizzie. She didn't normally drink beer, but tonight was special and she sipped the brown liquid, trying not to screw up her face at its bitterness.

Someone started to sing 'Roll Out the Barrel', and everyone joined in, following it with 'It's a Long Way to Tipperary', 'Goodbyee', 'Run, Rabbit, Run' and 'Pack Up Your Troubles in Your Old Kitbag'. Some of these were songs from the First World War but soon the more modern tunes began to be heard – Vera Lynn's famous 'We'll Meet Again', and 'The White Cliffs of Dover'. There were tears in many eyes at some of the lines, but before the celebration could become a wake the band struck up again with 'The Hokey-Cokey', and everyone crowded back on to the green to form a huge circle and put their left legs in, left legs out, left legs in and shake them all about . . . By the time they finished, they were all laughing again and dusk was beginning to fall.

'Light the fire!' someone shouted, and this time it was Eli who stepped forward with a taper, lit from his pipe, and set it to the base of the pile. It caught at once and there was a huge cheer as the flames licked skywards. The villagers grabbed each other's hands and danced around it, cheering and shouting, and then once again the church bells rang out, the band struck up and the cheers almost lifted the sky above.

'You should have made all this racket in the first place!' Floyd yelled in Lizzie's ear. 'You could have scared old Hitler away before he dropped a single bomb!'

'What?' she shouted back. 'I can't hear you!' And he shrugged and grimaced, and then caught her hand tightly and pulled her away from the throng and along the lane.

'It's bedlam back there,' he panted. 'I always thought you English were a buttoned-up crowd, but when you let your hair down you really go to town!'

'Well, it is quite a special occasion,' she said, allowing herself to be drawn into the wood. 'Where are we going?'

'Somewhere quiet, away from that lot.' It wasn't quite dark and they could still see where they were going. 'There's a clearing just along here, if I remember right. We can have a few minutes to ourselves, to talk. To say goodbye.'

Lizzie felt her joy evaporate. She had been trying to forget that this might be the last time she and Floyd would meet. After tonight, he would return to his base in Norfolk and then go to Germany. He might never come to England again.

'Floyd,' she said, her voice trembling.

He stopped and turned to her. They were in a tiny space, grassy underfoot and with low bushes and trees all about. The noise of the village celebrations was muffled by the foliage. There was a faint rustling in the undergrowth but apart from that, Lizzie thought, they were in their own silent space where nobody could reach them.

Floyd took her in his arms. She moved into them, slipping her own arms around his waist. For a long moment they stood close, feeling nothing but each other's warmth, hearing nothing but each other's breathing. She laid her head against his shoulder and felt his heartbeat against her breast. Her own heart was thudding and the tingle of danger was in her blood. Once again, she felt as if she walked a high and narrow path, separated from peril by no more than a fragile fence.

'Oh Floyd,' she whispered. 'I don't want you to go.'

'And I don't want to leave you, Lizzie,' he murmured. 'I sure as hell don't want to leave you.'

She turned her face up towards him, and he bent his head. His lips gently brushed hers, and she cried out and pulled him harder against her, a surge of passion sweeping through her body. I haven't felt like this for years, she thought wildly, and I *want* to feel like it! I've missed it so much – I've missed Alec and all our loving so much. I want some loving – I want it now. *I want Floyd . . .*

'Lizzie,' he muttered. 'We'd better get back.'

'No! I don't want to go back, I want to stay here with you.' She pulled him against her again. 'Floyd, kiss me again, please. Kiss me – make love to me. Oh Floyd, you can't go away, you *can't*. I love you. I *love* you, Floyd!'

'I love you too, Lizzie,' he said huskily. 'But you know I have to go. The war may be over but now we've got to win the peace, and it ain't going to be easy.'

'I don't care about that!' she cried. 'I've had enough of it, having to go without, having to do things I don't want to do, watching my life go by and having no loving. And now I've got to say goodbye to you too – and we've never really enjoyed being together, not properly. We've always been so bloody *good*!' She stared up into his face, almost invisible now in the darkness. 'I'm tired of being good, Floyd,' she whispered. 'I want to do what I *want*, for a change. I want to love you properly, just this once. It's a special night, Floyd. Let's make it really special.'

'Lizzie—'

'*Please*, Floyd,' she said, and drew him down on to the grassy floor of the little clearing. '*Please.*'

He lay beside her. She could feel his fingers tremble as he unbuttoned her dress. She lay back in his arms, looking up at the stars that showed through the gently shifting branches of the trees. The music of the church bells and the brass band, and the singing and laughter of the villagers sounded faintly in her ears and then faded as the fence gave way at last and Lizzie toppled into the dangerous depths she had flirted with all day.

Chapter Nine

After the celebrations of VE Day, things seemed a bit flat. The men weren't yet home and nobody seemed to know when they would come. There was no more threat of bombing, but otherwise not much seemed to have changed. Food and clothes were still on ration, you couldn't get an orange for love nor money, and none of the children under six had even seen a banana or a pineapple.

Dan had gone back to Portsmouth, still dazed by the news of Gordon's death. He and Ruth had told Sammy together the next morning and Sammy had seemed equally bewildered. Ruth, watching his frown as he struggled to come to terms with it, reminded herself that he hadn't seen his brother for five years – ever since Gordon had been sent to the approved school. The older boy hadn't come out to Bridge End when he'd been released at last; he'd spent two or three weeks in Portsmouth and then gone straight into the Army. Dan had never said much to Ruth about those weeks, but she'd sensed his disappointment. Gordon had been much more his father's son than Sammy, even working with him at the Camber, but after three years they'd grown apart.

Still, he had done well in the Army. After the approved school, he was accustomed to discipline and the life seemed to suit him. He had plenty of courage, enjoyed a fight and didn't mind living rough. He'd been transferred to the Commandos and had been in France for some time, or so Dan believed. Ruth knew that Dan was proud of his son.

For Sammy, however, his brother was not much more

than a vague memory and now he was dead. Ruth could see the thoughts and emotions chasing themselves across his face. There was no brother any more, no vague figure in Army uniform who would one day come home and claim his place in the family. She could see that Sammy couldn't make up his mind about what he was supposed to feel. Grief? The two boys had never got on. Relief? Guilt at feeling such relief? More likely, she thought, he felt nothing at all at the moment. Perhaps some grief would come later – they were brothers after all – but as he looked at Dan she could see that he was wondering what his father wanted him to say. She wished she could help him, but knew that at this moment he and Dan were sharing something beyond her help.

'Gordon's dead?' he repeated uncertainly. 'He's been killed? Does that mean he's a hero, Dad?'

Ruth sighed with relief. It was almost the best thing he could have said. She saw Dan's pain-creased face soften a little, and he reached out and laid his hand on Sammy's shoulder. 'I reckon it does, son. He already had one medal, so I reckon he must have been a hero. We can always be proud of him. We always got that to remember.'

Sammy glanced at Ruth, and she nodded. 'Your dad's right. Gordon died fighting for his country – for *you* – and nothing can ever take that away. It's something you can be really proud of.'

Sammy was silent for a moment. Then he said, 'Will they put his name on the war memorial? The one by the park in the Guildhall Square?'

'Blimey,' Dan said, 'I never thought of that. I'm surprised you remember that, Sam.'

'It's a soldier,' Sammy explained to Ruth. 'He's by the gate, with names underneath him – people that were killed in the First War. I used to look at them when Mum took me shopping and we went in the park for a picnic. Our

Gordon'll be there now.' He nodded. 'We can go and look at his name.'

'Well, I think you're looking ahead a bit there, Sam,' Dan told him. 'It'll be a while before they puts up war memorials – there's too much else to do first. But I reckon you're right – our Gordon's name'll be there when they do.' He stopped abruptly and his face twisted a little. 'Not but what I wouldn't rather have the boy himself back than a name chipped out of a bit of stone.'

'Of course you would, Dan,' Ruth said gently, 'but it'll be good to have something to visit, won't it? A place you can go and feel close to him.'

They went for a walk together after that, strolling along the country lanes and through the woods into the forest before Dan had to catch the train back to Portsmouth. Tomorrow the nation would be back at work after its two days' celebration, and the task of tidying up the mess and getting back on to its feet would begin. Ruth thought of all the bombed buildings, many hastily patched up only to be bombed again and again. There was all that rebuilding to be done; it would take a long time. And even before that, there was the rubble to be cleared away, ruined services to be repaired, roads to be mended. It was a huge and daunting task. And there were the homeless people, those who had been bombed out and spent years living with relatives or in rented houses and rooms. Where did you begin with a task like this?

'The schools are all going back now,' she said. 'Portsmouth Grammar, that's been out at Winchester, they've gone back already. There won't be any evacuee children left out here. There's no reason for them to stay now.'

'Am I going back?' Sammy asked. 'Brian Collins isn't. He says his mum doesn't want him any more and he's stopping on the farm. Do you want me to come home with you, Dad, now that Gordon's dead?'

Ruth felt a shaft of fear pierce her. She caught her breath

and glanced at Dan. He was striding slightly ahead, swinging a stick he had pulled out of a hedge, his back straight and his shoulders set. She knew that his face would be grim and shuttered, as if he had begun to push the fact of Gordon's death away; as if the emotion were too much for him to bear.

It would be only natural for him to take Sammy home now, she thought. He'd said he wanted the boy to stay for the summer but now, with this new grief upon him, wouldn't he want his company at home? He had lost so much during the past few years, and Sammy was all he had left.

Dan stopped and turned. He looked down at his son, his black brows drawn over his dark eyes. Ruth noticed a few grey hairs in them, and more in his thick hair. He looked older. He said, 'D'you want to come home, Sam?'

The boy met his eyes and then glanced at Ruth. She tried not to influence him. 'It's up to you, Sammy.'

'I don't want to go back to Portsmouth,' he said doubtfully. 'I like it here. I like living with Auntie Ruth. But if you want me, Dad . . .'

Dan was silent for a few moments. They both watched him anxiously, then he sighed and shrugged his big shoulders. 'No, son. It wouldn't be right, not the way things are now. I still got to work, see. There'll be ships coming in for repair. They'll be getting the Camber going again, more merchant boats in and out. I'd be out at work all day and away at sea some of the time, same as before. And Pompey's a mess. You don't want to come back there, the state it's in. You stop here for the summer, like we said. That'll be the best thing.'

Ruth let her breath out quietly. She glanced at Sammy and saw that he was still frowning a little. 'But you'll be lonely, Dad. You'll be all by yourself.'

'Well, that won't be no different, will it? I can still come out and see you regular. And I might freshen the house up

– do a bit of painting and papering, get on with the garden. I got some veg in already, told you that. Make it a bit better for you, for when – when you do come home.' His eyes slid momentarily towards Ruth's face, then moved away. 'We don't have to decide nothing in a hurry,' he said. 'We got all summer to make up our minds.'

They walked on. Ruth took Dan's arm and they strolled companionably together. She reflected that nothing definite had been said, nothing decided. Any decisions had been postponed. Dan needed time now – time to adjust to Gordon's death, time to consider what he wanted to do with his life – and with Sammy. Meanwhile, the situation was just as it had been before the war had ended, and with that she had to be satisfied.

At least she would still have Sammy. And as long as she had Sammy, then she would still have Dan.

'Our troubles are not yet over,' Mr Churchill warned a few days later. 'Remember why the war was fought.' He had been as delighted as anyone on VE Day itself, standing on the balcony of Buckingham Palace with the King and Queen and giving the crowd his famous V sign, but now he wanted the country to get back to work. There was a vast amount to be done to put to rights all the damage that had been inflicted on the towns and cities, to bring back men who had spent years away from home and to help everyone settle into an idea of peace that bewildered children and adults alike. But at the same time, he knew that people still needed to express their relief that the war was over, and on the first Sunday after VE Day church bells were rung all over the land for services of thanksgiving.

'I could learn to do that,' Sammy observed, watching Eli and the others emerge from the church tower after their performance. 'Tim Budd said he learned. The old vicar showed him.'

'Mr Beckett? I don't think he could have done, Sammy.

We weren't allowed to ring the bells when Tim was here. It was supposed to be an invasion warning.'

'They tied up the clapper so that it wouldn't strike. Tim told me. He says it's good.'

'Well, perhaps you can learn now. Ask Eli.'

Sammy turned down the corners of his mouth. 'I don't suppose they'll want any new ringers now. There'll be some coming back from the war. They won't want to teach kids.'

'I expect they will,' Ruth said thoughtfully. 'They won't all be coming back, you know, and those that do will probably be too busy.'

A day or two later she received a letter from Dan. He didn't often write during the week if he'd been out to Bridge End, and she opened it with some foreboding, wondering if he'd had more news of Gordon – a letter telling him how the boy had died, perhaps. Instead, she saw with some dismay that Dan wanted Sammy to go to Portsmouth on Friday.

'It's Navy Days,' she said. 'The first for six years. All the ships in the Dockyard are going to be open for people to go and look at, and there'll be entertainments and special band music and all sorts. Even HMS *Victory* is going to be open.'

'HMS *Victory*? That's Nelson's ship! Mum was going to take me to look at that once, but then she was poorly and then the war came and you couldn't go any more.' Sammy's eyes were alight with excitement. 'Oh, that'll be smashing! I can go, can't I, Auntie Ruth?'

'Yes, of course you can,' she said, though her heart had sunk at the idea of Sammy going back to Portsmouth, especially for something as enticing as Navy Days. Suppose he didn't want to come back . . . But he was Dan's boy, and Dan had the final say. 'You'll have to go on the train by yourself,' she added a little doubtfully, remembering Sammy's last adventure in train travel, when he had got lost. 'I'll see you on at the station and you won't have to get off till you reach Hilsea. Your dad'll be waiting for you there.'

Sammy looked at her. 'By myself? But – won't you be coming too, Auntie Ruth?'

'Me?' She stared at him, then looked again at the letter. The invitation was definitely for Sammy. 'Well, no – it's just you. Your dad wants to take you on the ships.'

'He could take you as well. You'd like to go, wouldn't you, Auntie Ruth? We could even take Silver. He'd like to go on a ship again.'

Ruth laughed. 'I don't think he would! Silver's sailing days are over. No, I think it's just you your dad wants, Sammy. And you can tell me all about it when you come back.' If you come back, she thought apprehensively. She didn't think this was a plot on Dan's part, to get the boy home and then keep him there, but she knew that once he had Sammy back with him he might find it hard to let him go. Jane warned me about this years ago, she thought. She warned me not to think of him as my own boy. She gave Sammy the letter. 'You'd better write back to your dad and tell him you'll be on the train. And I'll make sure your best shirt and that new blazer Mrs Greenwood gave you are clean and pressed.'

She gave him some writing paper and an envelope and Sammy sat at the kitchen table to write his letter. A few minutes later he asked for a penny for a stamp, and ran off down the lane to the village post office. Ruth watched him go and turned to Silver.

'I don't know, Silver. I can't make out what's in Dan's mind these days. I thought we had some sort of understanding, but you just can't tell how people will feel when the time comes. I don't think I could ever go to live in Portsmouth, and if he comes out here, what will he do? And now he's lost Gordon – well, in a way it ought to make it easier, but I can understand him not being able to put his mind to anything else just now. And I can understand him wanting Sammy back with him too.' The parrot cocked his head and blinked wisely at her but, for once, said nothing. She sighed. 'It'll seem funny without him, even if it's only for a weekend. I hope that's all it is, Silver – just a weekend.'

Silver seemed to agree. He fluffed up his feathers in the way he had when he was about to speak and she waited. Sometimes he came out with remarks that were quite appropriate. But this, it seemed, was not one of those occasions.

'Sod the little buggers,' he said, and stamped his foot for all the world as if he were stamping on the cockroaches that the phrase had originally meant. 'Ding dong bell. Tuppence in the well. I'm a little teapot, short and stout.' And then, wheedlingly, 'Let me call you sweetheart, Ruthie. I love you.'

Ruth laughed, though there were tears in her eyes. 'All right, Silver. I know I'll never be really alone as long as I've got you.' But a parrot, however much he could talk, had never been a real substitute for her husband Jack. Any more than he could now be a substitute for Sammy. Or Dan.

Chapter Ten

Alec Travers came home one cool, drizzly evening a week after VE Day. He had been in one of the first POW camps to be liberated and he had spent the time since then travelling across a torn and broken European landscape of ruined villages, neglected farmland and desolation. From the window, he had seen families trailing along the roads carrying their belongings in sacks and suitcases or piled high on carts dragged by thin, weary horses. In some places he saw lines of men and women in the fields, gleaning food. When the train ran through cities he witnessed a devastation even worse than that of London during the Blitz, and his heart, already like a lump of jagged metal scratching at the wall of his chest, shrank as if it rejected what his eyes saw.

He was almost two stone lighter than when he had been captured, dragged out of the sea after his ship had been blown up. His memory of that time was of cold water that was dark and sticky with oil, a mass of flotsam with men clinging to whatever they could find, crying out for help and choking on their words as oil slopped into their throats. There was blood too, and parts of men's bodies that had been torn apart in the explosion and now drifted grotesquely on the surface. A leg bumped against him, the leg of someone he must have known yet could not recognise, and then a part of a face with an eye staring . . . He pushed away the rest of the memories, knowing they would come back to him in nightmares as they so often did, and set his mind on what it would be like to be at home again. The warm kitchen, the fire, the farm with its well-fed animals and healthy fields. Lizzie in his arms, in his bed . . .

At last he was on the final leg of the journey, aboard the train that would bring him to Bridge End. He had been brought to Southampton on a crowded cargo boat and given a ticket for the last brief journey to the little station he had known so well. He stared at the town with its areas of devastation and wondered if he ought to go and see his parents first. But much as he wanted to see them, he knew that his appearance now, so thin and gaunt and dirty from the journey, would only distress them. And besides that, he wanted to be at home. Not his childhood home but his adult one, the one he shared with Lizzie.

Not that we've got a home of our own, not really, he thought, climbing wearily aboard the train. Just Lizzie's bedroom in the farmhouse. But that's where I want to be, just the same.

The train chugged out of the station and through the big town. He knew it had been hit hard during the Blitz, he had seen the damage caused then, but somehow it looked even worse now with the bombsites still a broken mass of bricks and rubble, and overgrown with weeds. Some of the weeds were quite pretty – tall pink flowers and a bush that looked a bit like lilac, with purple spires – but you knew that what they masked was misery and suffering and death. Alec turned his eyes away and the next time he looked out they had left the buildings behind and were running through green fields and woods.

Soon, they were at Bridge End. The signboard had been put back and two or three other people were getting out. Alec dumped his kitbag on the platform and climbed down and the train chuffed away. For the first time, he drew in a breath of country air, and he closed his eyes, suddenly dizzy.

He could smell flowers. The little garden that had always been kept at the station was in full bloom and the hawthorn hedge was smothered in creamy white blossom. From somewhere in its branches he could hear the trill of a robin, and a blackbird was singing full-throated in a tree. There were tits and finches twittering, and he opened his eyes and realised that they were scolding the station cat, who was lying stretched out in the sun.

'Blackie!' he exclaimed wonderingly. 'Are you still here?' He bent and scratched the cat's ears and it turned its head and gazed up at him. 'D'you recognise me?'

A shadow fell across the cat's body and Alec glanced up and saw Fred Knapper, the ancient stationmaster. The two stared at each other for a moment and then Fred's face split into a wide grin and he held out his hand.

'Why, if it ain't young Alec Travers! Come 'ome at last, 'ave yer? Tell me you bin a POW, that right?' He peered closer. 'Look as if you needs a bit of feedin' up. Dunno if I'da known you if you 'adn't spoke to old Blackie here.'

'I was so surprised to see him,' Alec said. 'I didn't think he'd still be alive.'

'He's only twelve or thirteen,' the old man said, a shade indignantly. 'No age for a cat, that ain't, not if it's fed right and looked after. Has a good life, he does. Anyway, better not stand 'ere chewin' the fat, your good lady'll be lookin' out for you. Be glad to see you back again, she will.'

'She doesn't know I'm coming,' Alec said. 'We didn't know when we'd arrive. Hope it won't come as too much of a shock!' He hefted his kitbag on to his shoulder. The journey had been long and hard, and he was dog-tired, but there was only half a mile to go now. And the bag wasn't heavy; it contained just a few items of clothes, his razor, and a book or two and the letters that Lizzie had sent him while he was in camp. Nobody had had any possessions to speak of in there.

The song was right about the longest mile being the last mile home, he thought as he trudged along the lane. Still dizzy with the sights, sounds and scents that had once been so familiar, he yearned to savour them yet at the same time felt impatient that the walk was taking him so long. And now that he was so close, he was beginning to feel nervous too. Suppose Lizzie had changed. Suppose she found *him* too much changed, with his thin body, his gaunt face and his nightmares. Suppose she didn't love him any more . . .

By the time he reached the farmhouse, he was exhausted. He trudged through the yard and leaned on the garden gate, too weary to unfasten the latch, and gazed at the neat beds of vegetables and soft fruit, edged with the flowers that Jane still insisted on growing. The kitchen window was open and he remembered the day he had once come home unexpectedly, just like this, and caught Lizzie standing there working at the sink. He had been full of energy then, he recalled, swooping her up into his arms and kissing her until they were both breathless. Now, he felt he had barely the strength to take the last few steps to the door.

As he stood there, he saw a movement inside the kitchen. His heart moved. He watched, frozen with his nervousness, and Lizzie's face appeared at the window. They stared at each other and then he saw her hand go to her lips.

'Alec,' she whispered, and then her voice rose in a cry that was almost of pain. *'Alec . . .'*

'He looks worn out,' Jane reported to her sister later that afternoon when she ran down the lane to tell Ruth the news. 'Just leaning on the gate, he was, as if he couldn't walk a step further, and when our Lizzie went out to him he sort of fell against her. Crying, she said he was, but then so was she, and when she got him indoors he collapsed into George's armchair by the range and sobbed like a baby. She hardly knew what to do for the best, but she just held on to him for a bit and then made him a cup of tea. He said it was the first he'd had all the time he was away. Oh Ruth, if you could just see him. He's a shadow of the man he was, a shadow.'

'I'm sorry,' Ruth said in a voice full of pity. 'Poor Alec. He must have had an awful time. But what d'you mean, Jane – if I could see him? I will see him, won't I? I mean, he's not actually ill, is he? And you'll be having a party for him, surely – a family party?'

'Well, that's what I thought we'd be doing too. I mean, I put by a tin of ham and a few other bits and pieces specially. But you can see he's not up to it. Maybe later on, when he's built up his strength. That doesn't mean you can't pop round and see him, of course, but better leave it a day or two, perhaps, just so he can get his bearings, like.'

Ruth looked at her uncertainly. 'He is going to be all right, isn't he? I mean, his mind's not affected, is it? You hear some awful things . . .'

'Oh no, I'm sure he's all right as far as that goes. He's just so thin and weak. Not like the old Alec at all. But nothing that some butter and eggs and fresh vegetables won't put right, I'm sure.'

Ruth said nothing, but she didn't think Jane was as sure as she made out. She watched her sister walk back along the lane and sighed. They'd been looking forward so much to Alec's return, and although he was safe at home again it seemed that he'd brought fresh worries with him. I wonder what happened to him in that prisoner-of-war camp? she thought. I wonder if they tortured him?

Lizzie wondered too, as she tried to reassure Alec that he was safe again. Somehow, he didn't seem able to accept that the war was truly over – at least in Europe. He jumped at every sudden noise and he hated having the doors closed. He wanted to be outside as much as possible, yet when he got there he seemed frightened, as if the sensation of space was too much for him. He seemed most content in the garden with the hedges bursting into leaf around him – enclosed, but not by a wire fence. He sat for hours on the wooden bench just outside the kitchen window where he could hear Jane or Lizzie at their chores inside, and as he grew a little stronger he began to do some work out there too.

Lizzie had left the hospital. The VADs were all expecting to be demobbed soon, and Madam had given her extended leave so that although she was still on the register she wouldn't actually have to go back again. Instead, she was at home, helping her mother indoors and looking after the calves. She looked out through the window sometimes and saw Alec sitting there doing nothing, and wondered how long it would take before he recovered, and what he would do then.

That first evening, she had quickly realised just how weak he was. Her mother had come into the kitchen to find them still weeping in each other's arms and naturally she had broken down too, and although George hadn't actually shed any tears he'd rubbed his eyes quite hard and couldn't seem to stop shaking Alec's hand. They'd agreed that they wouldn't pass the word round tonight, but tomorrow they'd have to think about killing the fatted calf – 'not that any of them are all that fat!' George had remarked with a grin – and get Ruth and young Sammy up, and Alec's mum and dad as well, of course, and ask in a few of the neighbours too, like the Knights, who were still waiting for Ian to be demobbed, and some of the other families Alec had grown up with.

Alec had said nothing to all this but later, when they were alone in their bedroom, Lizzie looked at him with concern and said, 'Are you sure you feel up to seeing people again yet, love? You were ever so quiet when Mum was talking about a party, and you look so tired.'

'I am,' he said, sitting on the bed and feeling its softness with wonder. 'To tell you the truth, Lizzie, I'm so tired I feel I could sleep for a year. I feel worn right out. I don't seem to have the strength to do anything.'

'You didn't eat your supper. You've got to build yourself up again.'

114

'I couldn't. There was so much of it. We didn't get big meals in camp – I just couldn't seem to manage it all.' He rubbed a hand over his face. 'I can't get used to it all, Liz – being home, being with you again, seeing all the old things around me. I'm sort of frightened to believe in it, somehow.' He looked up at her. 'I've dreamed about it so much, and it always seemed so real. I'd be here with you in our bedroom. Or out in the garden, or walking through the fields and the woods. I could see it all. I could hear the birds. I could smell the flowers. And then I'd wake up and there I was, back in that wooden shed with all the other blokes, and it wasn't real at all.' His voice trembled and he bent his head, his hands balled into fists on his shaking knees. 'Every time I dreamed it, it seemed more real. Once I even said to you, in the dream, "It *is* real this time, isn't it?" And you said, "Yes, it is real." And then I woke up – and it *wasn't.*'

Lizzie sank to her knees beside him. She put her hands over his and looked up into his face. His eyes were running with tears and she found a hanky and wiped them gently away.

'You won't wake up this time,' she said softly. 'This time it *is* real. Truly. You're home again. It's all over. We're together at last – and we're going to stay together.'

'Oh, Lizzie,' he said brokenly, and pulled her into his arms. She leaned lightly against him, feeling his thinness, almost afraid to hold him close in case she broke something, and her own tears brimmed over once more.

'Let's get you into bed now,' she said, and began to unbutton his shirt. 'I'll go downstairs and warm you some milk. You'll go to sleep in our own bed, and when you wake up in the morning you'll still be here, and I'll be beside you. It *is* true this time, my love. You're home and you don't ever have to go away again. Unless you want to go back to sea?' she added a little fearfully.

He shook his head quickly and she saw that his eyes were

haunted with memories that perhaps he would never be able to reveal, that he was filled with fear and horror, and she wondered briefly if he really was going to recover from whatever had happened.

'I'm not going back to sea,' he said huskily. 'I'm never going back to sea again.'

Chapter Eleven

On Friday morning, Ruth found the small suitcase she had had ever since she and Jack went on their honeymoon and packed it with Sammy's things for the weekend. There wasn't much to pack – just a clean pair of underpants and a shirt and pullover, a couple of blue hankies that Jane had given him for Christmas, his favourite book *Treasure Island* (which he liked because it had not only a parrot but a character called Silver) and this week's copy of *Dandy*. She also put in a few home-made biscuits which he could share with Dan.

'I'll meet you from school,' she told him as she kissed him goodbye, 'and we'll walk down to the station together. I'll bring some sandwiches but I expect your dad will have a nice tea ready. And I'll be at the station to meet you on Sunday, at teatime.'

'I wish you were coming too, Auntie Ruth,' Sammy said. 'I wanted to show you the ships.'

'Yes, it would have been nice, but I expect your dad wants you to himself. And I wouldn't have anywhere to stay, anyway.' She gave him a gentle push. 'Off you go now, and do your sums properly.'

'I always do,' he said with dignity, and Ruth smiled as she watched him run off up the lane. Sammy enjoyed school and did his work well, but after this term he would be back in Portsmouth and going to the 'big' school. He'd taken the scholarship exam in January and, since he was still an evacuee, been passed for the Northern Grammar School in Portsmouth. If he stayed in the village he would probably go to Southampton. If only we'd managed to get something settled, she thought with a frown. It's as bad for him not knowing where he'll be after the summer holidays as it is for me.

As it happened, Sammy wasn't at all bothered about which school he would go to. So much had happened to him in his life – moving from the pub in Old Portsmouth to the little terraced house in April Grove, seeing his brother sent to the approved school, being with his mother when she died, followed by the Blitz and his eventual arrival at Bridge End and Ruth's cottage – that he was quite accustomed to being wafted to and fro by events. Now, like any other eleven-year-old, he simply took life as it came and didn't trouble about anything further ahead than next week.

Ruth met him as promised after school, carrying his case, and they walked down to the station together. The train came puffing round the bend and groaned to a halt at the platform and Sammy climbed aboard one of the carriages. Ruth gave him his suitcase and kissed him.

'Now, you will be a good boy, won't you? And have a nice time. I'll want to hear all about it when you come back.'

He stared at her, sudden doubt in his eyes. 'You'll be all right without me, won't you, Auntie Ruth?'

'Of course I will,' she said, smiling although she could feel the tears in her eyes. 'It's only for two days anyway. And I've got Silver to look after me.'

'I wanted you to come too. Dad would have liked that.' He pushed the door, looking half inclined to get off the train. Ruth closed it again.

'I told you, he wants it to be just the two of you. Anyway, where would I stay?'

'You could stay with us. There's bunks in me and Gordon's room. At least, there were.' She saw him remember that there was now no Gordon and perhaps, therefore, no bunk. 'I expect they're still there,' he added doubtfully.

Ruth wished the train would go. Goodbyes were always difficult – she'd had enough of them with Jack – and she had no wish to get involved in a discussion with Sammy about bedrooms. 'Go and sit in the compartment,' she said. 'Look, there's a seat by a window. You go and sit there and you can wave as the train goes out. And I'll ask the guard to make sure you get out at the right stop.'

He pursed his lips but did as he was told and appeared a moment later at the window. Ruth caught the guard's sleeve as he walked by, flourishing his green flag, and indicated the boy in the compartment. 'Keep an eye on him for me, will you? He has to get out at Hilsea.'

The man nodded. 'I'll see he's all right. Your nipper, is he?'

'No,' Ruth said, wishing she could say he was. 'He's my evacuee, just going back to see his dad.'

'Ah, that's right. Best place for him, too, home with his family. You'll be glad to have him off your hands, I dare say.'

Ruth stared at him, but he had walked on and was slamming doors and calling out. A moment later, he blew his whistle and waved his flag and the engine began to get up steam. She turned quickly to the boy who was pressing his face against the window.

'Goodbye, Sammy. Have a nice time.' The train was moving now, gathering speed. She laid her fingers against her lips and waved with the other hand. Sammy gazed out at her, his face white and blurred behind the glass. 'Remember me to your dad,' she called and then, dropping her voice to a whisper that nobody could hear, 'Give him my love.'

Sammy sat in his corner seat, pressed against the side of the carriage. It was empty to begin with, but when the train

119

stopped just outside Southampton it filled with soldiers, all in battledress and carrying big grey canvas kitbags. They made a lot of noise as they crowded into the compartment and heaved their luggage on to the overhead racks. As they sat down they noticed Sammy and began to talk to him, asking where he lived and whether he liked being evacuated. Some of them had boys his age, they said, and one pulled a large bar of chocolate from his pocket and handed it over. 'You have that, kid. I bet you never seen a bar as big as that in yer life, eh?'

'Going home, then?' asked the one next to him. He was a big man, as big as Dan, but ginger-haired with a reddish complexion and a lot of freckles. 'Bet you'll be pleased to be back in your own place, eh?'

Sammy shook his head. 'I'm only going for the weekend. I live at Bridge End now.'

'That right? Don't your mum and dad want you back, then?'

'My mum's dead,' Sammy said. 'So's my brother. There's only my dad in Portsmouth now.'

'Well, he'll want you back then, won't he? Stands to reason. And the people you bin staying with, fostered like, they won't want you hanging about, not now the war's over.'

Sammy stared at him, feeling frightened. 'Auntie Ruth wants me back. She said so. She's meeting me on Sunday, off the train.'

The soldier laughed. 'Go on, that's just a tale. Told you that to keep you quiet, she did. You won't be going back, not once you're back in Pompey. The evacuation's over, son. All the nippers are going back now.'

The man on his other side nudged him. 'Knock it off, Ginge. You're upsetting the kid, can't you see that? Anyway, you don't know nothing about it.'

'I know enough to know that people don't want other folks' kids taking up space,' the red-haired man said a trifle bitterly. 'Seen it with my own, ain't I? Sent out to the country and treated like slaves, they were. My Flo couldn't believe her eyes when she went out to see them – took them straight back home with her, she did. You can't tell me this nipper won't be better off back home with his own family.' He glanced back at Sammy. 'You enjoy that chocolate, son, and be thankful you're going back where you belong, and never mind what the old woman you bin stopping with tells you. She's just frightened you'll tell the Authorities what's bin going on. I bet there's a few more the same, too.'

'But nothing's been going on,' Sammy began, but one of the other soldiers had got out a pack of cards and the red-haired man had lost interest. Sammy looked uncertainly at the chocolate and then put it in his pocket. He'd give some to Dad and take the rest back for Auntie Ruth. She hardly ever had any chocolate.

The men were playing cards now and Sammy stared out of the window, thinking about what the red-haired soldier had said. He couldn't believe that Auntie Ruth had been telling him lies and that he was going back to Portsmouth for good. She'd said he was going to stay till after the summer holidays. And he'd heard her and Dad talking once, when they thought he was asleep, about him staying for ever. Dad was thinking about getting a job out in the country. Or had that been a dream?

But that had been before Gordon had got killed. Somehow, without Sammy quite understanding how, that seemed to have changed things. His dad had been different, like he'd been after Mum had died. He'd gone back inside himself, like a snail going back into its shell. Perhaps now he wouldn't want to live in the country. Perhaps he wouldn't want Sammy to live there either.

Perhaps he really was going home for good.

The train stopped only a few times before arriving at Hilsea. The soldiers got off there too, jostling each other as they dragged down their kitbags, and pushing to get

121

through the door. Sammy was almost left behind and the guard was coming to look for him when he finally struggled along the corridor with his suitcase. Half afraid he was at the wrong station after all, he was relieved to find his father waiting on the platform but dismayed to see that Dan was scowling, his black eyebrows pulled together over his dark eyes.

'Blimey, I thought you'd missed it or got out the wrong place again,' Dan said. 'That your case? Big enough, ain't it? You must have all your worldly goods in there.'

Sammy looked at the suitcase. He hadn't taken any interest in what went into it, apart from stipulating that he wanted *Treasure Island* and today's *Dandy*, but now he wondered if Ruth had indeed packed it with everything he owned. Not that he owned very much. Most of the books and games and puzzles he had at the cottage belonged to Ruth herself or had been given him by Ruth's family, so weren't strictly his at all. He felt a sudden chill of fear as he remembered the soldier's words and thought of Ruth's face as she'd waved him goodbye. She'd looked as upset as if he were leaving for ever . . .

'Come on then,' Dan said brusquely. 'Don't want to stand here all night. We're getting fish and chips on the way home and if we don't get there sharpish they'll have nothing decent left.' He set off, striding along the platform and through the streets so briskly that Sammy had to trot to keep up with him. Once again, he felt a tremor of anxiety. Dad doesn't seem pleased to see me at all, he thought miserably. I'm in the way, just like I used to be. He only likes me when we're out in the country.

He trailed behind his father, his suitcase weighing more heavily with every step he took, and wished that he had never come. I hate Portsmouth, he thought bitterly. Nothing good has ever happened to me here. I hate it.

Dan was feeling as despondent as Sammy. He'd been

looking forward to having his son at home with him again, but now he was here he didn't seem to know what to say to him. Ever since the Christmas Sammy had spent in Portsmouth three years ago, they'd met only out at Bridge End where they both felt comfortable. They could talk about country matters – animals and trees, the things that were going on in the fields and woods. Sammy could show Dan bits and pieces he'd made at school or take him to see George's cows and pigs, and Silver could demonstrate his latest sayings. And Ruth was always there to welcome him into her cottage, to offer him a cup of tea, ask him to join them for supper and to sit sewing and chatting of an evening, by the fire in winter or out in the garden in summer.

I ought to have asked Ruth to come as well, he thought. He'd wanted to but hadn't had the courage. And it had seemed too difficult – where would she stay, for a start? And what would people think, him having a woman to visit? Not that Dan cared what people thought about him – he was used to them getting the wrong idea – but he cared what they thought about Ruth. He didn't want them putting two and two together and making half a dozen where she was concerned.

They arrived at the fish and chip shop and stood in the queue. Dan asked for two pieces of cod and twopenn'orth of chips, and handed the parcel to Sammy. 'You take that and I'll carry your case.' The grease was already seeping through the pages of yesterday's *Daily Sketch* and the parcel was comfortingly hot in Sammy's hands as they walked the last stretch down October Street and along to the end of April Grove.

Tommy Vickers was at his door, scraping off the old varnish. He turned and his crinkled face split into a grin as he saw Sammy. 'Well, if it ain't the prodigal son come back again! You're a sight for sore eyes, I must say.' He straightened up and stood with arms akimbo, surveying the

123

pair of them. 'Put on a good few inches, ain't he, Dan? Be as tall as you soon.'

'Maybe.' Dan was curt as he fitted his key into the lock. 'See you later, Tom. Got to go in now. We got fish and chips – don't want it getting cold.'

'No, you get it down you while it's hot.' Tommy winked at Sammy. 'Come in and say hello to the missus sometime, won't you? She'll be pleased to see you back again. Missed having you round the place, she has.'

Sammy followed his father into the house. He turned Tommy's words over in his mind. It sounded as though Mr Vickers was expecting him to stay. Perhaps he knew that Dad had brought him home for good. Perhaps everyone knew, even Auntie Ruth. Perhaps Sammy was the only one who didn't know.

Dan tipped the fish and chips out on to two plates and put them on the table. He gave Sammy a knife and fork and nodded at him. 'Go on, then. Eat up. You don't get fish and chips like this out at Bridge End.'

Sammy looked at his plate. The fish was encased in thick, yellowish-grey batter and the chips were soft and flabby. The man in the shop had smothered them in salt and vinegar and the smell stung his nose and eyes. He felt the tears start and sniffed, rubbing his nose with the back of his sleeve in the way that Ruth always scolded him for.

'Come on,' Dan said, and Sammy was suddenly transported to a time when his mother was still alive and he'd been unable to eat his dinner. Dad had shouted at him; he'd made him sit at the table until he'd swallowed the tasteless, gristly meat and then he'd sent him upstairs. Sammy could hear his mother crying downstairs and he'd lain on his bed and sobbed himself to sleep.

For a moment, he felt as if it was happening all over again. The past few years at Bridge End with Ruth and the others were no more than a dream. The times he'd spent with his father in the country, getting to know each other, getting to love each other, had been nothing but wishful thinking. He'd been here all this time, sitting at the table in front of a meal he couldn't eat, and nothing would ever get any better. Only this time, his mother wasn't there. He was never going to see her again.

'I can't eat it,' he said miserably. 'I'm sorry, Dad. I just can't eat it.'

The evening was over at last and Sammy was in bed. Dan hoped he was asleep. He sat in his armchair, staring at the empty fireplace and rubbing his hand over his face.

A hard lump of disappointment lay heavily in his chest. He wasn't over the shock of Gordon's death yet and he'd pinned all his hopes on Sammy's visit, hoping that his younger son could somehow fill the place inside him that had been left so empty.

I reckoned we got on all right now, Sam and me, he thought, pushing his fingers through his thick black hair. I know I used to think he was a bit of a cissy, a mother's boy and all that, but since he's been out at Bridge End he's changed a lot. Ruth's brought him on, letting him go roaming about in the woods and climbing trees and all that, and he's not a cissy at all. Different from Gordon, of course – always will be, I suppose – but shaping up all right, just the same.

But now he was back at April Grove, it was as if they'd gone right back to where they started. The kid didn't have a word to say for himself, and when he'd said he couldn't eat the fish and chips, it took Dan right back to those days when he used to sit picking at his food, tears dripping on to his plate, and Dan had felt the same old frustration, turning to anger, that he'd felt then. It had taken all his self-control not to shout at the boy.

Sammy had known, though. He'd looked up and seen his father's face, and he'd known exactly what Dan was thinking. And in that moment, as they stared at each other,

Dan had felt all their closeness slip away, and loss take its place. He had lost Sammy, just as surely as he had lost Gordon.

Chapter Twelve

'When's Daddy coming home?'

Heather and Pat were feeding the calves, holding buckets of milk and dipping their hands in for the animals to suck their fingers. Roger was scrubbing down the milking parlour and Teddy was pottering about close to his mother, leaning through the bars to rub the calves' heads as they fed.

'I don't know exactly,' Heather said. 'We have to wait for him to be demobbed.'

'What's demobbed?'

'Let out.' That sounds as if he's in prison, she thought. 'Discharged from the Army.'

'So he won't be a soldier any more?'

'That's right.'

'And he can come home and be a farmer again. And a daddy.'

'Yes.' Heather smiled at her daughter. Ten years old, and hadn't seen her father since she was five. 'That'll be nice, won't it? You'll like having a daddy again.'

'I don't think Roger will.'

'Don't be silly, of course he will.' Heather finished the last calf and went to swill out the bucket. 'We'll all like having your daddy back.'

Roger was just coming out of the shed as she walked across the yard. He was growing so fast, she thought. Already he was almost as tall as she was, and the work he did around the farm had developed his muscles. You could have taken him for fourteen rather than twelve. His straight, dark hair was falling over his forehead and she reminded herself that it was time to cut it again. He glanced round at her and she caught the expression in his dark brown eyes and realised how like Ian he had become.

'Your father's going to be so proud of you,' she said as she fell into step beside him. 'Doing so much on the farm. You'll be able to show him everything.'

He shrugged. 'S'pose so.'

'Are you looking forward to him coming home?' she asked, and went on before he could reply. 'Of course you are! We all are.'

Roger said nothing, and she glanced at him. 'I know it's a long time since we saw him, but he won't have changed, you know. He'll still be your dad.'

Roger nodded. His face revealed nothing. He seemed more interested in the cows that had shoved their way through the yard and were now grazing in the field. 'Daisy didn't give much milk today,' he said, frowning. 'Eli thinks there's something wrong with her.'

'Oh. We'd better keep an eye on that.' A small pang of anxiety pricked her. 'I hope nothing's going to go wrong with the animals, just as your dad's coming home.'

They went indoors. The Land Girls, who often came in to supper, had gone into Southampton to see a film. Arthur was in his chair by the range and Emily was just taking a pie out of the oven. Its crust was thick and golden, and an aroma of steak and kidney wafted through the air. She set it on the table and turned to fetch the dishes of steaming vegetables, giving Roger a severe look as she did so.

'I don't know what you think you're doing, young man, coming to the table in that state. Go and wash those mucky hands. You too, Pat, you've had your fingers in those calves' mouths this past half-hour, *I* know. And Teddy's been making mud pies by the look of him. He's got dirt all over his face.'

'We're all filthy,' Heather agreed cheerfully, going over

to the sink. She poured hot water from the kettle into the enamel bowl and washed her own hands with yellow carbolic soap, drying them on the roller towel as the children queued to use the same water. 'It's good, honest muck, though.' She sat at the table. 'It's nice to have the place to ourselves for a change. I mean, I like the girls but I do like just being ourselves – a family.'

'Yes, and it'll be even better when our Ian comes home,' her mother-in-law said. 'The family'll be complete again. Just like the old days.'

'Not quite,' Heather said with another look at Roger. 'We've got another young man in the house now. And Pat's growing up a bit more each day. He'll find quite a change in them.'

'And never even seen Teddy,' Emily nodded, putting her hand on the little boy's fair head as she passed his chair. 'But he'll soon get used to it all. Give us all a week or two and it'll seem as if he's never been away.'

'I hear Alec Travers is back,' Arthur said, helping himself to mashed potatoes. 'Nothing but skin and bone, so George Warren was saying when he looked in this afternoon. He was telling me their winter wheat's doing well, should be ready for harvest before ours. His field's in a better position, of course.'

'Have you seen Alec?' Heather asked, but the older couple both shook their heads.

'Hardly been out of doors, George said,' Emily answered, cutting into the pie. Rich brown gravy oozed out and chunks of beef and kidney glistened. It's a good job we're allowed to keep some of our own meat, Heather thought, with all these mouths to feed. Emily served Arthur a slice first, then put a piece on Heather's plate. 'Had a bad time in that POW camp, they reckon. He'll soon pick up, mind, with a bit of good fresh food and country air.'

Heather nodded and gave Pat some cabbage. 'Yes, you

do have to eat it. It's good for you. And you've got to have some swede, Roger. It's got vitamins in – as good as oranges, swede is.'

'Will we get more oranges now that the war's over?' Pat enquired. 'We won't have to eat swede then, will we?'

'Yes, you will. We're not throwing away good vegetables that we've grown ourselves to buy expensive fruit. Anyway, it'll be a while before they start bringing that sort of thing – we've got to get all the men home first.' Heather began to eat. After a long day working on the farm, including milking forty cows twice, she was ravenously hungry. Emily fed them well, providing cooked meals at noon and again at six, but they weren't able to eat like this every day. The pie was good but only half the size it should have been; it wouldn't have been much bigger if the Land Girls had been there as well. Most of her plate was filled with vegetables. Still, by all accounts it was a lot better than poor Alec Travers had been getting. She hoped that her mother-in-law was right and that good food and fresh air were all he needed to put him right.

At least Ian wouldn't come home nothing but skin and bone. The Army fed their men pretty well, knowing that they needed all their strength to fight.

She looked at the children. They were healthy and sturdy, and had suffered none of the bombing or disruption that many children had endured. They'd been able to stay at home with their family, eating as well as anyone could these days, helping on the farm and, apart from being able to see the glow of the flames as Southampton was blitzed, unaffected by air raids. They had missed having their father with them for four long years, but at least he had survived and would soon be home.

We'll settle down together again in no time, she thought, turning a blind eye as Roger tipped a spoonful of mashed swede on to his sister's plate. Mum's right – give us a week or two, and it'll be as if he's never been away.

It seemed to Lizzie that she and Alec would need a lot more than a week or two before it seemed as if he'd never been away.

Her joy at seeing him again had been touched with fear as he lay in her arms that first night, so thin she could feel his bones barely covered by his skin. She had looked forward so much to this moment – the moment when they would be together again, able to love each other as they had done before he went away. I haven't been as close as this to any man, she thought, not even Floyd – and she pushed away the thought of the big American and the memory of their last encounter. She was with her husband now, and at that very first sight of him all her love had flooded back. She wanted no one else.

But Alec didn't seem to want to make love. He lay in her arms, unresponsive as she stroked his body, his breathing shallow and uneven, and she knew there was no passion in him. He's tired out, she thought. He's come all that way and it's all been too much for him, and I've got to be patient. But her own body felt as if it were on fire. 'Oh Alec,' she whispered, 'I've wanted you so much. It's been such a long time . . .' And she pressed herself against him, longing for even the smallest response. 'Can't you love me just a little bit?' Just enough to banish Floyd from her mind, she thought. Just enough to push him away completely.

'Lizzie, I'm sorry. I'm too tired. I just want to sleep for a week – a month. Just so long as when I wake up again it's still true, and you're still here. That's all I want. Just to know it's true . . .' His voice was no more than a whisper, a gossamer of sound, and she felt ashamed of her desire, of her health and strength. It was as if she had somehow drained his away, by staying at home while he had had to endure so much.

'If you're too tired to love me, just give me a kiss', she

murmured. 'One of our special kisses.' And she moved closer and touched his cheek with her lips.

He turned his head, but his lips were dry and lifeless and she drew back, feeling rejected.

'I'm sorry, Lizzie. I can't seem to *feel* anything. It's all been – it's been so long, and – I don't know. I can't remember . . .' His voice was little more than a whimper, threaded with misery. 'All I've wanted all this time is to come home and be with you again and now I'm here, I can't—' To her dismay, his voice broke and she felt his tears trickle on to her cheeks. Instinctively, she pulled him closer, but he moaned as if she were hurting him and she eased her hold. He sobbed weakly, like a miserable child, and she cuddled him gently, murmuring comforting phrases in his ear. 'There, there, it's all right. Everything's all right. You're home now. You're with your Lizzie now . . . It's all right . . .'

Slowly, his sobs quietened and at last he lay still and she knew he was asleep. Occasionally, a long sigh would shudder through his body, but he didn't wake. He slept as though he hadn't been able to sleep for months; as if until now he'd been afraid to sleep.

My poor, poor Alec, Lizzie thought as she cradled him against her. Softly, she touched the dry, papery skin, feeling the sharpness of bones that seemed in danger of protruding through it, like butcher's bones through a paper bag. So thin, she thought. So weak. What have they done to you? Oh, my love, what have they done to you?

Alec stayed in bed the next morning. Jane was cooking bacon and eggs, and gave her daughter a look of disappointment as she came downstairs alone.

'Where's Alec, then?'

'Still asleep. He's worn out, Mum. I don't know what those Germans did to him, but he's like a little boy. He seems frightened to believe he's really here – says he kept

132

dreaming about being home and then waking up to find he wasn't, and he's afraid it's not true even now. He was crying last night.' Lizzie's voice broke and she sat down abruptly at the kitchen table. 'My Alec – *crying*. And he's so thin, Mum, you wouldn't believe. They must have kept those poor men on starvation rations.'

'Oh Lizzie, I'm so sorry.' Jane looked at the frying pan with the rashers laid out in it, crisp and brown, curling up at the ends. 'I know he's thin – that's why I did this. He'll be all right once he's had a week or two of good fresh food inside him. And of course he's tired, after that long journey. It's just tiredness that's making him cry, weakness and tiredness. He'll be a different chap in a week or so.'

'I hope so,' Lizzie said. She rubbed a hand over her face and Jane glanced at her.

'How did you sleep yourself?'

'Not very well. He seemed better with me holding him, and I didn't want to wake him up by moving. And I'm worried about him. Suppose it's more than just being tired. Suppose he's ill – got TB or something. Living in bad conditions, with not enough food, he could have caught anything. I'm surprised he hasn't had pneumonia.'

'Well, he hasn't,' Jane said briskly, 'and now he's home he won't, neither. As for TB – well, I don't suppose he's got that either, nor anything like it. The best thing we can do is make sure he gets plenty of food and rest and fresh air, and build him up. And the best thing *you* can do now is make sure you don't get ill yourself.' She slid the rashers and a fried egg on to a plate and set it in front of her daughter. 'You may as well eat this. No sense letting it go to waste. You can do some more for Alec when he comes down. I'm sure he'd rather have his wife cook his first breakfast at home than his mother-in-law.'

Lizzie smiled and picked up her knife and fork. She didn't feel a bit like eating the breakfast, but she agreed that food couldn't be wasted. 'I wonder how many other men are coming home in the same state as Alec,' she said, cutting a triangle of fried bread. 'Men who live in towns – men who are coming back to find their homes bombed or their families killed. Men who won't get a cooked breakfast or a warm bed. Oh Mum—' she laid down her knife and fork and put her hands to her face, suddenly in tears – 'they say the war's over but it isn't really, is it? I don't think it's *ever* going to be properly over.'

Chapter Thirteen

When Sammy woke up, he had no idea at first where he was. He lay in bed, staring at the ceiling so close to his face, listening for the sounds of Ruth clearing ashes out of the range and Silver squawking in his cage. There had been a thrush singing outside his window for the past few weeks, but all he could hear now was the squabbling of sparrows. He turned over, wondering why the window was in the wrong place, and then he remembered.

He was back in April Grove. He'd come home for the weekend, to see the ships at Navy Days. He was staying with his father in his old bedroom, the one he'd shared with Gordon, and because Gordon wasn't here any more he'd slept in the top bunk. It was Saturday and he'd be going back to Bridge End tomorrow afternoon.

At least – that was what he'd thought he'd be doing. Now, he wasn't so sure.

Sammy thought of the suitcase, packed with his things. His few clothes. His favourite book. His toy Spitfire that Terry had made him out of bits of wood, with the proper camouflage markings and RAF circles and everything. The other things, the ones that had been left behind, weren't properly his; they were things other people had given him, perhaps only for the time he was there. They hadn't actually *said* they'd want them back, but perhaps they hadn't thought it needed saying. They'd thought he knew the things were only lent.

Auntie Ruth had said he was going back, he thought doubtfully. She'd promised to meet him at the station,

Sunday tea-time. But then he remembered what the guard had said as he got on the train. *'Be glad to have him off your hands, won't you.'* And then the soldier, when Sammy had told him he was going back after the weekend: *'That was just a tale . . . Stands to reason people don't want other folks' kids foisted on them.'* And then Mr Vickers, next door, talking as if Sammy was going to have all the time in the world to run in and out of the house next door to see them: *'My missus'll be pleased to see you back. Missed seeing you round the place, she has.'*

Everyone knows but me, he thought. Everyone knows I've come back for good. They told me lies, all of them.

The bedroom door opened and his father's head appeared round it. 'You awake, Sam? I got some breakfast ready downstairs. Weetabix – you like that, don't you? And some toast and some of that jam your Auntie Ruth give me.'

Sammy gazed at him speechlessly and after a moment Dan withdrew and his feet could be heard going heavily downstairs. Sammy rolled over again and looked at the wall. Misery descended on him like a thick grey blanket. I want to go back, he thought desolately. I want to go home.

After a while, Dan called up the stairs, his voice touched with impatience, and Sammy scrambled out of bed, forgetting he was in the top bunk, and tumbled to the floor with a crash. He heard his father swear and then thump up the stairs. 'What the hell are you doing, Sam? Are you all right?'

'I fell out,' Sammy said, crouching back against the iron bunks. 'I forgot I was in the top.'

'You forgot you was—?' Dan stared at him, then burst into laughter. 'Blimey, if that don't beat the band! You forgot you was in the top! Well, you're a star turn, you are, and no mistake. Didn't hurt yourself, did you?'

Sammy shook his head. He looked cautiously at his father, still half expecting a cuff such as he would have

136

received in the old days. But Dan hadn't cuffed Sammy for years and it didn't look as though he was going to now. He shook his head, still chuckling, and when he shot out a big hand it was to lift the boy to his feet.

'Come on,' he said, his voice unexpectedly gentle. 'Breakfast's ready – you can eat it in your pyjamas. And then we're going down the Dockyard to see the ships, remember?'

They went downstairs and Sammy found the table laid with two bowls and plates, the box of Weetabix beside them, and a dish of butter and a pot of blackcurrant jam. The milk was in a bottle instead of a jug and the sugar was still in its blue paper bag, but apart from that it was just as Ruth would have laid it; and just as his mother would have laid it when she was well.

'Sit down,' Dan said. 'I've made you a cup of cocoa as well.' He brought in a cup each and put it beside their plates. Then he sat down and picked up the Weetabix. 'Two pieces?'

Sammy nodded. He was feeling sick and bewildered, but he dared not refuse another meal. He watched as the slabs of cereal were dropped in the bowls and then looked up at his father.

'I'm sorry you've only got me now,' he said. 'I'm sorry Mum and Gordon have both died.'

Dan had just picked up the milk bottle. He lowered it and stared at his son. 'What in the name of all that's wonderful brought that on?' he asked.

Sammy didn't know. He hadn't even known he was going to say it until the words came out of his mouth. He shook his head and mumbled, 'I dunno. I just thought it.'

Dan looked at him thoughtfully. There was an odd expression on his face, as if the hard lines were about to crumble. He said, 'You're not frightened something's going to happen to you, are you? Or me?'

Sammy considered this and shook his head again. It had

137

never occurred to him that he might die, and Dad was too big and strong. Gordon had been big and strong as well, but he'd been a soldier, and soldiers got killed whatever they were like. But Sammy hadn't ever been afraid that he or his father might be killed, not now that the bombing was over. 'The war's finished now,' he said. 'Nobody'll get killed any more.'

Dan laughed abruptly. 'Don't bank on it! People can find all sorts of ways of getting killed, even in peacetime. But you don't have to worry, Sam. Nothing's going to happen to you or me.' He looked at the boy again. 'I'm glad I've got you, Sam. You and me – we're all we've got now, ain't we? We'll take care of each other.'

Sammy swallowed. 'We've got Auntie Ruth too,' he said in a small voice, but Dan's face was suddenly shadowed.

'Yeah, well, we'll have to see about that, won't we? Things is different now, Sam. All sorts of things have changed. Anyway, we don't have to decide nothing now. We're going to see the ships, remember?' He picked up the milk bottle again. 'Come on – eat your breakfast. There's all sorts of things going on and I want you to enjoy yourself. You're home again, Sam! Home in Pompey, with your dad. Ain't that summat worth celebrating?'

The first thing Dan took Sammy to see was HMS *Victory*, Nelson's flagship. It stood in dry dock right inside the Dockyard, its masts and rigging visible from the harbour so that everyone could see that the German claim, made early in the war – that the historic ship had been destroyed and its timbers strewn all over the Dockyard – was untrue. Dan and Sammy joined the queue that filed slowly up its gangway and stood in a little circle to listen to the sailor who was to be their guide.

Sammy was so fascinated that he forgot to worry about whether he was going back to Bridge End. He fixed his eyes on the sailor, admiring his square collar and bell-bottom trousers, and drank in every word. He stroked the huge black barrels of the cannons, picturing the chaos of battle, and tried to imagine what it would be like to sleep in the hammocks strung to the low beams, close to all the other men, and to be woken by the swish of the cat-o'-nine-tails and shouts of, 'Show a leg, there!' He peered down into the dank depths of the hold and shuddered at the thought of being tossed down there as a punishment. He gazed at the spot on the deck where Admiral Nelson had been shot, and then at the dim little surgery below, where he had died.

'I'm glad I didn't have to be a powder-monkey,' he said, looking at the narrow runway where boys no bigger than he had scurried with gunpowder and balls. 'I don't think I'd have liked being in a battle.'

'No.' Dan couldn't help thinking of Gordon, who had been in a battle – not like the one on the *Victory* but probably just as chaotic, just as bloody – and wondered how his son had felt in those last few minutes. Had he died quickly or lain in his own blood, crying out for help that didn't come? 'Let's go and look at some of the other ships,' he said, turning away from the spot where Nelson had died, on a straw pallet on a floor painted red so that the blood didn't show. 'There's all sorts in harbour and an aircraft-carrier at the Southern Railway Jetty. I bet they've even got some planes on that.'

Together, they tramped around the Dockyard, filing up gangways, climbing ladders and pushing their way through the narrow companionways. Like most eleven-year-old boys, Sammy devoured all the comics he could get hold of, and he felt quite an expert as he surveyed the sort of instruments he'd read about in *Wizard* and *Hotspur*. Dan, who had worked on ships all through the war, was amused when Sammy held forth about them, but even he was impressed when they descended the conning tower of a submarine and stood listening to the sound of the ASDIC.

'It tells you when there's something outside the sub,'

Sammy said authoritatively. 'It's a bit like radar: a sort of beam goes out from the sub and if it hits something it bounces back. That's how they know if there's another submarine, or a ship, or even a torpedo coming. And then they can fire off torpedoes too.'

'Blimey, you know nearly as much as I do,' Dan said. 'I reckon you've been wasted out at Bridge End. You could've been our secret weapon.'

Sammy grinned and led his father through the cramped, narrow quarters. 'This is where they sleep. There's not much room, is there? Not much more than on the *Victory*. And here are the engines. I bet it feels funny being under the sea for days and days at a time, don't you? And when they can't come up they all die because there's no oxygen.'

'All right, Sam, that's enough.' Dan turned abruptly and began to squeeze back to the conning tower. He was feeling hot and anxious in the narrow space, and couldn't wait to get back to the fresh air. Daft, he thought, when he'd spent all that time working in ships' engine-rooms, but he'd never been in a submarine before and although he knew they were securely moored to the jetty he still didn't like the thought of being under water. He climbed the ladder and breathed a sigh of relief at the sight of the clouds scudding overhead.

'That was good, wasn't it, Dad?' Sammy chattered as they made for the next attraction. 'I liked the submarine. I wonder why they don't have windows, though, so you can look out at the fish. I bet that'd be really smashing, seeing the fish swim past.'

'Portholes,' Dan said, still breathing rather quickly. 'Windows on ships are called portholes. I thought you knew that.'

'Oh. Well, I did, but I didn't know if it'd be the same on a submarine. What shall we do next, Dad?'

'I reckon we'll go and get a bite to eat.' What Dan would really have liked would be to go to the Keppel's Head and have a pint, but he couldn't do that with Sammy tagging along. 'Better be fish and chips again, I suppose.' There was a fish and chip shop outside the Dockyard gates, and they headed there together, Sammy still chattering away about the ships. He seemed to have got over whatever it was that had been bothering him the night before, Dan was relieved to see, and looked as if he was enjoying himself. And so he should. Pompey Navy Week was something anyone ought to enjoy, and this year they'd really pushed the boat out – so to speak.

That's a good one, he thought, grinning to himself. I must remember to tell Ruth that. And he felt a sudden regret that she wasn't there too. I ought to have asked her to come down with Sam, he thought. She'd have liked all this too, and we could have enjoyed it together ...

By the time they got home at the end of the afternoon they'd seen every ship there was to be seen, and Sammy was flagging. So was Dan, to tell the truth. He couldn't ever remember spending such a long time on his own with his son, who he'd always thought of as a quiet little scrap, half afraid to open his mouth. It must be living with that parrot that's done it, he thought, and made a mental note that he'd have to tell Ruth that one as well.

After two lots of fish and chips in less than twenty-four hours, it was time for something a bit different. Freda Vickers often gave Dan a plate of Sunday dinner – he paid her for it, of course, and gave her his meat coupons so that she could get a better joint – and when she heard that Sammy was coming home she'd offered to make a meat pie for them. He knocked on the door and she came out, all smiles, and handed him the dish.

'We've got a bit of news too,' she told him. 'Our Cliff's got engaged to Gladys Shaw, down the road! We knew it was on the cards, of course, they've been friendly for years now, but she wouldn't say yes till the war was over. They went down to Pickett and Purser's and got the ring today. They're talking about a Christmas wedding.'

'Well, that's a bit of all right,' Dan said. 'You'd better give them my congratulations. She's a lucky girl – your Cliff's a good bloke.'

'He's lucky too,' Freda said, her face sober. 'He's had a rough deal, losing his mum and dad like that in the raids. Me and Tom were glad to give him a home here, but he'll be better off married with a place of his own. They're talking about going in for one of those new prefabs.' She looked down at Sammy. 'And how are you, love? Enjoying being back in Pompey?'

'We've been to see the ships,' Sammy said. 'We went in a submarine, it was smashing.'

'I bet it was! And are you going to the concert tomorrow?'

'Concert?' Dan said, and she nodded.

'It's on at the King's. There's going to be a special fanfare of music for VE Day – sounds ever so good. And there's things going on all next week as well.' She nodded at Sammy again. 'You won't want to miss those.'

'I've got to go back to work on Monday,' Dan began, but Freda interrupted him.

'Well, Sammy can come along with us! Tommy's got the whole week off and him and me are going to go to as many things as we can. We'll be glad to take Sam as well. And you'll be able to go to anything that's on in the evenings, won't you? We've got to make the most of it, after all this time.'

Dan looked at his son. 'That'll be all right, won't it, Sam? You'll enjoy that, with Mr and Mrs Vickers.'

Sammy stared at him. The joy of the day evaporated and he felt cold. 'But I'm supposed to be going back to Bridge End tomorrow.'

'Well, that don't matter. You can go back next week

instead. Your train ticket'll still be all right. I'll write to your Auntie Ruth and tell her.'

'But she's meeting me at the station—'

'I'll ring up the farm,' Dan said. 'Lizzie or someone'll run down and tell her. She won't mind.' He turned back to Freda Vickers. 'That's very good of you,' he said. 'Thanks. And thanks for making this pie as well. I'll do a few spuds and some carrots to go with it – I pulled out a few young 'uns this morning. That'll make a good, tasty supper.'

They went indoors. Dan went straight through to the kitchen to start peeling the potatoes and scrub the carrots. He turned on the bandy-legged gas oven and put the pie on the top shelf.

Blimey, he thought, I've come on a bit these past few years! I wouldn't have known how to do any of this when the war started. Always having women round me – Mum, and then Nora and her mum at the pub – I never had to do nothing at home. Took the view that working hard all day down the Camber entitled me to have a bit of a rest in the evenings, and so it did. But it didn't serve us well when my Nora was took bad. I was like a fish out of water then – couldn't understand why she didn't have a bit of decent grub on the table for me, or keep the place a bit clean and tidy.

It had taken Dan a long time to learn to look after himself. When Nora had died, he'd expected Sammy to do the work at home – the boy had helped his mother, after all, he ought to know what was what – and it had never occurred to him that it was too much to expect of a seven-year-old boy, especially in wartime conditions. Sammy would go to the shops and queue for hours on the pavement while women pushed past him, and when he finally got into the shop there'd be nothing left. Dan had even expected him to look after himself for three or four days at a time, while he went out to sea on the ships they were converting and the hastily built minesweepers. He could hardly believe now that he'd left the nipper on his own, all through the air raids and all. It's a wonder the authorities never took him away from me for good, he thought.

They'd taken him away, as it was. With Gordon banged up at the approved school, Nora dead and Sammy out in the country, Dan had felt as if he lived at the bottom of a deep, black pit.

It had taken him a long time to climb out of that pit. The Vickers had helped. Tommy had gone to the pub with him for a drink now and then, always with a cheery word, Freda had got his meat ration and even cooked him a meal sometimes, and Jess and Frank Budd had helped out as well. He had good neighbours, he thought, better than he deserved.

He owed Ruth a lot too. She'd never been to April Grove, so had never seen the mess it had been in, but Dan had been to her cottage often enough and noticed the difference. It was clean and bright, and smelled fresh, as if there were always flowers somewhere. Well, often there were, but even in winter there was a nice smell of polish and warmth and clean clothes. Dan used to come home and wrinkle his nose at the smell of oil and grease from the overalls he hardly ever washed, the odour of stale fish and chips, the general mustiness. And after a while he'd started to do something about it.

He'd never managed to get it up to Ruth's standards – well, he couldn't, could he, not when he was working down at the Camber all the hours God sent – but he scrubbed the floor when he had time, and he put a duster round now and then, and washed the dishes. And he took his clothes to the laundry. Never mind the cost, he couldn't go out to see Ruth in dirty clobber. And he stripped down every night for a wash and dragged in the old tin bath every Saturday and had a soak. Nobody could say he was dirty these days.

The vegetables were boiling now and he went into the back room to lay the table. That was another thing that had changed – he always used to make do with a few sheets of newspaper on the table but now there was a proper check tablecloth that Ruth had given him, and some cork mats as well. Good enough for anyone to eat off.

He came through from the scullery, feeling pleased with all he'd achieved, but at the door, he stopped short. Sammy was curled up in the armchair his mother had always sat in, and he was crying his eyes out. Dan stared at him and felt a brief surge of the old exasperation before concern took over. He crossed the room swiftly and put his hand on the boy's shoulder.

'What is it, Sam? Whatever's the matter?'

Sam shook his head but couldn't answer. He was shaking all over, tears streaming down his cheeks, and when he tried to speak the words seemed to fall to pieces in his mouth. He gave his father a look of despair and buried his face deeper in his arms.

'Sam, for cripes' sake, what's up? Got a pain?' The boy shook his head again. 'Is it your mum? Are you missing her again, coming back like this? Well, what *is* it, for God's sake? We've had a nice day, haven't we? Been on the ships – the *Victory*, and that submarine? So what on earth have you got to cry about?'

Sammy made a huge effort. He struggled up to a sitting position and took in several deep, shuddering breaths. At last, with his sobs more or less under control, he said, 'I thought I was going back to – to Bridge End. To – to Auntie Ruth.'

'Well, so you are,' Dan said, bewildered. 'You can go back next week. Don't you *want* to stop and enjoy all the things they're putting on in Pompey next week? The concert and everything, and going out with Mr and Mrs Vickers?'

'But Mr Vickers said about me stopping home for good. And the soldier on the train, he said people in the country didn't want us evacuees no more. He said they were glad to see the back of us. And you said you liked having me back here, so I thought – I thought now Gordon's dead – I thought I'd have to come back and be with you again.' He began to cry once more.

Dan stared at him. 'And you don't want to do that, then? Stop home and live with me?'

Sammy gave him a piteous look. 'I thought you'd come out in the country and live with me and Auntie Ruth,' he whispered. 'I thought we'd be a family together.'

Dan sat down heavily. It was what he'd hoped as well; it was a hope that had kept him going through all the dark months and years of the war, but now that the war was over it didn't seem so easy. Ruth seemed to have backed away from him somehow, and he didn't know why. Perhaps she regretted the half-understanding they'd had, or perhaps Dan had just imagined it all along. He didn't know how to broach the subject.

And what did he have to offer her, after all? A small, rented house in Portsmouth, where he knew she wouldn't want to live. The neighbours were good enough – most of them, anyway – and would help her along, but she'd be away from all her own friends and family. He couldn't ask her to give up all she had at Bridge End and come to Pompey.

Nor could he suggest coming to live in her own cottage. He knew that she owned it – it had come to her through her father, who had been given it when he retired from his job on the big farm. She might think that was all Dan was interested in – a free billet. And if she didn't think it, there'd be plenty of others who would.

He couldn't say any of this to Sammy, but he had to tell him something. Casting about for a reason the boy would understand, he said at last, 'But I've got a job in Pompey, Sam. I've got to earn the money for us to live. How could I move out to the country? There's no shipyards out there, is there?'

146

'There's shipyards in Southampton,' Sammy said. 'Some people go there on the bus to work. You could get a job there.'

Well, that wasn't such a bad idea, Dan thought. 'But will there be jobs for blokes like me? I mean, now the war's over, there won't be so many ships being built, will there? And I reckon there'll be plenty of local chaps coming back from the Forces who'll be looking for work too. I can't just chuck up the job I've got without looking into it a bit more.' He thought for a minute and then added, more to himself than to his son, 'I dunno as I wants to go on working on ships, anyway. If I went to live out in the country, I reckon I'd rather do a country job. But the same goes for that too,' he said quickly, before Sammy could speak. 'There'll be local lads coming back to take up those sort of jobs. They won't want a townie like me, that doesn't know one end of a cow from the other.'

Sammy was silent for a minute or two. Then he sighed and looked at his father again.

'I thought we were going to be a family after the war,' he said mournfully. 'Me and you and Auntie Ruth and Silver. I thought we were going to be a *family*.'

Chapter Fourteen

They're cutting the rations *again*!' Jane and Lizzie were in the farm kitchen, listening to the news on the wireless, when George came in for his dinner, and Lizzie turned to him at once. 'It's to share supplies with liberated Europe – that's what they said. Bacon's going down from four ounces a week to three, cooking fat's going from two ounces to one and soap's going to be cut by one eighth. Well, it's good to know they'll be able to wash themselves!'

'I don't know,' Jane said dispiritedly. 'I thought now the war's over things would get better, but they're getting worse. What have they been doing for food all these years? They must have been living on something. Haven't they got farms over there?'

'Yes, but we've been fighting all over them, haven't we?' Alec had come into the kitchen behind George. He'd been trying to help a bit around the farm, although so far he could only do light work. Lizzie was anxious that he shouldn't overstretch himself and they'd decided to stay in the farmhouse for the time being, until he was stronger. But he insisted that the only way to build muscles up was to use them. He sat down at the table. 'We've been tearing them to bits. There's nothing left of them. You ought to see what I've seen – men and women tramping the country, turned out of their homes, looking for somewhere else to live; nippers scavenging in the gutters, not knowing where their families are; people scratching about for a bit of turnip to chew on. All the food's gone to the fighting men, there's

148

been nothing left for the civvies, and now there's nothing for anyone.'

They stared at him uncomfortably. Jane glanced at the meal she was setting out on the table. It wasn't up to pre-war standards, when they had had plenty of produce – eggs in abundance, butter from their own milk, bacon and ham from their own pigs. Now, most of their produce had to be sent away and, although she knew that by keeping back a few eggs and some of the meat they still had more than townsfolk got, the table was poor in comparison. Yet it was still lavish compared with the conditions Alec described.

'Yes, but it's not like that everywhere, surely,' she said defensively. 'There must be plenty of places where there wasn't much fighting.'

'They were all rationed,' he said, 'just the same as you were here. Worse. They were occupied, weren't they? D'you suppose the Germans let them have easy lives?' He looked at the rashers of belly pork on his plate – thick slabs of meat, glistening with fat. 'I don't reckon people in occupied Europe have seen food like this for years.'

'But farmers—' Lizzie began, but he cut her off abruptly.

'I tell you, Lizzie, there aren't any farmers *left*. Not from what I saw, anyway. They're still growing a few crops, keeping some beasts, but the produce all went to the armed forces. And the land's sour. There's been thousands and thousands of men fighting all over the place. Though I suppose blood's a good fertiliser, when you come to think of it,' he added.

Jane uttered an exclamation of protest, and Lizzie turned on her. 'It's true, Mum! I know you don't like hearing things like that, but what Alec says is true. They've had a terrible time over there, worse than us. It's not just the Germans in Europe, you know. It's the French, too, and—'

'Well, I don't see as they've got anything to complain about,' her father said, sitting down and helping himself to cabbage and mashed potato. 'They gave in right at the outset. They didn't have to let the Germans overrun them.'

'But there's all those other countries too,' Lizzie objected. 'What about Holland? They didn't ask to be invaded. And Poland, that the war started over in the first place. They showed some poor souls on Pathé Pictorial last week at the pictures, trudging from one end of the country to the other, with nothing to their names but a suitcase or a few bags, trying to get home and not knowing what they'd find when they got there. And having to hide from Russian soldiers who might think they were German. The war may be over, but they still think they've got a few scores to settle. It's awful. And we complain about having to give them a rasher of bacon a week. *One rasher!*' she ended bitterly, staring at the meat on her plate. 'And a shaving off the end of a bar of soap to keep themselves decent.'

'Yes, well,' Jane said uneasily, 'it won't help them for us to waste the food we have got. Eat your dinner, Lizzie, before it gets cold. And you too, Alec. You won't build up your strength by throwing out good stuff.'

They did as they were told, but the food had no taste for Lizzie and to Alec it seemed too rich. His stomach seemed to have shrunk during his time as a POW and the sight of heaped plates sickened him. He ate as much as he could manage and then got up from the table. 'I'm going outside for a bit.'

'I'll come too,' Lizzie began, but he flapped a hand at her.

'You finish your dinner. I just want a breath of air.' He went out, shutting the door behind him, and Lizzie looked at her mother and sighed.

'He doesn't seem at all settled. I don't know what to do, Mum.'

'You've got to give him time. He's only been back a few days. It's bound to take a while to get used to being home again. We don't really know what he's been through, do we?'

'Well, he's told me a bit, but he doesn't say much, you know. And I don't like to go on at him about it. To tell the truth, I don't know if he's better talking about it or trying to forget – if he can forget, after all he's been through.'

'Put it behind him,' George advised. 'That's the best thing to do. That's what the men did who'd been in the trenches in the First World War. It don't do no good to keep rehashing it in your mind. It just keeps it all fresh. We've all got to get on with things now. Build a better world, like they keep saying on the wireless.'

'By handing over a quarter of our rations to starving Europe,' Jane said wryly. 'Well, I suppose it's a start. Now, we've got some nice fresh rhubarb and a bit of custard for afters. I'll put some by for Alec, shall I? I dare say he'll be glad to eat it later on.'

She spooned the pink, mushy fruit into a bowl and ladled a good helping of yellow custard on the top. We still don't eat too badly, Lizzie thought, watching her. Not out here in the country, anyway. Perhaps it's different in the towns and cities where they don't get so much fresh food and haven't even got gardens to grow their own, but nobody's actually starving. Not like those poor souls Alec talks about.

The sharpness of the rhubarb screwed her mouth up and afterwards her teeth felt rough. But the people gleaning the fields in Europe for a turnip to chew on would have been grateful even for that, she thought, and she wished she could give them more than a rasher of bacon and an ounce of lard. Once again, it seemed as if the war would never be properly over.

Ruth received the news that Sammy was to stay the whole week in Portsmouth with mixed feelings.

'It's not that I grudge the kiddy a holiday, specially with

his dad,' she told Jane when her sister came down to tell her about the telephone call. 'But I've just got this feeling he won't come back. I mean, Dan'd be within his rights to keep the boy now the war's over. He doesn't have to ask my permission. He doesn't have to come out here ever again if he doesn't want to.' She put the kettle on the range and poured a teaspoon of Camp coffee into two mugs.

'You're not really afraid he'd do that, surely? They both think too much of you to treat you like that.'

Ruth lifted her shoulders. 'I just don't know, do I? Once upon a time, I thought Dan and me had an understanding. I thought we'd do something about it, once the war was over. But now everything seems different, somehow. And him losing his older boy didn't help. It's driven him right back into himself. I tell you, Janie, I've laid awake these past three nights worrying about it all. Suppose he does decide he wants to keep Sammy in Portsmouth with him? There's not a thing I could do about it.'

'He won't do that, not without talking to you about it first. Anyway, I thought you said he wanted Sammy to stop on for the summer at least.'

'He did say that, but I don't know if he realised about the money.' Ruth saw Jane's puzzled expression. 'The billeting money. It'll stop now, won't it? There's no *reason* for Sammy to be evacuated now. Dan had to pay a bit, but I still got the government allowance on top. I don't know that he'll want to pay it all. He probably can't afford it.' She creased her lips. 'Not that I want money for looking after Sammy, but Dan's got his pride. He won't want me paying the kiddy's expenses.'

'And you don't think he'll come out to Bridge End himself after all?'

'I don't *know*, Jane. He hasn't said a word about it. And he never did say for sure that he wanted to do that anyway. What would he do? He's got a trade in shipfitting, toolmaking, that sort of thing. There's not much call for that out here.' The kettle began to whistle and she lifted it off the range hastily, before Silver could start to copy it, and poured boiling water into the mugs.

'Perhaps there's something else he could do,' Jane said doubtfully. 'He's a handy sort of chap. I don't know about farmwork though – I mean, he's never had much to do with animals, has he?'

'They had a cat once,' Ruth said. 'It's a bit different from a herd of cows or pigs.' She opened the larder door and took out a jug of milk to add to the coffee. 'Well, there's nothing I can do about it. I'll just have to wait and see. I'll put this beside you – there's saccharin tablets in that little pot. Thanks for coming down to tell me, anyway. Have you had any news about your Terry and Ben? They'll be home soon, surely?'

Jane smiled. 'You know what it's like. They arrive when you least expect them – like Alec did. I don't think they know themselves when they'll be able to come home, but I dare say they'll come strolling in any day now. It'll be so good to have them back.'

'George must be looking forward to having Terry back on the farm. What d'you think Ben will do? He was going to go to college, wasn't he, when he was called up. Will he be able to go back there?'

'I think so. They told him they'd keep his place. Mind you, that was a few years ago now, and they might have changed their minds.' Jane sipped her coffee. 'I mean, it stands to reason that there'll be a lot of chaps in the same boat, and then there's the ones leaving school now and wanting to go on to college. I don't see how there'll be room for them all.'

Ruth shook her head. 'Seems to me that everything's just as uncertain as it ever was, even though the war's over, what with even more rationing, and women having to give up the jobs they've been doing because the men are coming home and want them back – and *that's* not going to go down well with all of them. Lots of women have enjoyed doing the sort of jobs men usually do and aren't too keen to go back to the kitchen sink.'

'Well, that I can't understand,' Jane said firmly. 'Women should be satisfied to make a home for their husbands and families. They shouldn't be out driving buses and riding motorbikes and wearing trousers. It's all very well when there's a war on and the men have to go away and fight, but it's over now and the sooner we can get back to normal, the better. I don't say women shouldn't do the jobs that are suited to them – nursing, like you've done, and teaching in schools or working in offices – but once they're married they should give all that up.'

'I saw Heather Knight yesterday,' Ruth remarked. 'She says those Land Girls of theirs are going, just as soon as her hubby comes home and the men that used to work on the farm. But of course they've lost young Billy Burden, the boy that was killed early on, and that red-haired chap from over Fair Oak, he's a Japanese POW so goodness knows when he'll be home or what he'll be fit for when he does come. She told me one of the girls is stopping on anyway – the pretty one with the golden hair. Stevie, that's her name. Funny, because she just doesn't strike you as a girl who'd want to do farmwork.'

'And that's just what I'm saying,' Jane said. 'A girl like that – pretty, well-connected and nicely spoken – could get herself a husband as easy as a wink. Why does she want to be buried out in the countryside, slaving away with cows and sheep? It doesn't make sense to me.' She finished her coffee. 'Well, I'd better be getting back. I want to get out in the garden this afternoon. The fruit and veg are racing away now and the weeds with them.' She stood up and looked at her sister. 'Now, don't you go worrying about young Sammy, Ruth. I'm sure Dan'll send him back at the weekend. He'll probably bring him back himself and then you can have a talk with him. See what he's got in his mind.'

'I'll try,' Ruth sighed, 'but like I said, losing his other boy seems to have hit him really hard. He's gone right back to what he was like before, and I won't be a bit surprised if he wants to keep Sammy with him. And if he does, there's not a thing I can do about it.'

'Let's go for a walk,' Lizzie said to Alec. She had finished the washing-up and swept the kitchen floor while he sat in George's chair by the stove, staring at the newspaper. But every time she looked at him, his eyes were fixed on the same spot and they looked blank, as if they were seeing things far away.

'I don't know,' he said in a lifeless tone, still staring at the paper. 'I don't really feel like a walk.'

'Come on,' Lizzie said bracingly. 'You're not really reading that paper, and it's a lovely afternoon. We'll go up Top Field and back through the woods. It'll do us good.' She went over to him and laid her hand on his shoulder. 'Come on, love. I've been looking forward to this for years – you back home, and us able to go out for a walk together like we used to. Haven't you looked forward to it too?'

He looked up at her at last, and she saw with relief that his eyes had lost that emptiness. 'Of course I have. But I just don't seem to have the energy, Lizzie.'

'Well, come anyway. We don't need to go too far, but I'm sure once you're out you'll feel a bit better. The sun's lovely – not too hot, and there's a little breeze. I want to show you the primroses along the hedge. There'll be bluebells coming out in the woods, too. We could pick some and bring them back for Mum.'

Alec got up and shrugged into the old jacket Lizzie was holding out for him. It had been his favourite before the war but now it hung on him as if made for a much bigger man, and Lizzie felt the tears come to her eyes.

Blinking them away, she pulled on a cardigan and they went out into the sunshine. Jane had come back from Ruth's and was already at work in the garden, planting out lettuce seedlings. She gave them a smile as they went by and said, 'You might like to do a bit in the garden when you feel up to it, Alec.'

He nodded, and Lizzie took his hand. Alec had often pottered in the garden when he was home from sea before the war, but he seemed to have changed so much that she didn't know whether he'd still want to do it. She didn't know what he'd want to do, and she didn't think he knew either.

Alec had been home for a week now and still they hadn't made love. Every night, Lizzie slipped into bed beside him and drew him into her arms, but although he turned his head and kissed her there was no passion in his touch and she could tell that he wasn't aroused by her closeness. She tried to ignore the hurt and disappointment, telling herself that Alec had been through a terrible experience, that he needed time to recover just as if he'd been ill, and that the old loving would come back in the end, but she couldn't stop her own fears coming to the surface of her mind. Suppose he didn't love her any more. Suppose that the years of separation had changed him so much that he needed a different kind of woman – a different kind of loving, a kind she couldn't give.

She couldn't help thinking sometimes about Floyd. She tried to push away the memory of those few weeks when they had realised they were drifting into love, and that last evening when they'd been unable to hold back any longer, but when her longing for Alec's love was disappointed yet again, the sensations she had known so recently in Floyd's arms returned to torment her. I want to feel it all again, she thought, lying beside her husband's inert body. I want to be kissed and cuddled and excited. I want it to be Alec that does it to me, but I can't help thinking about Floyd . . .

They climbed up the narrow track through the woods and came out into Top Field. From here, they could look down on the village clustered round its little green, with the square tower of the grey church in one corner. Ruth's cottage was just along the lane, with the Warrens' farm at the end, and the Knights' farm lay a little way off on the opposite side. They could see Dottie Dewar's cottage with its garden cluttered with bits of an old motorbike that her eldest son had got from somewhere and was trying to mend, and a litter of bits of wood and old pram wheels that the younger boys were making into a cart. Dottie was outside hanging up some grey-looking washing and beside the door was the old pram that had seen her through umpteen children and now held the latest addition. Nobody knew quite whose baby it was; it certainly wasn't her husband Bert's, since he'd been away for the past year and a half.

'Some Yank, I suppose,' Alec remarked when Lizzie told him this. 'She's in for a black eye or two when he comes back, then. Bert was always a bit ready with his fists. Still, it's no more than she can expect.'

Lizzie felt uncomfortable. 'I don't suppose he'll be exactly pleased, but I don't think it gives him the right to knock her about.'

'What, when he's been away going through all sorts of hell and comes home to find his wife's been messing about with Yanks?' Alec turned away. 'You can't expect a bloke to laugh that off. Especially when there's a kid to show for it and the whole village knows. I suppose she'll expect him to feed and clothe it, along with all the rest.'

'Well, one more won't make much difference in that family,' Lizzie said, following him along the track. 'I'm not sure even Dottie knows exactly how many there are, and I'd bet my bottom dollar Bert doesn't!'

'He'll know that one's not his, though,' Alec stated

grimly and marched on. 'Even Bert Dewar can count up to nine.'

Lizzie was thankful that he was ahead of her and couldn't see her face. She could feel it burning and knew she must look the picture of guilt. He must never know about Floyd, she thought. He mustn't ever be given that humiliation. And it didn't mean anything, between me and Floyd – not really. We thought it did at the time, but I know now that it was just loneliness. It's Alec I really love.

They paused again a little further along the ridge and looked down at the fields. George Warren's sheep were dotted about the sloping meadow, their lambs capering amongst them. Late afternoon was their playtime and as Lizzie and Alec watched, they formed themselves into a little gang and tore madly across the field, wheeling at the hedge to race back again. One of them found its mother lying down and jumped on to her back, bleating in triumph, and then the lambs began running up a little hillock and leaping off the top of it. Lizzie and Alec sat on a grassy hummock and laughed at their antics, and she breathed a sigh of relief. The dangerous moment had passed and, better still, Alec was beginning to relax. There was a little colour in his thin cheeks and as they sat there he quite naturally slipped his arm around her and pulled her closer. She nestled against him, feeling her anxiety ebb away and a warmth flow into her heart.

I'm sorry I was unfaithful to you, she told him silently. It won't ever happen again, and you're never going to know. There's no point in ever telling you about Floyd.

She thought of Dottie Dewar, with the evidence of her faithlessness so impossible to conceal, and shivered with relief that she was not in a similar position. It might take time for Alec to recover his strength and his desire, but the love they shared was still there. And, as long as she never breathed a word about Floyd, nothing could destroy it.

Chapter Fifteen

Dan had gone into work on Monday but there wasn't much doing at the Camber and he asked if he could have one of his two weeks' holiday now instead of in the summer. The foreman hummed and hawed a bit but eventually said yes, and when Sammy came back from his day out with Tommy and Freda Vickers, he found his father with the *Evening News* spread out on the table, planning the rest of the week's activities.

'There's plenty on, son. There's a Gala at Southsea Common, an art exhibition at the Royal Beach Hotel, what they've been using for council offices – I don't reckon we'll go to that, never been much of a one for art meself – and the band of the Royal Marines is going to be out on the Common every night doing a Beat the Retreat. Must say, that don't sound very appropriate, but they're a good band, you got to admit that, one of the best. And there's a Combined Operations Demonstration every day on Southsea beach. Saturday, there's going to be a Grand Finale in the Guildhall Square, with community singing and bands and buglers and everything.' He looked up. 'Sounds all right, don't it?'

Sammy gazed at him. 'So I won't be going back till Sunday, then?'

Dan felt a mixture of disappointment and exasperation. 'Blimey, what do I have to do to please you? Perhaps you'd rather go back now, not stop here with your dad at all? Look, Sam, I've took a week of me holiday to spend with you. If you don't want me, just say so and I'll go in tomorrow same as usual.'

'No! I don't mean that, Dad – honest I don't.' Sammy came over to him and stood close, leaning his slight body against his father's bulk. 'It's just . . .'

'Yeah, I know,' Dan said with a sigh. 'You want your Auntie Ruth as well. But you'll be back with her next week, I've promised you that. Can't you just enjoy what we got here? You'll be able to tell her all about it when you do go back.'

Sammy nodded. He looked at the newspaper. 'What's a Combined Operation?'

'I dunno exactly, but it's bound to be worth seeing. I expect it's Navy, Army and Air Force all doing something together. Probably making out it's D-Day all over again, summat like that. There might be tanks and DUKWs.'

'Ducks? What did ducks do in the war?'

'Not that sort of duck, you twerp,' Dan said, grinning. 'It's those big tanks that can go on water as well as land. Amphibians, they're called. Like frogs.' He got up from the table. 'Come on, I got some sausages for our tea. Now, are you feeling all right about all this? Think you'll enjoy it?'

Sammy nodded. 'Yes, Dad. I'll be able to tell all the others out at Bridge End about it. And maybe we can send Auntie Ruth a postcard.'

'We'll send her one every day,' Dan promised. 'Now you come out to the scullery with me and we'll make some chips to go with the sausages. I thought we'd open a tin of baked beans as well – how does that sound?'

'Smashing,' Sammy said, and followed his father out to the tiny lean-to scullery that served as their kitchen. 'It sounds smashing.'

By Thursday, they had seen the Combined Operation, the Gala, the Beating the Retreat and even the art exhibition. They had been all along Southsea seafront and on the Pier, and had eaten sandwiches on the beach and on the Common. Dan had bought lemonade for Sammy and beer for himself and they'd had fish and chips three times. They trudged home, sat in the two armchairs by the fireplace and looked at each other.

'Well,' Dan said after a while, 'it's been a good few days, hasn't it? You enjoyed yourself?'

Sammy nodded. 'Yes, thanks, Dad. It's been nice.'

There was another short silence. Then Dan said, 'Tell you what. I'm not all that keen on seeing the Beating the Retreat again. I'm not all that keen on the Grand Finale in the Guildhall Square on Saturday, either. I dunno about you but I'd just as soon go back to Bridge End tomorrow. What d'you say?'

Sammy's face lit up and a broad smile broke out. 'Can we, Dad? Can we really? Tomorrow?'

'Don't see why not,' Dan said. 'It's only a couple of days early. Well, it's four days late if you look at it another way. I don't suppose your Auntie Ruth'll mind all that much.'

'Silver'll be pleased to see us. Can we go first thing?'

'No point hanging around. We'll catch the first train we can.' Dan found his heart lifting as he made the plans. I'm as bad as the kid, he thought. Just can't wait to get back. 'It's been good, though, hasn't it?' he said anxiously. 'I mean, you've had a good time in Pompey?'

Sammy nodded. 'I liked the Marines and the Gala and everything. And it was good being on the beach. But I like Bridge End better.'

'Yes,' Dan said thoughtfully, looking into the empty fireplace. 'So do I.'

'Dad?' Sammy said after a moment, his voice a little uncertain, and Dan turned his head.

'What, son?'

'Before we go back to Bridge End,' Sammy said, 'can we go and see Mum? In her grave, I mean? I'd like to take her

161

some flowers, like Auntie Ruth takes for her dad. I think she'd like to have some flowers from me.'

Dan stared at him and swore at himself. Wasn't he ever going to learn? 'Of course we can, son. I oughter thought of it meself. We'll go straight after tea. And we'll take some of them flowers in the garden, the ones your mum planted herself. She'd like that.'

It wasn't that he'd forgotten Nora, he thought as he put together a hasty meal. He'd been to her grave every week, as much as he could manage it. It was just that he'd never thought to take Sammy there. The boy had been away so long and got so fond of Ruth Purslow that Dan had almost forgotten Nora was his mother. It had never occurred to him that Sammy would want to visit the grave.

They went together after tea, Sammy carrying a rather straggly bunch of flowers. Neither of them knew what the flowers were called, but Dan had left them in their little patch, kept apart from the vegetables he'd planted, and looked after them as best he could. He walked with his hand on Sammy's shoulder, proud and thankful that the boy had remembered his mum.

At the grave, they stood in silence for a few minutes. Then Sammy knelt and put the flowers in the old tin Dan had left there for a vase.

'Hello, Mum,' he said softly. 'It's me, remember? Sammy – your boy. You used to call me . . .' his voice caught suddenly and he broke off, then went on, 'I'm going back to Bridge End tomorrow, Mum. I wish you could have come out there with me. You'd have liked it, with all the birds and the trees and everything. You'd have liked Auntie Ruth, too. And Silver. He's our parrot.' He paused and then added with a hint of mischief in his voice, 'He *swears*, Mum. He swears something *awful*.'

'I don't know as your mum would have liked that,' Dan said gruffly, clearing his throat. 'You know what she always said about swearing.'

'Yes, but Silver's a parrot. Parrots always swear.' Sammy stood up and looked down at the grave. 'Cheerio, Mum. See you again next time.'

They turned away and walked back, each silent. Next time, Dan thought. He means to come back, then. He don't mean to stop out at Bridge End for ever. Or does he think he'll only ever come back on a visit?

They were both up early next morning. The packing was all done, with Sammy's few things in the bag Ruth had lent him, together with a change of underwear and a clean shirt for Dan. He was hoping to be able to stay at the farm as he'd done before, but if they couldn't have him he'd just stop the day and then come home that evening. They'd also put their sweet coupons together and bought a small box of chocolates for Ruth. They ate a hasty breakfast of toast and a cup of tea, and then Dan passed the rest of the milk and bread over the fence to Freda Vickers, so as not to waste it, and they set off.

'I bet Auntie Ruth'll be pleased to see us,' Sammy chattered as they climbed on board the train. 'She didn't think I'd be coming back till Sunday. She'll be surprised, won't she, Dad?'

'Blimey, I meant to ring up the farm and let her know,' Dan said. 'Suppose she's not there! She might've took the chance to go off on a bit of a holiday herself.'

'She wouldn't do that. Where would she go? And what about Silver?'

'She might've took him too. Or left him with your Auntie Jane.'

Sammy was silent for a moment. Then he said, 'Well, anyway, even if she has gone away I'll be able to stop with Auntie Jane. I can help look after Silver. And Auntie Ruth'll be pleased to see me when she does come back.' He gave his father a confident look. 'It'll be all right.'

Dan looked at him, sitting in his corner seat gazing out

of the window at the fields and woods they were passing. I wish you could see him now, Nora, he thought. Your little angel, the nipper that wouldn't say boo to a goose, who used to creep about frightened of his own shadow, so sure of himself, so sure he'll be welcome. He's still quiet because that's the way he is, but he's not frightened of anything now. He knows he's part of the family out there. He's part of the village.

He thought of his other son, the big, brash Gordon who had never lacked confidence, who wasn't above a bit of thieving, who had broken his mother's heart by finishing up in an approved school. It was a shame she hadn't been able to see him, too – as a soldier, winning medals for bravery. And yet, if Gordon had lived and come back to civvy street, would he have been any different? He'd have been a spiv, Dan thought. He'd have been out for the main chance, same as before, and as likely as not ended up in prison.

I can't say I'm glad he died, he thought. No father could ever say that. But I'm glad he died a hero, because I'm not all that sure he'd have lived like one!

He looked again at Sammy. You couldn't have two more different boys than Gordon and Sam. He wasn't going to say Sam was perfect, mind, but he had a better chance than his brother of doing well in this new world that they hadn't got properly worked out yet. And for that, he had his mother to thank. Nora – and now Ruth.

He's better off at Bridge End, Dan thought, trying to ignore the heaviness in his breast. I wonder if she'll agree to keep him.

Ruth hadn't gone away. Instead of taking the chance to have a holiday, she was using Sammy's absence to get some gardening done. Somehow, with all the VE Day celebrations, she'd let it go a bit and the weeds were going mad. When Dan and Sammy came along the lane, she was on her knees in the vegetable patch, pricking out lettuce seedlings.

Silver was on his stand in the porch, where he could catch the sun but not the breeze.

Sammy saw her first and broke into a run. 'Auntie Ruth! Auntie Ruth, it's us! We've come home!'

She looked up and stared in disbelief. 'Sammy! Dan!' She scrambled to her feet, brushing soil off her hands on her old skirt. 'Whatever are you doing here? I thought you weren't coming back till Sunday.'

Sammy tore the gate open and rushed into her arms. 'We came back early. We wanted to see you. We missed you!'

Ruth held him tightly. She looked over his head at Dan, seeing him through a sudden mist. 'I've missed you too. Oh Sammy!' She bent and kissed the top of his head. Half laughing, half in tears, she said, 'I thought you might decide to stay in Portsmouth.'

Dan met her eyes. She felt a sudden quiver in her heart and turned away quickly. 'Come and have a cup of tea. You must be parched. And I've got a bottle of fizzy lemonade for you, Sammy, to celebrate you coming home.'

'Fizzy lemonade! Coo – smashing!' He dashed up the path and skidded to a halt at the porch. 'Hello, Silver. It's me back again. How are you, then? Say hello, there's a good boy.'

The parrot tilted its head and regarded him beadily. 'Sod the little bugger!' he said in a tone of astonishment, and then came out with one of the first phrases Sammy had taught him. 'Sammy, Sammy, shine a light, ain't you playing out tonight?'

Sammy gave a laugh of delight and vanished into the cottage. Ruth and Dan stood, one each side of the gate, still looking at each other.

'You don't mind us coming back early?' Dan said awkwardly. 'I mean, you don't mind me bringing *Sam* back early? It ain't a nuisance?'

'Sammy's never a nuisance, you know that,' she said

softly. There was a moment of quiet before she added even more quietly, 'Nor are you.'

Dan flushed and fumbled with the gate. 'I oughter let you know. Only I never thought of it, not till we got on the train this morning. I only made up me mind last night. We were going to stop for the Grand Finale but we seen the Gala and the Beating the Retreat and all the demonstrations and that, and – well, I knew the nipper was hankering to come home – I mean, back to Bridge End – and I thought about the trees and the birds singing – all we get in Pompey is sparrows and seagulls – and I just thought, Well, why don't we just go back? So I packed up our duds and that and—'

'Don't worry, Dan,' Ruth said, as he floundered on. 'I'm glad to see you – both of you. It's been quiet here without Sammy.'

'Well,' he said in a tone of relief. 'So long as it's all right, then.'

'Come and have that tea,' she said, and he followed her up the path. They went indoors, ducking past the parrot on his stand, and found Sammy already pouring boiling water into the pot. Ruth smiled and laid her hand on his shoulder. 'Thank you, Sammy. Now go and get that fizzy lemonade. It's in the larder. We'll take our tea outside, Dan. It's too nice to be indoors.'

They sat down on the old bench under the plum tree. Sammy brought out a stool so that he could sit beside Silver and they could hear his voice, recounting the week's experiences. For a few minutes, both were quiet and then Dan said, 'You bin doing a bit in the garden.'

'Yes,' Ruth said, looking at the neat vegetable and flower beds. 'The back needs a bit of attention, though. I want to clear out all those brambles in the corner before they get a hold. Somehow last year they overtook me and I don't want them to spread any more.'

'I could do that for you,' he offered. 'I mean, if you'd like me to. I could do a bit this afternoon, before I go back.'

Ruth turned her head and looked at him. 'Do you have to go back tonight, Dan? It's only Friday. Can't you stop on till Sunday?'

'Well,' he said, hesitating. 'If you think your Jane wouldn't mind putting me up. Only it's a bit short notice, and now Lizzie's hubby's back—'

'I wasn't thinking of you going to Jane's,' she said. 'I don't see why you shouldn't stop here, with me and Sammy.'

Dan stared at the cottage as if he'd never seen it before. He turned back to her. 'Here?'

'Well, why not?' she said. 'It's not as if I'm on my own. Sammy's here. And, well . . .' She lifted her head and looked him in the eye. 'We have got a sort of understanding, haven't we?'

'An understanding?' he said.

'I thought we had,' Ruth said quietly, still meeting his eye.

There was a short silence. They could both hear the twitter of birds in the hedgerow, the soft murmur of Sammy's voice and Silver's answering squawks, the clop of horses' hooves in the lane and the calls of farmworkers somewhere in the fields. Yet with all that, it seemed to both as if the world had stilled and was awaiting a reply.

'We got a lot to talk about,' Dan said at last. 'You and me.'

'There's no hurry,' Ruth said, and reached out her hand. He took it, almost swamping it in his own big fingers. Her skin was soft and smooth against his roughened, callused palm and he felt a sense of wonder, and a lifting of the spirit that had been so cast down. I've not felt this since before Nora died, he thought, and suffered a swift pang of regret that she had died so young. Yet he knew that she would not have begrudged him this second chance – a

167

chance that, in that moment, he swore he would not throw away as he believed he had thrown away the first. I'll do right this time, he vowed. I'll do all the things for Ruth that I ought to have done for Nora. I'll be a different man . . .

He cleared his throat. 'I'll start on that back garden straight after dinner,' he said.

Chapter Sixteen

Despite all the celebrations, the war was not yet completely over. The fighting in the Far East was as bitter as ever; even under heavy attack from firebombs, the Japanese refused to give in, and responded by sending kamikaze pilots to attack the Allied warships, losing over sixty planes but sinking two American destroyers. Even after the Emperor's own palace was bombed there seemed to be no hope of surrender.

In Europe, plans were proceeding for the new peace. Germany was to be divided into four, each quarter governed by one of the Allied powers. The British were to occupy Berlin and regular soldiers were to move in, early in July. Some of the Nazi leaders had been arrested and would be tried for war crimes; Rudolf Hess, who had parachuted into Scotland early in the war, would be tried with them. Himmler escaped by taking cyanide, as Goebbels had done before him, but Lord Haw-Haw, who had tried so hard to frighten the British with his broadcasts (and been laughed at for his pains), was captured near Hamburg and would be tried for treason.

The coalition government came to an end. Winston Churchill, who had led the country through its darkest hour and some of its finest, resigned as Prime Minister and the date of the election was set for 5 July 1945. And in mid-June, at long last, the demobilisation began of the conscripted servicemen.

'Ian will definitely be coming home soon,' Heather Knight said to her mother-in-law, and they gazed at each

169

other with tears of joy in their eyes. 'He's got through safely. He'll be coming home for good.'

'It's wonderful.' Emily, who had borne up so well all these years, sat down suddenly at the kitchen table and began to cry. 'Oh Heather, if you knew the times I've imagined him dead. My Ian, my son. There's been so many mothers lost their boys, I didn't dare think I might be one of the lucky ones.' Her words were lost in sobs, and Heather moved swiftly to kneel beside her, putting her arms around the older woman's shoulders and drawing her head down to her breast. 'My Ian, my little boy . . .'

Arthur Knight came in and stared at them in dismay. 'What is it? What's happened? Don't tell me there's been bad news about our Ian, not after all this time!'

Heather smiled at him through her tears. 'It's all right, Dad. We're crying because he's safe – he's coming home. They're starting the demob. There's sixty thousand coming out between now and August!'

'Oh, I see.' Arthur had grown used to women crying because they were happy. They would keep smiling through all sorts of bad times, and then crumple up like paper bags when something good happened. Not but what he didn't feel a bit choked up himself at the news that his son would be coming home at last. He cleared his throat and sat down in his armchair, shaking out the newspaper. 'Well, I suppose that means all these bits of girls will go home too. There'll be some work done round the place for a change.'

'Dad!' Heather protested, laughing, and Emily blew her nose and shook her head at her husband. 'You know we'd never have managed if it hadn't been for them.'

'All right, maybe they haven't been so bad,' he acknowledged. 'Easier on the eye than the blokes, I'll say that. It won't be near as pretty a sight, watching young Jim Hall and Mike Hutchins bring in the cows, as it has been seeing Stevie and the others around the yard.'

170

'I don't think Stevie's going to leave too soon,' Heather remarked, drying her eyes. 'She likes country life. And we'll need her for a bit longer, while the men settle in again.'

'Settle in!' he snorted. 'What do they need time to settle in for? Couple of days and it'll be as if they never went away.'

'Now then, Arthur, you know they're entitled to a bit of leave after all they've been through.' Emily, her moment of weakness over, got up and went over to the sink to start scrubbing potatoes. 'Though I dare say you're right and they'll be pitching in pretty soon. It'll be harvest-time before we know it, and I can't see any of those lads sitting back and watching while the women bring it in.'

'It'll be good for the children to have their father back,' Heather said, washing the soil off the new carrots she had just pulled. 'Specially Roger. He needs a man to look up to.'

'Oh, I see, he can't look up to his grandad, then,' Arthur objected, pretending to be offended, and the women laughed. 'Well, he might be in for a surprise. Ian's idea of discipline might be a bit different from what it used to be, after a few years in the Army.'

'Oh, he won't be hard on the children. He'll be too pleased to be back with them.' Heather dropped the carrots into a pan of cold water and started on the spring greens. She turned to look at her father-in-law. 'It's going to be lovely, being a proper family again, but don't think I haven't appreciated all the help you've given me with the children, both of you. I couldn't have done so much on the farm without all you've done.'

'Well, I dunno what would've happened to the farm neither, without all *you've* done,' Arthur said gruffly. 'You've been a good girl, Heather. A good mother to the youngsters and a good farmer too. Ian'll be as proud of you as I am.' They looked at each other for a moment and then he shook out his newspaper again. 'And now I think we've had enough of this mutual admiration society. When's my dinner going to be ready?'

Ian arrived on 4 July – the same day that the British moved in to occupy Berlin, and the day before the first General Election to be held in Britain for over ten years. The villagers had taken down the bunting strung around the houses to celebrate VE Day, and had now put up the colours of the political parties. The candidates had visited Bridge End and held meetings in the village hall, and there had been heated debates in the pub and on the green.

The Conservatives'll get in again easy, stands to reason they will. After all Mr Churchill's done for this country, it'd be a slap in the face if they didn't.'

'Yes, but being a good leader in wartime don't mean he'll be good for the peace,' others argued. 'He's a soldier when all's said and done. Time for a change, I reckon. Let Labour have a chance, bring in this new Welfare State they're talking about. Free doctor's treatment and a pension to look forward to.'

'That's right,' someone else applauded. 'Don't want to go back to the Thirties, do we? Had enough of the Depression – no jobs, folk chucked out of their homes and starving. Anyway, everything's different now. There's no upper class no more, with servants and all that. We're all equal.'

At the farm, they had been looking out for days, hoping to see Ian's tall figure come swinging up the lane. Heather had imagined him in his Army uniform, a kitbag slung over his shoulder, as he had been the last time she saw him, and when she first saw the man in the dark green suit and brown trilby stride up the path, carrying a cardboard suitcase, she didn't immediately realise who it was.

'Looks like someone wants to get us to fill in some more forms,' she remarked over her shoulder to Emily, and then

172

gave a shriek. 'It's *Ian*!' She dropped the rabbit she was skinning and rushed to the door.

'Ian? He's *here*?' Emily jumped up from her chair, letting her knitting fall to the rag rug in front of the stove, startling Fly, the collie dog. The two collided at the door and struggled to get through, laughing with excitement. Heather won and flung herself into Ian's arms just as he was about to come through.

'Ian! Oh, darling! Oh, my love! You're home! Oh, it's so good to see you!' They held each other tightly, lost in kisses, while Emily tried to put her arms around them both and Fly leaped about them all in a frenzy of barking. 'Why didn't you let us know?'

'I didn't know myself. The train times are all over the place. Anyway, I wanted to surprise you. I wanted to get off the train and walk home on my own and sort of *sniff* the place, and then just stroll in as if it was an ordinary day.' He turned to his mother and hugged her. 'You're looking as pretty as ever, both of you.'

'And look at you – so smart!' Heather held him at arm's length, studying him. 'Did they give you that new suit?'

'Well, they had to, didn't they. None of us had any civvies to come home in, and we had to hand in our uniforms. Couldn't send us on the train starkers, now could they?'

'Ian!' his mother protested, and Heather laughed. She hugged his arm against her side.

'Well, you look very smart. And just look at that trilby! All ready to start going up to the City on business.'

Ian made a face. 'A decent set of working clobber would've made more sense. How often do I wear a suit? I've only ever had one in my life, the one I got married in, and that would've lasted me the rest of my life. I hope you haven't given all my things away, Heather.'

'Oh yes, I did that as soon as you went off,' she said airily. 'Needed the space for my gentleman friend's

173

clothes . . .' She grinned at her mother-in-law's expression. 'It's a good job you left me with your mum and dad, or there's no knowing what I might have got up to.'

'Well, you can forget all that now,' he said, and kissed her again. 'You won't have time to go off gallivanting now I'm back. Are you going to let me in then, or am I going to be kept standing on the doorstep all day? How about a cup of tea? And what's for dinner?' He sniffed and wrinkled his nose. 'And what the dickens have you got on your hands, Heather?'

Heather lifted her palms and stared at them in dismay. 'Rabbit! Oh, I hope I haven't got blood on your nice new suit.' She snatched up a dishcloth and dabbed at his lapel. 'It looks all right.'

'Rabbit!' Emily's fingers flew to her mouth. 'Oh, what have we been thinking of!' She scurried back into the kitchen and moved the kettle on to the top of the stove. 'It's the rabbit for dinner. Heather was just cleaning it. At least . . .' She stopped, one hand still at her mouth, and Fly, who had ceased barking some time ago, crept guiltily towards the door. 'At least, we *did* have a rabbit. Oh, you bad dog! You bad, *bad* dog!'

Ian looked at the two furry ears that were all that was left of the rabbit Heather had been skinning. He looked at his wife's and mother's faces, dismayed by the dog's naughtiness. Then he dropped into an armchair and put back his head and roared with laughter.

'Oh, that's good, that is! The dog's eaten my dinner! Now I know I'm home. Now I really, *really* know I'm home . . .'

Not all the family was as welcoming as Heather and Emily.

Arthur and Teddy came in half an hour later from their walk around the woods, full of news about a family of fox cubs they'd come across playing by a grassy bank. Arthur greeted his son with a whoop of excitement, and almost

174

broke down in tears, but Teddy's tears were of a different kind. Scooped up into his father's arms, he creased his face, opened his mouth into a large square and burst into a howl of dismay.

'Teddy!' Heather exclaimed, and quickly took him away, holding him into her shoulder. 'He's just shy,' she apologised. 'He didn't expect you to be here, and he doesn't even know who you are.'

'Haven't you told him I'd be coming home? Doesn't he know I'm his daddy?'

'Yes, of course, but he didn't know it was you, did he? And what with everyone so excited – it's all too much for him. There, there,' she crooned to the sobbing child. 'It's all right, he's not going to hurt you. It's your daddy. You know about your daddy, don't you? You've seen his picture by Mummy's bed.'

Slowly, Teddy turned his head and took a cautious look at his father. Ian, almost as upset as his son, tried to smile at him and Teddy immediately hid his face again and broke into fresh sobs. 'I don't like him!' he wailed. 'Make him go away! I want my real daddy!'

Heather looked helplessly at her husband. 'I'm sorry, love. You'll just have to give him time.'

'*Time?* He's had four years—' He bit the words off. 'What does he mean, his *real* daddy?'

'I don't know. Perhaps he thinks you ought to be in uniform, like in your photograph. This *is* your real daddy,' she said to the crying boy. 'He's come home now. He isn't a soldier any more. Now come on, stop crying, there's a good boy.' She carried him to the armchair by the stove and sat down, still cradling him while Ian watched. 'He'll be all right in a minute. He'll soon get used to you.'

'I hope so. Looks to me as if a father's just what he needs. You've turned him into a mummy's boy.' Ian turned away from her distressed look. 'All right, I can see you've not had much choice. I'll take my things upstairs, shall I, and unpack. And then perhaps we can have a bite to eat. I haven't had anything for hours.' His amusement over the rabbit seemed to have evaporated. He went upstairs and Heather, Emily and Arthur looked at each other.

'Let me take Teddy,' Emily said. 'You go up with Ian. You want a bit of time on your own. Come on, Teddy-bear, come to Grandma.' She prised the boy's fingers away from his mother's arms. 'Let go, there's a good boy. Mummy wants to go and talk to Daddy.'

'I don't want her to!' Teddy screamed. 'I want her to stay here! Mummy! *Mummy!*'

Heather, on her way to the staircase, stopped and looked at him uncertainly but Emily shook her head. 'Go on, love. He'll be all right. He's got to learn he doesn't come first all the time. It's your husband needs you now.'

Pat and Roger arrived at the end of afternoon school. They came racing up the path, full of news of the day off they were to have for the General Election. 'They're going to use the school all day tomorrow, and everyone's going to vote, and it'll all be secret, nobody's allowed to say who they're voting for, and—' They stopped dead in the doorway, staring, until at last Pat cried, 'It's our *daddy!*' and threw herself across the kitchen.

Ian swept her into his arms, laughing. 'There's my girl, my little princess!' He hugged her to him and kissed her, and Heather felt a surge of relief that at least one of the children had given him the welcome he needed. He set her down again. 'Let me see you properly. My goodness, haven't you grown! A proper young lady. And pretty as a picture too, just like your mother.' He looked past her at the boy standing in the doorway. 'And there's Roger too, nearly as tall as me. Come and shake hands with your dad, son.'

Slowly, Roger came forwards. He met his father's eyes without a smile and put out his hand. Ian narrowed his eyes

176

a little and turned his head slightly to one side, still looking at the boy's face. There was a moment of silence.

'Say hullo to your father, Roger,' Heather said a little nervously.

'Hullo.'

'Well, you can say a bit more than that!' she exclaimed. 'He's come a long way to see you. He's been in the war. Haven't you got anything else to say to him?'

Roger looked at her. She gazed at him pleadingly, willing him to say something that would break the ice that seemed suddenly to have formed, but he appeared speechless. Perhaps he was shy too, she thought, and wished that boys were encouraged to show their feelings as girls were. Perhaps he really wanted to run to his father's arms as Pat had done, but didn't dare. Perhaps he was even a bit jealous of the attention she was receiving.

Roger turned back to his father. Ian was watching him too, and there was disappointment in his eyes. 'Oh, don't make him talk to me if he doesn't want to,' he said. 'I dare say he'll find his tongue again when he's ready. At least my daughter's pleased to see her daddy home, aren't you, my pet?' He hugged Pat again and she snuggled against him.

'You're a lovely daddy,' she said, smiling adoringly. 'The best daddy in all the world. You'll stay here now, won't you? You'll stay for ever and ever and ever.'

Heather glanced at Roger. He was standing quite still, staring down at his boots. He looked up, met her eyes, then turned abruptly and went to the stairs. They heard him clatter up to his room and slam the door.

'I can see there's another one who needs a father,' Ian said quietly. But Heather had seen the tears in Roger's eyes and knew that it was not so simple as that.

She had thought that it only needed Ian's return to make them all as happy a family as they'd ever been. Now she knew it needed something more; but she didn't know what it could be.

*

News of Ian's return flew round the village and over the next week there was a steady stream of people beating a path to the farmhouse door to see him for themselves. Ian had always been popular and the fact that he'd come home with medals added glamour to his reputation. Reluctantly at first, then more proudly, he laid them on the kitchen table for visitors to see.

'That's for good behaviour – or not getting found out, more like! This star's for serving in Africa. I've forgotten what this one's for.'

'It's the Military Medal,' Heather told them. 'It's the same as the Military Cross, except that that's for officers. He got it two years ago, didn't you, Ian?'

'Something like that.' He had never told her exactly what he'd done to be awarded this distinction but, looking at the ring of expectant faces, he sighed and said, 'It wasn't much. We just came across this hut. All the rest of the enemy had scarpered but there were about a dozen holed up in there and we took them prisoner. That's all. It wasn't just me, there were three of us.'

'But you were in charge,' Fred Hutchins said. He was bent and gnarled now, but he'd been in the First War and knew what war was like.

'Well, yes, but only because—'

'And they were armed, I reckon?' Fred persisted. 'A dozen of them and three of you? And they put up a fight?'

'Yes, in a manner of speaking, I suppose they did. I can't remember all that much about it.' He shrugged away other questions and after a while the visitors left, with several more claps on Ian's back and promises to meet soon for a drink in the pub. Ian swept the medals into the palm of his hand and looked at his father. 'It's all over now, anyway. I'm more interested in what's been happening on the farm. Heather and the girls been making themselves useful, have they?'

'Making themselves useful! I've barely had to lift a finger – and just as well, considering my arthritis.' Arthur made his way slowly to the door. 'I tell you, son, this farm would have gone to rack and ruin if it hadn't been for your wife there. Rack and ruin.'

He went out and Ian glanced at Heather. 'Thanks, love. I knew you'd do your bit. I'll take over now, though. You'll be able to sit back a bit. Help Mum round the house.'

Heather laughed. 'I already do that, as much as she'll let me! No, I'll be happy to go on working outside. I've got used to it now, and I like it. You'll need me to show you how things are, anyway.'

'I dare say I'll soon pick it up again,' Ian said, a little coolly.

There was a brief silence. It was broken by the arrival of the two older children from school. Pat made straight for her father while Roger, dawdling behind her, dumped his satchel on the table and started to fiddle with the straps.

'Daddy! I've missed you.' Pat rubbed her face against his sleeve and he laughed and ruffled her hair.

'You've only been gone a couple of hours.'

'I missed you all the same. I've got years of missing to catch up on.'

'Well, you'll have years to do it in.' He sat down and lifted her on to his knee and she snuggled into his chest. Ian looked over the top of her head towards Roger. 'How was school, then?'

'All right.' The boy's voice was indifferent.

Ian sighed but persisted. 'What've you been doing?'

Roger looked down at his shoe and drew a pattern on the floor with his toe. Reluctantly, he said, 'Reading and dictation. I can't see the point in dictation.'

'Did you make many mistakes?' Ian enquired, and Roger sent him a resentful glance.

'You can't help making mistakes in dictation. The words don't sound right.'

'Well, never mind,' Heather said. 'You've got the whole weekend off now. You don't have to go to school again till Monday.'

Roger leaned on the table, glowering at the scrubbed wood. 'I wish I didn't have to go back at all. I wish I could leave now.'

Ian spoke sharply. 'That's silly talk, Roger! A good education's going to be even more important now the war's over. You'll stay at school as long as you can.'

'Why? What use is stuff like dictation and all that going to be to me? I'm going to work on the farm. I'll be taking it over one day.'

'Not for a long time yet. And who knows what farming's going to be like, anyway? You take it from me, the world's changing and it's going to want men with a bit between their ears. I think I'd better have a word with your teacher, see how you're getting on.'

Roger opened his mouth indignantly and Heather intervened. 'There's no hurry, surely? It's two years before Roger can leave. Plenty of time to think about whether he'll stay on longer than that.'

'I shan't,' Roger muttered, and Heather sighed.

'Go and wash, there's a good boy. And you'd better take those muddy boots outside and clean them off first. I don't know how you get yourself in such a state.' She watched him trail resentfully through the door and turned to her husband. 'Go a bit easy on him, love. It's a big change for him, having you home again.'

Ian stared at her in astonishment. 'A big change? For *him*? And what do you think it is for me? I've been away for nearly four years. I've been to Africa and Italy and God knows where else. I've been fighting a *war*. It's a pretty big change for me, I can tell you, coming home again. Why, when I went away I had two little kids. Now I've got three, and young Roger's not so little any more. He's getting on for as tall as me!'

'I know, I know,' Heather said. 'It must be different from being in camp with other men all the time. But you're glad to be back, aren't you? We're glad to have you here again, I can tell you.'

'Of course he's glad,' Pat said from her position on her father's lap. 'He missed *me*, didn't you, Daddy?'

'I think he probably missed us all,' Heather said.

'Of course I missed you, pigeon. And your mum's right, I missed all of you. Now, how about going and changing out of your school clothes and then you can come and show me how you feed the calves. Then I'll start the milking.'

'You don't have to—' Heather began, and he turned quickly. 'I mean, why not have a few days off before you start work? You're supposed to be on leave, aren't you? Demob leave, like the other men?'

'Leave!' he snorted. 'You know what that means for most of them, don't you? It means they'll spend their "leave" walking the streets looking for jobs. There's not that many will find their places kept for them all these years. That's if the places where they worked are still there. But I've got a job – farming – and I want to get back to it. I don't want to kick my heels while you and those girls do my work.'

'All right, but you don't have to start with the milking. Why not just do the calves with Pat, and the pigs and hens to start with? Stevie and I can see to the cows.'

He looked at her, and she couldn't quite tell if he were joking or serious. During the few days he'd been at home he'd shown several unexpected flashes of temper, rising as swiftly as a flame and dying away again as quickly, and she told herself that this was a natural reaction to all he'd been through and nothing to worry about. He'd soon be back to the cheerful, placid Ian she'd known before the war. But it was the main reason why she wanted him to rest before starting work again.

'What's the matter?' he snapped. 'Don't you think I can do it after all this time?'

181

'Of course you can do it,' Heather said. 'It's just that – well, I think you ought to give yourself time to get to know the cows again. Some of them are different ones from when you went away, and even the older ones might not remember you at first. You know what cows are like; if they're not happy with who's milking them they won't let down their milk.'

'And of course, they will for *you*,' he said.

'Don't say it like that!' She moved quickly across the kitchen and laid her hand on his shoulder. Pat looked up at her, wide-eyed, and she spoke with gentle reassurance. 'It's not your fault, sweetheart. You've been away – it's bound to take time to get back into it all again. Why not let me go on doing it for a week or two? There's plenty else to get on with, if you really feel you want to work.'

'Yes,' he said with a touch of bitterness. 'Feed the chickens. Let the calves suck my fingers. *Children's* work. That's not what I fought a war for.' He lifted Pat off his knee and stood up. His voice was very low. 'All the time I've been away, I've thought about home. You and the kids – and the farm. It's kept me going, thinking what would be happening. They'll be drilling, or harrowing, or ploughing, I used to think. Or milking. Every day, twice a day, I could think about milking. It was what I looked forward to most. And now you don't think I can do it.'

'I didn't say that!'

'It's what you're thinking, though. You don't think the cows will let me have their milk.'

Heather glanced at Pat, standing on the floor between them, her eyes going from one face to another. 'Let's talk about it later. But just for now, why don't you go with Pat and let her show you all the things she does to help? She wants to do that, don't you, sweetheart?'

Pat looked up at her father and took his hand. 'Come on, Daddy. Come and see my calves. I want to tell you their names. Come on.'

Ian hesitated. Then he shrugged and followed his daughter to the door. As he pushed his feet into the old wellingtons that Heather had kept for him all these years, he turned and met her eyes.

'I'll start milking tomorrow. The sooner the cows get used to me again, the better.'

Heather said nothing. She watched them trudge across the yard to the calves' pen and then she sighed and started to put on her own boots.

He doesn't realise how tired he is, she thought. And I didn't realise how unsure he was of his place here at home. He's going to need a lot of help and reassurance before he feels settled again.

Coming home wasn't as easy as everyone thought it should be.

Chapter Seventeen

Slowly, aided by fresh country air and wholesome food, Alec began to regain his strength. The hollow look departed from his cheeks, his eyes brightened and his face began to fill out. The sunshine touched his skin with colour and as he worked around the garden and farmyard, his muscles began to harden again. Easily exhausted to begin with, he did a little bit more each day until Lizzie began to worry that he was overdoing it.

'There's no call for you to make a slave of yourself,' she said, finding him digging in the vegetable garden. 'We've still got the Land Girls till the summer's over. Ian Knight says we can borrow their Stevie and those others any time we like.'

'I'm tired of doing nothing,' Alec said. 'All these years in prison camp, I've felt useless. You'd think we could have been given some work to do, to keep our self-respect – though we wouldn't have done anything to help the Jerries' war effort. But we couldn't even do any work on our own huts.'

'Well, it wouldn't have been very sensible of them to hand out hammers and saws to you lot.' Lizzie had heard some of the tales of ingenious escapes from the German POW camps. At Colditz, it was said they'd even built a glider, although the camp had been liberated before they got a chance to try it out. 'You'd have been making ladders over the wire, or going on the rampage and killing all the guards. I wouldn't have given you so much as a screwdriver!'

'Well, maybe not, but I still feel I've wasted a lot of time. I want to feel useful again.' He stopped digging and leaned on his spade. 'Lizzie, I've been thinking about what I'm going to do. I can't loaf around here for ever.'

'You're still recovering. The doctor says you need time—'

'I've still got to *think* about it, though. I've got to earn a living for us – and for a family.' He glanced away, then said, 'I'm not going back to sea, Lizzie. I just don't feel the same about it, after being torpedoed like that. Floating about in all that muck of oil and blood and bits of bodies, bits of the blokes I knew—' He stopped abruptly. He didn't like talking about it to Lizzie, but the memories haunted him all the time. Sometimes, as he was working in the garden, watching the fat pink worms and listening to the birdsong, he was transported without warning to that terrifying night when he'd believed he was about to drown in the thick, viscous water. Once again, it was as real as it had been then, and he'd have to sit down quickly, just where he was, and wait for it to pass, feeling shaky and sick afterwards. Or it would come at night, in his dreams, and he'd be forced to endure it all again, waking only when he began to choke to find Lizzie cradling him in her arms, murmuring reassuringly in his ear. 'I can't go back,' he said.

'You don't have to,' she said quietly. 'Nobody's going to make you do that. I don't want you to go – I want you to stay here with me. You know you can work on the farm, Alec. Dad'll be pleased to have you, especially as poor Billy Burden isn't coming home.'

'I'm not sure that's what I want to do either,' he said restlessly. 'I don't mind doing what I can to pull my weight, but I'll never make a farmer, Liz. I don't understand the land like your dad and Terry do. I'm a town boy, me – I grew up in Southampton and I guess that's where I ought to go to look for work.'

She gazed at him. 'You mean you want us to live there? In the town?'

'It wouldn't be so bad, would it? I dare say my mum and dad would put us up to start with. Or we could find some rooms to rent. It's not that far away, Liz – you could come back on the bus to see your mum and dad whenever you want.'

'But what would you do?'

'Well, it's ships I know, so I reckon I could get work in the docks. Refitting, that sort of thing. They'll be bringing the big liners back into service soon – the *Queen Elizabeth* and the *Queen Mary*, all those. They'll all want refitting. And there's any amount of others. People will be wanting to travel again, Lizzie, and the only way they can do it is by sea.'

'They're talking about aircraft. Those new jets – they say they'll be flying to America.'

'Maybe, but not just yet. There'll always be a place for ships.' He jabbed his spade at the earth. 'I've got to get back my self-respect, Lizzie. I've got to earn a living for *us*. Us and our family.'

Lizzie looked down at the freshly turned soil. A large worm had come to the surface and was hastily burrowing out of sight. It's a bit like Alec, she thought, not wanting to face up to the light. Not wanting to face the truth.

'We don't seem all that likely to have a family yet awhile,' she said, trying to keep her voice light.

Alec's face darkened. He jabbed his spade again, almost cutting the worm in half. 'I've told you, it'll come right. It's no good keeping on.'

'I'm not keeping on.' She moved closer and laid her hand on his forearm. 'I love you, Alec. I just want us to be able to love each other properly.'

'And don't you think I do too?' he burst out. 'You don't know what it's like for me! I *want* to make love to you – I want it so badly I could burst – but it just won't happen. I

186

don't know why. God knows I've wanted you badly enough all these years. It's been all I could think about at times, and it was the first thing I wanted to do . . . but it just *won't* – I don't know—' He turned away, dashing the back of his hand across his eyes.

Lizzie moved after him, her hand on his arm again, trying to turn him to face her. 'Oh lovey, I'm sorry. I didn't mean to say anything. It was just when you said that about a family . . . I know it'll come right eventually, we just have to be patient. When you're properly strong and well again. But it's why I don't want you to think about looking for work yet. You're *not* properly over it all. And I don't think it's a good idea to go back to Southampton, I really don't, not amongst all those bombed buildings and everything. It's better for you to be out here in the fresh air.' At last she managed to get him to face her again. 'Don't let's think about it yet,' she said gently. 'Let's leave it for a few more weeks – till the end of the summer. There's plenty to do here to make yourself useful – the harvest and everything. Dad needs you on the farm, he really does.'

'He's got Terry. Terry'll be taking over in a few years. It'll be his farm then – there'll be no place for me.'

'That's not going to happen just yet.' She stroked his face, brushing away the streak of dirt that he had left there. 'Just let's have this summer here, love, and then see how you feel. You still need to build yourself up. It'll be all right, I know it will. But it's no good forcing it.'

'No,' he said, and thrust his spade into the earth once more. 'No, it's not.'

He began to dig again. Lizzie watched for a few moments and then went back into the house. She felt sad and empty. I want to love him so much, she thought. I want to feel his loving again. I thought it would happen straight away. I didn't know I was going to have to wait so long . . .

Although everyone had been to the polls on 5 July, the

results weren't announced for another three weeks while the votes from servicemen and women abroad were collected. When the announcement was finally made, the entire country was shocked.

'Mr Churchill pushed out, after all he's done! Whatever must he be feeling?' Emily was kneading bread when the news came through on the wireless, and she paused in the act of punching the dough into shape. 'It's so *ungrateful*.'

'General Elections aren't about being grateful,' Arthur said. He was sitting at the table cleaning the oil lamps. 'They're about looking forward, not back. Winnie's had a good innings, now it's someone else's turn. I think Clem Attlee will be a good Prime Minister. He's got the experience – been in the Cabinet ever since the start of the war, same as Churchill.'

'Well, I hope you're right. And this Labour Government – you know what they say, don't you? The minute they're in, they'll put up taxes. It's all very well talking about a Welfare State, but it's got to be paid for. I hope you're not going to get oil all over my table, Arthur, we don't want it in the bread.'

Heather and Ian came in and joined the discussion, standing at the door as they shucked off their boots. 'It'll be good that people can go to the doctor without having to worry about how they're going to pay the bills, though,' Heather said. 'I know plenty of people who haven't had the treatment they needed because they couldn't afford it. Look at old Mrs Miller, buried last week. She had that terrible lump on her chest and she never went to the doctor until it was too late. He said they could have done something about it if only she'd gone to see him when she first found it.'

'I don't suppose she'd have gone even if it was free,' Emily said. 'She was too frightened. She just tried to pretend it wasn't there, and when she did tell people about it and we tried to get her to go, she just said there was nothing he could do. Anyway, if you ask me, it was too late even at the start. That lump had been growing inside her for years.'

'It's not the doctor's bills I'm bothered about,' Ian said, 'it's this income tax. They've set up this fancy new way of collecting it from people's wages, and what does that mean? It means the poor bloke that employs them has got to do all the paperwork! That's for Eli and the men as well as for ourselves. We're just going to be nothing but unpaid tax collectors.' He hung his jacket on the back of the door and came to sit at the table. He rubbed his hand over his face and then pushed his fingers through his thick hair. 'And what happens if we get it wrong? We'll be the ones that have to pay.'

'Yes, but that's not this government,' Heather said, going to wash her hands at the sink. 'I mean, they were working out this system before Labour got in. Anyway, I can do that – I was good at arithmetic at school.'

'Now, that *would* be something useful you could do,' Ian said, and she turned and stared at him.

'What d'you mean by that?'

'Well, office work's a bit more suitable, you've got to admit that. After all, you don't have to be out in the fields now that me and some of the chaps are back.'

'I like being out in the fields,' Heather said, drying her hands. 'I've enjoyed working outside. And I think I've made a good job of looking after the farm while you've been away.'

'I'm not saying you haven't. All I'm saying is that you don't have to go on doing it now I'm back.'

'But if I like doing it—'

'There's no *need*,' he said sharply. 'Look, plenty of farmers' wives help with the hens and the calves, that sort of thing – I'm not saying you can't do that. But the heavy work, the milking and the ploughing, all that sort of thing – that's men's work. You and the Land Girls have done a good job these past few years, I'm the first to admit that, but *there's no need to do it now*. And I don't *want* you doing it any more. I want to get back into running the farm myself. I don't want you looking over my shoulder all the time, telling me how you've been doing this, that and the other, making out I don't know anything about it.'

'I don't do that!' she cried. 'All I've done is try to explain what we've had to do. Things have been different during the war; they've changed – I've had to tell you that. I'm not looking over your shoulder, or making out you don't know things, or anything like that! You're taking it all wrong.'

'Well, that's how it seems to me.' He sat at the table, his lips pushed out, looking very much as Roger had looked when he'd been told he'd got to stay at school. 'Ever since I've come back, you've been on at me, pushing your ways down my throat, chucking all my ideas out the window – that's when you let me come out round the farm with you at all. The first few days I was here you hardly let me put a foot out of doors.'

'That's because I thought you needed a rest! You seemed so tired. You'd been away fighting, as you never forgot to remind me, and I thought you needed a bit of a holiday. It wasn't because I wanted to stop you coming round the farm.'

'I'll believe you, thousands wouldn't,' Ian muttered, and Heather drew in a quick, angry breath. She took a step forward and then stopped abruptly as she caught her mother-in-law's expression. Emily had forgotten all about her bread. She was standing at the other side of the table, her face aghast, while Arthur's hands seemed frozen in the act of replacing the wick in the lamp. Heather bit her lip and took another breath.

'I think we ought to talk about this some other time,' she said quietly. 'I'm sorry, Mum – Dad. We didn't ought to be rowing in front of you.'

'I don't think you ought to be rowing at all,' Arthur said. He looked at his son. 'I told you when you first got home,

190

this young woman's made a fine job of looking after the farm and you ought to be grateful to her.'

'He's upset, Arthur—' Emily began, but Arthur lifted one hand to silence her.

'And now we're all upset. Heather's right. We ought to leave it for now, and they can thrash it out between them later on. I know what I think, that's all.'

'And so do we,' Ian said bitterly. He got up and walked to the door in his socks. 'I'll go down the pub for a pint.'

'Ian! You haven't had your dinner!' Emily took a step towards him but he waved her away.

'You can keep mine in the oven. I'm not hungry anyway. I won't be long – I'll be back in time for afternoon milking.' He threw Heather a sarcastic glance. 'That's if you don't mind me giving a hand! I think the cows are beginning to recognise me again now, don't you?'

He dragged on his boots and slammed the door behind him. The three in the kitchen looked at each other.

'Oh Mum,' Heather said, her voice shaking, 'I'm so sorry. I never meant all that to happen.'

'I don't even know how it did,' Arthur said. 'All we started off doing was talk about the election. I dunno how it got as far as arguing about the farm. It just seemed to blow up out of nowhere.'

Heather sat down at the table. Her knees were trembling. She said, 'It's not come out of nowhere, Dad. It's been building up ever since he first came home. It's as if I can't say a word without him losing his temper. He never used to be like that. He was always so nice-tempered and easy-going.'

'It's the war,' Emily said. 'It was the same after the First War – men came home different from how they'd been before. Some of them never got back to their old selves again. None of us knows what Ian went through and I don't suppose we ever will, not properly. We've just got to make allowances.'

191

'I try,' Heather said dispiritedly. 'I really do try. But I don't like him thinking that he's not wanted. And when I try to make him understand it's not like that, somehow it always turns into a row. And it's not just that – it's the children. Roger doesn't seem to like him, and Teddy acts as if he's frightened of him. And Pat's too much the other way!'

Emily left the bread and came round the table to put her arms round her daughter-in-law's shoulders. 'Don't worry, love. It'll all settle down in time. It's bound to be tricky at first, after he's been away so long, but once he gets used to being back and the children get accustomed to him again, we'll be the same happy family as we always were.' She held Heather for a moment and then went back to her dough. 'Well,' she said, surveying it ruefully, 'I think I might as well say goodbye to this! What with the door being opened and shut and all the argy-bargying, it's gone right down. It'll be more like concrete than bread now.'

Chapter Eighteen

In August, Dan had another week's holiday. Apart from the Bank Holiday at the start of the month, that would be all until Christmas, when he'd get three days off. He looked at the calendar and found that Christmas Day was a Tuesday.

'That means if I had Christmas Eve off instead of the day after Boxing Day, I'd get five days on the trot,' he said to Ruth as they finished breakfast. 'Unless they want us to do overtime on the Saturday, but I don't think they will.' Vospers was busy now refitting civilian ships like trawlers and ferries that had been requisitioned during the war. The Isle of Wight paddle steamer *Ryde*, which had been acting as a minesweeper, was back in service already, looking very smart in her new livery of black hull and white superstructure. Dan had taken both Ruth and Sammy to Portsmouth the day she'd made her first trip across the Solent and they'd stood on the Sallyport, waving and cheering with everyone else.

'What do you want to do, then?' Ruth asked, looking at her own calendar. Sammy had made it for her last Christmas from an old holiday postcard which showed a very large woman struggling to get out of a deckchair. She hesitated, then added, 'You know you're both welcome to come out here.'

Still nothing had been decided about Sammy's return to Portsmouth. He had stayed for the summer and finished school with the others. The last few evacuees had gone home and he was still at Bridge End. Dan had spent almost every weekend at the cottage with him and Ruth, and she was aware that tongues were wagging but she took no notice. Nothing untoward was going on, she'd told her sister; Dan slept on a camp bed in Sammy's room and the most they ever had was a kiss and a bit of a cuddle on the settee downstairs. But something would have to be decided soon, if only for the sake of Sammy's schooling. Wherever he was going to go, he'd need to know before September.

Besides that, Ruth was growing more and more anxious to know what was going to happen to her and Dan. Since he'd brought Sammy back in May, their relationship had grown stronger, yet, close as she felt they had become, there was nothing more definite, any more than there was over Sammy. Each weekend, she waited for Dan to say something, and each time he returned to Portsmouth with nothing said. Perhaps I'm imagining it, she thought uncertainly. Perhaps he just feels comfortable out here with me, but that's all. For some men, that might be enough – but she didn't know if it was for Dan.

She looked at the calendar again. 'Well, Dan? Are you going to spend Christmas at Bridge End?'

'Yes, please – if that's all right with you.' He glanced at her sideways. 'You getting fed up with me coming out here all the time, Ruthie?'

'I didn't say that. I just wondered if you'd thought about it.'

'Well, of course I've thought about it. I wouldn't have mentioned it otherwise.' He walked to the window and gazed out. Someone was coming down the lane towards the cottage. It looked like young Terry, who'd been demobbed a week or two ago, and he groaned softly. Just when he was getting up his courage to say what had been in his mind . . . Then Terry broke into a run and Dan looked at him more closely. 'Something's up,' he said. 'Your Jane's boy's charging down the lane as if the wolves are after him. We'd better see what he wants.'

'I hope nothing's wrong!' They ran out into the garden.

194

Terry had reached the gate and was fumbling to open it. He looked up as they came out of the cottage and they saw that his face was blazing with excitement. 'Have you heard the news? Auntie Ruth – Mr Hodges – have you heard the news?'

'No, what news? What's happened?'

'It was on the wireless. Japan's surrendered! The war's over! It's *finished*!' he grabbed Ruth by the waist and danced her up the path. 'Auntie Ruth, it's all finished and Mum sent me down to get you. Everyone's got two days' holiday – except for farmers, of course! – and we're having the biggest party you ever saw on the village green. It'll make VE Day look like a vicarage tea. And you've got to come and help get it ready, all three of you, and she says bring whatever you can to eat.' He stopped for breath, laughing at their faces. 'You should just see what you look like! And you should see our Lizzie too, and Alec – you'd think a bomb had hit them!' He laughed again, his voice high with excitement, and shook her arms. 'Auntie Ruth, the war's over! The Japs have given in!'

'Blimey,' Dan said when Terry hiccuped himself into silence at last. 'Who'd have thought it, eh? They always said the Japs'd never give in.'

'It's those bombs,' Ruth said in a muted tone. 'Those atom bombs. They say it's terrible, what they've done. There's nothing left of those two places, nothing. Portsmouth and Southampton and Plymouth were bad enough, not to mention London and Coventry and all those other places. And the ones we've bombed, over in Germany. But they say all that's nothing compared to what we've done to those people. It must be beyond imagining.'

'It's war, Ruthie,' Dan said. 'We'd got to end it somehow. And I don't suppose they knew much about it, if it was as quick as that.'

'The Emperor broadcast to the people himself, to tell them to give in,' Terry said. 'He's never done anything like

195

that before. He said that if they didn't, this new bomb could obliterate Japan and lead to – what was it – oh yes, the "extinction of human civilisation". Mind you, that's a bit strong, isn't it? I don't see how any bomb could do that.'

'The main thing is, he's surrendered and it's all over.' Dan looked at Ruth. 'What d'you want to do, love? Go straight up to the farm?'

She shook her head, smiling suddenly. 'If there's going to be a party, I want to dress up! I need to look in the cupboard too, see what I've got at the back. And Sammy's not home yet, he went over to play at the Moores' house.' She turned to Terry. 'You go back and tell your mum we'll be along in about half an hour. Dan, you might walk along and fetch Sammy, will you? Then I can get myself tidied up while you're gone.'

Dan nodded. 'I dare say we'll be getting the flags and bunting out again too,' he said. 'Here, I'm glad I was out here this time – not stuck in April Grove like when VE Day was declared.' He stopped suddenly and Ruth remembered that it was on that day he'd brought the news of Gordon's death. She touched his arm briefly and he gave her a wry grin. 'Anyway, it's something to celebrate, this is. All over, eh? I reckon there was times when we thought this day'd never come!'

He went off up the lane with Terry, and Ruth turned to go back into the cottage. Silver, excited by all the commotion, was dancing and squawking on his perch and she paused to give him a sunflower seed.

'Did you hear that, Silver?' she asked softly. 'The war's over. It's properly over at last. Now we'll really be able to settle back into our normal way of life.'

The words jolted her memory. Dan had been going to say something when Terry arrived – something important. But the news had driven everything from their minds. And she still didn't know what he meant to do about Sammy – or about Ruth and himself.

*

It was the new Prime Minister, Mr Attlee, who had broadcast the news. Even those who had been pleased by the election results couldn't help feeling for Winston Churchill, who had led them so doggedly through their darkest hours and now had this final victory taken away from him. Not snatched – Mr Attlee was a gentleman, for all he was a Socialist, and wouldn't gloat; it was said that he and Churchill were friends behind all their political rivalry – but taken away all the same, and only a couple of months after the end of the war, too. It did seem a bit hard.

The village party was to be held next day, when everyone had had time to prepare. Farmers' wives took down hams that had been hanging from the pantry ceilings and others found tins of corned beef and Spam that had been secreted at the backs of cupboards. Women stayed up late making rock buns and Victoria sponges while their men strung bunting and flags once again between all the houses. They all stopped, however, to listen to the King's speech at nine o'clock.

'*The world has come to look for certain qualities from the peoples of the Commonwealth and Empire,*' he said. '*We have our part to play in restoring the shattered fabric of civilisation. It is to this great task that I call you now.*' The cheers were so loud they almost broke the wireless set Terry and George Warren had made before the war began, and the news reporter had difficulty in making himself heard as he described how the Royal Family came out time and time again to the balcony of Buckingham Palace, where they were almost blown over by the cheers. Jane and Ruth wiped their eyes, Lizzie buried her face against Alec's sleeve and even the men cleared their throats and seemed to find they had something in their eyes that needed rubbing. And I bet it's like this in every home in the land, Ruth thought, meeting Dan's eyes as he took her hand in his. The war's over. We can't quite believe it. We have to keep telling

197

ourselves, and that's partly why we need to have a party – to help us believe it. After all this time, it seems impossible.

'Come outside for a bit,' Dan murmured in her ear. 'There's summat I want to say to you.'

Her heart skipping, she allowed him to lead her outside. The others were talking excitedly and only Jane saw them go. Ruth caught her eye and smiled a little, and Jane nodded, as if in approval. How can she approve, Ruth wondered, when she doesn't have any idea what he's going to say . . .

They walked through the yard to the paddock and leaned on the gate, watching the two big Clydesdale horses grazing quietly. It was still light; the sun wouldn't set for almost another two hours. But it was quiet, the sounds of the village muted as everyone sat indoors listening to the news and discussing the great events. Only a few rooks cawed as they made their way home across the fields, and the smaller birds twittered in the hedgerows.

'I was going to say this earlier on,' Dan said quietly, laying his arm across Ruth's shoulders. 'Only young Terry came pelting in and put it all out of me head. Not that I forgot, mind, but the right moment never come again.'

'The right moment for what?' Ruth asked softly after a moment's silence.

'Well, for a proposal, I suppose you might call it,' he said, and gave an odd, embarrassed little chuckle. 'Funny, that. I don't ever remember asking my Nora to marry me. It was just sort of always on the cards. But – well, with you I got to do it right. Ruth,' he turned her to face him and she looked up, seeing his dark face suddenly very serious, 'you know what I'm saying, don't you? We've both known it for a long time. I want us to get wed. I couldn't say much up to now because I couldn't see how we were to manage – I didn't want you to think I was after you for a house and home and all that, but well, I went along to see old Solly Barlow yesterday and had a talk with him, and—'

'*Solly Barlow?*' Ruth exclaimed. 'What on earth does *he* have to do with it? You didn't have to ask *his* permission to marry me!' She shook her head at him, half laughing in the midst of sudden tears. 'Dan, are you asking *me* to marry you, or Solly Barlow?'

'Blimey, you of course!' He shook her and then pulled her close. 'You will, won't you? You will say yes? You know what I think of you, Ruthie. Both me and Sammy – you know we both think the world of you.'

'I know,' she said soberly. 'And I think the world of you, too – both of you.' She reached up and pulled his head down so that she could kiss his lips. 'Oh Dan, of course I'll marry you! I was beginning to be afraid you'd never ask. In fact,' her laughter broke out again, 'I've been screwing up *my* courage to ask *you!*'

'That's all right, then,' he said, and bent his head to her again. They clung together joyously, oblivious to both of the big horses who were moving steadily closer and to the little group of people who had come to the door of the farmhouse and were standing watching them. 'It's what I was trying to get round to before, when I was talking about Christmas,' he went on. 'I reckon that'd be a good time for a wedding, don't you? Make it the Saturday before, eh? And – well, maybe if old Solly turns up trumps I wouldn't even need to go back to Pompey at all!'

Ruth drew back her head and looked up into his eyes. 'For heaven's sake, Dan – tell me what Solly Barlow's got to do with it, will you? *Ouch!*' She jumped away as Boxer shoved his big head between them, nuzzling at Dan's pockets for an apple or a bit of carrot. 'Go away, you silly horse!'

There was a roar of laughter from the group outside the farmhouse door and then a cheer as Dan caught her hand and raised it high in the air in a salute of victory. Then Sammy broke away and came running across the yard towards them.

'Are you getting married? Auntie Jane says you are!' He skidded to a halt and stood before them, his face alight. 'Are you going to be my mum now, as well as my Auntie Ruth?' And as she nodded, he turned and yelled to the others, 'They are! They are! They're getting married and we can stay here for ever and ever! *Hooray!*'

'Hooray!' they echoed, and as Terry called for three cheers Ruth turned to Dan again.

'Just tell me what Solly Barlow has to do with all this. Please,' she begged, but he grinned and shook his head.

'Tomorrow'll do. Let's just forget all that and enjoy tonight. I've got an idea your sister and that man of hers are planning a bit of a party all to ourselves.' He slid his arm around her waist and hugged her to him. 'Oh Ruthie, Ruthie – I reckon I'm the happiest man in England tonight.'

And that's saying something, she thought, smiling back, on the day that a world war finally comes to an end.

The village turned out again next afternoon, for a party that was even more joyous than the one held on VE Day. Once again there were races for the children, the men set up trestle tables and the women covered them with bedsheets and tablecloths and set out a spread of sandwiches, cakes and jellies. The big teapots were filled over and over again, and the children drank gallons of powdered lemonade. In the evening someone brought out a gramophone and played dance music, and as dusk fell Fred Barker and a few others carried out his Susie's piano and she sat down and played songs they could all sing along to. They started with the old wartime ones and then Susie played some of the old favourites – 'Daisy, Daisy', 'The Bells Are Ringing', 'Tavern in the Town', and 'The Ash Grove'. When darkness fell they were still singing and then she finished up with the stirring chords of 'Hearts of Oak', 'Rule Britannia' and lastly, 'Land of Hope and Glory' which they roared out so loudly that George Warren said they could probably hear it in Southampton. As the last notes faded away, old Arthur Knight, who had always been the one to make a speech when it was needed, climbed up on to a chair and lifted his arms for silence.

'We didn't ought to finish without a word for all those who can't be here tonight,' he said. 'The chaps we saw go off to war and not come back. Their names'll be put on the Memorial with the ones already there from the first time, but I want to say that I don't reckon we'll ever forget seeing them around the village, and they'll always be missed. I'm going to ask the vicar to say a little prayer for them now, and I know you'll all join in, and then perhaps Mrs Barker here'll be good enough to play the National Anthem for us.'

He clambered down again, assisted by Ian, and the vicar took his place. Nobody made a sound as he looked around at them all, waited as they bent their heads and then said in his quiet, but carrying voice: 'Oh Lord, in Thy mercy, look down upon us and accept our thanks for the deliverance Thou hast brought. Remember our brothers and our sisters who have given their lives in this great cause and who now sit with You in Heaven, and help us to remember them also all the days of our lives; and to live in honour and remembrance of their great sacrifice and to be worthy of it. Amen.'

There was a murmur of 'Amen' from the crowd; and then Susie played the first notes of 'God Save the King', and every person there lifted their head and sang from the heart, thankful beyond any words that this terrible time was over at last; that nearly six long years of war had come to an end; and that from now on, the world could live in safety and in peace.

Chapter Nineteen

Dan had been to ask Solly Barlow about the possibility of working with him as a blacksmith. 'I did my apprenticeship in a forge,' he told Ruth. 'It was what I wanted to be, but when I finished there was a closed shop and I couldn't get work, so I had to go into shipwork. But I've done plenty of metalwork at Vospers, and I've often walked down to Solly's with Sam when I've been here, to watch him with the horses and that. I reckon I could be useful to him. And he don't have no one else to help him now.'

Ruth nodded thoughtfully. Solly's son William was one of those whose name would appear on the War Memorial, and the old man had no other children. His wife had died before the war started, so she'd never known the grief of losing her only son, and Solly was alone in the world. 'Doesn't he want to take on an apprentice?' she asked, but Dan shook his head.

'He says he doesn't have the heart. It was Will he wanted to work for him, and seeing a boy around the place would bring it home to him what he's lost. He says he can soon put me in the way of working with iron, and it would suit us both. I can get on with him, Ruth.'

'I always thought it was trees you wanted to work with,' she said, but again he shook his head.

'That's no more than a dream. I know I've often thought how good it would be to work in the forest, but there's too much to learn and I'm too old to learn it now, to be of any use. I'll help out a bit on the farm, if George'll have me, but that's as near as I'll get to being a real countryman.' He gave her his dark smile, the one that seemed to have a twist of irony behind it. 'Will that be good enough for you, Ruthie?'

'You'll be good enough for me whatever you do,' she said, and reached up to kiss him. They stood quietly for a moment and then she said, 'Will you be happy to live here in the cottage with me, Dan? You don't want us to move somewhere different?'

'If that's all right with you, Ruthie. It's been home to me all these years now – more than April Grove ever was, nor even the pub.' He looked around at the small room with its low, beamed ceiling, its stone-flagged floors covered by home-made rag rugs and its range burning brightly with the kettle singing softly on the side. 'I couldn't imagine seeing you anywhere else. I reckon you'd wither away if you was made to leave here.'

'Well, perhaps,' she said. 'But you mustn't feel it's just my house, once we're married. It'll be *our* home – yours and mine and Sammy's. That's how I want it, Dan.'

'Then that's how it'll be,' he said, and instead of kissing her he gave her his hand. 'And this is how *we'll* be – till the end of our lives.'

The news of Dan and Ruth's engagement had come as little surprise to the family at the farm. They talked about it the day after the VJ Day party. 'Not that it's a proper engagement till he's given her a ring,' Jane remarked, 'but Ruth doesn't seem bothered about that. Told me she'd got rings already, and it was the wedding ring that's most important.'

'And so it is,' George said. 'Anyway, if they're getting married at Christmas she wouldn't have much time to wear an engagement ring on its own. Hardly worth having one.'

Jane and Lizzie looked at him and then at each other with an expression that said, 'Men!' Lizzie was looking a bit peaky, Jane thought. Tired, probably, and maybe a bit worried about Alec. He still wasn't picking up all that well – couldn't seem to eat a decent meal, didn't talk much, had funny moods – but it would pass in time, Jane was sure. He'd been through a terrible time, after all. But it was hard on Lizzie, who was doing her best to help him yet didn't seem to be getting all that much thanks for it.

'Are you all right, love?' Jane asked her later, when the men had gone back outside. 'You're looking a bit pale.'

'Well, it was a late night last night.' Lizzie brushed her hand across her brow. 'I'm quite glad we haven't got any more wars to win; I don't think I can stand any more victory parties!'

Jane laughed. 'We're all going to have to start buckling down to ordinary life now. Has Alec thought what he wants to do? The doctor'll be signing him off soon, so he'll have to make his mind up if he's not going back to sea.'

'I don't know, Mum. He was talking a while back about going to Southampton and working on the ships – refitting, that sort of thing. He's determined not to go to sea, but he says he wouldn't mind doing that. But that'd mean moving there and I can't say I'm keen on that.'

'Couldn't he go on the bus?'

'I suppose he could, but it adds on to the day, doesn't it? He'd have to leave home before six and he wouldn't get back till gone seven, and later still if he had overtime. It's too much, after all he's been through. I wish he could find something to do out here, but he says he's not a farmer and that's that.'

'He helps out. He seems to enjoy that.'

'I know. But he wouldn't ever be any more than a labourer, would he? I mean, Terry'll take over the farm when Dad gives up, and then there's Ben. Alec'll never have a real part in it. And he's an engineer – he was good at his job. He'd never get the same satisfaction out of being a farm labourer.'

'Talking of Ben,' Jane said, 'there was a postcard from

him this morning. He says he's got a weekend pass and he'll be home this Friday. He's got some news for us. I meant to say so at dinner-time but we were all so taken up with Ruth and Dan.'

'News?' Lizzie said. 'Perhaps he's getting married!'

'Oh, I hope not! Not till we've had him at home for a while, anyway. I expect it's about his demob. Your father'll be pleased – Ben will be able to go back to college.' Jane took another look at her daughter. 'Why don't you go out for a bit of a walk, Lizzie. Get some colour into your cheeks. I can see to things here.'

Lizzie pulled on her cardigan and went out. She knew she wasn't looking well, but unlike her mother, she knew why. And it wasn't going to be long before everyone else knew too.

She walked down the lane with no real idea as to where she was going but as she passed Ruth's garden she saw her aunt working amongst the flower beds and stopped to say hello. Ruth came and leaned over the gate to talk to her, and Lizzie thought how lovely she was looking. Ten years younger, and with a bright light in her eyes. That's how I thought I'd be looking when Alec came home, she thought, and misery seemed to settle over her like a dark grey cloud.

'Lizzie!' Ruth exclaimed in concern. 'Whatever is it? You look as if you've got the weight of the world on your shoulders.'

'I'm all right. It's just a reaction after all the excitement. I'm tired, that's all.'

'Tired, a young girl like you?' Ruth studied her face and then said gently, 'Are you sure it's not a bit more than that, Lizzie?'

To her consternation, Lizzie's mouth crumpled and she began to cry. At once, Ruth swung open the gate and pulled the girl into her arms. 'Come indoors. I'll make you a cup of tea and you can tell me about it.'

'What about Dan? And Sammy?'

'They've gone fishing in the river. They won't be back till tea-time, and probably not then. Once those two get out with their rods they forget there's such a thing as time. Now, you sit there in the armchair while the kettle boils.' She bustled about, sliding the kettle across to the hob where it began at once to sing, and taking a tray of fresh scones from the oven. 'Good job you came when you did. I was just about to come in and see to these and I'd have missed you.' The kettle whistled and she poured a drop of boiling water into the fat-bellied brown teapot, swished it round and tipped it into the sink, then put in two teaspoonsful of tea and filled it with boiling water. 'I'll just butter a couple while it's brewing. You can have a bit of blackberry and apple jam too, if you like. It's the last pot till we get some more fruit in a month or so.'

'I'm not hungry,' Lizzie wept, but she took the tea gratefully and sipped. 'Oh, Auntie Ruth . . .'

'I don't think you need tell me what's the matter,' Ruth said quietly. 'But it's no cause for tears, surely? You must be pleased – and Alec, too.'

Lizzie looked at her wildly. 'Alec? He doesn't know!'

'Well, he'll be pleased when you do tell him. Or didn't you want it to happen so soon? I know you're not properly settled yet, with him talking about leaving the sea, but there's always a home for you at the farm, and when your mother knows you're having a baby—'

'That's just it!' Lizzie cried. 'I didn't know I was having a baby, not till a week or so ago, and I'm not even sure now. I mean, I haven't been sick or anything – I've just missed, that's all. But I feel sore up here,' she touched her breasts, 'and I keep wanting to go to the lavatory, and I do feel tired. And I know they're signs as well. And I can't tell Alec, or Mum, or anyone. I didn't even mean to tell you.'

Ruth looked at her with concern. 'Well, I am a nurse, and I've brought quite a few babies into the world around here. I'm bound to know the signs. But there's nothing to worry about, Lizzie. I know it can be a shock at first – but you must be pleased about it really. Look, the best thing for you to do is tell Alec the first minute you can, and then everything will be all right.'

'It won't be,' Lizzie said woefully. 'It won't be all right at all. It'll be all wrong.' She looked at her aunt and her voice dropped to a whisper. 'You see, it isn't Alec's baby.'

There was a silence. The grandfather clock could be heard ticking out in the hall and from the porch came the sound of Silver muttering to himself on his stand. Ruth took a breath, then said at last, 'Are you sure about this, Lizzie?'

'I couldn't be more sure,' Lizzie said. 'Alec and me – well, we haven't been able to – you know – ever since he came home.'

Ruth stared at her. 'Not even once?'

'No. He can't, you see. He's tried – we've tried – lots of times, but even when we think it's going to be all right . . .' Lizzie was blushing furiously '. . . it all goes wrong at the last minute. So you see, he'll know. And he's going to be so hurt, Auntie Ruth. He's going to be so upset and hurt.'

'Yes,' Ruth said thoughtfully. Her brows came together and she spoke slowly. 'I can see he is. But if it's not his, whose . . . ?' Her frown cleared, only to leave her looking even more worried. 'Of course! That young American you were friendly with. Floyd.' She sat down suddenly, the scones forgotten. 'Oh Lizzie!'

'I know. It's dreadful. But we didn't mean it to happen, Auntie Ruth. We really didn't mean it to happen. We said we'd just be friends and that's all we were until VE night. And then – well, everything was so different and everyone was going mad and we just – we just couldn't hold back. I thought I loved him. I knew I loved Alec too – I never stopped loving Alec – but I thought I loved Floyd as well. And I thought he loved me.' She ended in a small, doleful

207

voice, and then sat looking at her aunt. 'What am I going to do?'

Ruth was nonplussed. She couldn't think of a thing to say. She sat gazing at her niece in silence and then said at last, 'I don't know, Lizzie. I honestly don't know.' For want of anything else to do, she held out the plate on which she had buttered two scones. 'Here. Have one of these while I think. Have some jam as well.'

Lizzie laughed a little, though her laughter sounded very near to crying, and did as she was told. She spread the lumpy, glistening purple jam on the two halves of a scone but then left it on the plate. She looked at Ruth with frightened eyes. 'I've been thinking for weeks, ever since I started to wonder, and it hasn't got me anywhere yet. I'm almost at my wits' end, Auntie Ruth.'

'I'm sure you are.' Ruth studied her again. 'How far on would you say you are?'

'It must be just about three months, mustn't it? That was the only time, you see.'

'But you still don't know for sure? I mean, you say you haven't been sick or anything. It could be that you've just got a bit irregular, and the other things are just coincidences. There might be nothing at all to worry about.'

'I know. I kept telling myself that. But I think there is. I can feel it, somehow. I just know that's what it is.'

There was another silence. Ruth drank some tea and reached out absently for the other scone. 'And you haven't told anyone else? No one at all?'

'No. I didn't dare.' Lizzie looked up with sudden hope. 'Are you thinking there's something we can do about it? I mean, is there something I could take to – to bring it on, sort of thing? Or someone I could go to?'

'No!' Ruth's voice was shocked. 'No, of course not. We can't do anything like that. It's against the law, for a start.'

'But if nobody knows,' Lizzie said pleadingly. 'I honestly

208

haven't breathed a word. It would be just between you and me. *Please,* Auntie Ruth.'

'No,' Ruth said sternly. 'Don't ask me again, Lizzie. I can't be a party to anything like that, you know I can't. And it's not just the law. You've been a nurse yourself. You know it's dangerous. Women have died trying to get rid of babies.'

Lizzie flinched at the words. 'But it's hardly a baby yet. It's only three months – it's not much more than a lump of jelly.'

'It's not jelly. It's a baby. It might be tiny, but it's more or less formed by now. You know that as well as I do.' Ruth looked her niece in the eye. 'It's murder, Lizzie. You'd be murdering your own baby.'

'No!' Lizzie cried. 'No don't say that! Don't! I can't bear it!' She covered her face with her hands. 'I've been trying not to think of it – trying not to think of it being a real baby. It's the only way I can manage. Oh, Auntie Ruth, you don't know what it's *like.*' She flung herself to her knees, throwing her arms around Ruth's waist as she sat opposite her. 'I've nearly gone mad trying to think what to do. How can I tell Alec this? How can I hurt him so much? It'll kill him.' Her shoulders shook with sobs. 'If I don't kill the baby, I'll kill my husband,' she said brokenly. 'How can I do that?'

The two women stared at each other. The grandfather clock struck the hour and Silver began to squawk excitedly. Voices sounded in the lane outside the open door and they knew that Dan and Sammy were on their way home.

'Oh Lizzie,' Ruth said. 'What a mess. What a terrible, terrible mess.'

Lizzie sat back on her heels and brushed the wet strands of hair from her face. 'I'd better go. I don't want anyone to see me like this.'

Ruth nodded and helped her niece to her feet. 'You won't go doing anything silly, now will you?' she asked anxiously. 'Why don't you come down and see me again tomorrow? Dan's going back to Portsmouth and Sammy'll be at the Knights' farm. He and young Roger have got quite pally these holidays. We can have a chat on our own.'

Lizzie nodded. 'Yes, I will. Thanks, Auntie Ruth.' She hugged her aunt swiftly, pressing her wet face against Ruth's cheek. She's going to break down again any minute, Ruth thought and gave her a push towards the door. 'Go on quickly, before they come in. You can slip out through the back gate. And try not to worry too much. We'll have a good talk tomorrow and see what can be done.'

I don't want to give her false hope, she thought, watching as Lizzie hurried down the back garden path and out through the little wooden gate, vanishing behind the tall rows of runner beans. But I had to say something, just to get her through the next twenty-four hours. Poor girl. Poor, silly girl.

It was only a second or two after Lizzie had disappeared that Sammy and Dan came round the side of the cottage, their faces beaming and burned by the sun. Both had Jack's old fishing-rods over their shoulders and Sammy was swinging Ruth's shopping basket. He held it up for her to see.

'Look! We've got three fish! One each for our tea. They're trout, see? I caught one and Dad caught two. And we saw a kingfisher. It's been smashing!'

Ruth smiled at him. 'They're lovely,' she said. 'We'll fry them. Go on indoors now and put them in the sink.'

Sammy went in and Dan put his hands on her shoulders and kissed her. 'It's been a smashing afternoon,' he said. 'I can't wait to be out here for good, Ruthie.' He paused, then said, 'I looked in on Solly on the way back. He says I could lodge in his spare bedroom for the time being. He needs my help pretty soon, and I've only got to hand in a week's notice at Vospers. What d'you say?'

'Oh yes!' she said. 'If that's what you really want to do.

210

Sammy would be thrilled to have you living so near. And you could come here for your tea every evening.'

'It'd take care of everything,' he said. 'I'd have to pay Solly rent, of course, and I wouldn't want you feeding me for nothing. Nor Sam, neither. But I wouldn't have the rent to pay at April Grove, so that'd be all right. And Solly's going to give me a decent wage. He reckons there'll be plenty of work coming along, with farm machinery wanting repairs and people buying new stuff. I wouldn't be surprised if we didn't start making a bit ourselves. I've had a look at some of it and I reckon we could do it. Start off with hurdles and such. We could build up quite a solid business – might even get Sam in on it when he's a bit older.'

Ruth laughed. 'Dan, I've never heard you say so much all in one go! I can see you can't wait to be a blacksmith. But you'll have to shoe horses and repair carts as well. It'll be quite a while before the farmers round here go in for anything more up-to-date than that.'

'I don't mind,' he said. 'I don't mind what I do. It'll be the sort of work I enjoy. And I like the horses too. It'll be good to work with something that's alive.'

Sammy burst out through the back door. 'Auntie Ruth, there's some scones in here. Can I have one? Can I have jam on it? There's one already spread.'

'Yes, that was Lizzie's. She wasn't hungry. You can have it.' She followed them indoors, the laughter fading from her face. Her own life was going so well now; she hadn't been so happy since Jack had been alive. Yet in the midst of her joy there was this looming worry about her niece. A worry that wasn't going to go away.

Chapter Twenty

On the Knights' farm, the harvest was almost finished. Sammy and Roger had been building stooks all afternoon and were now lying in the shade of a large oak tree in the hedge a little way away from the others, eating slabs of cake and drinking lemonade that Emily had brought out. Roger had asked for cider but his grandmother had refused. 'You're not old enough for cider. It'll make you sleepy.'

'Well, you ought to give it to me when I go to bed, then,' he'd argued, but she'd given him a light cuff on the head and an extra slice of cake and taken the cider jar to the men. After a bit of grumbling, he and Sammy drank their lemonade and forgot about it.

'My dad's going to come and live out here soon,' Sammy said, gazing up at the sky through the gently shifting leaves of the oak. 'He's going to be a blacksmith with Mr Barlow.'

'I wish *my* dad would go away again,' Roger said morosely. 'It was better when he was in the Army.'

'Don't you like having him home again?'

Roger was silent for a moment, then burst out, 'He seems to think he's in charge of everything! We were getting along all right before. Mum and Grandad looked after the farm, and we had Eli and the Land Girls. Now they've got to go away, and Eli says he'll only work some of the time, and Dad says Mum's got to stop indoors or just come out to feed the hens. As if she was a *prisoner*!' Roger's voice was high with indignation. 'She's done *everything* all this time. She knows much more about the farm than Dad does. But he won't take any notice of her and they keep arguing and he's made her cry lots of times, and I just wish he'd go *away*. I wish he'd been killed!'

Sammy was horrified. 'You don't! You can't wish your own dad was killed.'

'I can. At least we could feel nice about him. We could be proud of him and have his name on the Memorial and tell people how brave he was and all that.'

'He was brave, wasn't he? He got all those medals.'

'It'd still be better if he was dead,' Roger said.

They were silent for a few moments. Sammy could hear a lark singing high above. He squinted into the blue, trying to focus on the tiny dark spot but failed. After a few minutes, he said, 'My mum's dead. And my brother. I don't think it is better.'

'That's different. Your mum was ill, wasn't she?'

'Gordon wasn't. He was killed. My dad's still upset about it.' Sammy paused for a moment to consider whether he was upset as well, but he couldn't decide. It was so long since he'd seen his elder brother, and they'd never got on well when they were both at home in April Grove. He remembered when Gordon had stolen and eaten the bar of chocolate Sammy had been saving for his mother's Christmas present. 'I expect your mum would be upset if your dad had been killed.'

'Not if she'd known what he was going to be like when he came home,' Roger said grimly.

It was too difficult for Sammy. He was sure there was something wrong with this argument but couldn't think what it was. He said, 'Are all the Land Girls going away? I thought the one with the yellow hair was staying.'

'Yes, she is, for a while. Just till the other men are demobbed.' The farm had had several men working on it before the war, and not all were yet home. 'And Mum's going on for a while as well, but Dad says when they're all back she's got to stop and Stevie will go home. He's going to run the farm himself, with just men, like before.'

'Perhaps you'll get to like him better after a while,' Sammy suggested. 'I didn't like my dad all that much once, but now he's all right and I'm pleased he's coming to live at Bridge End and marrying Auntie Ruth. I think it'll be good, being a proper family.'

'You're lucky, then.' Roger sat up and threw a stone at a rabbit that had ventured out of the hedge and was feeding amongst the stubble. 'I don't think I'll ever like my dad, not really. Pat does,' he added with a sneer. 'All over him, she is. Daddy's little girl – Daddy's little princess! It's enough to make you sick. I wish she'd go away, as well. They could go off together and leave the rest of us in peace.'

He got up and packed the empty lemonade bottle and the greaseproof paper from the cake into the bag his grandmother had brought out. 'We might as well go and look for tiddlers in the stream. They can finish the stooks without us.' He marched off along the hedgerow and Sammy followed him. He had been feeling anxious about Roger's revelations, but now he dismissed them from his mind. It would probably turn out all right, and if not there was nothing that he or Roger could do about it. In his eleven years of life, Sammy had learned to take things as they came.

Heather saw the boys go and thought of calling them back, for there was still plenty to do, but then decided against it. They were still children and needed to be able to go off on their own pursuits. Ian wouldn't agree – he said that Roger was old enough and big enough to do a decent day's work on the farm, since he wasn't at school. That was what school holidays were for. But although Heather wanted to keep the peace between herself and her husband, she wasn't inclined to give in to him all the time.

'You don't make Pat work,' she said when Ian complained later, as she'd known he would, about the boys' defection. They were sluicing down the milking parlour.

Emily was in the house getting supper and Pat was helping her. Nobody had seen Roger since he'd slipped off with Sammy Hodges.

'Pat's a girl and she's younger. It's not the same at all.'

'She's still used to helping round the farm. She's done almost as much as Roger at times.'

'Well, I don't want her working now. It's all right to help with the calves and the hens, that's what women have always done on a farm, but slaving out in the fields is men's work.' Ian pointed the hose at the milking stalls and sent a fierce jet of water at a patch of dung, swishing it into the gully.

'Roger's not a man. He's a boy – a child. And he worked right up till tea-time.'

'He's not far off being a man,' Ian stated. 'His voice is starting to break and it won't be all that long before he starts shaving. He's got to learn to do a full day's work.'

'He'll learn well enough when the time comes. For now, I think he ought to be allowed to be a child as well. It won't be all that long before his childhood's gone for ever, and goodness knows it's been interfered with enough already with the war and everything.'

'*His* life interfered with!' Ian exclaimed. 'What about *my* life? Hasn't that been interfered with? God almighty – I've been in the Army, I've been all over the world fighting! All that boy's done is stay at home, living in the lap of luxury and coddled by you women. I don't see that his life's been interfered with at all.'

'He hasn't had his father,' Heather said quietly, sweeping the last of the straw into a corner.

'And he hasn't *wanted* him, as far as I can see! He doesn't give much sign of missing me. In fact, if you want the truth, I think he'd rather I hadn't come home at all.'

'Ian, don't say that! Of course he wanted you home.'

'Oh yes? Have you ever seen him so much as give me a friendly look? A civil word? He comes in looking like

215

thunder, sits at the table and eats his meals without saying anything and if I speak to him he just glowers. He doesn't want me here, Heather. If you ask me, he's jealous.'

'Jealous? Whatever do you mean? Who's he got to be jealous of?'

'He's jealous because he thought he was the man of the family. Now he's had to give that up, and he's had to give *you* up. He thought he came first. Well, *I* come first with you – or ought to – and he doesn't like it. And he's jealous of Pat too, because she does like having me home. His nose is right out of joint, that's what it is.'

Heather knew that there was some truth in what Ian was saying. She had seen Roger's reaction to his father and grieved over it. 'All the same,' she said, 'Roger is still a child and you're a grown man. You're the one who has to put it right, not him. He's not old enough to understand it all. And maybe it would help if you made a bit less of Pat. It's not really good for him to think she's your favourite.'

Ian set his mouth. 'So I've got to push her away when she comes to give me a kiss? Not let her sit on my knee? That's not very fair, is it?'

'No, it isn't,' Heather admitted. 'But you could give Roger a bit more attention. Make him feel he's important too.'

'But that's just what I'm saying!' he exclaimed. 'That boy feels *too* important! He's been cock of the walk all the time I've been away and he doesn't like taking second place. He's got to get used to it, that's all. He's got to realise that the sun doesn't rise and set just for him. I tell you, Heather, if he had to join the Army like the boys I've seen, not that many years older than him, and do what they had to do, he'd soon learn what was what. A few weeks in the front line would teach him about being *important*.'

'You can't really want him to have to do that,' Heather said quietly. 'You can't want him to have to go to war and risk being killed.'

Ian shrugged. 'Well, perhaps not.' They had finished cleaning and he walked to the door. 'But he needs a sharp lesson and if he doesn't mend his ways soon he'll get it. I'm warning you, Heather!'

He marched out into the evening sunlight. Heather sighed and followed him. It was all so different from what she had expected. She'd looked forward to their being a close, happy family again, with herself and Ian working as partners. Now, not only was she expected to go back to the kitchen as soon as the rest of the men were home, but there was all this trouble between father and son. It shouldn't be like this, she thought, walking across the yard. It shouldn't be like this at all.

That Hitler had a lot to answer for. He'd spread his poison everywhere – even into the villages of England. You just couldn't get away from what he'd done.

Roger came in late for supper. He was dirty, his face was scratched and his hair full of twigs. Heather stared at him. 'Whatever have you been doing? You look as if you've been pulled through a hedge backwards!' It was a phrase used to describe anyone who looked a bit untidy, but Roger really did look as if that was what had happened.

'I've been down the woods, that's all. Birds'-nesting. And getting tiddlers with Sammy Hodges.' He went to sit down at the supper-table but Ian stretched out a hand to stop him.

'Oh no, you don't, my lad! You go and get yourself washed and tidied up before you sit down with us.'

'But I'm hungry—'

'Then stay hungry,' Ian ordered. 'Your mother's been worried sick about you, stopping out like this. Last she saw of you, you were stooking. And don't say you were with Sammy Hodges, because Pat went down there an hour ago and Mrs Purslow said Sammy had been home since half-past five.'

'Yes, she did,' Pat chimed in. She was sitting next to her father and she moved a little closer and gave Roger a smug look. 'And I know she was telling the truth because I saw him.'

'And that's enough from you, too,' Heather said sharply. 'Mrs Purslow wouldn't say it if it wasn't true. She doesn't tell lies. The idea!'

'I never said she did,' Pat began in an injured tone, but Heather gave her a quick, angry look and she subsided with a resentful scowl. Ian put his arm round her and squeezed her shoulders and she slanted a grateful glance upwards to him. Heather sighed.

'There's no need to take it out on Pat,' Ian said. 'It's Roger who's done wrong. Now, young man, where were you and what have you been up to?'

'I haven't been up to anything. I've just been in the woods, that's all.'

'He's not that late,' Heather said. 'He often goes out roaming in the woods and fields. All the boys do. You must have done so yourself when you were his age.'

'So I might have done, but not without letting Mum know where I was going. And I didn't do it at harvest-time, when I was needed.'

'Well, you must have been a perfect little boy, then!' Heather flared. 'Just as you're a perfect man now! And it's a bit hard on Roger to expect him to be perfect, too. He's just an ordinary boy.'

'There's no need to be sarcastic!'

'And there's no need to go on at Roger, either. He's worked hard all this week and now he's had a few hours off and got in a bit late and in a bit of a mess, and that's all there is to it. He's done no more than any boy does, and if you tell me you never did the same I just won't believe you. Now, Roger, do as your father says and go and get washed and tidied up a bit, and I'll keep your supper hot for you. Go along, now.'

Roger hesitated, then went out to the back kitchen where he could be heard pumping water into the sink. Ian's face had darkened. '*I* give the orders in this house. I say he'll go without his supper.'

'And I say he won't.' Heather faced her husband. 'I'll not let him go to bed hungry. He's a growing boy. He needs his food.'

'Give him bread and milk, then.'

'*No!*' Her voice made them all jump. Teddy started to cry and Arthur and Emily, who had been sitting silent during all this, began to protest but Heather lifted her voice above them. 'Roger's done nothing wrong. I won't have him punished like that. He often goes off in the summer, and why not? He works hard enough the rest of the time, on the farm and at school. He's a good boy but you're treating him like a criminal and I won't have it!' She drew in a breath. 'I don't know what it is you've got against him, Ian. Anyone would think you hated him. Your own son!'

'And what about him? Doesn't he behave as if *he* hates *me*? He's been against me from the moment I walked in. I've told you, Heather, he's jealous and that's the plain fact of the matter.' Ian came to his feet, glaring at her. 'All right, it's obvious there's not room for the two of us at this table and you're determined to go against me, so I'll be the one to leave. Let the boy sit down, feed him like a king, if that's what you want to do – I'm going outside!' He pushed his chair back so violently that it toppled over and clattered on the stone-flagged floor. Heather cried out and flung up a hand to prevent him, but he ignored her and stamped out of the kitchen. Pat, with a quick glance at her mother, wriggled out of her chair and made to follow him but Heather grasped her arm and dragged her back.

'Oh no, you don't, my lady. We haven't had pudding yet. You stay where you are.'

'Don't want pudding.'

'Then you'll sit there while the rest of us eat ours!'

Heather snapped, and then sat down abruptly, looking at the older couple. 'I'm sorry, Mum and Dad. I didn't mean to let fly like that. We just seem to get aeriated all over nothing these days.'

'It's not easy for him, getting used to being at home,' Emily said peaceably. 'He thought everything would be the same as when he went away, and it's not. The children are different, the farm's different – and I expect he finds you different too, Heather. Taking on all the responsibility the way you have, it's bound to have changed you.'

'I'm not the only one who's changed, then,' Heather said, taking Teddy from Emily and cuddling him against her. 'Ian's changed as well. He's changed a lot.' She looked at her mother-in-law. 'Sometimes, he just doesn't seem to be the man I married at all.'

Ian strode down the yard and across to the field gate. He leaned on it, staring across the meadows where the corn stood in stooks, their golden colour burnished almost to copper by the evening sun. Beyond the stubble the pasture rolled gently away to the distant woods where Roger had said he'd spent the past few hours. What had the boy been doing all that time, he wondered. What was it about the woods that made them better than being at home?

He heard light footsteps behind him and braced himself for another row with his wife. But it wasn't Heather who came to stand beside him; it was Stevie, the Land Girl who had offered to stay on until all the men were back. She gave him a quick smile and leaned on the gate, her shoulder not quite touching his.

'Lovely, isn't it,' she said dreamily. 'You know, when I first came out here I hated the country. I just wanted to be back in the city streets, with a pavement under my feet and shop windows to look in. It took months before I got used to the idea that I was here for the duration and even longer before I started to enjoy it. Now, I just don't want to leave. I feel as if it's home.'

'You're lucky, then,' Ian said morosely. 'It doesn't feel like home to me.'

She turned to him, startled. 'Ian! Whatever do you mean?'

'Oh, it doesn't matter. Forget I said anything. I'm just in a bad mood, that's all.'

She looked at him closely. 'But why? Don't you like being back on the farm? Would you rather have stayed in the Army?'

'God, no!' Ian said with a short bark of laughter. 'I hated the Army! I hated everything about it – the marching, the uniform, the fighting – everything. The only thing I was good at was shooting, because I'd always been a good shot, but there's a hell of a lot of difference when you know it's a man on the end of your bullet and not a fox or rabbit. At least, there was for me. You're not supposed to think about it like that, but I couldn't help it.'

'That's because you're a nice man,' Stevie said. 'You don't like killing people. But it was them or us, wasn't it?'

'So they said. Well, yes, I know it was. And I didn't hold back when it was me or the other bloke, so maybe I'm not as nice as you think. But apart from all that, I hated being away from home. All this –' he waved his hand at the fields before them – 'and the family as well. Mum and Dad, Heather and the kids. I hadn't even seen Teddy – I didn't even have a photo, with there not being any film for cameras. But it was them I thought of all the time I was away. It was them I wanted to get back to. I couldn't have got through it all if I hadn't had them to come back to.' His voice cracked a little and he stopped speaking and fell silent.

Stevie looked at him. After a bit, she said, 'But you're back now.'

'Oh yes,' he said with the same little bark of laughter. 'I'm back now.'

'So what's wrong?' she asked carefully after another pause. 'Why are you so miserable?'

'Because I don't feel as if I've come back to the same place!' he said violently. 'Because I don't feel as if I've come back to the same people! They *look* the same, more or less, but they seem to be sort of out of focus, as if someone's tried to copy them and not got it quite right. I don't know how else to explain it. But I don't feel welcome. I don't feel as if they wanted me back. They've got on all right without me, and they don't mind telling me that!'

'Ian, that's not true! Of course they wanted you back. They've thought about you all the time as well. We all have. And Heather's been looking forward so much to having you home again. She's been talking for months about how good it would be to work with you on the farm—' She stopped, shaken by the sudden anger in Ian's face.

'That's just it! I don't *want* her working with me! That's not how it used to be. She used to look after the hens and I didn't mind her helping with the calves, but she never did the milking or worked in the fields or anything like that. Those are men's jobs. I don't want my wife doing them.'

'We've all had to do men's jobs,' Stevie pointed out. 'I'm doing a man's job.'

'Yes, but you'll go back to a normal life. You'll get married and have a family and stop at home and look after them, as a woman should. You won't be talking nonsense about working as partners like Heather is. I don't know where she's got these ideas from,' he finished despondently. 'It's as if she's joined that women's thing they had at the beginning of the century – suffragettes or whatever they were called.'

'Well, a lot of women do feel quite strongly about it,' Stevie said. 'Women getting the vote and being able to be doctors and lawyers and that sort of thing. And look at Lady Astor, getting into Parliament. You're not against all that, surely?'

'I don't know. It seems to me it's all going too far. It may be all right for some – the sort of women who go to posh schools being lady doctors, I don't say there's not a place for them. But I'm talking about *Heather*. She's just an ordinary farmer's wife, and if you ask me this war's gone to her head. It's given her ideas above her station. I'm not saying she hasn't made a good job of running the farm, though I don't agree with everything she's done, and she had Dad to help her when all's said and done – but now that I'm home she ought to be satisfied to hand over the reins. There's plenty to do indoors, and as far as I can see it's my mum who has to do it all, and if Heather wants to take over from anybody she can take over from her.'

'But she likes the farmwork.'

'And so do I! Oh, what's the use. You're bound to be on her side.'

'I'm not on anyone's side,' Stevie said quietly. She laid her hand on his sleeve. 'It's not just that, though, is it? It's the children as well. Heather told me you were having a few problems with them.'

'Not with Pat – she's as good as gold. It's that boy who's the trouble.' Ian's face darkened again and he kicked his toe against the bottom bar of the gate. 'He's as jealous as a cat. Used to having his mother to himself, that's his trouble, and hasn't been given any proper discipline. I'd have thought Dad would've helped a bit there but he don't seem to have lifted a finger to put the boy right. He was hard enough on me when I was that age, I can tell you! But young Roger seems to get away with murder.'

'Does he? I've always thought what a helpful boy he was. He's always been ready to give a hand when his school-work's done.'

'Well, he's not now. Look at this afternoon. Brought that

young Hodges boy, the evacuee, along to help with the harvest, but what did they do as soon as they'd had some cake and lemonade? Skived off into the woods and never came home till half an hour ago. And didn't even have the manners to say they were going!'

'That's boys for you, isn't it,' Stevie said comfortably. 'Didn't you ever do anything like that when you were twelve years old?'

'My dad would've had the hide off me if I had! Why, I remember once I nipped off for a whole day with Bill Wain from over Ashwood; we walked as far as Botley and never came home till it was almost dark.' He stopped as Stevie began to laugh. 'All right then, I did, but my dad gave me the feel of his belt when I came in. Young Roger wasn't even made to miss his supper. You see? Spoiled, that's what he is. A proper Mummy's boy. And I mustn't say a word, oh no.' Ian kicked the gate again. 'Have you seen the way he looks at me? As if I was dirt! I tell you, he doesn't want me here at all. He'd rather I hadn't come back.'

'Ian, that can't be true – you're his father!'

'You wouldn't know it,' he muttered, and then drew in a deep breath and squared his shoulders. 'Look, Stevie, I'm sorry about going on like that. I shouldn't be sounding off to you about it all. You're Heather's friend and you're being a big help, stopping on for the summer. Don't take any notice of me, all right? Just forget what I've said.'

'I won't do that,' she said. 'I'm really sorry, Ian. I can see that you're all a bit upset. But I'm sure things will sort themselves out. Heather and the children – well, they're bound to be different from when you went away. And you're different too. It's going to take a bit of time to settle down.'

'Maybe.' He scowled at the gate for a moment, then looked up and grinned at her suddenly. 'Well, so long as I've got you to come and moan to, maybe it won't be so bad.'

'Come any time,' she said quietly. 'I'm always ready to listen, Ian. But I won't take sides. Heather's my friend too – remember that.'

He nodded and she laid her hand on his for a moment, then turned away and walked across to the main gate out of the yard. He watched her slim figure in the worn green pullover and brown breeches of the Land Army uniform, and wondered why such a lovely-looking girl should want to bury herself in the country when she could be going back to the town. He hoped she'd stay as long as possible, all the same. She understood.

Pity his wife couldn't be as understanding.

Chapter Twenty-One

By the middle of September Lizzie could no longer pretend to herself that she wasn't pregnant. Her breasts were fuller, her waistline thickening and she was forever popping out to the privy. She was feeling tired too, although she dared not show it. Ruth was still the only person she had confided in.

'You'll have to tell him soon,' Ruth said when Lizzie came down to the cottage one afternoon. 'People are going to notice. I'm surprised your mother hasn't already.'

'I'm not sure she hasn't,' Lizzie said miserably. 'She's been looking at me a bit funny lately. But of course she'll think it's Alec's, so she'll wait for us to tell her. Oh, Auntie Ruth, what am I going to *do*?'

It had been her constant cry for weeks now and they were still no nearer an answer. Together, they'd talked over all the possibilities: Lizzie going away to have the baby in secret, giving it up afterwards for adoption. Lizzie telling Alec and then offering to do the same. Lizzie going away altogether so that she could keep her baby. Lizzie stopping at home, having her baby and leaving it to Alec to decide what to do. But none of these solutions was satisfactory. There was no possibility of Lizzie going away without telling Alec, and no guarantee that Alec would agree to her doing so. In any case, Jane and George would want to know why and where she was going. Even if they all knew and agreed to keep it a secret there would be talk in the village. And there was no question of Lizzie simply staying at home and giving birth to another man's baby. It wasn't fair to expect Alec to put up with this.

'He'll leave me,' she wept. 'He'll just walk out and go back to his parents in Southampton. And I can't blame him, can I! Any man would do the same.'

'He might not,' Ruth said doubtfully. 'After all, he loves you.'

'He won't, though, when he finds out what I've done! He'll hate me then. Oh Auntie Ruth, why did I do it? I never meant to. Neither of us meant to – it just sort of happened. It was as if we were in some kind of bubble that night, what with the end of the war and the party and everything, and Floyd going away. I thought I loved him then, I really did. And then when Alec came back – oh, I don't know, it was as if I loved both of them. You can't do that, can you, love two men at once?'

'I'm not so sure. I think you can.' Ruth was thinking of herself. 'I mean, I loved Jack all the time he was alive and I've loved him all the time he's been dead. But I love Dan as well now, and it doesn't seem to make any difference. Jack's still there in my heart. It's as if there's room for both of them.' She looked pityingly at Lizzie. 'It's just your bad luck that both of your men are alive. Oh, I didn't mean that! I meant—'

'I know what you meant. And it is my bad luck.' Lizzie lifted her face from her hands. 'But it's Alec's bad luck too. He's been through such an awful time. He doesn't deserve to come back to find his wife's a whore.'

'Lizzie! Don't say that! It's not true!'

'It is. It's what he'll think, anyway. I've been unfaithful to him, and I'm going to have another man's baby. Why should he believe it was only once? Why shouldn't he think I've been off with every man I could get, all these years? He knows I like – well, all that side of marriage.' Lizzie blushed. 'Why shouldn't he think I just couldn't wait? Or didn't even bother trying.'

'He won't think that.'

'He might.' Lizzie looked at her. 'You've seen Alec,

Auntie Ruth. He's not the man he was. He's like a hurt dog, frightened he's going to be hurt again. And I'm going to do it – hurt him even more than the Germans did.'

Ruth said nothing for a few moments. Then she asked, 'And you still haven't been able to do any more together? In bed, I mean?'

'We've almost given up trying,' Lizzie said miserably. 'We just go to bed and kiss each other goodnight and turn over, like an old married couple. I don't even like to hold him now, in case he thinks I'm trying to – oh, I don't think we're ever going to be able to make love again. Especially when he knows about this.' She touched her stomach.

'And what d'you feel about it yourself?' Ruth asked.

'I've been going over and over it all in my mind. I lay awake every night, thinking about it. And I reckon he'll just leave me. He'll go back to Southampton. He's been talking about going to work there anyway, once the doctor says he's fit. Only he won't take me, and when Mum and Dad know . . . I expect they'll turn me out, don't you?' Lizzie looked up with huge, woebegone eyes. 'They won't want me bringing trouble to the house.'

'I'm not so sure,' Ruth said, wondering if Lizzie knew that her mother had been expecting her when she married George. Not that it was the same thing – they'd been engaged anyway, and had just anticipated the wedding. Still, it ought to give them a bit of understanding. 'But we don't know how anyone'll react till the time comes. All I do know is, you're going to have to tell them the truth soon, and the first one you've got to tell is Alec.' She hesitated. 'Unless you'd like me to do it.'

'No, I'll have to do it myself.' Lizzie got up and brushed back her hair. 'There is one thing you could do for me, though. Offer me a bed if they turn me out. I might be glad of somewhere to come.'

'Of course you can come here! I'd offer to take you in permanently if it came to it – well, until Christmas, anyway, when Dan and me are getting wed. But I'm sure it won't come to that. Your mum would never shut the door on her own daughter, and you know your dad thinks the world of you.'

'Until now,' Lizzie said wryly. She opened the door and stood looking out. The summer glory of the garden was fading now to the tints of autumn, although the dahlias Ruth had planted in the spring were showing a few bright spots of colour amongst the gold. She thought of that dull, drizzly day in May when the world had seemed suddenly lit with the brightness of joy and she had turned to Floyd because he was there and she needed so desperately to express her relief and thankfulness with physical ecstasy. It had seemed so right. It *was* right, she told herself fiercely. Lovemaking was the right thing to do that night – it was just that Floyd was the wrong person to do it with.

And yet she hadn't been sorry. Not then. Not until Alec came home and she realised what it would mean to him if ever he knew. Not until she realised that he would have to know.

'You're right,' she said dully. 'I'll have to tell him. I just have to wait for the right moment – and find the right words.'

She went slowly down the garden path and Ruth watched her with pity in her heart. Then she went back inside and shut the door against the September chill, and began to get supper ready for Sammy and Dan.

I wonder if there could ever be a 'right time' to tell a man something like that, she thought as she started to peel potatoes. Or the 'right words' either.

Poor Lizzie. Poor, poor Alec.

Lizzie was right in thinking that her mother had begun to suspect she might be pregnant. After bearing three children herself, Jane knew the signs well enough and was just waiting for Lizzie to tell her the news. She hugged herself with joy. It was exactly what they needed – a new life coming into the family, bringing hope for the future. And it would be so good for Alec, who was still in a very fragile state after his imprisonment.

There was another reason why Jane needed some good news. Ben had come home as promised two or three weeks ago but, instead of telling them he was to be demobbed from the RAF and would be going back to college, he had surprised them all by saying he intended to stay in the Air Force and make it his career. They'd all stared at him, astonished, and all began to talk at once.

'Stay in the Air Force? But you always said you wanted to be an accountant or something to do with figures. It's what you've always been good at!' Jane had exclaimed in dismay.

'I thought you were going to finish your education,' George said. 'They've kept your place for you in college and all. They're not going to be best pleased.'

'They won't be bothered. There's plenty of others wanting a place. It'll give some other chap a chance.' He'd looked at them with glowing eyes. 'I don't need to go back to college. I can learn all I want to learn in the RAF. I've found something I really like doing – something I'm good at. I'm a pilot now! And I'm a good one. There's not many who've got through the whole war like me.'

'That's as much luck as anything else,' George began, but Ben shook his head.

'Luck comes into it, yes, but skill matters more. And they're developing new planes now – jet planes. They'll be wanting pilots to test them, and there's no better place to train than in the RAF. I've got a far better future there than if I go back to college and just learn to add up. And a much more interesting job too.'

'But you'll still be risking your life,' Jane said unhappily. 'These new planes – nobody really knows what will happen to them. They go faster, don't they? How does anyone know how safe they are? I thought once the war was over you'd be in a nice job on the ground.'

'Where I could get run over by a bus,' Ben said with a grin. 'Look, Mum, nobody's really safe, you know that, whatever they're doing. And I don't mean to take any silly risks. I keep telling you, I'm a good pilot. I want to stay alive, you know!'

George sighed and knocked out his pipe against the hearth. 'It's your life, son, and you're old enough to make your own decisions now. I don't say we're happy about it, but we'll support you all we can, same as we've always done. Just make sure you keep in touch with us, mind. Come home and see us as often as you can, and don't let your mother worry too much.'

Ben beamed at him and then squeezed his mother's shoulder. 'You don't have to worry at all, Mum. I won't be fighting, after all – just flying. One of these days I might even take you up and show you how marvellous it is!'

Jane shuddered. 'Oh, no you won't! If God had meant us to fly, He'd have given us wings.'

'Go on,' her son said with a twinkle. 'I bet you've got a pair tucked away under that cardigan. You're an angel, after all!'

'Get away with you,' she said, giving him a push. 'You've learned bad ways in the RAF. Flattering your mother like that!'

Jane smiled whenever she remembered that conversation. Ben had always been able to wind her round his little finger, just as Lizzie had always been able to get round George. As for Terry, he was everyone's favourite with his open face and cheery grin. We've been lucky with our family, she thought as she sat at the kitchen table polishing a few bits of brass. Never an ounce of trouble between the lot of them. And although I'm sorry Ben isn't coming home to live, I'm glad he's doing something he enjoys so much.

And it does mean there'll be a bit more room here for when the baby comes . . .

The back door opened and Lizzie came in. Her shoulders were drooping and she looked pale and exhausted. Jane looked up. Their eyes met, and there was an instant of communication. Then Lizzie turned abruptly and went to the staircase.

She doesn't want to tell me yet, Jane thought, resuming her polishing. She wants to tell Alec first, and quite right too. But she knows I know, and she'll tell me properly soon. I expect they'll tell me together.

She went on with her work, thinking and planning ahead. Alec had come home in June, so the earliest the baby could be coming would be next March. A spring baby – the best time of year to be born. The natural time, when other animals were having their young and the farm would be alive with calves and lambs and chicks. Or it might be April, or even May, two lovely months. It gives a child such a good start to be born then, she thought. The whole summer to be out in the fresh air in its pram, getting strong, ready for winter. And then the year after it'll be on its feet, toddling about and into everything. It's going to bring us all to life, she thought, and was still smiling to herself when Alec came in. He had been out with George in the barn and looked almost as worn out as Lizzie had done.

'You look happy, Mum,' he said, and dropped into a chair. 'Had some good news?'

Jane looked at his tired face and longed to tell him. But no – that wasn't her place. Instead, she said, 'Not exactly, Alec, but I've got a feeling there's some to come for us all. Why don't you go upstairs and ask your wife? I've an idea she's nearly ready to tell you.'

He stared at her for a moment. 'What on earth?' His brows came together in a frown. 'I don't know what you mean. What good news?'

'Well, what do you expect when a man comes home from

232

a long time away?' Jane asked, unable to prevent her joy from showing in her face and voice. 'I can't say any more – it's for Lizzie to tell you. You go up and ask her now, there's a dear, and then we can all celebrate. Go on!'

He looked at her again, still baffled. Then he turned and went up the stairs. She heard his footsteps on the landing above, and then his voice as he called to Lizzie. The bedroom door closed and there was silence.

I wonder if they'll tell us straight away, Jane thought. Or maybe they'll want to keep it quiet for a while. It doesn't matter – *I* know, and they know I know. And I can keep it to myself until they're ready.

Lizzie was lying on the bed when Alec came in. She'd heard him come into the house but the bedroom was at the other end of the house from the kitchen and she'd not heard the voices. When he opened the door she lay with her eyes closed as if she were asleep. I can't face him yet, she thought. I can't even look him in the eye.

'Lizzie,' Alec said, and as she heard the strange, tight note in his voice she felt a twinge of alarm. 'Lizzie, don't pretend. I know you're awake.'

'I was just resting,' she said, opening her eyes. 'I felt a bit tired, that's all.'

'Is it?' he said.

Lizzie glanced up at him cautiously. 'Is it what? What d'you mean?'

'I mean, is that all? Just a bit tired?' He sat down on the edge of the bed and looked at her gravely. 'There's nothing else wrong, is there? You would tell me if there was?'

'Of course I would.' She tried to meet his eye but found herself having to look away. She looked down at her hands, pleating the edge of the coverlet between her fingers, folding it tightly over and over again. 'There's nothing wrong, Alec.'

'There is!' She jumped at his tone. 'Don't lie to me,

233

Lizzie! There is something wrong, and I've got a pretty good idea what it is. And so has your mother.'

'Mum?' Lizzie sat up sharply. 'Why, what has she told you? I haven't said a word to her!'

'It doesn't look as if you needed to. And she hasn't told me anything, not in so many words. She just looked at me when I came in, as if the sun had come out, and told me you might have some good news for me. *Good* news, she said! So tell me, Lizzie, because I could really be doing with some good news.'

'Oh God,' she whispered. 'This is awful. Oh Alec . . .'

'Well?' he said after a moment. 'What is it then? It doesn't seem as if you think it's such good news as your mother does.'

She shook her head blindly. 'I don't know how to tell you. I never meant it to happen. It was only once, I swear it was only once – and neither of us meant it to happen, only it was VE night and everything was so different. We all went mad – it was like VJ night, you remember that, everyone celebrating. And – well, I was sorry afterwards, especially when you came home and I knew it was you I loved, I knew it all the time really – and then I began to wonder if – if—' She looked up at him piteously. 'Oh Alec, I'm going to have a baby!'

She broke down then in a storm of weeping, her head buried in her arms, her shoulders shaking, while Alec sat watching her. He was like a man turned to stone; although he was only inches away, he could no more reach out and touch her than he could have sprouted wings and flown. He felt as cold as ice.

At last he said, 'No wonder you were so disappointed when I couldn't make love to you. You could have pretended it was mine then, and I would never have known.'

'Alec, no! I wouldn't have . . .' She faltered into silence. 'I'm sorry,' she whispered at last. 'I'm really sorry.'

'I bet you are. And you would have, wouldn't you? Pretended it was mine? *For God's sake be honest with me!*' he shouted, leaping to his feet. 'You've been living a lie all these weeks. For God's sake be honest with me now.'

'Alec, please!' She was crying hard, kneeling up on the bed and lifting her arms towards him. '*Please* don't be angry. I never meant it to happen. It was just a stupid, stupid mistake – it was you I loved really, but it was so long since I'd seen you, and it was the VE Day party and – and we were friends, we got on well and – well, it just *happened*! I'm so, so sorry.' She laid her hands against his chest and he took them in his own and held them away from his body. 'Oh Alec, *please*!'

'What the hell do you expect me to do?' he growled. 'What the hell do you expect me to *be*, if I'm not to be angry! I get torpedoed at sea, spend years in a German POW camp, and then come home to find my wife's been messing about with other men and is having a baby. What am I supposed to do – congratulate you? Start knitting little bootees?'

'No! No, of course not.' She looked up at him imploringly. 'I know it's awful for you, especially . . .' She stopped and bit her lip, tears once more spilling from her eyes.

'Especially since I can't deliver the goods myself,' he said crudely. 'That's what you were going to say, isn't it?'

'I don't know what to say,' she whispered.

'Well, you could try telling me the truth. That'd be a start. Or did you have some other plan in mind?'

Lizzie shook her head forlornly. 'I knew I was going to have to tell you eventually. I just didn't know how to do it. I knew you'd be hurt.'

'You can say that again!' he said with a bitter laugh.

'And I couldn't bear it. Things are bad enough as they are.'

'I'm glad you realise *that*, at any rate!'

'Oh Alec, please! I'm trying to tell you. It isn't easy.'

'And you think *I* should make it easy for you?' He looked at her. 'D'you realise, I don't even know who it is? You might at least tell me that. I could have been talking to him this very afternoon, for all I know. D'you have any idea how that makes me feel? To know that someone in this village, someone I know, maybe even someone I think is a friend of mine, is laughing at me behind my back. D'you have any idea at all what you've done to me?'

'Yes,' she said. 'I do. I've lain awake every night since I began to suspect, worrying about it. It's been driving me mad. But it's not anyone in this village, Alec. It's nobody you know at all. It was an American.'

'An American? You mean a GI?'

'No. He was an airman.' She drew in a breath. 'He used to come here for Sunday dinner, him and another one. A lot of them did – they were sort of billeted on houses in the area, so that we could give them a few home comforts.'

'Blimey! You did that all right!'

'And we became friends. He put on some square dances at the base and invited us all to go along. It was just *fun*, Alec. We never meant it to go any further. But then it was VE Day and he was going away, and the party—'

'All right,' he broke in, 'don't go over it all again. You had some cider and he had some beer and you got carried away. You forgot me. You forgot your marriage vows. Or maybe you just didn't care. Was that how it was? Well?'

'Alec, don't say it like that. I never forgot you or our marriage vows.'

'You just didn't care about them, then.'

'I did! I *did*! Alec, please, you've got to understand.' She put up her hands again, pawing at his chest, and he gripped her wrists and held her away. '*Alec!*'

'I don't think,' he said contemptuously, 'that *I've* got to do anything. *You* got yourself into this mess, Lizzie – you and your American boyfriend.' His lip curled. 'What is it

236

they say about girls' knickers? One Yank and they're off? I never thought that would apply to you!' He flung her hands away from him, pushing her back on to the bed. 'You'd better ask him what he intends to do about this. It's his baby, after all. Or maybe you were planning to go to America with him? Well?'

'No,' she said, crouching on the bed. 'I told you, we never meant it to go so far. He was going away. I haven't even seen him since that night. I don't know where he is now.'

'So it was going to be *my* baby. If I'd only been able to come up to scratch, I'd never have known. You probably wouldn't have been too sure about it yourself.'

Lizzie said nothing. She curled herself up on the bed, her knees drawn close to her chin. Her tears made a dark, spreading patch on the coverlet. She shook with sobs.

Alec looked down at her, a variety of expressions chasing themselves across his face. Slowly, almost tentatively, he put out one hand towards her; then he drew it back and took a step towards the door. Lizzie raised her head and stared at him. Her eyes were swollen and red, her mouth distorted, her whole face ravaged. For a long moment they remained quite still, eyes locked. And then Alec turned and jerked open the door. She lifted herself and stretched one hand towards him, but he ignored her entreaty. He flung himself out and slammed the door behind him.

As she heard his footsteps going down the stairs, she collapsed once more on the bed in a storm of despairing tears.

Chapter Twenty-Two

It had taken Dan longer than he'd expected to move from Portsmouth to Bridge End. It was true that he had only to give a week's notice, both to Vospers and the landlord of his house in April Grove, but he'd reckoned without the business of sorting out all his belongings, getting rid of those he didn't want and packing up those he did.

'I never realised I had so much claptrap,' he said to Tommy Vickers as they had a pint together in the pub at the top of March Street. 'It's not all mine, either – there's all Nora's things, and Gordon's as well. I dunno what to do with it all.'

'I dare say someone'll be glad of it,' Tommy said. 'There's the old clothes shop up September Street, and that junk shop, they'll take almost anything. And what they don't want, the rag-and-bone man will. There's not much goes in the rubbish bin these days.'

'I know.' Dan rubbed his hand over his face. 'It's the sorting out that's the worst. I mean, I've never had the heart to touch Nora's things – it brings it all back. And now there's Gordon's as well. It's a sad job, Tom.'

Tommy wrinkled his face. There were plenty of wrinkles there, mostly created by laughter. Most people in Portsmouth who knew him – and a lot knew Tommy Vickers – thought of him as a bit of a card, always with a joke on his lips. The fact that he looked a lot like the popular comedian Arthur Askey didn't help, either. They didn't see him as someone with serious feelings, who might have his own troubles and griefs.

But Tommy had seen as much pain and distress as anyone else during the six years of war. He had been one of the firewatchers on top of the Guildhall when it was bombed and gutted in the first big Blitz of 1941. He'd been in an air-raid shelter in Old Portsmouth when the Whitewoods' furniture store was burned down, jollying people along with songs. He'd put out incendiary bombs, fought fires and stood guard over live bombs until the Bomb Disposal Squad arrived to deal with them. He'd risked his life time and time again, without ever making a fuss about it, and when he'd lost his own sister and her husband in the bombing he'd offered his nephew a home without a second thought.

'D'you want me to come in and give you a hand, Dan?' he asked. 'And I dare say my Freda would too, if we asked her. She could see to Nora's things for you if you like.'

'I dunno. I feel I ought to do it meself really. As a sort of last goodbye, you know. But – well, I won't say I wouldn't be glad of someone to do it with me. Must be getting soft in me old age!' Dan finished with an attempt at a grin. 'If you got the time, Tom – and your Freda, too – it'd help me put me mind to it, if nothing else.'

'That's settled, then.' Tommy went to buy another pint, thinking how Dan had changed in the years that they'd known each other. Nobody had liked the big, dark man when he'd first come to April Grove, and everyone had felt sorry for his pale, quiet little wife Nora. There'd been a suspicion that he drank and knocked her about, especially when she started getting those bruises all over her. But it had turned out that they were all part of her illness – leukaemia, the doctor called it, a sort of cancer in the blood – that had eventually killed her. And you couldn't say but what Dan hadn't been proper cut up about losing her. He'd had a funny way of showing it, but once you realised that was what was eating him you could see he'd thought the world of his wife and didn't hardly know how to manage without her.

It was only after he'd finally agreed to let the boy be evacuated, and then gone out to Bridge End to see him, that he'd started to come out of his shell. Now, he was a different man. The Dan Hodges that Nora must have known and loved when they were young had begun to emerge. And Tommy knew that the credit for that went to Ruth Purslow.

He'd be all right out there, married to her, Tommy thought, handing over a florin for the drinks. Doing blacksmith's work like he always wanted, living amongst the trees and having a proper family life with his boy. It was a shame he'd lost his other boy too, but when all was said and done Gordon would probably have brought him more trouble, so maybe it was just as well. This way, he could at least be proud of the lad.

He took the drinks back to the table. 'Me and Freda'll come in tomorrow evening, after tea. We can start sorting stuff out then. It won't take long, not with three of us at it.' He gave Dan his perky grin. 'We'll listen to the wireless at the same time. *ITMA*'s on – we can't miss that.' And then, in quite a good imitation of the charlady Mrs Mopp, 'Can I do yer now, sir?'

Dan's face, which had been in danger of settling into its old morose lines, brightened and he laughed. 'Don't mind if I do,' he answered in the whisky-sodden tones of Colonel Chinstrap. 'Thanks, Tom. You're a good mate. You'll have to come out and see us when we're properly settled in Bridge End.'

'Come and see you?' Tommy echoed. 'I'll tell you what, we'll be expecting an invitation to the wedding!' He was pleased to see Dan smiling again. Tommy Vickers liked to see people smiling. In fact, if it had ever occurred to him that he had a mission in life, this would have been what it was – to make people smile.

Better than bombing them to smithereens, he'd have said with his characteristic cheery wink.

As Tommy had said, with three of them working at it, Dan's belongings were soon sorted out. Freda took charge of Nora's few clothes and said that she'd take them straight up the road and see what she could get for them in the second-hand shop, and if it was all the same to Dan she'd rather like this pink jumper for herself. She'd always liked Nora in it. She'd give him a couple of bob if he thought that was fair. Dan said no, he didn't think it was fair at all after all Freda and Tom had done for him and he didn't want a penny, and if she said another word about it he'd take it as an insult, straight up he would. 'And you can help yourself to anything else you've a mind to,' he added. 'I've got a lot to thank you for, you two. I've not forgotten all you did for my Nora, nor for young Sam.'

Tommy had a few sacks by him and they crammed all the stuff to go to the second-hand and junk shops into these. They put the rubbish into the dustbin to be taken away next week, and Dan packed his and Sammy's things into a selection of suitcases borrowed from Ruth and her family, and anyone in April Grove who had one to offer. The Budds had a couple from when Jess and the children were evacuated, Bob Shaw brought his Army kitbag along and Tommy himself contributed a canvas grip from his Navy days. Dan looked at them and shook his head. 'I dunno how I'm going to carry this lot. And there's me bike as well! Reckon I'm going to have to make two trips.'

'Well, that's not the end of the world,' Tommy said. 'You can bring young Sammy back with you to say cheerio. We ain't seen him since he was here for Navy Days, back in May.'

There was more celebration in April Grove before Dan finally left the street. Ted and Annie Chapman's boy Colin, who had been a Japanese prisoner of war, finally came home and everyone got out their bunting for the third time that year to welcome him back. Dan saw him coming along March Street with his family, who had virtually camped on the railway station so as not to miss him, and thought he didn't look too bad, considering what he'd been through. He stopped Frank Budd, who was hurrying past with his own tribe, and said, 'Your nephew, isn't he?'

'That's right. Annie is Jess's sister.' Frank looked at him. 'You never met Colin, did you? He was gone before you came to April Grove.'

Dan nodded. 'I heard about him, though. It's good to see him back. I dare say the women'll make a fuss of him.'

'I dare say he deserves it too,' Frank said grimly. 'When you think of the way they got treated out there . . . Well, mustn't stop, Dan. Got to add my congratulations. You're off soon, are you?'

'Tomorrow. Got to come back for the rest of the bits and bobs, but I've worked out me notice at Vospers and paid me last week's rent.' Dan hesitated, then stuck out his hand. 'Just in case we don't run into each other again – thanks for all you done, Frank. I'd never have got this house in the first place if it hadn't been for you. And I know you and your missus done a lot for my Nora when she was poorly, and Sam too. So thanks, mate.'

Frank shrugged. 'It was only what anyone else would've done. Anyway, good luck, Dan. Tell you what, I wouldn't mind being in your shoes meself – I've always fancied living out in the country. But there you are,' he grinned a little ruefully, 'have to make do with me back garden and the allotment! Reckon we got a lot to be thankful for, eh?'

'Reckon we have,' Dan said and his eyes went to the excited group clustering round Annie Chapman's front gate. 'Reckon we have.'

He turned and went back into the house. It looked empty now, with almost all the furniture gone and his possessions packed into the assortment of bags and cases. All it needed was a sweep through and a bit of a scrubbing, and the landlord wouldn't have anything to complain about. It was in better nick than when Dan and Nora had first moved in.

I hope you don't mind me going, love, he thought, conjuring up his favourite picture of his wife as she had been as a young girl, her hair curling around her laughing face, her eyes bright and her lips waiting for his kiss. And I hope you don't mind me getting wed again. I won't forget you. Me and Sam, neither of us is ever going to forget you.

Before they left, he and Sammy would take a last bunch of flowers to her grave. And he'd come back every year, on the anniversary of the day she'd died. He would never, ever, forget.

For Sammy, it was a strange feeling to come back to April Grove knowing that this time he would leave it for ever. The house looked different with just the last few bits of furniture that would be taken away after they had left, and the bags and cases already packed. Dan had brought home the empty ones belonging to the Budds and Bob Shaw and he and Sammy returned them, saying goodbye at the same time.

'I hope it'll all go well for you out in the country,' Jess Budd said, standing at her clean white doorstep. She looked at Sammy. 'I dare say it's more home to you than Pompey is now, after all this time.'

Sammy nodded. Apart from the kindness of the neighbours, the little street held few good memories for him, and it was only the bond with his mother that connected him to it now. He wondered if, once he had left for good, that bond would be broken.

Gladys Shaw came out of the house next door. She was engaged to Clifford Weeks, who was Tommy Vickers's nephew, and they were getting married soon. She looked bright and happy, and she gave Dan and Sammy a glowing smile.

'It's good to be starting a new life,' she said, ruffling Sammy's fair hair. 'And you're getting married too, Mr Hodges, so I've heard. Well, congratulations. I hope you'll be as happy as Cliff and me are going to be.'

'Thanks,' he said, his dark face brightening. 'I reckon I will be. Both of us will, won't we, Sam? It was a good day for us when he was first took out to Bridge End,' he added, turning back to Jess. 'I didn't think so at the time, mind, but I wasn't thinking straight about anything then. What with the war, and Nora and everything, life didn't seem much worth living. It's wonderful how things can change.'

'It is,' Gladys said soberly. 'When I think about the way poor Graham Philpotts died, helping me with the ambulance, and my poor mum, strafed in the road by that Jerry plane, and Cliff's parents killed by a bomb – well, there were some horrible things happened. But it's over now and we've got our own lives to live, and it won't do the people who died any good for us to sit around moaning about it all. We're going to build a new world – a *better* world!'

She flashed another bright smile at them and swung off up the road, her coat flying out behind her. Jess and Dan watched her and then smiled at each other.

'That's the right attitude,' Jess said. 'It's too easy to look at all the bombsites and think of the people who've been killed, and wonder how we're ever going to put it all right again – but there's plenty of us left. We can do what Gladys says. We can build a better world.'

'You don't think I'm running out on that?' Dan asked, suddenly anxious. He liked this friendly little woman who had always been so good to him and Sammy, and didn't want to lose her good opinion. 'I mean, leaving Pompey and going out to the country.'

'No, never!' She gave him her warm smile. 'You're making a better life for you and Sammy. That's all part of it. It's the kiddies who're the future, after all, and young Sam deserves the best start he can have.'

'He's got that now,' Dan acknowledged. 'I'm not sure he had it in the beginning – when we were here in April Grove.' He turned to go. 'Anyway, I just wanted to say thanks for all you've done for us, specially when Nora was bad and when Sam was on his own. And I'll be coming back from time to time to see to her grave. Maybe I'll look in.'

'You do that,' she said. 'You come in and have a cup of tea and tell us all about Bridge End. Don't forget, I was evacuated out there myself for a while. I'd like to hear how they're all getting on.' She watched them walk up the road; the big, powerful man and the slight figure of his son with those fair curls that he'd got from his mother.

She'd always thought of April Grove as a happy little street, but it hadn't been like that for the Hodges family. I hope they have a good life now, she thought. I hope they'll be happy, out at Bridge End.

Dan and Sammy didn't stay overnight in the little terraced house. All they needed to do was say goodbye to a few people and collect their things, then catch the train back. After having a bite to eat with Tommy and Freda Vickers next door, they walked up to the little churchyard where Nora was buried. They put a bunch of flowers into the tin vase Dan had bought specially and stood for a few moments looking at the grave, each thinking his own thoughts. Then they walked back and collected their bags,

'Well, that's it,' Dan said, shutting the door for the last time. 'I just got to drop the key in through the door and we've finished with it. It's not our house any more.'

At the sound of the door closing, Tommy popped out of the next house with Freda behind him. Clifford Weeks and Gladys were there too and as they crowded round to shake hands and slap him on the back, Dan realised that people were coming out of all the other houses in April Grove as well. Frank and Jess Budd and their family – Bert and Bob

245

Shaw – the Taylors, who had been bombed out of their own place and come here to live, together with that bloke Polly was going round with and the young aircraft spotter Chris that was going to marry young Judy Taylor – and even toothless old Granny Kinch and her scrawny daughter Nancy, who made her living round the gates of the Dockyard. They were all there, waving and shouting goodbye, wishing him and Sammy good luck.

Dan felt a lump in his throat. He folded his lips tightly, biting on the inside, and nodded at them. When he tried to speak, the words came out gruffly and he was almost afraid he was going to break down in tears. He grabbed Sammy's hand and bent to pick up one of the bags.

'Thanks,' he said to them, and it was all he could manage. 'Thanks.'

Then he turned and began to stride up March Street, with Sammy beside him. He heard a little cheer go up, a ragged chorus of good wishes, and he thought of the day he and Nora had first come here and found the squalid little house they were to live in. He thought of how he'd hated it, and hated his neighbours too, how he'd believed they looked down their noses at him and wished the Hodges would go away and live somewhere else. And then he thought of how they'd helped Nora and then young Sam; how they'd offered him friendship and help; how he wouldn't have got through without them.

'It wasn't such a bad place, April Grove,' he said to his son as they reached the little station and waited for the train. 'It wasn't such a bad place at all.'

Chapter Twenty-Three

Both Lizzie and Alec knew that something would have to be done about their situation, and time was not on their side. Jane already suspected that Lizzie was pregnant and believed the baby was Alec's. Ruth knew the real story, but she wouldn't tell anyone else. Before long, Lizzie's figure would swell, as it had already begun to do, and then everyone would know.

'I don't know what to do,' the girl wept as she told her aunt about the terrible row she and Alec had had. 'I'm at my wits' end, I really am. I wish I'd got rid of it when I first realised. I know you don't approve, Auntie, but it would have been the best thing all round. I mean, what sort of a life is the baby going to have, with its parents at loggerheads all the time? That's if Alec stays with me at all,' she added mournfully. 'I'm still not sure but what he's going to just walk out and go back to Southampton. And I don't know what my mum and dad will do then. They'll turn me out, I'm sure they will, for bringing such disgrace.'

'I don't think they will, honestly,' Ruth said, hoping she was right. 'You're not the only one this has happened to, you know. There's quite a few men coming home to babies that aren't theirs, and in a lot of cases they're just getting on with it.'

'And in a lot of others, they're not. And even if they do, what's it going to be like, watching the kiddy grow up, having to pretend to be its father, having to feed and clothe it? It must be miserable for them all.'

'I don't know. I just don't know. Perhaps after a while

they just forget about it. But in any case, it's not them we're talking about, it's you and Alec. And when it comes down to it, it's you two that's got to decide. You know you can always come here and talk it over, but it's for you and Alec to make up your own minds.'

'Yes, but he hasn't even spoken to me since it all came out. He just walked out of the house without another word and when he came in he looked awful. White as a sheet, and as sickly as when he first came home. He went straight to bed and when I took him up some supper he just turned over and pretended to be asleep. And he hasn't said a word to me since.'

Ruth sighed. She was waiting for Dan and Sammy to come back from Portsmouth and had prepared a special supper for them – rabbit pie with mashed potatoes and the last of the runner beans. She didn't want them coming in to Lizzie's tears, yet in all humanity she couldn't turn the girl out. 'What's your mother making of all this?' she asked. 'I haven't seen her these past two or three days. I'd have thought if she was worried she'd have come down to me herself.'

'I don't know. She hasn't said anything at all, but she knows there's something wrong. She keeps looking at us both and you can see she's having to bite her tongue not to ask what's up. I suppose she thinks Alec's upset because a baby's coming so soon, before he's got himself sorted out. And she knows he's been funny since he came home – flares up at the slightest thing, goes off at a tangent when you least expect it. But I expect she thinks he'll come round.' Lizzie sighed and shook her head. 'If only it was that easy!'

'Well, I don't know what to advise. Except to try and talk to Alec again. He might not feel like talking about it but he's got to at some point. And you've got to help him, Lizzie. I know it's hard for you, and you're upset too, but it

248

is your responsibility after all, and you're the one who's got to do the mending.'

'Not only me!' Lizzie retorted, suddenly angry. 'It takes two to tango! I wasn't the only one who made this baby.'

'No,' Ruth said quietly, 'but you're the one who's carrying it, and you're the one who's married to Alec.' She hesitated. 'Have you heard from Floyd at all since he went away?'

'No.' Lizzie was despondent again. 'He's probably forgotten all about me by now. But we did agree that we wouldn't keep in touch. He said he'd write to Mum now and then, to thank her for all the times he came to our house, but he hasn't done so yet. I suppose they're busy over there in Germany, putting things to rights.'

'Suppose he came back?' Ruth asked carefully. 'Suppose he wanted you to go away with him? It does happen. What would you do?'

'I don't *know*! I want to stay with Alec – it's him I really love. But I thought I loved Floyd as well, and if Alec didn't want me, and Floyd did . . . I honestly don't know, Auntie Ruth!' She started to cry again. 'I hope he doesn't come. I hope he doesn't even write! It would only make things worse, and they're bad enough already.' She repeated the cry that had tormented her ever since she had first suspected she might be pregnant. 'I don't know *what* to do!'

Alec wasn't in when Lizzie returned to the farm. Her mother, making pastry at the table, looked at her uncertainly as she came in. 'You're looking bone-weary, Lizzie. Is everything all right?'

'I don't know, Mum.' For a moment, Lizzie was tempted to tell her everything, but until she'd talked to Alec again she didn't dare. 'It's just that everything's so different from what I'd expected. Heather Knight says the same. She and Ian aren't getting on too well, and Roger doesn't like his father and Teddy still hasn't come round to him. We thought the men would just slip back into their old ways and everything would be like it was before, but it doesn't seem to be working out that way at all.' She gave her mother a lopsided grin. 'It's just tiredness, that's all. Alec's still having nightmares and it's wearing us both down a bit.'

'Well, if that's all . . .' Jane hesitated. 'You'd tell me if there was anything wrong, wouldn't you? Anything serious, I mean.'

'Yes, of course I would.' Lizzie stood beside her mother for a moment and leaned her head against her shoulder. 'It's just a reaction after all those years when we haven't known what was going to happen next. I expect a lot of people are feeling the same.'

Slowly, she climbed the stairs to the bedroom she and Alec shared. It was the only place where they could be private; perhaps after all it would have been better, she thought, if we'd moved into the cottage where we could have had all the rows we wanted! But with Alec's future still so unsettled, it hadn't seemed worthwhile. She sat down on the bed and stared despondently at her linked fingers. I'll end up there on my own, she told herself, me and my baby; and she wondered if that might, in the end, be the best solution.

Downstairs, Jane went on rolling out the pastry and thinking her own thoughts. A lot of people were feeling sort of let down, especially the women. They'd had to keep cheerful all through the war and manage on the rations, although she knew that it hadn't been so difficult in the country as in the towns, and try not to worry too much about their men. And now it was all over, and after all the waiting and anxiety the end seemed to have come so suddenly. They had to pick up the pieces, and there seemed to be just too many of them. It was no wonder people just felt like sitting down and crying their eyes out. And for girls like Lizzie, having their man come home in an even worse state than they expected – well, it must be such a bitter disappointment.

When she'd first begun to suspect that Lizzie might be pregnant, she'd been overjoyed, thinking that this would cheer them both up and give Alec something to live for. A new life. A son or a daughter. But instead, he seemed even more miserable and that must be upsetting Lizzie too. And until they told her their news, so that she knew officially, as it were, she couldn't do a thing to help.

They'll tell me before long, she thought. They'll have to, because Lizzie'll be showing soon. And then me and George will be able to help. We can show them what good news *we* think it is . . .

Lizzie was sitting on her bed, crying yet again. For her and for Alec, it wasn't good news at all. When she heard him come into the house and up the stairs, his footsteps slow and heavy, her heart sank even lower and the face she turned to him as he opened the door was white and woebegone.

As he stood in the doorway looking at her, she couldn't read the expression on his face, couldn't tell if he were angry or in despair. She knew how hurt, how betrayed he must feel, and knew there was nothing she could do about that. You couldn't call back the past, however desperately you wanted to.

'I'm sorry,' she whispered. 'I'm really, really sorry.'

He stared at her for a moment longer. Then he came into the room, closing the door behind him, and took the two strides that were all that were necessary to bring him to the bed. He dropped to his knees and flung his arms around her waist, pulling her against him, burying his face against her stomach. 'Lizzie! Oh *Lizzie*, I've been so miserable.'

'I know,' she wept, stroking his head, hardly able to believe he had come to her at last. 'I know.'

His shoulders shook; his voice was thick and muffled. 'I hated you at first. At least, I *wanted* to hate you. But then –

it was like looking into a huge black hole. There was nothing there. Nobody to love. Nobody to love me. Oh Lizzie, say you still love me!'

'I do! I do love you – I always have done. I loved you all the time. I never, never stopped loving you, Alec, not for a minute.'

He lifted his face and searched her eyes. She met his gaze steadily. Then she said, 'Do – do you still love me, Alec?'

'Yes,' he said. 'I do.'

They stayed very still for a few moments, still meeting each other's eyes, and then he dropped his head once more into her lap. She sat stroking his hair, a great feeling of relief washing over her. She could feel the warmth of his cheek against her stomach, the wetness of his tears. At last she said, 'What do you want to do?'

He lifted his head again. 'Do? What do you mean?'

'What do you want to do about us?' She took a deep breath. If she asked the question, he would have to answer, and even though he'd said he loved her, the answer might not be what she wanted to hear. 'Do you want us to go on being married?'

He stared at her. 'Go on being married? Well, of course I do! What else could we do?'

Relief washed over her again and she felt the tears flood her eyes. Her voice was no more than a breath of sound. 'I thought you might leave me. I thought—'

Alec looked at her, his face sober. 'I can't leave you, Lizzie. I did think about it, but when I tried – I walked across the fields, away from you, and tried to imagine I was walking away for ever. And I couldn't do it. I had to come back.' He paused for a moment. 'We belong together, Lizzie. We've got to face this out together. For better, for worse, isn't that what we promised? Well, I reckon we've been through the worst, and now things might get a bit better.'

'And – the baby?'

He met her eyes again. 'What do *you* want to do? This baby – will you want to keep it? Because if you do, Lizzie,' he hurried on, seeing the panic in her face, 'if you do, I just want you to know – well, it'll be all right by me. I mean, if we're going to make a go of it – well, we can't start by giving away your baby. It wouldn't be right. And you might never forgive me.'

She stared at him. 'But how would you feel about it? Having someone else's baby about the place? Watching it grow up – wouldn't it remind you all the time? Wouldn't it be worse for you?'

'I don't think so,' he said. 'It's not the baby's fault, is it? And it might be the only child we'll ever be able to have.'

'Alec!'

'We don't know that I'm ever going to get better,' he said. 'Look, Lizzie, I've been doing a lot of thinking these past few days. The way I am – I might never be any different. I might never be able to love you properly again. Can you put up with that? If you can't, it might be better to go our separate ways now. You've got to think about it.'

'I don't have to. I love you. If that's the way it is, that's all there is to it. It's like a man losing his arms or legs. I'd still love you just as much then as I do now.'

'Tell you what,' he said, 'let's say this baby's been sent to us, shall we? From now on, it's ours. How about that?'

Lizzie began to cry again. 'I don't deserve you. I don't deserve any of this.'

'Well, if you knew about everything I've done in foreign ports you'd say I didn't deserve you either!' he said wryly. 'Don't cry any more, sweetheart. We're together, that's all that matters, and we're having a baby. There's been times when I thought we never would. Let's forget what's happened, and go on from here, shall we?'

'But what about other people?' she asked. 'Mum and Dad and everyone. What shall we tell them?'

'What do we need to tell them? Just that we're having a

baby, of course. They'll think it's mine – and to tell you the truth I don't mind if they do. It's better than them knowing I'm not up to the job myself.' His mouth twisted a little and she hugged him fiercely.

'Don't say that! It'll be all right. I know it will.' She smiled at him. 'I dare say we'll have about ten babies before we're finished. You don't have to worry about that.'

'We'll see.' He frowned suddenly. 'You haven't told anyone else, have you? About the baby – and about me?'

'No – well, only Auntie Ruth. And she won't say anything. She's been a good friend to me, Alec. I don't know what I'd have done without her.'

'All right. I don't mind her knowing. But nobody else?'

'Nobody,' she said, and he bent forwards and kissed her. They clung together and then he lowered his head to her lap again. For a minute or two he stayed very still and then he lifted his head.

'What was that? That sort of twitching?'

Lizzie stared at him. 'I don't know. I felt it too. Like a sort of fluttering inside.' Sudden excitement gripped her and she caught his head and held it close to her stomach. 'Alec, it's the baby! It's moving! I can feel it again – very faint, like a butterfly. Can you feel it too? Can you really?'

'I think I can,' he said softly. 'At least, it's not so much a feeling as a – a – well, I don't know what it is!' He stayed very still, waiting for another tiny movement, then shook his head in wonder. 'It's our baby, Lizzie. It's our baby. It's alive – and it's *moving* . . .'

Chapter Twenty-Four

In October, the vicar decided to hold a Harvest Festival service in the church. The whole village came along and afterwards there was a supper for everyone in the village hall. The long trestle tables were put up again and benches lined up beside them, and some of the women came round with big pans full of winter vegetable soup and baskets of home-made bread. Afterwards, some of the produce that had decorated the church was packed into boxes for the old folk, and Arthur Knight auctioned off the rest. Jane bought a huge marrow to make into jam, with a bit of ginger to give it a kick, and Alec bought a gallon jar of the Knights' home-made cider. 'To wet the baby's head,' he said with a grin.

Lizzie and Alec had told the family that a baby was coming soon. They had agreed that Alec needed a little time to get used to the idea, and that they should wait a week or two, but by then nobody could fail to see their glowing faces, and put their own interpretation on the cause. By the time the news became official, it was an open secret.

'Crikey, we're not waiting that long!' Terry exclaimed, reaching for it and filling everyone's glass. He lifted his in a toast. 'To Lizzie and Alec.'

'Lizzie and Alec,' everyone echoed. 'And the baby.' They drank and congratulated the couple all over again, and those in the village who hadn't heard the news also crowded around to wish them well. 'You didn't take long over that, young Alec!' one of the farmers said with a wink.

'Wish my old bull could do as well. He's gone right off the idea just lately.'

'Go on, that bull of yours is so old he's forgotten what it's for,' someone else jeered. 'Time you put your hand in your pocket and got yourself a young fellow with a bit of go about him.'

'That's right,' old Eli chimed in. 'Once a bull's gone off like that he's no use to man nor beast. Leave it much longer and he'll be too tough even to stew!'

Lizzie glanced sideways at Alec, half afraid that he might take their ribald comments amiss, but he was grinning broadly and joining in. She drew in a sigh of relief. I wouldn't have dreamed he'd take it so well, she thought. After the first shock, he's really turned up trumps. And it even seems to have done him good. He's more relaxed – as if he felt he had to make some sort of showing, and now he doesn't have to. He hasn't even had any nightmares this past few nights.

He'd even begun to pull her close to him in bed and cuddle her. And Lizzie too felt as if the pressure had been taken off. She was content now to lie in his arms, savouring their closeness and no longer hungry for more. It would come, she felt sure, but the desperate anxiety they had both felt was gone.

She glanced around the room and observed Heather Knight. The other woman was looking pale, she thought. Pale and tired, with unhappy shadows in her eyes. She was sitting beside Stevie, who was laughing and joking with Ian on her other side. The older children, Roger and Pat, were there too, but neither seemed to be enjoying themselves. Pat was looking sulky and Roger sullen, hardly speaking to Sammy Hodges who sat beside him, with Ruth and Dan looking like young lovers at the end of the table.

I hope there's nothing going on there, Lizzie thought, glancing at Stevie's laughing face and the way Ian seemed to be hanging on her every word. Heather was joining in their conversation and Stevie seemed to be doing her best to include her, but Ian had half-turned his back, so that it was difficult for Heather to get in. After a while, she gave up and turned her attention back to the children, but Pat wouldn't answer her and although Roger spoke readily enough to his mother, he kept darting bitter glances past her at his father.

'It doesn't look as if anything's better there,' Lizzie murmured to Jane. 'Heather's told me how difficult Ian's finding it to adjust to being back on the farm. She wants to help him settle in and of course she's got to show him what changes have been made, and explain about the new regulations and all that – but he just doesn't want to listen to her. If you ask me, he's being downright unreasonable.'

'Well, it can't be easy. He was used to working with his father before he went away and he expected to be boss when he came home. No man likes taking second place to his wife.'

'Heather doesn't want him to take second place! She wants them to work together. She likes farming, and with Mrs Knight still able to look after the cooking and young Callie Dewar doing the rough work, she's got the time to do it. You'd think Ian would be pleased.'

Jane shook her head. 'I don't think it works like that. Men want to be in charge and they want their women indoors, not out making decisions and running things. That's the way it's always been.'

'I don't think it's going to be like that any more,' Lizzie said. 'The war's shown us women that we can do a lot of the things men have always kept for themselves – and we're good at them. Women aren't going to go tamely back to scrubbing floors and peeling potatoes, not after they've been in the Services and driven cars and buses, even flown aeroplanes. They've proved that there aren't many jobs a woman *can't* do, and they don't want to give them up. If

257

you ask me, the men are scared. They're frightened they don't matter any more.'

Alec heard the last few words and leaned past her. 'What's that? Men don't matter any more? Who says?'

'*I* don't,' Lizzie said, squeezing his hand. '*I* think you matter more than ever. Being apart from you all these years has shown me that – not that I didn't know it already. I'm just saying that women can do a lot more jobs than they ever thought, but that's not what matters. It's just being together that matters – being together and loving each other.'

She smiled into his eyes and he gave her a sudden quick kiss. Lizzie felt a swift tremor of excitement. It was only a peck, but there was something in it that made her feel that perhaps their long period of abstinence was coming to an end at last. Not tonight, perhaps, but soon – tomorrow, next week, next month – they would be able to turn to each other and let their love flow freely once more. The fears and torments of the long separation would finally be over.

Heather saw the kiss and the smile, and felt her own loneliness deepen. Everyone seemed to be happy, she thought, everyone except herself and Ian. Lizzie and Alec, Ruth and Dan – why, even Dottie Dewar was looking like a cat that got the cream, probably because her Bert had come back and, if he'd noticed the latest baby and done his sums, must have decided not to mention it. He must know what Dottie's like by now, Heather thought, and from the way he's acting tonight there'll be another on the way soon. I dare say there's a few little Dewars in France or wherever he's been, as well.

'Are you going to have some apple pie?' she asked Pat as the soup bowls were taken away. 'Granny and I made most of them. Come on, lovey, look cheerful. Aren't you enjoying yourself?'

258

'I wanted to sit next to Daddy,' Pat said in a surly tone. 'You knew I wanted to and you pushed me out.'

'No, I didn't. And I wanted to sit next to him myself. You could have sat the other side, between him and Stevie.'

'No, I couldn't. He wanted Stevie there. He'd rather sit between Stevie and me.'

'Pat! That's a spiteful thing to say.'

'It's true. He's not talking to you, is he?'

Heather felt tears come to her eyes. She bit her lip and looked down at the plate that had just been put before her, with a slice of her own apple pie. Ian had barely addressed a word to her all evening, despite Stevie's attempts to draw her into the conversation. 'All right,' she said, getting up, 'we'll change places now. See if he'll talk to *you*.' Pat slid along the bench, a smug look of triumph on her face, and Heather sat down beside Roger. She looked at him with a little more sympathy, knowing that he was as miserable as she was.

'Come on, Roger,' she said gently. 'You're not having any fun at all.' She was aware that her tone of voice was different from when she'd spoken to Pat, but she couldn't help it. 'Don't you and Sammy know any jokes tonight?'

'Don't feel like jokes,' he muttered. He'd eaten his soup and was now munching his way doggedly through a large slice of pie. At least misery didn't put boys off their food, she thought. 'I'm fed up.'

'What are you fed up about?' She knew pretty well, but she wanted Roger to say it. Until he admitted what was wrong, they couldn't discuss it, couldn't even begin to put things right. 'Is it school?' He shook his head. 'Your friends, then? You haven't quarrelled with anyone?' Another shake. 'It's home then, isn't it? Tell me, Roger, please. What's upsetting you so much? I don't like to see you so miserable.'

'You know what it is!' he burst out and several people looked round. Lowering his voice to a mutter, he went on angrily, 'It's him! Coming home and spoiling everything. We were all right before. We don't need him coming back. And he's nasty to you,' he said even more quietly, so that she had to bend her head to catch his words. 'I've heard him.'

'Roger, no!' The words were out quickly, before she had time to think about whether they were true or not. 'You mustn't say that about your dad. He's not nasty to me.'

'He is. He says horrid things to you. I heard him the other day – he said you were an *interfering nuisance*, and that you didn't know anything about farming and if he hadn't come home we'd be going bankrupt. It's not true, is it?' He looked up and met her eyes and she saw the anger in his face. 'You're *not* an interfering nuisance, Mum, and you *do* know about farming, and we *wouldn't* be going bankrupt. It's him who doesn't know anything – he's been away for years. Now he's come back, he thinks he knows it all, and he doesn't. And I *hate* him.'

'Roger! You mustn't say that – it's wicked.'

'I don't care,' he said. 'It's true.' He got up suddenly, climbing back over the bench. 'I don't want any more to eat. I'm going home.'

Ian looked round and saw him. 'Sit down at once! You're not going anywhere.'

'I feel sick,' Roger said, staring at him defiantly. 'I'll *be* sick if I stay here any longer.' He ran for the door.

Ian smothered an exclamation and started to follow him, but Stevie laid her hand on his arm. 'Leave him alone, Ian. He'll be all right.' Her voice was soft, yet it stopped him and he sat down again slowly, still looking angry. Pat slipped her hand through his arm and cuddled her face against his sleeve.

'It's all right, Daddy,' she said. 'You've still got me.'

There was a moment of silence at the table. Then everyone began to talk at once and Heather was able to take out her handkerchief and surreptitiously wipe her eyes. She sat staring at her plate, messing the pie around with her spoon until it looked as if she'd eaten some of it. As the meal dragged on to its end, with cups of tea being passed along the tables, she got up.

'Come on, Pat. Time you were home in bed.' She ignored her daughter's protests. 'No, don't argue. People are only going to sit around and talk, and you've got school tomorrow. I'm going home now, and you're coming with me.' She glanced at Ian. 'You won't be too late, will you?'

'No,' he said casually. He was talking to Stevie again and didn't even bother to turn round as he tossed the words over his shoulder to his wife. 'No, I don't suppose I'll be late.'

Heather walked home with her daughter. Her back was straight, her legs felt stiff and she had to keep her chin high and blink rapidly to force the tears away. Beside her, Pat was scuffing her feet and grumbling, but she took no notice. All she wanted was to get back home to her bedroom, where she could give way to the misery in her heart.

Oh *Ian*, she thought. Where have you gone? And who is this stranger that's come to take your place?

The party broke up about an hour later. The women did the washing-up while the men put away the tables and benches and someone swept the floor with the wide broom. Then everyone walked home by the light of the hunter's moon.

'It's been a lovely evening,' Stevie said as Ian saw her back to the cottage. 'I'm not sure Heather enjoyed it, though.'

'Heather's in a funny mood lately,' he said indifferently. 'Nothing pleases her and whatever I say she takes it the wrong way. I tell you, Stevie, I sometimes wonder why I bothered to come home at all. They seem to have managed better without me.'

261

'Oh no! Heather was always saying how good it would be when you came home. And the children too, they were always talking about their dad. They're all very proud of you, Ian.'

'Maybe they were – *then*,' he said. 'But I don't think they're so keen now I'm home. I reckon young Roger would be pleased enough if I went away again.'

'He's at a tricky age, that's all. It'll blow over.'

'I wish I could be as sure as you are.' He stopped and laid a hand on her arm. 'I'm not sure I even want it to blow over. I'm disappointed in that boy, Stevie. To tell you the truth, I'm disappointed in all of them – all except Pat.'

'Ian, I'm so sorry,' she said softly.

They stood together for a moment. The big, yellow globe of the moon went behind a cloud and there was an instant of darkness. Ian bent towards her and then the cloud passed and she moved away.

'Mrs Clutter will be wanting to go to bed,' she said in the same quiet tone.

'You've got a key, haven't you?'

'Yes, but I promised I'd be back in time to tell her about the Harvest Supper. It's the first one she's ever missed, but with her bad back she didn't think she could manage to sit on those hard forms. Take me home, Ian.'

He sighed, and they walked on. Nothing more was said about Heather and the children, but as they stopped at the cottage gate he put his hands on her arms again and looked down at her.

'I don't know what I'd have done these past weeks without you, Stevie. You're the only one I can talk to – the only one who understands.'

Stevie looked up at his face. She could see the gleam of his eyes in the moonlight, the taut lines of his face. She felt very, very sorry for him, and very aware of his closeness.

262

For a moment, she could not breathe. Then she put her hand on the gate and unfastened the latch.

'Goodnight, Ian,' she murmured, and went through and up the path to the cottage door.

Chapter Twenty-Five

The date of Ruth and Dan's wedding was coming closer. Dan was now working with Solly Barlow, turning his skills to those of the blacksmith's trade. Solly had always done a variety of jobs and had a workshop for wood as well as metal, making gates and hurdles at the same time as shoeing horses and fashioning anything you wanted in iron and steel. He showed Dan sketches of the garden ornaments he used to make before the war – rose arches and arbours, obelisks for plants to climb up, even pergolas. 'Folk'll be wanting these again in time,' he said. 'Get their gardens back in order, stop growing all those dig for victory veg. They'll be looking to prettify them up again.'

'I can do those,' Dan said, studying the sketches. 'I trained in wrought iron and I haven't forgotten how to do it. It'll make a nice change from ships.'

He lodged with Solly and had his evening meals with Ruth and Sammy, cycling through the lanes and revelling in the autumn colour of the trees. You never saw this in Pompey, except in the parks. You just didn't realise that in October the woods and indeed the whole of the New Forest would look as if it were in flames, the leaves a blaze of bronze and golden glory against the blue sky. He'd seen real flames in plenty during the Blitz, but this was different; this lifted your heart and reminded you what life was all about, what really mattered. You wondered how people could bomb and shoot and smash each other when the world was as glorious as this.

Dan gave up trying to make it out. It had happened, and

millions were dead because of it, but what you had to do now was get on with the peace. Dan's world was small and very different from what it had been before the war, and he supposed that that must apply to a lot of other people too. They all had to sort out their own little corners, rescue what was left and put it together again.

He seemed to have come a long way from enjoying the autumn colours, he reflected, wheeling his bike into Ruth's front garden and leaning it on the fence. He'd never had these deep thoughts before, not when he was in Pompey working down the Camber all the hours God sent and then firewatching in the evenings. He didn't have time to think then, and the streets and buildings and the noise of traffic and the racket in the workshops and ships' engine-rooms didn't give you the space, somehow. You needed peace and quiet and natural things to let your mind flow and bring all these thoughts to your mind. Dan did, anyway.

He went indoors to find Ruth making curtains. Her treadle sewing-machine, which stood in a corner of the living room, was draped in material and she was working away at it, her feet going like little pistons and the wheel whizzing round. She looked up and smiled as Dan came in.

'I've been to Southampton,' she told him. 'Look at this lovely material – I thought it'd do for our bedroom. Those curtains have been up for donkey's years, they're nearly falling apart.'

'It's pretty.' Dan touched the fabric. It was thick and strong, and the colours were those he had been enjoying as he cycled along the lanes – brown and gold, with touches of dark red. 'Nice for winter. Nice and warm.'

'That's what I thought.' She smiled at him and lifted her face for a kiss. 'I might be able to get some lighter stuff for summer next year. Depends on the rationing, of course. I was lucky to get this. I'll just finish this seam, and then I'll clear away and get supper. It's shepherd's pie. There's

265

some tea in the pot, I only made it ten minutes ago, if you don't mind pouring yourself a cup.'

'Smashing.' Dan did as she said. 'You got a cup?'

'I've had one. I'll have another one when I've done this. Sammy's just popped over to Roger Knight's to get something he needs for his homework. A protractor or something.' She concentrated on her work for a moment, then eased the material away from the sewing-machine and broke off the thread. She folded the new curtain and laid it on top of the one she had already made. 'There, that's finished. I'm a bit worried about the Knights, Dan. Heather looked proper miserable at the Harvest Supper – and did you see the way Roger dashed out? Ian's face was like thunder. There's something wrong there, if I'm not much mistaken.'

'Well, it's none of our business,' Dan said, sitting down in the armchair. He didn't know the Knight family well, though he liked young Roger all right and thought he made a good friend for Sam. 'It's hard for a bloke to come home and find everyone's managed without him. Solly says young Mrs Knight's made a good job of the farm. His nose is probably a bit out of joint, that's all.'

'You mean he'd rather have come back and found the place in a mess?'

'Not a mess, perhaps, but I dare say he'd have liked something to get his teeth into. As it is, it don't seem as if there's all that much for him to do.'

'There must be plenty of work with the Land Girls all going back – except for that yellow-haired one. I don't really know why she's stopping on so long.'

'Perhaps she's got her eye on the main chance,' Dan suggested, drinking his tea. 'Thinks if things go wrong she might step into Heather's shoes. They seemed to be getting on pretty well at the Supper.'

'Oh Dan, I hope not!' Ruth gazed at him in consternation over an armful of gold and brown material. 'That would be awful. But I must admit, the thought did cross my mind as well. And I don't suppose we're the only ones. You know what villages are like.'

It didn't seem to Dan that they were all that different from little groups of city streets. April Grove, March Street and October Street, with September running along the top, had been a bit like a village. Everyone knew everyone else, and everyone knew everyone else's business, and what they didn't know they made up. He could remember when he himself had been the subject of gossip and almost accused to his face of knocking his wife about.

'Maybe we're reading more into it than we should,' he said. 'Nobody knows what really goes on in someone else's life. I like the Knights – the old couple are good folk, and the young ones are just having a bit of trouble settling down. I expect it's the same for a lot of others. Take your Lizzie – she and Alec didn't seem to be getting on too well to start with, and now look at them, with a baby coming and all. Happy as sandboys, the pair of 'em.'

Ruth looked at him thoughtfully. She had kept her promise to Lizzie and not told even Dan the truth about the baby, and she'd been surprised and delighted when Lizzie had told her that Alec had decided to accept it as his own. There was no need ever to tell Dan, although she didn't like keeping secrets from him and had already made up her mind that this would be the only one. I just hope Alec and Lizzie go on being happy, she thought.

Roger had taken Sammy up to his bedroom to find the protractor. It was a small room over the porch of the farmhouse, with a big oak beam in the ceiling and uneven walls. Roger said it was in the oldest part of the house.

'Do you mean the house was built at all different times?' Sammy asked. 'I thought houses were built all in one go.'

'It was, to start with. It was just the middle bit, see – the front door, where you come in, and this room which is over

267

that, and the rooms at the back. But all the bits on the other side were added later on. You can see they're different by looking at the walls. Grandad says the old bit goes back nearly three hundred years. The new bits are only a hundred years or so old.'

Sammy blinked. A hundred years still seemed quite old to him. But it explained the odd shape of the house, with rooms at the end of short passages or leading out of each other. It was the sort of rambling house you read about in Enid Blyton books, where children went for holidays and had adventures. He could see that the Knights' farmhouse would be ideal for adventures.

'I think it's smashing,' he said, putting the protractor in his pocket. 'You're lucky to live in a big house like this.'

Roger shrugged. 'It's all right, I suppose. I'd rather have a cottage like yours. It's cosier. That's what I'll have when I'm grown up.'

Sammy stared at him. 'But you'll live here, won't you? You'll have to work on the farm.'

'What, with my dad?' Roger gave a short, bitter laugh. 'Not on your life! I'm going to get away. I might go to sea like Alec Travers, or maybe be a pilot like Ben Warren. Anything. I'm not stopping here, that's all I know.'

Sammy felt uncomfortable. Roger had talked like this before but he'd thought it was just a squabble that would blow over. But as he looked at his friend's face now, dark and scowling, he could see that it was more than that. Doubtfully, he said, 'I didn't used to like my dad much but we get on all right now.'

'Your dad didn't go away for years and then come back expecting everything to be done his way. He's always been around.'

Sammy thought of the times after his mother had died, when Dan had had to go to sea for two or three days, leaving him to fend for himself. He remembered how he'd tried to cook his meals – putting a whole egg into the frying pan and getting spattered all over with hot fat and bits of shell, or trying to cook potatoes with no water in the saucepan – and how he'd gone down to the Anderson shelter all by himself when the siren went and sat there on his own in the dark, petrified with fear as he heard bombs dropping all over Portsmouth. If it hadn't been for Mr and Mrs Vickers telling Dan he was being neglected and then getting the Authorities in to have him evacuated, he didn't know what might have happened. I'd have set the place on fire and burned to death, he thought. That's what I'd have done.

Dan hadn't been around much then, and when he had been home Sammy had crept about the place like a shadow. Even after he'd started to come out to the country to see how Sammy was getting on at Bridge End, it had taken a long time for them to get to know each other.

'Yes, but your dad couldn't help going away,' he said to Roger. 'He had to fight for his country, and he got all those medals. I think you ought to be proud of him.'

Roger shrugged and opened that week's *Wizard*. 'There's a good story in here,' he said. 'It's all about a boy who joins the Commandos and goes to France and helps sabotage German bases and things. I wish I could do something like that, then I could get medals too. I wish the war wasn't over. If it had kept going for another two or three years I could've joined up and been in the Commandos.'

'You still wouldn't have been old enough,' Sammy said, adding up dates in his head.

'I'd have lied about my age. That's what this boy did. If you're tall enough, they believe you. And once you're there they can't send you back, specially if you're good at sabotage.' He threw the comic down on the bed. 'I wish they'd kept it going a few more years. It's spoiled everything, having peace come.'

Sammy still felt doubtful, but he didn't want to lose

Roger's friendship by arguing with him. He borrowed the comic and walked home, thinking that perhaps a small cottage was better than a big, rambling farmhouse after all. At least he and Dad and Auntie Ruth were going to be a proper family soon.

As he walked past the end of the lane leading to the Warrens' farm, he saw Lizzie and Alec strolling home, their arms around each other's waists. Lizzie didn't have so much of a waist now, he observed. That was because she was going to have a baby. Sammy had lived long enough in the country and seen enough calves and lambs being born to know about what people called 'the facts of life'.

He opened the back door of the cottage and found his father and Ruth waiting for him. The shepherd's pie was steaming in its brown dish on the table, its aroma wafting to meet him as he came in.

'There you are, Sammy,' Ruth said, getting plates from the rack above the range where they'd been keeping warm. 'Wash your hands now, and sit down. It's all ready.'

Sammy did as he was told. He watched as Ruth helped him to a hearty pile of meat and mashed potato. He returned his father's grin and felt warm all over.

'I'm glad I live here,' he said, picking up his knife and fork. 'I'm glad I live in a cottage.'

The atmosphere at the Knights' farm was uneasy. Somehow, without the family realising it, they seemed to have drawn up sides. Heather, Roger and Teddy were on one side with Ian and Pat on the other. Arthur and Emily had tried hard to stay out of it, but you couldn't live in the house and not get dragged in, and when they talked about it in their bedroom they found that Emily supported Heather while Arthur, who had been so appreciative of her work on the farm while Ian had been away, now had more sympathy for his son.

'I know she's done well, I've always said that. But it's a

man's place to be in charge when all's said and done, and it was understood from the first that it was only for the duration. Tell him what's been going on, show him the changes we had to make, that's fair enough, but after that she's got to be satisfied to take a back seat. There's enough for her to do, what with the cooking and work in the house and the children to look after. Best thing of all would be for her to have another kiddy – that'd take her mind off the farm, and it'd stop young Teddy from getting spoiled too.'

'I don't mind doing the indoors work,' Emily said. 'I've got young Callie Dewar to help, and Heather does a lot, you've got to admit that.'

'Yes, and it's too much,' Arthur said. 'Look at her, up at five and working all hours. She's dog-tired by evening and she don't need to do it *all*, that's what I'm saying. It's as if she can't bring herself to give up the farm, and it's *Ian's* job now he's home. She's taking away all his self-respect.'

Emily sighed. 'Well, they've got to sort it out for themselves. It's no use us sticking our five eggs in. It's young Roger I'm most worried about. Trailing around the place looking as if he's lost a shilling and found sixpence. And the way he looks at his father! I don't like to say it, but you'd think he *hated* him.'

'He'll get over it. I'm sorry for our Ian, though. He must've been really looking forward to coming home and getting on with the farm with his wife glad to take her rightful place in the house, and instead he seems to be at loggerheads with half the family. You can't blame him for feeling fed up.'

'I don't blame him, not really. I don't blame Heather either. She's done her best and she feels he doesn't appreciate her. I just hope neither of them does anything silly.'

Arthur stared at her. 'What – like old Bob Hammond over Ashwood? But he was going bust, everyone knew that. It's a different thing altogether.'

Emily shook her head impatiently. 'I don't mean anything like that! It's just – well, I'd be happier if young Stevie was off the place. I've seen them a time or two, her and Ian, and they're getting on a bit too well. I know she's Heather's friend and I don't think she'd do anything wrong for a moment, but – well, when people aren't too happy at home they sometimes look elsewhere for a bit of comfort, that's all.' She folded her lips. 'I'll not say any more. I shouldn't have said that much. We'll just have to hope they come to their senses soon, the lot of them!'

Stevie too was feeling uneasy about the relationship between herself and Ian. She had been on the farm for almost five years now; she had known Ian before he went away, but she had been Heather's friend during those years and had worked with her while Heather was pregnant with Teddy. They had become very close then, and Stevie had been proud to be asked to be Teddy's godmother. She had offered to stay on at the farm until all the men were home and she wasn't needed any more, but in truth she didn't want to go back to the city at all.

'I'd like to be a farmer's wife, like you,' she'd told Heather. 'I like it out here in the country. I like waking up in the morning and hearing the dawn chorus. I like being out in the fields in the sun and the wind. I like the lanes and the woods. I like the animals and I like the whole idea of producing food for people to eat. I mean, there can't be any more important work than that, can there!'

'And d'you like getting up at five in the morning when it's dark and cold and the rain's pouring down?' Heather asked slyly. 'Or the snow's a foot deep? And the mud everywhere, and having to tramp backwards and forwards across the fields with the horses when you're ploughing and harrowing? And hardly ever being able to go to the pictures or a dance, unless it's a hop at the village hall? And having no big shops for miles?'

Stevie laughed. 'Yes! I even like those things. Not *quite* as much, perhaps, but they're all part of it so I have to like them too. Honestly, Heather, I don't want to go back to the town. I'd rather stay here. But I can't see how I can do that unless I find some nice young farmer to marry me!'

Heather looked at her friend's blonde hair and blue eyes, at the skin that somehow hadn't become weatherbeaten but had retained its smooth, pearly glow, and thought that Stevie should be able to find a husband easily. Yet in all the time the Land Girl had been at Bridge End, she hadn't even had a serious boyfriend. Of course, apart from the Americans there hadn't been all that many young men around, and even now, when they were coming back, there wouldn't exactly be a crowd. Bridge End was only a small village and most of those returning from the Services were labourers rather than farmers. Stevie deserved something better than life in a tiny farm cottage.

Stevie, too, knew that her chances of finding a farmer to marry her were slim. One day soon she was going to have to make a decision about her future. There would be no job for her at the farm once all the men were home, and she wouldn't find work on any other farm either. She probably wouldn't even have anywhere to live. Mrs Clutter was getting old and although she'd taken several girls in while the war had been on, and welcomed Stevie's company now, she wouldn't want to go on cooking for a lodger much longer. Her legs were getting very bad and one day soon, Stevie thought, she wouldn't be able to get about at all. Her daughter was already talking about having her over to live with her.

There would be no place for Stevie in the country. She would have to go back to the town, but the idea filled her with misery. I'll feel trapped back there, she thought.

She told Ian this as they carried out the morning milking together. She felt sorry for him, understanding that he was finding it difficult to adjust to life at home, just as she would find it difficult to return to life in the town. The difference was that Ian *wanted* to be here, but she could still appreciate the problems.

'It must be hard to go back anywhere,' she said thoughtfully. It was warm in the milking shed, the big bodies of the cows steaming as they stood in their stalls. Stevie particularly liked morning milking, when everyone else was still in bed and she and Ian had the world to themselves. When they went into the shed it was still dark and nothing was stirring; when they came out the farmyard was light and the kitchen full of bustle, with the smell of bacon and eggs and fried bread. She knew Heather felt the same about the morning milking, and she was a little uncomfortable about sharing this time with Ian, when Heather would have liked to be doing it, but this was one argument Ian had won. 'You've got the children to get ready for school,' he'd stated, 'and there's Teddy too. It's time Mum was able to take it a bit easier of a morning.' And Heather had had to give in.

'He's right, I know,' she'd said privately to Stevie. 'And it's not just that – I'm afraid he might say we don't need *you* any more. I don't want to see you go, any more than you want to leave!'

Ian finished with Buttercup and moved on to Primrose, on the opposite side of the long shed. All the cows had flower names – Daisy, Clover, Teasel, Hyacinth, Angelica – and each had its own personality. You got to know them when you worked with them every day, Stevie thought, laying her head against Bluebell's warm, damp flank and beginning to squeeze the rubbery teats. Milk frothed into the bucket, thick and creamy, and she thought how different proper milk, straight from the cow, was from the milk that came to city doorsteps in bottles with cardboard discs stuck into their necks. I really don't want to go away from here, she thought, and felt tears come to her eyes.

Ian had heard what she'd said about the difficulties of

'going back' but he didn't answer at once. Then, as he settled himself at Primrose's side, he said, 'It depends on the people you go back to. If they want you, it must be easy.'

Stevie turned her head. He was only a few yards away across the shed, concentrating on what he was doing. 'That's all right, then,' she said. 'Everyone wants you back.'

'Do they?'

'Ian! Of course they do. I keep telling you, they never stopped talking about how good it would be when you came home.'

'Yes, but that was before.' Primrose shifted her back foot and he grabbed the bucket to stop it falling over. 'Keep still, you daft creature! It's different now I'm here.'

'That's just what I was saying,' Stevie said firmly. 'It's not easy to go back anywhere. It's always different from what you expect. But that doesn't mean they don't *want* you. It just means – well, it's different, that's all, and everyone has to get used to it.'

'I tell you what,' Ian said after a pause, 'it would've been a lot easier if everyone had been as welcoming as you.'

There was a silence in the milking shed. Stevie laid her face against the cow's flank and squeezed the teats, staring at the froth of milk. At last she said, 'Perhaps it was easier for me. I'm not one of your family.'

'And why should that make it easier? They're the ones who ought to find it easy, if they've been looking forward to it as much as you say.' He got up, taking the bucket of milk to tip into one of the metal churns that stood in a row by the door. On his way back, he paused beside her. 'You and Pat are the only ones who've made me feel it was worth while coming back,' he said quietly. 'All the rest make me feel as if I'm in the way. But you – you've always got a smile. And you listen to me. You understand what it's like.'

Stevie stared up at him. Her heart was beating fast. She looked at his strong body, his square, handsome face with the straight dark eyebrows, and the black hair damp on his forehead. She met his eyes, eyes so dark that they looked almost black, and felt a shiver ripple across her skin.

'It's because I'm away from home too,' she said at last. 'And I don't have children to think about as well. It's not easy for Heather either. She's had all this responsibility, and now—'

'And now I can take it off her shoulders. But she won't let me! She wants to go on running the farm herself. She doesn't *want* me here, Stevie. Oh, she made a good show of being pleased when I came home, and I really believed everything was going to be just as it used to be. But as soon as I started wanting to take over . . .' He looked at her again. 'You aren't like that. You don't keep telling me what to do and how to do it.'

'But it's not my place to do that, is it? I'm just a farm labourer. Heather's your wife. She's been looking after things – she's been in charge.'

'And she's not in charge now – that's the problem. You and me, Stevie, we work well together. But when Heather's around she just has to keep on: *this is the way we do it now, this is what we've been doing.* I'm fed up with it, Stevie, I really am.' He went back to Primrose and settled himself once more on his stool. 'And Roger's no help. Honestly, if that boy doesn't mend his ways soon I'll – well, he'll be sorry, that's all.'

Stevie squeezed the last few drops of milk from Bluebell's udder and carried the bucket along the shed. As she tipped the milk into the churn her thoughts seemed to be frothing and bubbling as much as the warm, creamy liquid she had just drawn from the cow. I shouldn't have started this conversation, she reproached herself. But it seemed just lately as if every conversation she had with Ian ended up this way. He really is upset, she thought – but so is Heather. So is the whole family.

'I'm sure it'll be all right,' she said, taking her stool to

Crocus, always the last to be milked. 'They're just finding it difficult, that's all. Everyone is. We've had six years of war and now suddenly we've got peace, and it's not what we expected. It *can't* be like it was before, can it? Things *aren't* the same. There's so much to be put right. There's so much to *do*. It's going to be years before we get the bombed buildings rebuilt. Years before we get everything working properly again – and even then it'll all be different. It must be just the same with people. We've *had* to change – we couldn't help it. We've got to learn about each other again.' She set the bucket in the right place beneath the cow and felt for the teats. 'It doesn't mean we don't still love people as we did before,' she said in a low voice.

Ian said nothing for a moment. He finished Primrose and stood up, the bucket in his hand. But instead of taking it to the churns, he came over and stood beside Stevie.

'Perhaps not,' he said. 'But it doesn't mean we *do* still love each other, either. Sometimes people change more than you expect. Sometimes you find you've changed yourself. Sometimes,' he said, even more quietly, 'you find you love somebody else.'

Chapter Twenty-Six

Although Lizzie's baby was due in February, she and Alec had told everyone that it would be born sometime in March. A month early wasn't so unusual, after all. Only Ruth was aware of the real situation, and she realised that it was a lie that had to be told. She didn't like it, all the same. Once you've told one lie, she thought, it leads to others, but in this case, the truth would only hurt a lot more people. However Alec, who was the most important person involved, knew the truth, so maybe it didn't matter too much about the rest.

Except for Alec's parents, who would be welcoming a grandchild that wasn't really theirs, and Jane and George, who didn't know what their daughter had done. And the baby itself, who would grow up believing in a father who was really no relation at all.

Did it matter? So long as the love was there, so long as Alec could accept the child and treat it as his own, did it matter?

Ruth didn't know. She tried not to think about it, but she still had the uneasy feeling that a lie told was a lie that might be found out. And it was always worse then than if the truth had been told in the first place.

October drew to a close. The trees erupted in a final explosion of volcanic colour and then shed their leaves in a sudden storm, spreading a carpet of shimmering auburn over the ground. The children shuffled to school along the lanes, kicking up the scraps of colour before they were swept to one side and gathered up by old Jonas, the roadsweeper. The men started to build a bonfire on the village green, ready for Guy Fawkes Night. There was even talk of a few fireworks, the first for six years.

'We haven't had a bonfire in all that time,' Ruth said, 'and now we've got three in a few months! I'm glad this one hasn't been forgotten, though.'

'We'll get all the traditions back,' Jane told her. 'It's part of getting back to normal. It takes more than a few Germans to stop us having a party!'

She was feeling particularly excited because she'd had a letter that morning. It was in her pocket now and she was dying to tell Ruth about it, but she'd been sworn to secrecy. It wouldn't be too long before everyone would know, she thought, hugging the knowledge to herself, and what a lovely surprise it would be. Especially for Lizzie.

Ruth was busy altering a suit for her wedding. Clothes were still rationed and she couldn't afford the coupons for a new frock, so she'd taken her dark red costume out of the wardrobe and considered how to make it look a bit more dressy. Emily Knight had given her a black fur collar, taken from a coat she'd had for years, which she had decided to trim and attach to the lapels, and there was enough left over for a narrow band around the cuffs. It looked really smart, she thought. And she could wear her mother's jet brooch on one shoulder, which would pick up the colour, and the little black hat with a tiny veil. It was suitable for a winter wedding, especially as she was a widow. And since she wasn't wearing white, she wouldn't be having any brides-maids, so there was no need to worry about that.

Sammy had a new blazer and grey flannel shorts. He'd begged for long trousers and Ruth had been almost inclined to give in, but Dan had been against it. 'Fourteen's soon enough to go into long trousers,' he said. 'If he has them now, he'll have grown out of them by then and they'll never be used again. It's just a waste.'

It was Dan who most needed new clothes. Not having

been in the Services, he didn't have a demob suit and as far as Ruth could make out, he'd never actually had a suit at all. All he seemed to have was working clothes, and a pair of grey trousers and an old sports jacket for best. 'I never realised it all this time,' she said. 'What with you coming out here on your bike, you never needed anything smart, but I thought you might have something at home.'

'We never had nothing at home,' he said. 'I thought you knew that.'

Ruth had known really, but she still hadn't quite realised the depth of poverty in which Dan and his family had lived. There had been four of them living on his wage which, before the war, had been poor money, and Nora's medical treatment had cost a lot. Since she had died and Gordon went into the Army, money hadn't been quite so tight, but it had never occurred to Dan to spend his overtime money on clothes for himself. Now, looking at his scanty wardrobe, he felt ashamed. Ruth deserves better than this, he thought, and counted out his coupons to go into Southampton to get himself fitted out.

'I dunno when I'll ever wear a suit again,' he complained to George Warren. 'I reckon a decent sports jacket and a pair of good trousers'd make more sense. But I know Ruth'll look like a queen, and I can't let her down, can I?'

'You could borrow my suit,' George suggested. 'I wore it for our Lizzie's wedding and it's only been out a few times since then – Joe Sellers's funeral was the last time. Come and try it on.'

'And what will you wear if I do? You're giving her away!' The two men looked at each other and shrugged. It looked as if Dan would have to buy a suit. They went to Southampton together with Jane and stared in a depressed sort of way at the few suits that were available. In the end, Jane hit on the solution.

'Look, there's a Moss Bros. over the road. Why don't you hire something?'

'It's all posh stuff,' Dan began, but she dragged him across the street and through the door before he could finish. A pale, slender floorwalker approached them, looking down his nose at Dan's old trousers and sports jacket. Reluctantly, he produced a few dark suits and they looked at them carefully.

'This one looks as if it would fit,' Jane said, picking out the biggest. 'Try it on, Dan.'

Dan threw her a hunted look and disappeared into the changing-room. After about ten minutes, during which Jane and George stood silent under the floorwalker's disdainful gaze, he reappeared. They stared at him.

'Well!' Jane said at last. 'What a difference! You look really smart, Dan.'

'Just the ticket,' George nodded. 'I reckon Jane's hit on the answer.'

Dan looked down at his sleeves and then glanced self-consciously into a tall mirror. 'I dunno. It seems a bit daft, paying money to borrow clothes.'

'Not if you're never going to wear it again. And it'll save on clothing coupons. You'll be able to give them to Ruth to buy a nice new frock for her trousseau,' Jane said cunningly.

'That's an idea,' Dan agreed. He looked at the floor-walker. 'All right. I'll have this one. You can have it ready for the Friday before Christmas.'

'Not until then? I don't know if we can—'

'Nobody else has put in an order for it then, have they?'

'No,' the man admitted. 'But someone might want—'

'Well, you can tell 'em they should have come in sooner. First come, first served.'

'I'll need a deposit,' the assistant said, looking as if he thought Dan wouldn't be able to afford it. 'And I'll need to take your name.'

But Dan had regained his self-confidence. He moved closer to the pale young man, looming over him. 'Hodges is the name and I'll pay you a deposit if you want it, but I want that suit for my wedding. I'm marrying the best woman in the world – begging your pardon, Jane – and I want to look me best for her. So make sure it's here ready for me, all right?'

'Yes, sir.' The floorwalker looked up at Dan, impressive in his dark suit, and decided not to argue. 'You can rely on me, sir.'

'I'd better be able to.' Dan went into the little cubicle to change back into his own clothes, then handed over the money required for the deposit and marched out of the shop, followed by Jane and George. Outside, they stopped and grinned at each other.

'I must say, you soon set him right,' George declared. 'He was all ready to take a high hand till he saw you in the suit. You looked like the Lord Mayor himself!'

'I wasn't having a little pipsqueak like him treating me like dirt,' Dan snorted. 'What's *he* been doing for the past six years, I'd like to know? Mincing about in a gents' outfitters, asking "which side Sir dresses"! I'll give him "someone else might want it" – as if I didn't have any rights at all! I mean to say, some of us have been through two world wars so that he could walk about and look down his nose.'

Jane giggled. 'And I'm sure he's very grateful. Now, what about getting a cup of tea? There's a Cadena café down the street and they always have nice toasted teacakes there.'

The men tagged along. When you went shopping with a woman, you were under her orders. But when they finally returned home, festooned with shopping bags, they had to admit that Jane was a good woman to go shopping with. She knew what she wanted and where to get it, and she didn't hang about staring in windows at stuff she couldn't afford – not that there was much of that in Southampton's shop windows at the moment. Things were as short as ever, and it didn't look as if Christmas was going to be any more lavish just because hostilities had come to an end.

'It'll take a long time before things are back to normal,' Jane sighed as they sat in the bus with their purchases on their knees.

There was still plenty to look forward to, though. Not only Christmas, but the wedding and then Lizzie's baby – and there was still that letter she'd received, with the news she was keeping secret. A nice surprise for the whole family, she thought, and smiled to herself.

Lizzie and Alec were coming to terms with their new life. The joy and relief of their reconciliation had calmed down now and they were beginning to think more seriously about their future. There were still times when Alec's depression returned and Lizzie could see that it wasn't going to be all roses. And he still hadn't been able to make love to her.

'I'm sorry, Lizzie,' he groaned, lying back on his pillow and staring at the ceiling. 'I want to love you so much it hurts – but nothing happens. I'm useless!'

'You're not!' Lizzie was just as disappointed, but knew she must overcome her own feelings to comfort him. 'You're *not* useless, and it'll be all right one day, I know it will. We've just got to be patient.' She moved closer and slipped her arms around him. 'Maybe we should stop trying so hard. Just cuddle instead. Come on, love. It's nice just to be here together after all those years apart. Let's just be content with that.'

He put his arm round her but she knew he wasn't content. How could he be? A man wanted to be able to make love to his wife. If he couldn't, he didn't feel like a man. And he wanted to be able to father his own children, too.

'Do you think it's because of the baby?' she whispered a little fearfully. 'Is that what's putting you off?'

'No. I was like this before I knew about the baby, you know that.'

'It can't help, though.' Lizzie was frightening herself, talking like this. She was still afraid that Alec would revert to his original anger and hurt about her betrayal; if he did, she was sure that would be the end of their marriage. But she had to keep probing, like putting her tongue into a tooth after the dentist had attended to it, to make sure it really was better.

Alec rolled over and put both his arms around her, holding her close. 'Lizzie, stop it! It's *not* the baby. I've got over that, I have really. I'm going to be its father – I'm here now, I'll be here when it's born, I'll be here when it's growing up. It's going to be our baby. And at least no one else will ever have to know what a useless bloke I am.'

'Alec!' She pulled herself out of his arms and sat up, looking down at him. The moon was half full, shining a faint light through the curtains. 'Now you listen to me.' She spoke slowly, almost spelling the words out. 'You are *not* useless. You're my Alec, my husband, the man I love. You've had a horrible time and you're not properly over it yet. That's all it is. Everything will come back. All we have to do is be patient – and I still think we shouldn't try so hard.' She lay down against him again. 'Just forget about it, and let's enjoy being together again. That's the only thing that really matters.'

'Yes.' He held her close, his hands moving slowly over her body in a tender caress. 'Yes, that's what really matters.' She felt his lips against her hair. 'Let's go to sleep now, Lizzie. Let's just go to sleep . . .'

It wasn't just their lovemaking that they had to think about. Both knew that they couldn't live for ever at the farm, helping out with the work but not really earning a living. And although Jane and George insisted that there was a home for them for as long as they needed it, both Lizzie and Alec wanted a place of their own. Before the war, with Alec away at sea, it hadn't seemed so urgent, but that was six years ago. It was time they had their own home – especially with a baby on the way – but before they could do anything about that, Alec needed a job. And if he were not to work on the farm, the cottage George had offered them would be needed for someone else.

Alec was still adamant that he could never go back to sea. 'It's not just the memories, I don't want to leave you again for months at a time. But I don't know what I could do out here. I don't mind helping out on the farm, but it's not the sort of work I'm good at. I'm an engineer, Lizzie. That's what I'm trained for.'

'So it's the shipyard?' she said doubtfully. 'You want to go back to Southampton?'

He looked at her. 'What do you think about it? I know you're not keen to live in town.'

'I'm not keen for you to have to travel in and out on the bus either,' she said. 'You'd be working a long enough day without that. And we'd still have to find somewhere to live here. There's not that many places in Bridge End.'

'I don't want to move in with my mum and dad,' Alec said. 'They've only got the one spare bedroom. It wouldn't be fair on any of us. What would be nice is one of those new Phoenix houses – the prefabs. But I expect they'll be given to people who are already living in Southampton. We'd probably have to start off in rooms and go on a waiting list.'

'Well, plenty of people have to do that. The main thing is to be together. Anyway, we need to know you can get a job first. You'd better go and see about that.'

Alec went into Southampton the next day. With the great liners coming back into commission after their time as troopships there would be plenty of work for qualified engineers and he came back with a beaming face and the news that he was to start work the following Monday. 'I'll be starting a bit lower down the ladder, but I can soon work my way up. The main thing is, I'll be bringing home a wage again.'

'And I hope you'll stop here till the spring at least,' Jane said when she heard the news. 'I know you want to get your own place, but why not stay until the baby's born? The weather'll be better then and Lizzie'll be more up to it. I don't like the idea of you in rooms in a strange place as things are now.'

'I don't want Alec doing that bus journey—' Lizzie began, but he put his hand on her arm to stop her.

'I don't mind. Your mum's right – you're better off here for the time being. There's no sense in you sitting in a room all through the winter with nothing to do all day, and suppose something happens? The baby might come early – anything. You'd have nobody to turn to. I'd be happier if you were here.'

'All right,' she said, feeling secretly relieved. 'Just until the baby's born, then.' She gave her mother a severe look. 'And no saying why don't we stop till it's six months old – or crawling – or walking, all right?'

'Or going to school, or out at work,' Alec added with a grin. 'We know what you're up to!'

'I'm not up to anything,' Jane protested. 'I can't say I want you to leave Bridge End but I can see you've got to go where the work is. It's not as if Lizzie herself has been at home all these years, after all. We got used to her being away when she was nursing. Just as long as I can keep an eye on her until the kiddy's born, that's all.'

They smiled at each other. It'll be born earlier than she expects, Lizzie thought, so it's just as well I'll be at home. She'll be all the more concerned when she thinks it's early.

It would probably be a bit big for a 'premature' baby, and she hoped that Jane's suspicions wouldn't be aroused. She hoped too that it wouldn't look too much like Floyd! But Floyd had been away for long enough now for the family not to make any connection with him. And so long as he didn't come back, it was unlikely that anyone would notice any resemblance there might be.

There was no reason for Floyd to come back. He was safely out of the way in Germany. He wrote occasionally, but that was all. He would probably never come back to Bridge End.

Chapter Twenty-Seven

Guy Fawkes Night was wet, the bonfire refused to light and the fireworks turned out to be literal damp squibs, but the determination of the villagers to enjoy it whatever happened turned it into a jolly affair anyway, with lots of laughter whenever something went wrong. And at least nobody had got hurt, George remarked as they walked home, and none of the cottages caught fire!

'There's a dark cloud to every silver lining, Dad,' Lizzie teased him. 'You always manage to see the black side, don't you! He was just the same when we were little,' she said to Alec. 'If we fell in the stream he'd say at least we hadn't been drowned, and if we fell out of a tree he'd say we should be grateful we hadn't broken our necks.'

'I wouldn't say that was looking on the black side,' George protested, but they all laughed at him and went indoors for a cup of cocoa to drive away the chill of the evening.

The Knights had been at the bonfire too, but their walk home was more silent. Roger was sulking because his father hadn't allowed him to light a rocket and he blamed Ian because it hadn't gone off. Ian, whose feelings were steadily mounting inside, like a pan of water coming to boiling point, was annoyed because Heather had argued with him over one of the cows, who wasn't giving so much milk as usual, and Pat was dragging her feet because her father had pushed her away when she was pretending to be frightened by a jumping jack that one of the boys had thrown at her. Ian was beginning to feel irritated by his daughter's clinging and ashamed of his irritation, which increased his annoyance, and Heather was just generally miserable about the atmosphere which was spoiling the family's life.

Arthur and Emily hadn't gone to the bonfire. Arthur said standing about on wet grass wouldn't do his arthritis any good, and Emily said she'd rather keep an eye on the potatoes which were baking in their jackets, ready for supper. When the rest of the family trailed indoors, she had a pot of thick beef stew ready to go with the potatoes, and the smell wafted out to greet the family as they opened the door. Teddy was already in bed.

'Oh, that smells lovely,' Heather said, giving her mother-in-law a hug. 'Whatever would we do without you, Mum?'

'Yes,' Ian said, standing on the doormat as he removed his boots and feeling his anger boil over at last, 'that's what *I* often wonder! Because *you* wouldn't be getting our supper and washing our clothes and keeping the house clean and warm and comfortable, would you, Heather? You'd rather be out in the cowsheds looking after the beasts than indoors looking after your family. You'd rather be a farmer than a farmer's wife. You're not a proper woman at all.'

There was a dead silence. Heather turned white. Arthur stared at his son in astonishment and Emily pressed the back of her hand to her mouth. Roger rolled his eyes at the ceiling and crossed the room to his mother's side, and Pat began to cry.

'Perhaps you'd rather I wasn't here then,' Heather said quietly. 'If I'm such a nuisance to you, and no use as a wife, perhaps you'd rather I went right away.'

She put her hand briefly on Roger's shoulder and walked across the kitchen to the staircase door. Emily gave a little cry and reached out, but Heather took no notice. Her back stiff, she opened the door and went through, closing it very quietly behind her. They heard her feet going slowly, almost carefully, up the stairs.

'Oh, Ian,' Emily said at last, her voice breaking. 'Oh, *Ian* – whatever have you done?'

By the middle of the month, the first cold snap had taken hold. There was a frost for three days and then a gathering of clouds. People began to talk about snow, but the clouds hung about for a while as if not quite certain what they were supposed to do, and then drifted away, leaving blue skies again. The ground was hard and dry.

Stevie was aware of the fact that she wouldn't be needed much longer. She was scarcely needed now, but when she mentioned the subject to Ian he shook his head. 'Don't go yet. You don't really want to, do you?'

'You know I don't,' she said. They were walking across Top Field, looking down on the farm and the village. 'I'd like to stay here for ever. But I can't do that, so I have to think of what I am going to do. It's back to Portsmouth for me, I'm afraid, and some sort of office job.'

'You can't do that! You'd hate it, being stuck indoors all day sitting at a desk, typing or pushing bits of paper about.' He stopped and turned to face her. 'You'd just wither away.'

Stevie laughed. 'I don't expect so! It's what I was doing before the war, after all. Anyway, I expect I'll find Mr Right and get married, and then I won't have to work. I can stay at home and be a lady of leisure.'

'I don't think you'd like that either,' he said. They were standing on the edge of the wood and there was a fallen tree nearby. He took her arm and drew her across to it. 'Stevie, don't you ever think that perhaps you've already met Mr Right?'

Stevie sat down on the log. She stared out across the view. The trees were almost bare, the woods no longer a tapestry of crimson and gold but a pencil sketch of branches and twigs. The recently ploughed and furrowed fields were like corduroy, ribbed in brown. A few rooks cawed overhead.

'Why ever should you say that?' she asked at last. 'I haven't even got a boyfriend.'

'You know what I mean.' He put his hands on her shoulders and twisted her to face him. His eyes were very dark. 'Stevie, ever since I came home I—'

'No!' she said forcefully. 'Don't say it, Ian. Don't say *anything*.' She tried to get up but his hands kept her down. 'Ian, *please*.'

'You've got to listen to me,' he cried. 'You've got to! Stevie, don't run away – don't leave me. You know what's happening between us—'

'No! *Nothing's* happening. Ian, stop now, please. Don't say any more. Don't say something you might regret.' Her last words came in a whisper as their eyes met. She turned her face away, but she knew he had seen her expression. 'Ian, please let me go . . . '

'You don't mean that,' he said quietly, with a note of triumph in his voice. 'You know very well what's happening and you can't deny it. Look at me, Stevie,' as she began to protest again, 'Look me in the eye and tell me there's nothing between us. Come on. *Look*.' There was a brief pause. Stevie could feel her heart kicking in her breast. She drew in a deep, ragged breath and stared at the ground. 'There, you see? You can't. You can't do it, because you know I'm right.' Suddenly, before she could draw back, he pulled her roughly against him so that her face was buried against his jacket and she felt his lips moving over her cheeks and neck. 'Oh Stevie, I love you! I love you!'

'No!' she cried, struggling to be free. 'No, Ian, you don't. It's Heather you love. Heather, your wife. You *don't* love me – you can't! You *mustn't*!'

'It's not a case of mustn't, or can't,' he said, still holding her against him. 'I do, and that's all there is to it. We can't help our feelings, Stevie.'

'We can!'

'We can't. They just happen. Look, you know what it's been like for me since I came home. My wife doesn't want me, my son hates me, my little boy's frightened of me – Pat's the only one who cares and she's just a little girl: she'll turn against me the minute I don't give her what she wants – don't think I don't know that. But you – you've been beside me all the time. Whenever I've needed someone to turn to, someone to talk to, you've been there. Of *course* I love you. Didn't you want me to?'

'No,' she said, half in tears. 'No, I didn't want you to. I just wanted to try to make things easier for both of you – you and Heather. What do you think I am? I'm Heather's *friend*. I wouldn't steal her husband.'

'It's not a question of stealing,' he said, 'not when the husband wants it.'

There was a tiny silence. Stevie struggled for words. At last she said, 'Ian, you've got to stop this. You have a family who love you, whatever you might think now, and there's a farm to run. You can't put all that at risk over a silly misunderstanding between you and your wife.'

'It's not a misunderstanding.'

'It is. You're just taking a little while to adjust to being at home, that's all it is, and Heather's taking a little while to adjust to having you here. And the farm—'

'Oh yes, the farm,' he said bitterly. 'You say I've got a farm to run. But Heather's the one who's been running it and it's more her farm now than it is mine. I thought at first she'd be pleased to hand it over, but she won't. She just won't let it go. Do you know how that makes me feel?' he demanded, his voice rising. 'It makes me feel *useless*, that's what! As if there was no point in me coming home at all. I might as well have stayed in the Army.'

'She just wants to work with you.'

'She doesn't. She doesn't want me at all. But *you* do.' He pulled her against him again. '*You* want me, Stevie, I know you do. I've seen it in your eyes. I can hear it in your voice. I can *feel* it.' He ran his hand down her body, from the crown of her head, down her neck and breasts to her thigh.

'*Ian!*' With a tremendous effort she thrust him away from her and leaped to her feet. 'No! Don't touch me.' He came after her and she warded him off with both hands held palm outwards towards him. '*Please* – don't touch me! You mustn't say these things – you mustn't even think them. You've got to think about Heather, your family.' She backed away. 'Leave me alone, Ian. Let me go. Please, please, just let me go!'

Sobbing in earnest now, she turned and ran away from him, careering wildly through the trees, along the narrow, twisting path that led from the ridge and down to the village, away from the Knights' farm. For a few minutes she was afraid that he was following her. Then she realised that the thumping she could hear was the thudding of her own heart, and that her footsteps were the only ones to be heard.

She slowed to a walk and then leaned against a tree, her hand to her side as a stitch almost doubled her up with pain. Tears streamed down her face and she shook and heaved with sobs.

I'll have to leave Bridge End, she thought. I'll have to go away. I can't stay here now.

Oh, Ian. Ian – my love.

It wasn't so easy to leave Bridge End, though. When Stevie returned to the farm next morning Ian was nowhere to be seen. He'd gone to Romsey to see a feed merchant, Heather explained. It had been Stevie's morning off so Heather and Ian had done the milking and Stevie was concerned to see that her friend's eyes were red and swollen, as if she'd been crying.

'What is it?' she asked, dreading the answer. 'You look awful.'

'Thanks.' Heather tried to smile. They were feeding the pigs, carrying buckets of warm mash from the kitchen to the sties where the pigs were standing with their front trotters up on the low walls, screaming for their breakfast. There was no point in even trying to talk until the animals quietened, and the two girls tipped the mash into the troughs and watched as the snouts delved into it. The noise of slurping and gobbling was almost as loud as the screaming, and Heather laughed a little. 'I always think they're so funny. Look, you could swear they were smiling.'

'I like the pigs too,' Stevie agreed. They leaned on the low wall for a moment and then she said quietly, 'It's Ian, isn't it?'

Heather sighed and nodded. Tears came to her eyes. 'Oh Stevie, I don't know what to do. He's so angry and so bitter, and all I've done is try to keep the farm going. I thought I was doing so well—'

'You were. Everyone says so.'

'Sometimes I think it would have been better if I hadn't,' Heather said gloomily. 'Maybe Ian would have been happier if he'd come home to a mess.'

'Oh no! He'd have been really upset to find the farm run down and everything gone wrong.'

'Yes, but he would have been able to put it right, wouldn't he? He'd have been able to take charge and tell people how useless his wife was.'

'Ian wouldn't have said that.'

'Not in so many words, perhaps. But he would have felt that he was the only one who could run it properly. He'd have felt *useful* then. He would have been the big strong man of the family, the hero come back from the war to save the business. Oh, maybe I'm not being fair to him, I know he wouldn't have been pleased to find things in a mess, but it wouldn't have been as bad as it is now.' She pushed herself away from the wall and picked up her bucket. 'If only he realised that all I want is to work *with* him. I want to be his partner. But he just can't see it.'

'It's a lot for a man to get to grips with,' Stevie said. 'Things have changed such a lot since the war started. Perhaps it's not you at all, Heather. Perhaps it's just his reaction to all he's been through in the past six years, and if he hadn't had this to pick on he'd have found something else to blame.'

'Like Roger,' Heather said. 'I feel so sorry for that boy. I know he's behaving badly but he's still just a child, for all he's so tall and strong. It's difficult for him too, but Ian won't make any allowances at all. He just says I've spoiled him and he needs some proper discipline.' Her voice shook and she suddenly dropped the bucket and burst into tears, covering her face with both hands. 'Stevie, I don't know what to do! The way he talks to me now – and looks at me – I think he really *hates* me! It's as if he just can't bear the sight of me. I sometimes think I'll have to go away, right away, where he doesn't have to look at me any more. But where could I go? What could I do?'

Stevie stared at her, appalled. She dropped her own bucket and put both arms round Heather's shoulders, holding her close and murmuring in her ear. 'There, there, I'm sure it'll all come right. It's just a phase, it'll sort itself out. Don't cry, Heather, please don't cry. It'll all be all right. You don't have to go away. I *know* he doesn't want you to go away.'

Guiltily, she wondered if that were true. Ian had made his feelings very clear to her; he wanted Heather to go and Stevie to stay. But that's not what he really wants, she told herself. It's just what he *thinks* he wants, because he's upset and unhappy and maybe even frightened. Because he isn't finding it so easy to run the farm, whatever he says, and he's taking it out on Heather because she's closest and the safest. If she weren't here, he'd be totally lost.

'Oh Stevie,' Heather sobbed, clinging to her, 'I'm so

thankful you've stayed on. You're a good friend – the best friend I've ever had. You won't go away, will you? You'll stay as long as you can?'

'I'll have to go sometime,' Stevie said gently. 'As a matter of fact, I was thinking I ought to go soon, before Christmas. In some ways, you know,' she hesitated, 'it might be better if I did.'

'No!' Heather gripped her arms tightly and stared into her face. 'No! You can't go! You mustn't! I need you here – we all need you. Promise me you won't go, Stevie. *Promise me!*'

Stevie looked at her distraught face. I can't leave her, she thought. I shall just have to cope with it all as best I can, but I can't leave her now. I'm her friend.

But what sort of a friend could she be, feeling as she did about Ian?

Chapter Twenty-Eight

December brought the first flurries of snow. The children greeted it with whoops of glee, remembering the war winters when snow had lain three or four feet deep and drifted to the tops of the hedgerows. Everything looked magically different, shrouded in white. School had been suspended and you had to dig your way out of your own front door to get to the village street. Snowball fights had raged in the fields and once an enormous snowman had been built on the village green. He had frozen solid and stood there long after the rest of the snow had melted, gradually losing his shape until in the end he was just a grotesque lump. By that time even the children were fed up with snow, but they had forgotten that now and remembered only its mystery and its joy.

The adults weren't excited at all. They'd hoped that they wouldn't have to suffer another bitter winter, with all its extra work and hardship, but there was nothing you could do about the weather so they just shrugged their shoulders and got on with it, as they'd done all their lives whether 'it' was weather or war. If you had any sense, you'd done something every day during the summer and autumn to prepare for winter, anyway – mended thick curtains, got in some wood, knitted new gloves out of old jumpers, bottled fruit and made pickles. So by the time December came you were ready, like an armed guard waiting to repel invaders.

Lizzie was beginning to feel her pregnancy. She'd been lucky in the early days, with no sign of morning sickness, but now she seemed to be getting bigger every day and her back ached. She had heartburn and the baby also seemed to be lying against a nerve so that she had sciatica, like toothache all down one leg. When she was up and about she just wanted to lie down, but she couldn't get comfortable in bed either. She sighed and counted the weeks and wished it were all over.

'I'm beginning to wonder if you might be carrying twins,' Jane said, studying her swollen stomach. 'You seem to be getting very big.'

'Maybe I am.' Lizzie knew that she was big because the pregnancy was over a month further on than her mother guessed, but she couldn't say so. 'Can't they tell?'

'The midwife might be able to feel it. But it's not always easy. Sometimes one gets sort of hidden behind the other and they stick their arms and legs out at all sorts of angles. Remember Mrs Parker, down the other end of the village? She was sure she was only having one and so was the midwife, but when it came to it, two popped out. You'd better ask your Auntie Ruth what she thinks.'

Lizzie nodded, thankful that Ruth was to be her midwife and wouldn't ask any awkward questions about dates. She knew as well as Lizzie when the baby was due. All the same, the next time she was at the cottage Lizzie mentioned her mother's idea about twins, just in case Jane said anything to her sister about it.

'I wouldn't like her to think I hadn't asked you. But it isn't, is it?'

'Not as far as I can tell.' Ruth still wasn't happy about the lies they were telling, but she knew there was no help for it. 'You're about the right size for seven months. We'll just have to hope it doesn't come even earlier. That really would make tongues wag!'

'You don't think it will, do you?' Lizzie asked anxiously.

'No, I don't. Everything seems to be going along perfectly well. I know you're uncomfortable, but that's to be expected and the baby will probably turn again soon and get away from those nerves. It's still moving all right, isn't it?'

'Never stops!' Lizzie said ruefully. 'He's going to be either a footballer or a boxer. I don't think he ever goes to sleep.'

'You're in for a few disturbed nights, then.' Ruth smiled at her niece. 'You've made up your mind it's a boy, have you? You mustn't get too set on it, you know. Just because it kicks a lot doesn't mean anything.'

'I know. I don't mind what it is, so long as it's healthy. Neither does Alec. Well, to tell the truth, if I had a choice I'd say it would be better for him if it turned out to be a girl. Then *our* first baby might be a boy – his son. It means a lot to a man, having a son.'

Ruth gave her a quick look. 'So are you and Alec . . . ?'

Lizzie shook her head. 'No, not yet. We're not even trying just now – he's afraid it might hurt the baby. But I'm sure it'll come right soon. Once the baby's born.'

'It wouldn't hurt if you did want to make love now,' Ruth said. 'The doctors advise stopping about six weeks before it's due. You've still got a bit of time.'

'Well, we've decided not to think about it any more for a while. Not unless it comes right all by itself. And Alec seems a lot better since we made up our minds about that. More settled.'

Ruth nodded. She didn't want to go any more deeply into Lizzie's private business; it was only the fact that she was a nurse and already knew the truth about the baby that had led them to talk so intimately. Instead, she turned the conversation to the other subject that was uppermost in her mind these days – her own wedding. There were only three weeks to go now and there still seemed to be a lot to do.

'I didn't think there'd be so much to arrange, what with us both being widowed and having the cottage and furniture and everything already. But what with my clothes, and Dan's and Sammy's, and organising the church and the hymns and the wedding breakfast – it's lovely to be having it at the farm – and then Christmas coming on top of it all, well, I wonder sometimes if I'm on my head or my heels. It's a shame you can't be my matron of honour.'

'What, looking like this?' Lizzie let out a hoot of laughter. 'Talk about a ship in full sail! And I'll be even bigger by then. You don't want me giving birth in the church!'

'You're not going to do that. And at least if you do, you'll know your midwife's handy.' They both laughed and Ruth went to make some tea.

Silver stood on his perch and winked at Lizzie. 'Georgy-Porgy, pudding and pie,' he said conversationally. 'Kissed the girls and made them cry. Let me be your sweetheart. I love you, Ruthie.'

Lizzie smiled. 'You're an old rogue, you are. Always got to join in any conversation. Does he imitate Dan at all?' she asked as Ruth came back into the living room.

'Oh yes, quite a bit. You know how he picks up things that people say quite often. But Dan doesn't go out of his way to teach him anything special. He says Silver's got enough to say already.'

'It must be funny for him, hearing Silver talk in Jack's voice – specially when he says things like "let me be your sweetheart". It's a reminder that you've been married before, isn't it?'

'Well, Sammy's a reminder that Dan's been married before!' Ruth said with a smile. 'And that doesn't bother me.'

'You've had Sammy here for a long time, though. He's almost like your own.' Lizzie hesitated and Ruth gave her a perceptive glance.

'You're still worrying about Alec taking to this baby, aren't you?' she said quietly. 'Well, I can't tell you for sure that it'll be all right – nobody knows how they'll feel until a thing actually happens. But I can tell you that babies bring

300

their love with them. I've seen it time and time again, mothers and fathers who didn't want a child right up to the time it's born, and then when it's here they'd do anything for it. And all I can say is, you've got a good start. You've told him the truth and he's accepted it. I don't think you've got too much to worry about.'

'I hope not,' Lizzie said. She spread her hands on her stomach as if protecting and comforting the child within. 'I really do hope not.'

Jane was busy in the farm kitchen, making Ruth's wedding cake. It was a bit late to be doing it, but dried fruit had been in short supply and even with contributions from the whole family it wasn't going to be what you might call a proper rich fruit cake. And there wasn't any icing sugar to be had yet – not that it was illegal to ice cakes now that the war was over, it was just that you couldn't get it, so it wasn't going to look much like a wedding cake anyway, to Jane's mind.

She creamed together the butter and sugar and whipped up a dozen eggs to beat into it. They hadn't been easy to come by either, with most of the hens off lay, and for a few days she'd had to give the family scrambled eggs for their breakfast, made from dried powder. Lizzie always said she thought they were just as good, if not better, but George screwed up his face and said he could tell the difference and Terry declared that it was worse than NAAFI canteen rations. But neither of them really meant it. Everyone wanted Ruth's wedding to go well.

The flour was sifted into a bowl ready, and she began to add it to the creamed mixture. The dried fruit had been washed last night and left soaking in a drop of brandy in another bowl by the stove. The big square tin was greased and ready. The cake would be in the slow oven nearly all evening, driving them mad with its fruity smell, and could be taken out just before they went to bed and left to cool overnight.

Just as she finished folding in the flour, someone knocked on the door. Jane clicked her tongue in annoyance. A few more minutes and the mixture would be ready to go into the tin. She hesitated, wondering who could be there, but before she could move the door opened and a tall figure walked in. He stopped and grinned at her and Jane gave a cry and dropped her wooden spoon in the bowl.

'Floyd!'

'That's me,' he said, and held out his arms.

Jane ran into them, not even stopping to wipe her hands on her apron. She hugged him tightly and kissed him, forgetting that her face had flour on it from where she'd brushed her hand across her brow a minute or two before, and he hugged her back. 'Floyd, how lovely to see you! Why didn't you let me know you were coming?'

'I did. I wrote you a letter. Didn't you get it?'

'Oh yes, I got that but I didn't know exactly when you'd be here. And I haven't told anyone else – I kept it as a surprise.' She stood back, surveying him. 'You look well. They're feeding you all right then, over in Germany? I was afraid there wouldn't be enough rations.'

'Uncle Sam always looks after his airmen,' Floyd said. His grin was so wide it seemed in danger of splitting his face. 'Gee, I can't tell you how good it is to be here again. When I went away, I thought it'd be years before I got the chance to see you all. I thought you'd have forgotten me.'

'We'll never forget you, Floyd. Nor Marvin. How is he? Is he coming too?'

A shadow crossed the airman's face. 'No, poor old Marvin's had to go home. He went down with pneumonia a month or two back and they said he'd got TB. They flew him back as soon as he was fit to travel, but they say he'll be OK. Caught it pretty early. A year or two in the mountains and he'll be right as rain again.'

'Oh, that's awful. I'm sorry. You'll have to tell me his address so that I can write. And how long will you be here?'

Jane was bustling about, filling the kettle, the cake forgotten. 'Can you spend Christmas with us?'

'No such luck, I'm afraid. We're just back at the base, clearing out a few things, and then it's off to Germany again. But I've got a weekend pass. I can stop a couple of days – I'm not asking you to put me up, I can sleep at the base, but I can come over for the day tomorrow and Sunday.' He looked at the bowl of cake mixture. 'Is this for Christmas?'

'Goodness, I'd almost forgotten it!' Jane came swiftly back to the table and folded in the rest of the flour, then added the dried fruit and stirred it all together. 'No, it's Ruth's wedding cake. She and Dan are getting married the Saturday before Christmas. Oh, what a shame you can't be here for that.'

'Yeah.' He watched as she tipped the mixture into the tin and then took the bowl from her and started to scrape out the few bits that were left. 'Say, that's good! I'll wish her well now. And how're the rest of the family? How's Lizzie?'

Jane looked at him, suddenly remembering that he and Lizzie had been special friends. His voice was very casual, but you could never tell . . . Still, he knew that Lizzie was married and he wasn't the sort of young man to play about. 'Oh, Lizzie's very well. She's expecting a baby.'

The kitchen seemed very silent all at once. Floyd stared at her. 'Lizzie's *expecting*? But—'

'Alec came home in June,' Jane said, beaming. 'The POW camp he was in was one of the first to be liberated. He looked awful when he first arrived, but he's doing so well. He's got a job in Southampton, working on the liners. Refitting – he doesn't want to go back to sea. Once the baby's born they'll look for somewhere to live in Southampton, but they're staying here until then.'

'Yeah,' Floyd said slowly. 'I guess that's best. And – they're pleased about the baby? I mean, it's pretty quick.'

'It's the best thing that could have happened,' Jane said and there was another small silence.

'And how about the rest of the tribe?' he asked after a minute. 'Terry, is he back? And young Ben? I'm hoping to have a yarn with him, swap flying stories, you know.'

'You'll have to catch him first,' Jane said ruefully. 'He's decided to stay in the RAF and make it his career. George and me weren't too pleased at first but we've come round to the idea. It's what he's good at, and he's done so well. As I tell George, you can't live their lives for them. But Terry seems happy to be back. He's working with his father on the farm, settled back into it without any trouble at all, and he's courting a girl from over Ashbrook way.'

'That's great.' Floyd spoke absently. He finished scraping the bowl and handed it back. 'I don't think I can get any more out of that.'

'No, I don't think you can,' Jane agreed. 'It looks so clean I'll think I've washed it! Now, you're staying to supper, aren't you?'

He hesitated. There was a bag at his feet and he bent and lifted it, pushing it across the table towards her. 'There's a few bits and pieces in here – a sorta contribution. But maybe I ought to be getting along now. I'll come back tomorrow when you've had a chance to tell the others I'm here.'

'You can't do that! They'd never forgive me.' Jane looked in the bag, 'Oh Floyd, that's kind! Tinned fruit and salmon, and look at all that chocolate! Oh, and nylons! Lizzie'll have to wait a while before she can wear hers, mind! Can we save some of this for the wedding? We're having the breakfast here – it'll make a lovely spread. So long as you don't mind us not using it while you're here.'

'Sure you can. I meant it for Christmas anyway, so that's fine. But look, I really think I ought to slip along now. You're busy and—'

He was on his feet, but before Jane could protest again

they heard footsteps outside. The door opened and they both turned round.

Lizzie stood on the mat. In her winter coat, she looked bigger than ever. She stood very still for a moment, outlined against the pale winter sky, and then she took a step into the kitchen.

'*Floyd* . . .' she whispered, and crumpled to the floor.

Chapter Twenty-Nine

'She's all right now,' Jane said in relief. She and Floyd had both leaped forward and caught Lizzie as she staggered in the doorway, helping her to a chair by the table. Now she was in George's big armchair beside the stove, her coat unbuttoned and a glass of water in her hand, smiling weakly at them.

'I'm sorry. I don't know what came over me. It was such a surprise to see Floyd there – and coming into the warm from the cold air. I just felt a bit giddy for a minute. I'm fine now.'

'Your colour's coming back,' Jane said, taking the glass. 'I'll get you a cup of tea now. It's my own fault, I should have told you Floyd was coming.'

'You mean you *knew*?' Lizzie stared at her. 'You knew he was coming, and you never said anything?'

'I wanted it to be a surprise – a nice surprise for you all. I didn't know you were going to be so surprised you'd pass out, did I!'

'I told you, it was coming in out of the cold.' As Jane moved away across the kitchen, Lizzie glanced at Floyd, meeting his eyes for the first time. 'So how are you, then? And how come you're here? I thought you were in Germany.'

'I am. Well, not at this moment, obviously! But I'm still stationed there – just came back to tie up a few loose ends, that's all. Couldn't do that without paying you all a visit, could I?' His eyes were saying something quite different and Lizzie let hers drop. She could feel her colour rising and she pushed her coat away from her.

'It's really hot in here, Mum. I'm surprised you haven't come over faint yourself. What have you got in the oven?' She met Floyd's eyes again and flushed scarlet. Not the most suitable choice of words, she thought, and looked away again.

'Your Auntie Ruth's wedding cake,' Jane said, handing her a cup of tea. 'There you are, I've put in an extra spoonful of sugar. You should see what lovely things Floyd's brought us,' she went on, reaching for the bag. 'Tins of pineapple – why, I haven't tasted pineapple for years – and peaches and apricots. *And* half a dozen tins of salmon. Are you sure it was all right to bring us all this, Floyd? I wouldn't like to think we were getting you into trouble.'

Again, Lizzie felt her colour rise. Everything that was said seemed to have a double meaning. Her mother was still delving into the bag. 'And look at these lovely nylon stockings. We'll have to put a couple of pairs back for you, Lizzie. You'll never get into them now!'

'Why, Lizzie, I haven't even congratulated you yet,' Floyd said, breaking into her chatter. 'When's the baby due?'

She glanced at him and then quickly away. 'In March. About the end of the month.'

'March,' he said, and she knew that he didn't believe her. 'Looks like you're going to have quite a big baby, then.'

'Yes, that's what Auntie Ruth said. We were wondering if it might even be twins.' She met his eyes again. 'But Alec's mother told me big babies run in their family.'

'Did she? You never told me that,' Jane remarked. She finished tidying away the cake bowls and whisks. 'Now I'm going to love you and leave you while I pop upstairs and have a wash. There's a nice beef stew wants putting on the hotplate, Lizzie, and I shall be very put out if you don't

307

stop and share it with us, Floyd. And you two can have a good gossip while I'm gone. There'll be nobody else back for a while so you've got the place to yourselves. I dare say you can find plenty to talk about!'

She whisked out and they looked at each other. Floyd drew a chair over from the table and placed it close beside Lizzie's. He sat down and took her hand.

'Does your mother know?'

Lizzie looked at him dumbly, and he added a little impatiently, 'Don't fool with me, Lizzie. It *is* my baby, isn't it?'

'Yes,' she whispered. 'Yes, it is.'

The silence this time was longer. Floyd gazed down at her hand. He held it between both of his, tracing the blue lines of the veins with the tip of his finger. He turned it over and bent his lips to her palm. She snatched it away at once.

'Don't do that, Floyd!'

He raised his eyes. 'Why not?'

'You can't! I'm married!'

'I don't recall that that stopped you on VE Night,' he said drily, and she flushed crimson.

'You know that wasn't meant to happen. Neither of us meant it to happen. At least, I didn't mean it to, and I didn't think you did. Perhaps I was wrong about that.'

He sighed. 'No, you weren't wrong, Lizzie. I didn't mean it to happen either. I never wanted to cause you any trouble. I knew you loved your husband.'

'I loved you too,' she said in a low voice. 'I really did, that night.' She lifted her eyes to meet his gaze. 'I think I still do, but I love Alec as well, and he's the one I'm married to.'

'And it's *my* baby you're carrying,' he said. 'I guess that kind of complicates things. Though I don't suppose he knows, does he?'

'Yes, he does. You see . . .' she felt the blush begin again

308

'. . . Alec hasn't been really well since he came home. He – he can't—'

'OK, I get it,' he said after a pause. 'It can't be his kid, that's what you're saying, isn't it? So he knows it's another guy's. Does he know who the guy is?'

Lizzie nodded miserably. 'I had to tell him, otherwise he'd have thought it was someone local – someone we both knew.'

'Shit,' he said, and rose abruptly to his feet.

'I'm sorry, Floyd.'

'So'm I,' he said tersely. 'So'm I sorry, Lizzie. What a bloody mess.'

They were silent again. Upstairs, Jane could be heard moving about. The sound reminded Floyd of his original question. He sat down again. 'Does your mother know? She can't do, or she'd never have welcomed me the way she did. But what she said about us having things to talk about. It sounded to me . . . '

Lizzie shook her head. 'She doesn't even suspect. I never told her about Alec. She knew we were good friends – she just wanted us to have a talk on our own. The only person who knows is Auntie Ruth.'

'Ruth? She knows?'

'I had to tell *someone*,' Lizzie cried desperately, and then glanced up at the ceiling and lowered her voice. 'Anyway, she's a nurse – she noticed I was pregnant. And she's my midwife too. I couldn't have hidden it from her. She won't tell anyone.'

'And what about Alec? Has he given you a hard time over it? Because if he has . . .'

'Well, you could hardly blame him, could you! But as it happens, he hasn't, not once he got used to the idea. He was upset at first, of course he was, but then he thought about it and said he wanted to keep the baby and let everyone think it was his. That's how we think about it

309

now, Floyd.' She met his eyes again. 'Our baby. Mine and Alec's. You don't have to worry about it at all.'

He stared at her. 'I don't have to *worry* about it? Your husband's going to call *my* kid *his* and I don't have to worry?' He gripped both her hands tightly and brought his face close to hers. 'Lizzie, you don't know how I had to wangle to get this trip back to England. I came back because I couldn't stay away any longer. I had to tell you how I felt. I had to ask you to make a choice.'

'A choice?' she whispered. 'What – what choice?'

'Me or him,' he said bluntly. 'I was going to ask you to come away with me. Ever since that night . . . oh God, Lizzie, I knew I was in love with you before, but after that there was no hope for me at all. I couldn't get your face out of my mind. I couldn't get your voice out of my head. I lie in bed at night and go over it all again, every moment of that night when we loved each other. I *know* you loved me then. You love me now, too – I know you do. *Don't you*!'

'Floyd, no – you mustn't talk like that. Mum'll hear you – she'll be down any minute. Dad might come in, or Terry. Or Alec. Please, Floyd, you'll have to go!'

'I want you to come with me,' he said urgently. 'Not now, not today, but soon. Look, if Alec can't be a husband to you now, you've got grounds for a separation, maybe a divorce. I don't know your English laws, but we can find out. You can come to Germany – we can get married. And then I'll take you back to the States with me. We can be happy together, Lizzie, you know we can. You're having my baby. You've got to say yes!'

'I can't! I can't say anything! It's all happening too quickly.' She felt the baby move and laid her hands on her stomach. 'Floyd, please – I can't answer you now. You've got to give me a chance to think.' She cast a frightened glance at the door. 'Go away, please – go now!'

'All right,' he said. 'I'll go. But I'll come back tomorrow, and I'll want an answer. You've got to think about this,

Lizzie. Think what it's like for *me*.' He paused and then said quietly, 'I don't like doing this to another man. But see it my way – he's got the woman I love, and now he's going to have my baby as well. And nobody's given me any say at all. As far as I can see, nobody's given me a thought!' He stood up, looking down at her. 'All right, I'll go now. But remember – I'll be back. And I'll need an answer. That's my baby you're carrying, Lizzie. It could be the only kid I'll ever have. You can't shut me out of its life.'

He walked to the door and pulled it open. Outside, darkness had fallen. A flurry of snow blew into the kitchen and he stepped through the doorway and closed the door behind him.

Lizzie lay back in her chair, breathing heavily. She felt sick and shaken. She groped for her tea and drank it quickly, desperate to be looking more normal when her mother came back. By the time Jane came down the stairs again, she was at the stove, stirring the stew.

'Don't tell me he's gone after all!' Jane exclaimed in disappointment. 'I was sure he would stay for supper.'

'He couldn't, Mum. He was due back at the base. He said he'll call in again tomorrow.'

'Oh well, we'll have to be satisfied with that, I suppose.' Jane came a little closer and gave her daughter a searching look. 'You know, you're still looking a bit off-colour. I wouldn't be surprised if you've got a temperature. Why don't you go up to bed and I'll send Alec up with your supper on a tray?'

'Yes,' Lizzie said, thankful for the chance to be away from the family and all their chatter. 'Yes, I will, Mum. Thanks.'

She handed over the wooden spoon and went slowly up to the room she and Alec shared. Why did this have to happen, she thought, sitting heavily on the edge of the bed. Why did Floyd have to come back now, of all times? Why did he have to come back at all?

311

And why did her emotions have to be turned upside down all over again, just when she'd thought she had them under control?

When the family came in from their various chores around the farm, Jane was ladling stew into a large bowl which she set in the middle of the table. Once they were all seated, she would divide it between their plates and anyone who wanted seconds could help themselves. As they queued up to wash at the kitchen sink, she told them the news about Floyd.

'And he's brought us some lovely things! We can make a real spread at the wedding, and still have some left over for Christmas, I wouldn't be surprised. It was a shame he couldn't stop to supper but he says he'll be back tomorrow and you'll all see him then. He's looking forward to meeting you, Alec,' she told her son-in-law, embroidering a little because Floyd hadn't said that at all. 'He and Lizzie were good friends.'

'So she's told me,' Alec said slowly, wiping his hands on the roller towel. 'Where is she now?'

'She went up to bed, said she felt a bit tired. She looked it, too. Why, when she came through the door Floyd and me thought she was going to pass out! We had to run to catch her. She was better again in a minute,' Jane added hastily, not wanting Alec to worry. 'It was just the cold, and her back was playing up again. But I thought she'd be better lying down. I said you'd take her supper up on a tray.' She ladled a helping of stew on to a warm plate. 'There, you can take it now.'

Alec carried the tray up the stairs and balanced it on one hand while he opened the bedroom door. Lizzie was lying in bed, her brown hair loose on the pillow. She heaved herself up and cast him a wary glance. 'Hello.'

'Hello,' Alec said. He put the tray on the little table beside the bed and sat down beside her. 'Are you all right?'

'I think so.' Her eyes filled with tears and her mouth wobbled. 'Oh *Alec*!'

'There, there,' he said, pulling her into his arms. He patted her shoulders gently and murmured into her hair, 'It's all right, Lizzie. It's all right. I'm here now. I've got you. Everything's all right.' He held her away from him and looked at her gravely. 'It must have been a shock for you, coming in and finding him here.'

'It was. I thought – well, I didn't know *what* to think! And Mum *knew* he was coming – he'd written and told her, and she never breathed a word. She thought it would be a nice surprise.' She laughed a little. 'It was a surprise all right! I thought I was going to faint.'

'So did they, apparently.' He hesitated. 'Does he – did he realise? About the baby?' He laid his hand on her stomach and she nodded.

'Yes. I wouldn't have told him, but he knew straight away. I couldn't lie to him, Alec. I'm sorry.'

'So your mum knows as well?' he asked, and then frowned. 'She didn't seem upset. I'd have thought—'

'No! No, she doesn't know anything. She left me and Floyd together and he asked me then. I'm so big, he knew straight away it couldn't be yours.' She began to cry again.

Alec watched her helplessly. There were so many questions he wanted to ask but he could see that she was still shaken and upset. He patted her shoulder again and looked in the drawer for a clean hanky. She took it with a wavering smile and mopped her eyes and nose, and he indicated the tray. 'D'you think you can manage something to eat? It'll do you good.'

'I don't know,' she said. 'I don't think I can eat anything.'

'You've got to think of the baby as well,' he said, and she sighed and nodded.

'All right, then. I'll try.' She pulled herself up again and he arranged the tray on her knees. 'You go down and have yours.'

'Are you sure? I don't want to leave you like this.'

'Yes. I'm all right. *Please*, Alec.' There was a sudden edge to her voice and she put her hand to her brow. 'I'm sorry, I didn't mean to shout. I just – I just need to be by myself for a bit, to – to think. You go and have your supper with the others. And don't let Mum worry. I don't want her to start wondering, and putting two and two together.'

He nodded and went to the door, glancing back uneasily as he pulled it shut behind him. Once on her own, Lizzie leaned back against her pillows and closed her eyes. She took several very deep breaths.

Floyd would be coming back tomorrow. He would be expecting an answer to his question. He would be expecting her to say she would come away with him.

How could she send him away, when she was carrying his baby? What would he do if she did? And what would it do to Alec if she abandoned him now, after all he had suffered?

Worse still – how could she keep her secret from the rest of the family when the two men finally met?

Chapter Thirty

It was years since Dan had done his apprenticeship in the blacksmith's forge in Old Portsmouth but he could still remember the pleasure of working with the big Shires which pulled the brewers' drays and the carthorses that were used by many of the tradesmen delivering bread, milk, coal and so on around the city. He soon found himself getting back into the way of it and grinned as he saw Stevie coming down the lane leading the two Clydesdales that the Knights used.

'Boxer and Barty need new shoes,' she said, halting in front of Solly's forge. Yesterday's snow hadn't come to much after all and there was only a white rime along the foot of the hedges to show that it had ever fallen. 'Can you do them now?'

'Can I do you now, sir?' Dan quipped, in imitation of Mrs Mopp, but Stevie only smiled politely. Usually, when anyone quoted one of the characters in *ITMA* it led to a whole flurry of responses, but the pretty Land Girl obviously wasn't in the mood this morning. Dan looked at her closely and thought she seemed paler than usual, with shadows under her eyes and a sad droop to her mouth. 'Here, are you all right?' he asked. 'Not catching flu, are you?'

'No, I'm OK.' The girl looped Boxer's lead rein over one of the hooks in the wall and led Barty into position. Dan took the horse from her, stroking its nose and murmuring in its big brown ear. This was one of his favourite jobs and he liked the big Clydesdales and Shires best of all. He bent

315

to feel amongst the long, feathery hairs that covered the fetlock and hoof, and lifted Barty's hind leg.

'Every inch the countryman,' Stevie said wryly. 'I bet nobody in the village would have believed this six years ago – two townies doing jobs like this.'

'I used to shoe horses when I lived in Pompey as a boy,' Dan said mildly. 'There's plenty there even now, doing deliveries and such. They still need shoes put on their feet.'

'I suppose so.' Stevie sat down on the bench beside the cottage wall. Solly lived at the back of the forge, with a couple of rooms upstairs overlooking the green, and Dan was lodging in one of these until the wedding. 'You don't miss living in the town, then?'

'Not on your life!' Dan had removed the old shoes and began to heat the bars of metal in the furnace. 'I've had enough of city streets! I dare say there's parts of Pompey where it's a pleasure to live, but you got to have the money to live there. Mind, April Grove wasn't so bad – there wasn't much money about, but the folk that lived there were decent enough and looked after their places. But the house me and Nora moved into had been let go right down, and was no more than a hovel. Not that we made it much better. Nora wasn't up to it and I never had time.'

He stopped, surprised to find himself talking like this to a girl he scarcely knew. Probably it was because they were both from town and so had something in common, though he didn't think Stevie had ever lived anywhere like April Grove. She talked more as if her father was a doctor, or a teacher, or solicitor or something. Not the sort of person Dan would ever have mixed with back in Portsmouth. He wondered why she stayed on in the country, working on the farm and bringing horses to be shod.

'I've had enough of the city too,' she said, almost as if she'd read his mind. 'I hated it out here at first, but now I can't imagine living anywhere else. You seem closer to real life in the country, somehow. Seeing the seasons go by – I mean, winter's just horrible in town, with all the wet streets and slush, and summer's hot and noisy, and you don't even notice spring and autumn. Not like you do out here. I love seeing the first snowdrops in the hedge, and then the primroses and violets, and the bluebells and the hawthorn blossom. And the animals – the lambs and calves, and the wild ponies in the Forest having their foals. You don't see any of that in the town.'

'People have gardens though,' Dan said, feeling he ought to stick up for Pompey a bit even if he had left the place behind him. 'You've got to know the seasons, to plant your veg. And flowers, too,' he added, thinking that this girl must come from a home with a big garden. 'I bet you had plenty of spring flowers in your garden.'

'Yes, but they were tame,' she said, dismissing them with a wave of one hand. 'Flowers out here are wild. They're natural.'

Dan worked for a while in silence. He finished Barty's shoes and started on Boxer's. The big horse stood patiently, unmoved by the application of the hot iron to his foot and the smell of burning hoof. It was just the same as a toenail, Dan had told Sammy, and didn't have any feeling in it. Having his hoof cut away didn't hurt the horse any more than cutting your own nails. He tossed a piece to Solly's spaniel, Susie, who loved nothing better than a bit of hoof to chew.

'You'll have to go back soon, though, won't you?' he said to the girl, who was giving Barty a carrot as a reward for his patience. 'I mean, all the blokes are back now, aren't they? There's no Land Girls out here any more, only you.'

'I know, and I'm not really a Land Girl any more. I've been demobbed. I just stayed on because Ian and Heather seemed to need me –' she stopped and coloured a little, then went on '– and I like it here. But you're right, I'm going to have to go back.' She scuffed the cold earth with the toe of her boot. 'Mrs Clutter wants to go and live with her daughter, so there'll be nowhere for me to lodge. And they don't really need me at the farm now. I suppose I'll have to go and work in an office or something.' She stared disconsolately at the pattern she had made in the dust.

'You got a home to go back to, though, haven't you?' Dan wondered suddenly if the young woman had a mother and father or even a home in the town. Perhaps they'd been bombed out or even killed. 'You got *someone*?'

'Oh yes. No worries about that. I just like it here better. I like being in a village. All my friends are here now.' Dan had finished his work and she stood up and took Boxer's rein. 'Thanks, Mr Hodges. It's been nice talking to you.' She gave a wistful glance around the forge. 'You've been lucky, haven't you? I wish I could find some proper work to do in Bridge End.'

'I been luckier than that,' Dan said. 'I've found a good woman. What you want is a bloke as good as my Ruth. Pretty girl like you shouldn't have much trouble.'

She smiled ruefully. 'It's not as easy as you might think, Mr Hodges. Especially in a little place like Bridge End, with half the men away at war for the past six years. And perhaps I'm a bit too choosy.' She gathered the horses' reins in her hands and began to lead them away.

'Well, at least there'll be more to choose from in the town,' Dan said, and she turned and gave him another sad smile.

'I dare say there will. But they won't be country boys, will they? They won't be farmers.'

She walked away down the lane, a slender figure between the two big horses, her blonde hair gleaming in the pale winter light. Dan watched her for a moment, then went to get the big broom to sweep up the bits of hoof and tidy the forge before starting on the next job.

'You needn't think you're going to get all those bits of hoof to chew,' he said to Susie, who was staring at him expectantly. 'One bit's all you're allowed. It'll make you sick if you eat any more.'

He felt sorry for the pretty young woman who looked as if she'd be more at home in the city where she'd grown up, yet had found her place in the country. I didn't want to stop in Pompey after the war, he thought. I've been really lucky, finding Ruth and then this job with Solly. But what is there for a girl like young Stevie?

The war had shown her the kind of life she really enjoyed. But the peace was taking it away.

Stevie had to walk fast to keep up with the two big horses who, with their long legs and powerful bodies, just weren't capable of going any more slowly. With a plough or harrow behind them, walking on soft earth, they went at a more stately pace but on the hard metalled surface of the lane they strode along as if determined on some great purpose.

'You're babies just the same,' she said to them. 'If a paper bag blew out of the hedge you'd jump out of your skins!' The horses bowed their heads but took no other notice. 'You're only brave as long as there's nothing to be brave about,' she told them, stroking their warm necks.

Stevie had had a bad night. She didn't really know whether she'd been asleep and dreaming or awake and worrying, but she seemed to have spent the entire night in frantic conversation with either Heather or Ian. Tossing and turning, she'd seen first one face then the other, heard both their voices begging her not to leave, was tormented by her own churning emotions. This morning, she felt like an old dishrag, used and wrung out for the last time. I'll have to go back home, she thought – yet how could she bear to leave the people she'd come to love best in the whole world?

Until she came to the farm, Stevie had never really known what a happy home was. As Dan had surmised, her father was a doctor and the family lived in a large house in one of the better areas of Portsmouth. Her mother gave dinner-parties and her father often went to London, where he shared a practice with another doctor in a fashionable street. Stevie and her younger brother James had their own playroom with all the toys they could need, and when they grew old enough they were sent away to boarding-school. During the holidays, they were entrusted to the care of a succession first of young girls, and then of young men who were training to be teachers and needed to earn some money for their vacations. They saw very little of their parents.

Stevie often thought this was no loss. Their mother always seemed to be wearing the wrong sort of clothes for doing anything with her children, examining their hands for signs of stickiness before allowing them to touch her. Their father was cold and unapproachable and expected impeccable behaviour at all times. There were no jokes between them and they seldom played games together.

The Knight family had been a revelation to Stevie. Warm, loving, their conversations peppered with jokes and banter, they had welcomed the three Land Girls into their life, entertaining them to supper at least once a week and to Sunday dinner as well. You had to remember they were girls away from their own homes, Emily had said, and they were doing work they'd never been accustomed to, in all weathers. They'd work a lot better for being treated right, and she hoped that someone would be doing the same for her Ian, wherever he was.

Stevie had slipped into her niche as if it had been carved especially for her. Bridge End was more her home than her father's house had ever been. In Emily and Arthur she found the warmth for which she'd always hankered, and in Heather she found a sister. After her brother James, who had joined the RAF, was killed when his Hurricane was shot down, it was the Knights who had given her comfort. Her own parents seemed unable to express their own grief, let alone help with hers, and when she tried to offer them consolation they brushed her away.

I can't go back there, she thought, leading the two horses to their field and removing their head collars. I *can't* go back.

Heather and Ian were standing by the gate of Lower Meadow. Winter wheat had been sown there but as yet it still lay dormant. Sometime in early spring it would begin to shoot and the brown earth be misted with green but at present even the air seemed quiet, as if everything waited.

'We had to plant barley and oats during the war, of course,' Heather remarked. 'Everyone had to. And we gave over Middle Meadow to potatoes, and—'

'Yes, I know,' Ian interrupted. 'You've told me. Over and over again. You've left me in no doubt about what you did during the war. What am I supposed to do, go down on my knees to thank you?'

Heather bit her lip. 'No, of course not. I was only saying—'

'Well, maybe you could find something else to say. I *know* how well you did while I was away. If you're not telling me yourself, Mum and Dad keep reminding me. What you don't seem to realise is that I'm back now, there's no war and the farm's going to be run my way from now on. Why can't you get that into your head? What do I have to do to make you understand?'

'I do understand,' she said. 'I just want to help you. You need to know what's been happening, you need to know about all the new rules and regulations. Ian, I *want* you to run the farm – but I want to run it with you. I want us to work together.'

'*I* want, *I* want,' he mimicked. 'It's all what *you* want, isn't it! You say you want me to be in charge, but you don't mean it. You say you want us to work together – but what you really mean is that *you'll* be in charge. You just won't

321

give it up.' He flung himself away from the gate and began to stride away. 'Why can't you leave me alone? You're like a bloody dog, following me around wherever I go. You're there all the time, looking over my shoulder, going on and on about what you did during the war. I can't even *think*, because you're there in my head, wanting to know what I'm going to do next and telling me it's wrong.'

'Ian, no! I'm not doing that. You're not being fair.'

'Sorry,' he said. 'I didn't realise I had to be *fair* as well as everything else.'

'Oh, for God's sake!' Heather stopped and brought both hands up to her mouth, clenching them into fists of frustration. 'How long are you going to keep this up? You've been home for months now. I can understand it being difficult for you to start with, but you seem to have just got stuck in this – this dreadful *bitterness*. You seem to think everyone's against you, that we don't want you here. Why? What have we done to make you feel this way? What have *I* done?' She uncurled her hands, covering her eyes with her fingertips. 'I don't know what to do any more. I just don't know what to *do*.'

'I keep *telling* you, don't I?' For a moment, as Ian turned and saw her distress, he faltered, but then his own anger and frustration surfaced once more. 'Leave me alone – that's all I ask. Leave me alone to run my farm my way. Go back to what you were doing before this bloody war started. Be a *wife* again. Do your own job, instead of always wanting to muscle in on mine. That's what I was looking forward to, it was what I wanted all the time I was away. I never dreamed I was going to have to *share* it.'

'But that's what marriage is – sharing. The vows—'

'Not *work*!' he exclaimed. 'Worldly goods, yes. You can share those, such as they are, till the cows come home. *But I don't want you sharing my work*. Do you see Lizzie Travers going into Southampton with Alec to share his work? D'you see Ruth Purslow going down to the forge to

322

work the bellows for Dan Hodges? So why should you want to share mine?'

'Because it's our life,' she said. 'Farming's different. It's a way of life and I've found out that I'm good at it. Why can't I do what I'm good at? Why have I got to go back into the kitchen and not be allowed to walk the fields, milk the cows or make decisions any more? Why must all that be taken away from me?'

'Well, you could think yourself lucky you've had your own way for nearly six years,' Ian said. 'You wouldn't even have had that if it hadn't been for the war. And maybe that would have been a good thing. You wouldn't have got all these ideas into your head.' He had begun to walk on, but he stopped again and wheeled round. 'Look, Heather, the war's over. Women have done a lot of men's jobs but now they're not needed any more. They can go back to doing what women are supposed to do – looking after their homes and families. And that goes for you too!'

He marched away down the track and Heather stood looking after him. A heavy lump of despair seemed to settle somewhere between her chest and her stomach. Her shoulders drooped and she turned away to lean on a gate, laying her head on her arms.

We're never going to get out of this argument, she thought. Not unless one of us gives in. Ian obviously isn't going to, so it's up to me as usual. But I don't *want* to give in! I don't see why I should. There's nothing wrong with wanting to be a partner, to work together. And if I do give in, what sort of marriage will we have? I'll be a submissive little wife in the kitchen, saying yes sir, no sir, three bags full, sir. And he'll know he can win. He'll turn into a bully.

She lifted her face and stared across the field that she had ploughed and harrowed and harvested during all the years of the war. She felt a powerful sense of ownership, of pride in all she had achieved. Was all this to be thrown back in her face? Was she to be treated as nothing better than a caretaker?

I don't believe women will tamely go back to what they used to do, she thought. None of us is going to want to give up the freedom, the independence, the responsibility we've had for the past few years. If that's what men think, they've got another think coming. They're in for a big surprise.

Not that it would help her in this quarrel with Ian which, from an initial irritation, had developed into a war of their own. It threatened not only the farm but their marriage, too. And, therefore, the whole family's entire way of life.

Ian came across Stevie as she closed the field gate on the two horses and set off to go back to Mrs Clutter's cottage for her dinner. Her landlady always cooked something at midday and Stevie usually saw to supper. In fact, as Mrs Clutter grew older and more frail, Stevie had taken over quite a lot of the household chores. It wasn't what Land Girls were supposed to do, but Stevie wasn't strictly a Land Girl any more and she didn't like to see the old woman struggling to cope with scrubbing and sweeping.

'Been to the forge?' Ian asked, pausing beside her to look at the horses.

Stevie nodded. Her heart was thumping, as it always did when she saw Ian, but she was determined not to let her feelings show. She began to chatter, her voice a little high and slightly ragged. 'They've both got nice new shoes on now. Barty was so funny when he had his – making a fuss about picking up his feet. He always behaves as if they're too heavy. I told him he's just a big baby.'

Ian nodded, but he didn't smile. She gave him a nervous glance. He's had another row with Heather, she thought, and sighed, moving away a little. She didn't want him to tell her about it; she didn't want a repetition of the scene up on Top Field. Since then, she'd managed to avoid being alone with him, handing the milking over to Heather in the hope that the closeness of the milking parlour would help her and Ian to resolve their differences. From the expression on Ian's face, it didn't look as though it had worked.

'Stevie,' he said abruptly. 'I need to talk to you.'

'Oh? Something interesting?' She wished she hadn't said that, but pinned a bright, enquiring smile on her face and looked up at him expectantly. 'Or are you giving me the sack? I've been thinking about that. It's time I moved on anyway and now that all the men are back . . .'

'Stevie, shut up!' He gripped her arms and she gave a little squeak. 'You know what I want to talk about. We've got to get something sorted out.'

She stared at him, suddenly afraid. 'I don't know what you mean. What do we have to sort out?'

'Us,' he said, and glanced hastily round the yard. There was nobody about but they were in full view of the farmhouse windows. 'Not here, though. Come into the barn.'

'I was on my way home. Mrs Clutter will have dinner on the—'

'That can wait. Come *on*.' He dragged her across to the big barn. It was over half full of hay and he pulled her into a corner, hidden from the doorway. Stevie looked up at him in alarm but before she could speak, he pulled her into his arms and kissed her savagely. For a moment, all her own feelings and desires surged to meet his kiss; then she began to struggle, trying to pull back her head and pushing at his body with all her strength.

'Don't do that, Ian! Let me go! Whatever's come over you?'

'You know what's come over me! You know how I feel about you. I've told you plainly enough.' He was still holding her by the arms. 'Stevie, we can't go on like this. You know what it's like between me and Heather now. She's so different these days. And she thinks I'm different

325

too. We just don't get along together any more, we're always bickering and arguing, and it's affecting the whole family. Mum's upset and Dad hardly says a word and the kids – well, you know what Roger's like. Never a word to say for himself. And Pat hardly knows which way to turn. And Teddy won't even let me pick him up.' He let her go suddenly and ran both hands through his thick dark hair. 'It's a mess, Stevie, it's just a mess and – and you're the only person I can turn to. You're the only one who even tries to understand. You're the only one I really care about.'

'I'm not.' She tried to speak steadily but her voice shook and tears were not far away. 'I'm not the only one. You care about them, too – all of them. And you care about them more than you care about me.'

'I don't! I've told you—'

'You do,' she said firmly. 'Of course you do. They're your *family*. Everyone cares most about their family.' She thought briefly about her own parents, locked in their own chilly emotions. Deep down, they probably grieved endlessly for their dead son; deep down, perhaps they even cared about her, missed her. Her father had written only a day or two ago, asking her to come home and work as his receptionist . . . She turned her thoughts away and went on: 'All families go through bad patches. I expect lots of people are having the same problems. The war's over and the men are coming back and everyone thought it would be wonderful – and so it is, but there are a lot of things that aren't wonderful at all. Things are still on ration, and people are still homeless, and the bombsites are still there, and it's going to take years to put it all right. And it's a reaction to all the strain – a bit like waiting for a birthday: afterwards, everything seems a bit of an anticlimax. You feel let down and flat and miserable, and you don't really know why.'

'Oh yes, I do,' Ian said bitterly. 'I know why, all right! I

326

feel let down because I've come back to a wife who doesn't want me.'

'That isn't true, Ian,' Stevie said quietly. 'It just isn't true. Heather loves you. She's never stopped loving you.'

'Well, she has a funny way of showing it. Not that it matters,' he said with sudden energy, 'because I don't love her. It's you I love, Stevie – you! You're the one who listens, who understands, you're the one who's always there when I need you—'

'No!' she cried. 'You mustn't say that – you mustn't. There's no future for us, Ian – how could there be? You're married to Heather, you've got children, you've got a *farm*!'

'I could leave it,' he said, and she gasped. 'Or Heather could leave. People do get divorces, Stevie. They do start again. *We* could start again.'

Stevie took in a very deep breath. She gathered together all her courage, all her determination, and said, 'No, Ian. We couldn't. It's impossible. You can't turn Heather out of her home.'

'Then I could leave. It's more her farm than mine now, anyway – she's made that very plain. I could get work somewhere – somewhere far away.' He caught at her arm again. 'We could emigrate – we could go to Canada! We could start a new life there and forget all this.'

'And how could you forget your children?' she asked. 'And your parents, and all your friends here? You're talking nonsense, Ian.'

'Are you saying you don't love me?' he demanded.

Stevie opened her mouth but she couldn't reply. She knew he was watching her, knew that he was setting a meaning to her silence, but she couldn't tell him the truth and she couldn't lie. She shook her head miserably and managed to whisper at last, 'Don't ask me that.'

'You do,' he said. 'I know you do.'

There was a short silence. Then she said, 'Ian, it doesn't matter what I feel. The point is that you can't break up

327

your marriage or leave your farm. Too many people will be hurt.' With a sudden flash of anger, she looked up and met his eyes. 'Don't you care about that at all? Don't you even care about your children?'

'All I care about,' he said, bending his head towards her, 'is you.' And he kissed her on the lips.

Stevie was too exhausted to resist. Her own feelings rose again and she pressed herself close against him and let her mouth answer his. For a long moment, and without saying a word, they were at last completely honest with each other.

'You see?' he muttered, lifting his head at last. 'You see, you can't lie to me about that.'

Stevie looked into his eyes. She could feel the tears hot and stinging in her own. She shook her head speechlessly but, before either of them could move, a sound made them both turn their heads.

Roger stood a few yards away, between them and the door of the barn. How long he had been there, how much he had heard, neither of them could tell. But from the expression of shock and disgust which was frozen on his face, they knew that he had seen their kiss.

Stevie gasped in dismay and Ian let her go and stepped towards his son. 'Roger—'

But the boy backed away. The frozen look left his face; his mouth was working with misery. Tears streamed down his cheeks, and he turned and fled.

Chapter Thirty-One

Lizzie knew exactly which way Floyd would come to the farm. He had walked over from the base often enough with Marvin, and she thought it was likely that he would take the same path, enjoying the familiarity. She went to meet him, setting out in good time to encounter him in the woods, well away from the village, and sat on a stile leading to the far fields to wait.

On the way, she had met Heather and Ian walking round their fields and Stevie taking the two Clydesdales to be shod. She had also run into Dottie Dewar, attended by the usual raggle-taggle tribe of children, and Joyce Moore on her way to the village school, where she worked as a dinner-lady. She met a number of other villagers too, and thanked heaven that she didn't have to confront Floyd in front of all these inquisitive eyes.

She hadn't been at the stile for more than a quarter of an hour when she saw his tall figure approaching along the footpath. He saw her and his face lit up. He quickened his step and made to put his arms around her.

Lizzie backed away. They were on opposite sides of the stile. She held out her hands, laying them against his chest, keeping him at arms' length. 'No, Floyd. Don't do that. Just – stay where you are for a moment. We have to talk first.'

'Too darn right we do.' He began to climb the stile, but she shook her head violently and pushed harder against his shoulders.

'*No*, Floyd. Stay there – please. Don't make things even more difficult than they already are.'

He stared at her. 'What are you saying, Lizzie?'

'You know what I'm saying,' she said wearily. 'I told you yesterday. Alec is accepting this baby as his, and nobody else knows any different.'

'I thought you said your Aunt Ruth—'

'Except for Auntie Ruth. And she won't tell a soul, not even Dan. Nobody is ever going to know.'

He was silent for a moment. Then he said, 'Not even the baby?'

Lizzie hesitated. 'I can't think that far ahead. But why should I tell him – or her? Alec will be the baby's father, from the moment it's born and all through its life. There's no need for the child to ever know any different.'

He looked at her. 'No need for a child to know who its real father is?'

'No – why should there be? Alec will be the baby's father, just as if it was adopted.'

'But it won't be *his* blood in my son or daughter's veins,' he said. 'It'll be mine. This baby will have *my* inheritance. *My* father and mother will be his grandparents, as well as yours. D'you mean to say you'll never tell him all that?'

She stared at him. 'What good would it do? It'll only upset everybody.'

'What *good*!' he exclaimed. 'Lizzie, this kid isn't always going to be a baby. It'll grow up, be a man or a woman. Don't you think he or she will want to know the truth? Don't you think they'll be *entitled* to know? Doesn't truth matter?'

Lizzie looked down at the ground. She had wrestled with these questions all through the night and still didn't know the answer. 'Perhaps there's more than one kind of truth, Floyd.'

'Not in this case,' he said and repeated, 'That baby is going to have my blood running through its veins. *My*

330

blood, and my father's and mother's. There's a whole lot of history there, Lizzie.'

'Yes, but—'

'My great-grandmother,' he said, 'was a Red Indian.'

Lizzie stared at him. 'A – a Red Indian?'

'That's what I said. She married my great-grandfather and they had ten kids. There's a lot of us about, Lizzie. You might almost say it's a *tribe*! And this baby,' he reached across the stile and placed his hand against her coat where it covered her stomach, 'is one of them. One of *us*. It's got Red Indian blood in its veins.'

Lizzie swallowed. 'I don't see what difference that makes.'

'Of course it makes a difference! It makes a hell of a difference!'

'It doesn't. It doesn't make any difference who your great-grandmother was. She could have been French or Italian or an Eskimo. I've got ancestors too, you know! I might be descended from a Norman duke or – or King Henry the Eighth, or anyone. It doesn't make any difference to this baby.' She met his eyes. '*My* baby.'

'Mine too,' he said quickly.

'No,' Lizzie said. 'It's not yours too. Oh yes, you needn't look like that, it was conceived that night. It's yours in that sense. But you didn't make this baby because you wanted it, or even because you loved me. It just happened. It was an accident – you didn't *mean* it to happen. And then you went away and – and never gave it another thought.' To her dismay, her voice began to shake and tears came to her eyes. 'You never even wondered whether I might be – be – and you came back yesterday, expecting to walk back into our lives as if nothing had happened. You didn't come to see me specially, whatever you say; you'd probably forgotten all about what happened that night. You must have known Alec would be home by now. You knew, and you didn't think it mattered. It didn't mean a thing to you until you realised I was carrying your baby.' She was crying in earnest by the time she finished, but her words were still clear and her tone as scathing.

There was a long silence. Lizzie felt for a handkerchief and Floyd silently handed her his. She blew her nose and wiped her eyes, then handed it back.

'Keep it,' he said.

'No. I can't. Take it, Floyd, please.'

'All right.' He stuffed it into his pocket. 'Now you listen to me, Lizzie. You've had your say, now it's my turn. First, that night didn't "just happen". I'd wanted to make love to you for a long time, and you knew it. Yes, you did, and you wanted to do it, too. Let's be honest about that, at least. Second, you say I didn't love you. You're wrong. I *did* love you. I'd loved you for months. I still do.' He paused, but Lizzie said nothing. She stared down at the dry ground. After a moment, he went on. 'Third, I didn't go away and never give you another thought. I've thought about you all the time. I've lived that night in my head every night since, but that's not all I've thought about. I've thought about you on the farm, feeding the calves and the chickens, handing me the roast potatoes at Sunday dinner, dancing with me at the square dance. I've never stopped thinking about you, Lizzie.' He paused again and then finished quietly, 'And I didn't come back yesterday thinking that none of this mattered. It matters a hell of a lot. I came back to see if you were happy.'

At last, Lizzie raised her eyes to his. 'To – to see if I was happy?'

'That's right. I'd made up my mind that if you were happy with your man, I'd simply wish you well and go away. I wouldn't say a word about how I felt. But if you weren't happy, then I'd move heaven and earth to take you away from him, to give you the life I think you ought to have. With *me*.'

The silence was longer this time. The woods were quiet,

with only the faintest breeze stirring the bare twigs. A robin trilled from a nearby hollybush. Lizzie glanced up and caught sight of its red breast, echoing the scarlet of the holly berries. Floyd followed her glance.

'Very seasonal,' he said dryly. 'Remember last Christmas, Lizzie? The carol-singing round the village? We were all looking forward to the end of the war then.'

'A lot had to happen before we got there,' she said.

'And something very important happened that night.' He leaned across the stile again and gripped her hand. 'Lizzie, you're right, I didn't mean to give you a baby. It was damned careless of me and I'm sorry it's brought you trouble. And I didn't expect it when I came yesterday. It was a complete shock.'

'A shock?' Lizzie repeated.

'Yeah, a shock. What d'you expect? I'm not beating around the bush, Lizzie. It never even occurred to me. I suppose, if I'd thought about it at all, I'd have thought you'd let me know.'

'I didn't think you'd want to know,' Lizzie whispered.

'Maybe you were right. But when I saw you standing there in the door, and realised you were pregnant – and when I realised it must be *my* baby you were expecting, well, a whole lot of feelings I'd never have dreamed of came flooding over me.' He stopped and grinned. 'Sorry, getting a little carried away there. But you see, I've never had a baby before!'

'You're not having one now,' Lizzie said tartly, and he laughed. 'And I don't know what you think is so funny. It's me that's having the baby, not you, and it's not funny at all.'

'I know. I'm sorry.' He looked down at her hand and said humbly, 'Please, can I come over this damned stile? I promise not to do anything to upset you.'

'Oh, all right then,' Lizzie said, and stepped back as he

vaulted over. She looked at him uncertainly and he leaned back against the stile and regarded her gravely.

'We've got to thrash this out, Lizzie. I swear I don't want to do anything to hurt you, but we can't just leave things as they are. I can understand why you didn't let me know. You'd no way of knowing I'd do anything to help, or even that I'd accept the baby as mine. You didn't know if you'd ever hear from me, or see me, again. But now, I *do* know – and that changes everything.'

'I told you – Alec wants to accept the baby as his.'

'OK, OK, I heard you, and I guess there's not too much I can do about that. I don't know about your laws here, but back home I reckon a guy in my situation would have a fight on his hands if he tried to claim a baby as his own. And I don't want to fight you, Lizzie. I don't want to cause you any more grief.'

Lizzie looked down. Her stomach was very swollen now and the baby was kicking. Her baby. Floyd's baby. A baby whose great-great-grandmother had been a Red Indian. How peculiar that is, she thought. But it still doesn't make any difference.

'It was awful,' she whispered. 'Knowing I had to tell Alec the truth. If it could possibly have been his baby . . .'

'He might still have realised,' Floyd said gravely. 'Lies don't ever help, Lizzie.'

'But you have to tell lies sometimes. Everyone would be so upset if they knew the truth. Mum and Dad, and Terry and Ben – what would they all think of me? And then all of them knowing about Alec, how he can't make love . . .'

'He'll get over that,' Floyd said. 'It's just the result of being in POW camp all those years. It affects everyone, one way or another – this is just his way. And there's no need for them to know that, is there? That's private, between you and him. What is it you're really afraid of, Lizzie – hurting people or having them think less of you?' And as she hesitated, he leaned forward and said, 'The important person in all this is the baby. People have a *right* to know about their parents, Lizzie. They have a right to know where they come from. This is my baby in here,' he laid his hand on her stomach. 'OK, Alec can be its father to all intents and purposes, and I hope he's a good father and the kid'll appreciate that. But one day, that kid will want to know its real father – *me* – and I want it to be able to come and find me, if it wants to. And that means telling the truth. Right from the start. To *everyone*.'

Lizzie stared at him. 'You can't make me do that.'

'No, I can't.' Floyd drew back a little. His gaze was very intense. 'I can't make you do anything, Lizzie. I can only ask you. I'm not going to see the baby grow up. I'm not going to have anything to do with him or her. All I can ask is that you tell my son or daughter, about me – and say that I'm always there, ready and waiting. I won't come here, but I'll always be waiting.' He took both her hands. 'That's all I'm asking, Lizzie.'

'All?' she said. 'It seems an awful lot to me. You're asking me to tell Mum and Dad. Everyone . . .'

'They'll get over it. You're not the first. And you've got your Alec to stand beside you.'

'Yes,' she said. 'He will, too. We've talked about this, Floyd. He knows I'm here now. He let me come, even though he must have been afraid . . .'

'Then he's a fit man to bring up my kid,' Floyd said, 'and you can tell him I said that.' He paused, then said, 'I think it'll be better if I don't come to the farm after all. Tell your ma and pa I'm sorry I can't see them again. Say I've had to go back.' He stopped and gave a twisted grin. 'Here am I, talking about the truth and telling you to lie! Hell, you're going to tell 'em the truth, aren't you! They'll understand why I couldn't come . . .' His voice faded and he stood looking down at Lizzie, his face very grave. 'Oh Lizzie, it hurts like hell to be leaving you now.'

Lizzie couldn't speak. She nodded, and tears slid from

her eyes again. He felt in his pocket and drew out his hanky, wiping her eyes tenderly. 'Here, keep it. Keep it till my kid comes looking for me. You can send it back then.' He bent his head and drew her close. 'Just one kiss, Lizzie,' he whispered. 'Just one last kiss . . .'

They clung together, their tears mingling. When they broke apart Lizzie was sobbing. She held out her hands, but he moved away and climbed back over the stile.

'Goodbye, Lizzie,' he called. 'I'll write every Christmas, so you'll always know where I am. And let me know when it's born, will you? Keep me in touch, just a little bit.'

She nodded blindly. 'I'll write every year. I'll tell Alec – he'll understand. Goodbye, Floyd.' She closed her eyes and covered her face with her hands. When at last she let them drop, he was gone. She was alone again by the stile.

For a while, she stayed there, letting the tears flow and wiping her eyes with the big white handkerchief. Then she turned and walked back the way she had come, scuffing her feet through the fallen leaves until she was close to the village again.

'Lizzie.'

She looked up. Alec was waiting for her by the lane. He held out his arms and she broke into a clumsy run. He came towards her and pulled her close, and she buried her face against his jacket.

'It's all right,' he murmured, stroking her hair. 'It's all right. Everything's all right now.' He kissed her wet face and then held her close again. 'Let's go home, shall we?'

'Yes,' Lizzie said, 'I'm ready to go home.'

Chapter Thirty-Two

The wedding was only two weeks away. Sammy hardly knew whether to be most excited about that or about Christmas. In the end, he decided that the wedding was the best because it would only happen once, while Christmas came every year. And because then he and his dad and Auntie Ruth would be a proper family at last, all living in the same house.

Dan had carried out his promise to invite Tommy and Freda Vickers and, having invited them, he thought he ought to invite the Budds as well, Frank having been a mate of his for years and Jess having been so good to Nora and young Sam. To his surprise they all accepted, and Jess wrote to ask if he'd mind the children coming too. *We can't very well come without Maureen*, she explained, *and Tim and Keith were friends of Sammy's and they'd like to see some of their old pals from Bridge End*. And Rose was coming too, so as not to be left out, although she'd only been evacuated to Bridge End for a few weeks, right at the start of the war. But Jess had kept in touch with the people she'd stayed with then and had often come out to visit them when the boys were living at the vicarage with old Mr Beckett, and Rose had usually come with her.

'Blimey, that's upped the guest-list a bit,' Dan said in some consternation. 'What with Tom and Freda and all the Budds, that's another eight, all coming from April Grove. I never knew I had so many friends there.'

'Of course you did!' Ruth said. 'And very welcome

they'll be too. We'll have to find beds for them round the village.'

'Beds! Can't they come and go back on the day?'

'Well, I suppose they could. The wedding's at twelve so they can come that morning, and the meal and speeches and so on will last until about four. Then Jane thinks everyone will go home to tea and we can have a party in the evening for the family. So the April Grove people could catch a train about five. Yes, that would work out all right. Mind you, the Budds might like to stay. They've got lots of friends here they'll want to catch up with.'

'They can offer them beds, then,' Dan said. 'Honestly, Ruth, I hope I'm not being mean but we can't expect your Jane to put them up, not with doing all the food and all, and I don't see that we can ask anyone else either. To tell you the truth, I never thought they'd come, not with it being so near Christmas.'

'Now you know how popular you were,' Ruth said with a smile, but he shook his head. He hadn't been popular at all, especially in the early days when folk thought he knocked his wife and kids about, and Gordon had got into all that trouble. He didn't really know what had changed their minds. Still, he had to admit he was pleased. It would be good to see Tommy Vickers and Frank Budd again and show them the forge and the village, and women always enjoyed a good wedding.

And that's what this is going to be, he promised himself. A good wedding and a good life to follow. He was a lucky man.

Ian Knight didn't feel at all lucky in *his* marriage. He was convinced now that he and Heather could never find their way back to each other, and he didn't even want to try. His mind was filled with thoughts of Stevie. If only I'd known her first, he thought as he paced the fields. If only she could have been the one who bore my children and waited for me

338

all these years. If only I could have come home to *her*. If only, if only, if only . . .

Heather knew that the situation had become even more serious, though she couldn't really understand why. Their last quarrel had been no different from the others; but perhaps it wasn't just one quarrel but the accumulation of all of them. We've argued too much, she thought desolately. We've pushed ourselves too far.

She didn't even seem to be able to talk to Stevie about it any more. The blonde girl had almost stopped coming into the farmhouse for the odd meal or cup of tea, saying she needed to get back to the cottage because she was anxious about Mrs Clutter. If Heather tried to start a conversation, she made some excuse to cut it short – the hens must be fed, the cows needed attention, Boxer had seemed a little lame that afternoon and she was wondering whether to take him to the blacksmith again . . . There was always something. And if she did happen to be in the farmhouse and Ian walked in, she was out like a shot. She didn't even pay much attention to the children.

Everything seems to be falling apart, Heather thought sadly.

Stevie herself was making definite plans to leave Bridge End. She had started to look in the Portsmouth *Evening News* and the Southampton *Echo* for job advertisements and spent her evenings writing letters of application. Nobody wanted farm girls, of course, so she gritted her teeth and applied for secretarial posts, nannying or even shopwork. I don't care what I do so long as I can support myself, she thought. I could go and work for Dad for a bit, but that would be taking a step backwards. The past six years had taught her the value of independence and she wasn't prepared to give it up easily.

She was walking across the yard one morning, about twelve days before Ruth and Dan's wedding, when she encountered Roger. It was a Monday and Ian had gone to

Fareham market with a couple of the men. Heather was milking with Eli, and Emily, Arthur and Teddy were indoors in the warm.

They both stopped. Roger stared at her, took a quick breath, and then turned away. Stevie shot out her hand and grasped him by the sleeve. 'Don't go, Roger! Please – you haven't said a word to me for days.'

'Got nothing to say,' he muttered, trying to wriggle away from her grip.

'You must have.' She pulled him round to face her. 'Roger, I know what you must be thinking. You saw us, didn't you – your dad and me. You must let me explain.'

'I don't want you to! I don't want to talk about it.'

'But *I* do,' she said firmly, and led him round the corner and into the very barn where she and Ian had been seen kissing. She stood just inside, gripping both his arms, and faced him. He met her eyes and then looked away, his face blushing a fiery red.

'Listen to me, Roger,' she said quietly. 'What you saw – it meant nothing.' She saw his eyes come back to hers, filled with scorn, and felt her own cheeks flush. 'All right,' she amended quietly, 'it did mean something. But not what you think.' She hesitated. Just what did a twelve-year-old boy read into a passionate kiss between his father and another woman? Probably quite enough, she acknowledged. She went on, trying to make a case that was truthful and that Roger would understand. 'Your father's very unhappy just now. It's been very hard for him to get used to being at home again. He doesn't feel welcome in the family. And when people are unhappy in their own family, sometimes they do silly things. Things they're sorry they did, afterwards.'

'Mum's miserable too,' he said angrily. 'She's worked hard and he doesn't care about that at all. He doesn't care about *her*.'

'Roger, that's not true. He does care about her!'

340

'He doesn't. He cares about *you*.' He glared at her and she saw the tears glitter in his eyes. 'Everything's spoiled!' he shouted, stamping his foot. 'Everything! And it's all because of you! Why didn't you go away when the war stopped? All the others did, so why didn't you? Why don't you go away *now*? We don't want you here. Mum and me don't *want* you here!'

Stevie felt as if she had been struck with a rock, full in the middle of her stomach. Her breath left her in a gasp and she almost doubled up with the sudden pain. She shook her head, trying to clear the blur of tears in her own eyes, and looked at him, forgetting that he was only twelve years old. 'Roger, I'm your mother's friend. She's asked me to stay. She does want me here.'

'She won't when I tell her you've been kissing Dad,' he said bluntly.

Stevie pressed the back of one hand to her mouth. She tried to speak quietly, to keep her voice steady. 'You must not tell your mother about that. You mustn't tell *anyone*. It would only upset her, and cause a lot of unnecessary trouble. Promise me you won't tell her.'

He shook his head. 'You only want me to promise that so she won't hate you and send you away,' he said scornfully. 'I *want* her to hate you. I want you to go away. *Now*.'

'I am going away. I've been looking for a job—'

'Go away now,' he repeated. 'Go away and leave us in peace, then Mum and Dad will stop hating each other and we'll all stop being miserable.'

Stevie doubted that. Ian had only turned to her because of the argument between him and Heather over running the farm. Even if she went away, and she knew she must, that situation would still be the same. But at least I don't have to make it worse, she thought. Roger's right – I should go away as soon as possible. Then they might start to sort out their real problems.

'Let's strike a bargain,' she said. 'If I go away, will you

341

promise never to tell your mother what you saw? She doesn't have to hate me if I'm not here, does she? It's horrible to hate people, Roger – really hate them, I mean. It makes the person miserable and angry inside and they can't get rid of it. You don't want your mum feeling like that, do you?'

He hesitated and she waited a moment, then added, 'It's making you miserable, isn't it – hating me? It's like something eating your insides – a mouse gnawing away at your stomach.'

'A rat,' he said. 'That's what it's like – a rat.' He looked up again and she saw the helpless misery in his face. 'It's chewing all the time.'

'Oh *Roger*,' she said, and took his hands. This time he didn't try to snatch them back. The tears were streaming down his face. 'You've got to let go of it. Stop hating me. You never did before, did you? We were good friends. We can be friends again.'

'No!' he shouted, stamping his foot again and twisting away from her. 'We can't! We can't ever be friends again! I hate you! I'll *always* hate you! You've got to go away!'

Stevie sighed. She had lost control of his hands but he hadn't run away. She couldn't think what to say next, so tried another approach.

'All right. You hate me and you always will. But listen for a minute. When your dad kissed me, I didn't want it to happen.' No, that wouldn't do. Blaming Ian wasn't right – she couldn't leave the boy hating his father. '*Neither* of us meant it to happen. It was just that we were both upset and sometimes when grown-ups are upset they do kiss each other like that. It didn't mean anything else. But if you tell your mother, it will cause a lot of trouble and upset her a lot. You don't want to do that, do you?'

'It's not me who'd be causing the trouble,' he said, sniffing and wiping his nose with his sleeve. 'It's you.'

'Yes,' she said. 'And I've already told you I'm going

away. I've been looking for another job, somewhere else to go . . .'

'I want you to go now,' he said, and planted his feet very firmly apart. *'Now.'*

'And if I do,' she said, 'will you promise never to tell your mother? And will you stop hating your father and help him to be happy, too? So that you can all be a family again, as you want to be? Will you try – *really* try?'

There was a long moment of silence. Then he dropped his eyes, scuffed his toe in the dust of the floor and muttered, 'Yes. All right. I'll try.'

'You promise?' Stevie knew that promises were very important to children but they didn't always consider a promise made unless they said the word itself. Once Roger had said it, she was sure he would stick to it.

'I promise.'

She sighed with relief. 'Good. Thank you, Roger.'

'And you'll go now? Today?'

'I'll have to talk to your mother and father. I'll have to tell them—'

'But you'll go *today*? That's our bargain.'

She looked past him at the door of the barn. Outside, the pale winter sunshine glittered on the ice over the puddles. She had let out the hens earlier and they were scratching for the corn she had thrown down for them. She could hear one of the pigs snorting in its sty, and from the milking shed came the clatter of churns and buckets and the occasional lowing of one of the cows.

This is going to break my heart, she thought, and looked back at the anxious young face.

'Yes,' she said, 'I'll go today.'

'I'm going to miss her so much,' Heather said later as the family sat round the supper-table. 'She's the best friend I ever had. She's been like a sister to me. I knew she'd have to go eventually, of course – she wouldn't want to stay around a farm, working like she's been doing for the rest of her life. But I just wanted her to stay a bit longer while,' she glanced across the table towards her husband, 'while we got things sorted out. And I always hoped she might marry someone in the village and stay for ever.' She poked disconsolately with her fork at a lamb chop. 'I never expected her to go at a moment's notice like that.'

'Well, it is Christmas,' Emily said reasonably. 'It's only natural that she should want to be with her own family. And her poor mother and father must be feeling the loss of their boy, with the war over and so many mothers having their sons back. I can see why they'd want Stevie home.'

'For Christmas, yes. But she's gone for *ever*.' Heather put down her fork. 'I don't think I can eat this.'

'Now, that's just being silly. You'll need to keep up your strength – Ian's going to want your help on the farm more than ever, with Stevie gone. I know we've got the men back, but she was still doing a lot around the place, wasn't she, Ian?'

Ian cleared his throat and nodded. Since he had come home from market to find Stevie gone, he had barely spoken. Heather had been in tears and Roger looking half sulky, half afraid. For a sick moment he'd wondered if the boy had blurted out what he'd seen, but from the way Heather had run to him the moment he appeared, it didn't seem likely.

'She's had a letter from her mother. She wants Stevie home. This is the first Christmas since her brother was killed, and they're feeling it badly. And she says she's not coming back. Oh Ian, Stevie's not coming back!'

'But why?' His eyes had gone to Roger again. There was definitely something odd about the boy's expression – a sort of defiant triumph. But that might be just because something had happened that he knew Ian wouldn't like. It didn't have to mean that he'd caused it.

'She says it's time she moved on.' Heather moved away

from him and found a handkerchief. She blew her nose and mopped her eyes. 'She only stayed on because she thought she was needed, but now everyone's back she's not any more. And she thinks her father might need some help. You know he's a doctor, and apparently the woman who was his receptionist wants to retire, and Stevie says he wants her to do it. So she's packed up all her things and gone. She said she was sorry not to be able to stay and say goodbye to you, but she knew you'd understand.'

Ian stared at her. I understand all right, he thought bitterly. She's walked out on me. She's chucked everything back in my face. She's left me to pick up the pieces and carry on without her.

'She'll come back to see us, though,' he said, feeling he was clutching at straws. 'She's not that far away.'

'Oh, I hope she will. She'd better!' Heather said with an attempt at a laugh. 'But she said she wouldn't come back for a while, or she'd never leave again. She thinks it's better to make a clean break.'

A clean break, Ian thought, turning away. A clean break from me, that's what she means. And I'm still not sure that boy didn't have something to do with this . . .

Now, sitting at the supper-table, he replied to his mother's remark. 'But we *haven't* got all the men back, Mum. I haven't had a chance to tell you, what with all this upset about Stevie, but while we were at the market today, young Ollie told me he's leaving in the New Year. Going up to Lincolnshire, apparently. He was stationed up there when he was in the RAF and got friendly with a local girl, and they're getting married at Easter. Her uncle runs a market garden and he's going to work with him. So after Christmas we'll be a hand short again.'

There was a brief silence. Then Roger said, 'Well, Mum can do it, can't she? You don't have to get anyone else.'

They all looked at each other. Heather stared first at her

son, then at her husband. She couldn't read his expression at all and dared not speak. Her heart was thumping.

'Seems to me that's a good idea,' Arthur said from his end of the table. He had finished his chops and there were only a few bones left on his plate. 'She knows the work and she can do it as well as any bloke. You'd be a fool not to let her, Ian.'

'And you do need someone to help with all the paperwork,' Emily added. 'Heather can do that. She knows just what's what, having done it all these years.'

'Can I still help with the calves?' Pat asked. She was sitting next to Ian and she snuggled against him, looking up into his face. 'I like it when Mum and me do the calves together. And she can teach me to milk. My hands are big enough now.'

Ian looked round the table. He saw the ring of faces, each one expecting the same answer. But he was not ready to give it – not yet. He didn't know if he would ever be. All he could think of was that Stevie had left. She had left the farm. She had left *him*.

'I don't know,' he said, getting up abruptly and pushing back his chair. 'I'll have to think about it.' He gestured at his half-empty plate. 'Sorry, Mum, I'm not very hungry. We had a good feed at the market. There's something I want to see to outside . . .' He trod to the door and shoved his feet into his boots, dragged on his jacket and pulled the door open. A gust of cold air blew in and then he slammed it behind him and was gone.

Chapter Thirty-Three

It was almost Christmas. Preparations were even more hectic this year, with the wedding coming first, and the village seethed with excitement. Sammy had been practising his bellringing and been declared steady enough to join in with some rounds for the wedding, as well as on Christmas morning. His pride knew no bounds and his conversation was peppered with phrases like 'call-changes', 'Grandsire Doubles' and 'double dodging', that nobody else could understand. Ruth wasn't sure that he understood them either but she was pleased that he had found a new hobby, something that he could do in the village and that would last him all his life.

'My dad used to do a bit of bellringing, years ago,' she said when Lizzie called in to show off her new maternity smock. 'I'd have liked to have a go myself, but women weren't allowed.'

'I bet they will be now!' Lizzie said with a grin. 'Women aren't going to be pushed into second place any more, not now we've proved we can be as good as a man.'

The smock was a warm, dark red with box pleats that would allow plenty more room for growth. Lizzie was going to wear it for the first time at the wedding and then it would be her main item of clothing until the baby was born. The rest of the time, she would make do with one of Alec's shirts and a skirt she had made bigger with some elastic in the waistband. She spent most of her time knitting clothes for the baby; the whole family had chipped in with coupons for the wool, although she'd had to compromise a bit on colour. As well as pink or blue, and white, the baby would find itself arrayed in a rainbow of orange, yellow, green and mauve.

'It's a good job you're not superstitious,' Ruth observed, watching Lizzie count the stitches in a second-size matinée jacket in pale green. 'A lot of people wouldn't put a baby in green.'

'I don't suppose it'll care what colour its cardigan is,' Lizzie said. 'And neither do I, as long as the baby's healthy.'

Ruth smiled. She was doing her ironing. The cottage had been cleaned to within an inch of its life, the curtains and cushion covers washed and all the furniture polished, ready for the wedding and Christmas. 'Your mum and dad have come round all right, then?'

'Yes.' Lizzie laid her knitting in her lap for a moment. 'I was frightened they'd be upset – well, they were, of course – but they took it better than I expected. Couldn't do much else, really, with Alec making it plain that he was happy with the situation. Well, maybe happy isn't quite the right word!' She twisted her lips a little ruefully. 'And yet, you know, Auntie Ruth, I think he *is* happy. He's really looking forward to this baby and he doesn't even object to me writing to Floyd to tell him when it's born. I think he agrees that it's best to have the truth out in the open right at the start. And with Floyd all those thousands of miles away in America, once he leaves the Air Force, it's not likely to be much of a problem, is it? The baby will grow up looking on Alec as its dad, even though it will know it's got another dad in America.'

'I suppose so.' Ruth was a staunch believer in truth, but she thought Lizzie and Alec were being very brave in letting the rest of the family know what had happened. Plenty of people adopted babies, of course, and some of them told their child the truth; this situation wasn't really all that different. And if anyone should understand a young

348

couple getting carried away, it ought to be Jane and George, who hadn't been married all that many months before Lizzie herself was born. 'All's well that ends well,' she declared. 'And nobody will be surprised now when the baby comes in February instead of March.'

'Only a few weeks now,' Lizzie said, covering her stomach with her hands. 'And Alec's so much better now, too. He likes his new job, and guess what, Auntie Ruth! He's found us a nice little place to move into after the baby's born. It's the ground floor of a big Victorian house, with a living room at the back and a bedroom at the front, and a good-sized kitchen. There's even a little bathroom too, so we'll be really private. It just wants a bit of doing up and he's going to do that at weekends so it'll be ready. Our Terry's giving him a hand.'

Ruth stopped ironing. 'Oh Lizzie, that's good news! Why ever didn't you tell me before? Sitting there knitting and not saying a word!'

'I wanted to save it. It's lovely, isn't it? I'll miss Bridge End, of course, but I can come out on the bus whenever I want to, and you'll come and see us, won't you? It's handy for the shops, so you can call in for a cup of tea and rest your feet.'

Ruth seldom shopped in Southampton, but she nodded. 'You'll wish you'd never said that. I'll be on the doorstep all the time.'

'I'll never wish that,' Lizzie said. 'You've been a good friend to me, Auntie Ruth. I don't know what I'd have done without you.' She hesitated and then said, 'I know this seems a bit like jumping the gun, but me and Alec would like you to be the baby's godmother. Will you?'

Ruth stared at her. Her face turned pink and tears sprang into her eyes. She came round the ironing-board and dropped to her knees beside Lizzie, putting her arms round the bulky figure. 'Oh, yes!' she cried. 'I'd love to!'

'I want you to be a real godmother, mind,' Lizzie warned

her. 'You'll have to help me with the baby – help me to bring her or him up right, and teach them the proper way to live, like it says in the prayerbook. It's not just a matter of wearing a hat at the christening and giving the kiddy a silver mug or something.'

'I'll be the best godmother a baby ever had,' Ruth declared, and then, her normal modesty returning, 'I'll do my best, anyway. Oh Lizzie, thank you for asking me. I'm so pleased.'

'It'll be good practice for you,' Lizzie said with her familiar wicked grin. 'You might be having a baby of your own by this time next year.'

'Lizzie!' Ruth's colour deepened. 'What a thing to say.' But secretly, a tiny hope had been stirring for some time now. Suppose she and Dan did have their own child? She wasn't too old. Women had had babies in their early forties before. First babies, even. 'We'll have to leave that to the Almighty to decide,' she told her niece primly. 'Now, I'm going to put this ironing away. There's nothing that can't wait until later. You and me are going to sit down and have a cup of tea and a piece of the "taster" Christmas cake, and talk about *this* baby. Have you decided on a name yet? I wondered if you might call it George, after your dad, if it's a boy? It's a name the Warrens have always used, isn't it?'

Lizzie frowned and shook her head. 'Maybe for a second name, but I want the baby to have a name of its own – a name nobody in the family's ever used before. I thought of Malcolm for a boy and Hilary for a girl.'

'Malcom or Hilary,' Ruth said thoughtfully. 'They're both nice. And as you say, if the second name's George your dad will be happy. That's if it's a boy, of course,' she added hastily. 'Even he wouldn't want you to call a girl George!'

Silver, who had been unusually quiet for almost half an hour now, decided that it was time he joined in. 'Georgy-Porgy, pudding and pie,' he declared and then, with a tilt of

350

his head, 'Mary, Mary, quite contrary. Tom, Tom, the piper's son. Little Jack Horner sat in his pie—'

The two women burst out laughing. 'He's suggesting his own list of names,' Ruth said, going to make the tea. 'I'll say this for that bird – he always tries to help.'

Lizzie got up and scratched the top of the parrot's head. 'I'm going to miss you,' she told him. 'I'm going to miss you most of all.'

The day of the wedding came at last. Ruth woke early and lay in the darkness, listening to the wind that blew around the cottage roof. This was the last time she would wake alone in this room. For the past sixteen years of her widowhood she had slept by herself and now she was about to become a married woman again. Tonight she would fall asleep in Dan's arms, and tomorrow morning he would be beside her. Tomorrow, and the day after that, and every day until death did them part.

She felt a surge of panic. Was she doing the right thing? Suppose it didn't work? How well did she know Dan, after all? He wasn't an easy man – he had dark, difficult moods and she knew that he still grieved for Nora, just as she still grieved for Jack. And that was another thing – what would Jack think of his Ruthie marrying another man? I've waited a long time, she told him, straining to reach through the darkness for the feeling that he was still with her. I've waited so long. And I'm sure you wouldn't mind. You'd like Dan. You'd get on well with him, you could talk about ships and – she sat up abruptly and felt for the matches and candlestick. Never mind talking to ghosts, there's a lot to do, she told herself sternly, watching the flame quiver and then steady. Time I got up and started doing it.

It had been decided that Sammy would stay at the farm until Christmas Eve, to give Ruth and Dan some privacy since they weren't going away on honeymoon, and the cottage was unnaturally silent. Even Silver was still asleep in his cage when she went downstairs. If it hadn't been for him, Ruth would have accepted her sister's urging to stay at the farm as well, and be married from there, but she couldn't leave the parrot alone and refused to take him to the farm with her. It was too cold out and would be too unsettling for him, she said. And Dan knew he was going to have to share her with the bird, so he might as well do so right from the beginning. She could still be married from the farm if she went up there in the morning.

She took the chenille cover off Silver's cage and he woke up and stretched his claws and wings. He eyed her beadily and croaked a greeting: 'Hello, Ruthie. Poor little sod. It's a bleeding eagle!'

Ruth laughed, but there was a tear in her eye as she remembered Sammy coming out with that phrase on his first ever sight of Silver. She opened the cage door to take out his food and water bowls. 'You'd better make the most of this,' she told him. 'You won't get much more attention today. But you'll be seeing a lot more of Dan from now on, and you'll like that. You like Dan, don't you?'

'Dan, Dan, dirty old man,' Silver said obligingly. 'Washed his socks in a frying-pan. Went to bed, cracked his head, didn't wake up till he was dead.'

'Yes, well, I don't think you'd better repeat that too much. It's a pity Sammy ever taught you to say it, in my opinion.' She filled the bowls and put them back. 'Now, I've got a lot to do, so if you want to talk you'll have to talk to yourself.'

She had had a bath last night and Terry had come over to drag the tin bath back into the yard and tip the water over the vegetable plot. After he had gone, she had tidied the kitchen and she had her breakfast there now, looking at the range with its fresh blackleading and the shining pots and pans on the dresser. Then she went upstairs and changed the sheets on the bed, and packed a small case with the few things she would need at Jane's. Her wedding

352

costume was already there, and there was nothing more for her to do here. She could spend an hour or two helping with the last-minute preparations for the wedding breakfast.

She walked up the lane. Dan had been given strict instructions to keep out of the way, so as not to see her on the morning of the wedding – Ruth wasn't quite as bold as Lizzie in discarding the old superstitions. She waved to a couple of the men working in the fields, but apart from that the village was quiet. Everybody's getting ready for the wedding, she thought with a quiver of pleasure, for although only family and close friends had been invited to the farm afterwards she knew that almost everyone in the village would be at the church.

This is my last walk as a widow, she thought and then paused. Jack had died abroad and there was no grave for her to visit, but there was one particular spot in the woods that had always been theirs. It was a small clearing, with a fallen tree where they had often sat for their last goodnight kiss when they were courting. The trees were taller now and the log had almost rotted away, but Ruth had got her father to make a rough wooden bench and drag it up the lane to set where the log had been. On its back he had carved the one word 'Jack', and she had gone at least twice a year to clear away the brambles and tree seedlings that might encroach on this special place.

She turned aside and walked along the little path. The clearing was empty, the sun dappling through the bare branches to spread a latticework of shifting light on the grass. Ruth walked across to the seat and sat down, lifting her face to the tentative warmth.

It isn't goodbye, Jack, she thought. You'll always be here in my heart. Dan will be here as well – he's been here for a long time now – but there's room for you both. Plenty of room for you both.

Dan was in a panic. When he'd unpacked the parcel containing the suit he'd hired from Moss Bros, he'd found they'd given him the wrong one. It wasn't that it wasn't as good – it was *too* good. It was a pale grey, with tails, and he had been given a top hat to wear with it. He put it on and stared at himself in the mirror with dismay.

'Coo, what a smasher!' Tommy Vickers exclaimed. He was to be Dan's best man, and he and Freda had arrived on the first train. Freda had gone with Jess Budd to look round the village and meet some of Jess's old friends, and Solly was in the other bedroom getting himself dressed. 'You look like the Duke of I Dunno Where! You'll put us all to shame.'

'I don't want to put you to shame,' Dan growled. He adjusted the wing collar of his white shirt. 'I feel like a flipping monkey on a stick. I can't go looking like this, Tom.'

'Well, it's either that or your working clobber, and you definitely can't turn up in that. Thank your lucky stars it fits. Suppose they'd got you mixed up with some little squirt five foot tall!'

'I dunno what to do.' Dan stared despondently at the resplendent vision in Solly's speckled mirror. 'If I had time, I'd go and change it – and give 'em a piece of my mind at the same time.'

'Well, you ain't got time. Wear it and be thankful you ain't the other bloke – the one what's having a posh wedding today and got to wear *your* suit! I bet he's spitting red-hot nails.'

'Yeah, I suppose it's worse for him,' Dan agreed, not sounding all that sure. 'Though I can't see why anyone would want to dress up like this. Oh, I *can't* wear it!' he burst out again. 'What's my Ruth going to think? And her sister and George Warren, they'll think I've gone barmy. The whole village will. They're all coming, you know,

Tom. The whole flipping lot of 'em will be there in the church. I'll never live it down, never.'

Tom tried to repress his laughter. 'Come on, Dan, see the funny side. And if you can't do that, try and forget it. You're getting married, remember? Somehow or other, God knows how, you've managed to find a woman who's willing to take you on, a woman any bloke'd be glad to marry. What does it matter what you're wearing?'

'Well, if it doesn't matter, maybe I *could* put on my working clothes—'

'It matters a bit more than that,' Tommy said hastily. 'Listen, Dan, you look really smart in that suit. You do, honest. Nobody's going to laugh at you. Their eyes'll pop out of their heads when they see you. Now, stop making a fuss and stand still while I do this bow tie up. Good job my old man used to wear these or I wouldn't have a clue . . . Stand *still*, man, for goodness sake!'

At last both were ready. Freda had come back and they could hear her voice downstairs, talking to old Solly. Like her husband, Freda could talk to anyone, and she'd taken to Solly at once. In fact, she'd taken to Bridge End altogether and told Jess she could understand why the Budds were so fond of the place and often came back to visit.

'Well, not everyone's as nice as the Greenberrys and Edna Corner,' Jess said. 'The Woddis sisters were really nasty to poor little Alan and Wendy Atkinson when they were out here, and Martin Baker had a terrible time with that Mrs Hutchins. But most people are kind. Now, where are those boys? I knew I shouldn't have let them go off on their own – they'll get their new shoes all muddy. The only reason they've come is for a piece of wedding cake and a sausage roll!'

She went back to Mrs Greenberry's house, where she had stayed herself when she was first evacuated in September 1939. Six years ago! Such a lot had happened since then, and here she was for a wedding that would join

April Grove and Bridge End as well as Ruth Purslow and Dan Hodges. I wonder how many other weddings there are like this one, she thought – people from the towns and cities marrying countryfolk they would never have met if it hadn't been for the war. It just showed how true the old saying was: it was an ill wind indeed that didn't blow good to somebody.

By a quarter to twelve the church was already almost full. Sammy, with his best jacket hanging on a hook, was in the tower ringing one of the bells and Tim Budd had persuaded his mother to let him come along too. Tim had been taught to ring during his evacuation by old Mr Beckett, with the clapper tied to the bell to keep it silent, since the sound of a bell was supposed to mean the German invasion had started, and he had kept it up since returning to Portsmouth. The sound of the six bells, their notes tumbling over each other, made joyous music in the crisp cold air, and people smiled as they made their way along the lanes to the church. The first wedding in the village since the end of the war. It must be a good omen.

Dan had been persuaded to come out of the forge wearing the grey tailcoat and trousers. He'd flatly refused to put on the top hat, saying he couldn't wear it in church so what did it matter, but Tommy and Freda between them had convinced him that he couldn't go to church for his own wedding without a hat under his arm, and he'd given in. He shambled along as if hoping nobody would notice him.

'Stand up straight, for Gawd's sake,' Tommy told him. 'Hold up your head. Blimey, anyone would think you were going to your execution.'

'I wish I was,' Dan grunted. 'I wouldn't have to see the grins on people's faces for the rest of me life if I'd had me head cut off. I'll tell you what else I wish, too, Tom – I wish I was the blacksmith at Gretna Green. I wouldn't have to step outside the forge to get married then. I could just stop inside and Solly could do it for us over the anvil!'

'Stop thinking about yourself,' Tommy said. 'Think about Ruth instead. Blimey, if I wasn't married to the best wife in the world meself I might try and cut you out. And think about that boy of yours, too. You've got a nipper to be proud of there. Give him summat to be proud of too!'

Dan didn't look as if he thought a daft suit and a top hat would give Sammy anything to be proud of, but all the same as he walked into the church and saw the congregation sitting there, waiting to see him marry Ruth, his heart lifted and he raised his chin almost without thinking about it. All these people, waiting to wish him and Ruth well! He'd never have dreamed, when he'd lived in Old Pompey and then in April Grove, that he could ever have all these people ready to stand by him and wish him luck. His eyes misted for a minute and when they cleared he found his son standing before him.

'Gosh, Dad,' Sammy said in a voice of awe, 'you look smashing!'

Dan looked down at him. He saw Sammy's fair, curly hair and bright blue eyes, so like Nora's. He saw the straight, strong body that had once been so puny with poor nourishment and neglect, and the confidence where once there had been a cringing fearfulness. He felt the pride that Tommy had meant him to feel.

'Do I, son?' he asked. 'Well, so do you. Let's go into the church together, shall we? You're sitting in the front row with Tommy and me. You can both be my best men.'

He put his hand on the boy's shoulder and they marched up the aisle together, and he heard the little gasp that ran round the church. It wasn't laughter, he realised with a warming heart. It wasn't mockery. It was a genuine welcome.

I'll be one of them now, he thought. A villager. Part of Bridge End.

The Knight family were almost the last to arrive at the church before the Warrens. They filed into pews towards the back of the church, knelt briefly and then sat together in a row.

Arthur sat at one end, with Emily beside him. Roger was beside her, with his mother and then his father. Teddy was on his mother's knee and Pat on the other side of Ian. They sat still and quiet, looking at the arrangements of holly and chrysanthemums by the pulpit and on the altar. The organ was playing softly and in the tower they could hear the bells ringing their final peal. The ringers – apart from Sammy, who had come down early to be with his father – would come in after the bride and take the pew at the back, slipping out again just before the wedding party emerged from the vestry to sound the bells in triumph and joy as she and Dan came out of the door.

Heather sat very still, listening to the organ and the bells and thinking of her own wedding. It hadn't been in this church; Ian and the family had come to Sussex, where she had been brought up. But the service would be the same and the same vows exchanged. I hope they'll be happy, she thought. Ruth's a lovely person and Dan is a fine man. I hope they'll have a good life together.

She turned her head slightly and looked at her husband. He too was sitting very still, his eyes gazing straight in front. Since Stevie had left, things had still been strained between them, yet she was beginning to think she noticed a slight thawing in his coldness. He'd allowed her to help him with several of the farm jobs and in return she had given way to his ideas instead of trying to impose her own. He'd even asked her advice last night, over one of the pigs, and she'd given it more as a suggestion and noticed that he found this easier to accept. Maybe that's the way to do it, she thought. Maybe this way we can find our own path forwards.

She missed Stevie sorely, yet she couldn't help noticing

that without her there was less tension in the atmosphere. Even Roger seemed more relaxed, and Pat was less clinging with her father, while Teddy, for no reason that anyone could fathom other than that it was what kiddies did, had exhibited a complete change in his attitude, discarded all his fears and followed Ian everywhere like, as Emily remarked, a puppy-dog.

Perhaps it will all come right after all, she thought. We just have to give it time.

The note of the organ changed and the bells stopped ringing. As the first notes of 'The Wedding March' sounded, everyone rose to their feet. They turned as one to see Ruth, her face lit by the sunshine pouring through the south window, standing in the doorway. Then, with George beside her, she began to walk up the aisle.

Dan, sitting in the front pew, stiff and nervous in his smart suit, stood up. Nudged by Tommy, he stepped out into the aisle and turned. He saw Ruth in her costume and knew by her smile that she had taken in his own appearance. And then it was as if everything around them had melted away. It didn't matter what they were wearing; they could have been in their working clothes, fancy dress or bathing costumes. They were just Ruth and Dan, and they were getting married, and nothing else mattered at all.

Heather felt her eyes grow hot with tears. Without thinking what she was doing, she felt for Ian's hand. He gripped it in his and she turned to look at him. Their eyes met; his fingers tightened. Tentatively, she smiled at him, and as he smiled back a great flood of relief washed over her and her eyes filled with tears of thankfulness.

Lizzie and Alec, near the front of the church, were also holding hands. They had their own special reason to give thanks; on the previous night Alec had, at last, without any effort at all, made sweet, tender love to her. And not just to her, she had thought, lying in his arms afterwards, but to the baby as well. *Their* baby. They were a family now, and always would be.

'I now pronounce you man and wife,' the vicar said, holding Ruth and Dan's hands together in his. And then, in tones that rang to the very top of the rafters in the church roof, 'Those whom God hath joined together let *no* man put asunder!'

The carol-singing this year was held on Christmas Eve itself. So many people came to this first peacetime carol-singing that there were almost not enough cottages occupied with people to be sung to – but they all trooped round just the same, singing all the well-loved carols, and ending with the old favourites that weren't Christmas carols at all but were always included.

> *'We wish you a Merry Christmas,*
> *We wish you a Merry Christmas,*
> *We wish you a Merry Christmas,*
> *And a Happy New Year.'*

And then the one that Sammy, standing between his father Dan and his new stepmother Ruth, liked best of all:

> *'Christmas is coming, the goose is getting fat.*
> *Please put a penny in the old man's hat.*
> *If you haven't got a penny, a ha'penny will do,*
> *If you haven't got a ha'penny a farthing will do.*
> *If you haven't got a farthing*
> *God ... Bless ... You!'*